20ᵗʰ Anniversary Edition

PATRICK THOMAS

PADWOLF PUBLISHING INC.
WWW.PADWOLF.COM
www.facebook.com/Padwolf

WWW.PATTHOMAS.NET
www.facebook.com/PatrickThomasAuthor
twitter.com/I_PatrickThomas

EXILE AND ENTRANCE
a Xiles novel
20th Anniversary Edition
© 1997 and 2017 Patrick Thomas

Book edited by John L. French

Cover Art by Patrick Thomas

Rick Wagner, Susie, Burke, Kerr, Red, Sasha, and all related characters
and settings are © & TM Patrick Thomas

10-digit ISBN 1-890096-74-1-, 13 digit ISBN 978-1-890096-74-8
Printed in the USA
First Printing

For Mom and Dad

RICK

I stood, one among the multitudes. For so many people, it was deathly quiet. Forced to become faceless masses, fear kept us silent and still. My ears strained for some comforting sound, but all that greeted them was the noise of my pounding heart. I didn't want to be here - who among us did? The public at large probably still has no idea what's happening. I wish I could still count myself in their number. I should wish for a million dollars and a Jacuzzi – I'd have a better chance of getting them.

Something pulled on the pant leg of the gray coveralls which we were all forced to wear. I'd been so deep in thought I'd forgotten I wasn't alone in my misery. Looking down to see who had disturbed my despair, I found myself absorbed into the depths of a twosome of blue eyes.

"I'm scared, mister." This profound statement was issued by a blond girl. God, she reminded me of Deborah. She was slightly younger and had her hair pulled back in a ponytail, but the resemblance threw me. Staring down into that innocent face, anger stirred within me. How could one so young be subjected to this? What kind of a world do we live in that children are not allowed to grow up and be happy? I wasn't the first to ask these questions and hopefully wouldn't be the last. Maybe someday someone will find the right answers; I already know the wrong ones.

My emotions concerning this girl were both new and familiar. I could do nothing to help myself, but perhaps I could help her. My protective instincts toward this girl were growing by leaps and bounds. A sucker for a damsel in distress, that's me. As long as the dragon was not too big, that is. The one we were facing was enormous.

"Don't worry; everything is going to be okay," I lied. The likelihood of anything ever being okay again for either of us was too slim to mention. She didn't need to know that. I was so scared that it was taking all my concentration to keep control of my bowel and bladder. She didn't need to know that either. If it came to that, she'd be the second to know.

I didn't want to scare the kid, at least no more than she already was. Besides, kids are used to being lied to - ask Santa Claus. Okay, I was rationalizing, but it worked.

"My name's Rick Wagner. What's yours?" I asked, extending my hand to shake hers. Amazingly, my hand didn't tremble as much as I thought it would.

"I'm Susie Jonas," she replied as her tiny hand unexpectedly crushed mine; for a minute I wasn't sure if I'd get it back. Finally, with great reluctance, her grip softened.

"Susie. That's a very pretty name. A pleasure to meet you," I said, hoping to distract her from the events occurring around us. I had a better shot at trying to distract piranha during a feeding frenzy, but it still might do some good. If I was really lucky, I might distract myself.

"Thank you. It's nice to meet you too, Mister Rick," she replied.

Polite kid. Her parents raised her well. Too bad the same can't be said for them or their kid wouldn't be here.

Susie told me she was eight and a half, almost three-quarters, years old and was in third grade. Her best doll's name was Betty, her favorite color was sky blue, not to be confused with "that icky navy blue". She loved dogs, cats, hamsters, and chocolate chip ice cream.

"Do you think they will have ice cream where we are going, Mister Rick?"

"I don't know, Susie." I had no idea what was going to happen. I could think of a multitude of possibilities, many of them ending in our deaths, none of which I wanted to tell an eight-year-old girl.

Susie broke into my gruesome thoughts with another tug to my pants' leg. "Mr. Rick, is it okay that I'm talking to you? Mommy said I shouldn't talk to strangers, but she's not here. I know they told us to face front only, but I was so lonely and you looked like a nice man, so I talked to you. Is that okay?"

"It's okay, Susie. Besides I'm not a stranger anymore. We introduced ourselves, remember? So we can't be strangers if we know each other, right?"

She pondered the logic of my statements for a moment, then thoughtfully nodded in agreement. "I guess so, Mr. Rick."

She bought it. "So it's okay to talk to me. And Susie, can I ask you a favor?"

"Sure," She replied brightly.

"Don't call me Mister Rick. It makes me feel old"

"But you are old. You must be twenty years old."

"Twenty-six," I smiled. "But just call me Rick."

"All right Mister um...I mean Rick. Can I ask you a favor now?"

I turned my head as little as possible to look around. They weren't paying attention to us yet. Still too busy making their damn preparations.

"Sure, Susie."

She hesitated, then shyly asked, "Can we be friends? I know that sounds like something a little kid would say, but I mean it."

I could feel my face broaden, my smile mirroring her own sweet one. "There is nothing I would like better."

Susie gave a melodramatic sigh of relief. "Thank you. You know, Mommy told me to go with those scary men with the suits and the guns, but they're strangers, even if she said they weren't. She said they would take care of me." She fell silent for a moment, then softly said, "I don't think she knew what they were going to do to me."

She knew, kid. She just didn't care enough to stop it.

Susie continued, eyes fixed on the ground. "She was crying when she said goodbye. I told her not to, that I'd be fine, but she didn't stop. Daddy just stood in the corner like a zombie. He didn't even say goodbye. I miss him and Mommy," she quietly confessed to her feet.

"I'm sure they miss you too, Susie." Maybe they did, but they had no right to. They gave her up to the government of their own free will. If they really cared, they would have done something, anything but give up their child. At least, that's what I would have done ... or did do.

"Those men must have lied to Mommy because they didn't take good care of me. They put me in a stone room with bars on the windows. It was like a jail," She exploded tearfully. "Did I do something bad so locked me away?"

"No Susie." I struggled for an explanation that both of us would buy, but all I could come up with was, "Sometimes bad people do bad things to other people without a good reason."

"Why?"

I helplessly shrugged. "I wish I knew."

She told me more about her cell: it was dark, damp, and smelled like a toilet overflowed. At least her living conditions were better than mine had been.

"And I thought I saw a rat." She shuddered. "I hate rats! They scare me."

"Me too." As I was trying to think of a way to change the subject to something more pleasant, perhaps a light discussion of nuclear holocaust, Susie changed it for me.

"Do you know what I want to do when this is all over?"

"No, Susie, I don't."

"I want to have a tea party. I had them all the time at home. Betty and all my stuffed animals and I would play dress up with Mommy's clothes."

"That sounds like a fun game."

"Oh, it is," she agreed. "Will you come to my tea party, Rick?"

"It depends." I could not keep from grinning. "Do I have to play dress up with your mother's clothes?"

"No, silly," she giggled. The happy sound was out of place in this abode of horrors.

"Then I would love to go." As a matter of fact, I would have given anything I owned to be at that tea party with Susie, anyplace else but here. Of course, that wish meant nothing. I don't think I own anything anymore except for the clothes on my back and I was having doubts about even that.

The dessert air some two hundred feet in front of us unexpectedly lit up and all talk of tea parties disappeared. The light was dazzling and incredibly beautiful - almost blinding in its brilliance. It was without a doubt the most horrifying sight I have ever witnessed in my life.

It was also our signal to begin. The government troops had given us instructions to walk into the light and not to stop for any reason. Susie slid her hand into mine and gripped it tightly. If it was not for that little girl's hand I think I would have broken down and cried hysterically. Some guy four rows to my right was doing just that.

As I turned my head to look, I recognized the man. He was a small-time movie hero from my childhood. He always played the rip 'em up and shoot 'em up hero who selflessly risked his life for others - so much for life imitating art. This former idol of thousands was now a quivering mass of jelly. He was yelling at the top of his lungs, "You can't do this to me! Don't you know who I am? I'll give you money, anything! Just let me go!"

So much for my childhood illusions. They were fading away fast; no heroes selflessly charging to the rescue here. A real shame; such lousy timing for heroes to become extinct. If there were any such creatures left, wouldn't they be here to save us?

How long would Susie be able to maintain her innocence in this place? I would try to make that as long as possible, which from the looks of things would be about another three minutes.

And so it came to pass that nine hundred people, too terrified to do anything else, moved forward like so many cattle. Without hope, without choice. I know that in theory we always have a choice, however in practice many times the options would move us out of the frying pan and into the microwave. This was one such situation.

Before this ordeal began, we were graciously informed that resistance was futile and those who disobeyed orders or strayed from formation would be shot down. These orders were issued by the government troops stationed so bravely behind us under cover of sandbag piles, holding their automatic weapons. They apparently were not bluffing, for no sooner did the actor go berserk, than he was riddled by more bullets than the victims in his films. Unlike them, he would not get up when this scene was over. The rest of us decided not to improvise or stray from the script. The masses trampled over him as if he didn't exist. Technically, I guess he no longer did.

Susie had kept her eyes front the whole time so she did not see the horror, but I felt her flinch when the gunshots rang out.

As if the threat of painful and immediate death wasn't enough of a deterrent, the government threw in an added bonus at no extra charge. If anyone disobeyed or somehow escaped, not only would they be killed but so would their families.

If I found a way to escape I would have taken it without a moment's hesitation. My family could go rot in hell for all I cared. They meant nothing to me... except for Deborah.

Deborah is a ten-year-old living example of joy in motion. Pretty, brilliant, a straight A student in fact. She also happens to be my kid sister. I love her more than anything in the world.

The government had demanded that my parents turn Deborah over to their custody. The officials informed my parents that they would never see their daughter again. These powers that be regretted that they were unable to inform us as to why they required my sister: a matter of grave importance, of national security they said. Don't tell anyone, they said. We had forty-eight hours to comply, they said. Fat chance, I said.

The only decent thing my parents did during this whole nightmare was to call me. The story they told was too much for me to take. I was as patriotic as any citizen, but there are some things a government has no right to ask.

I expected my parents to share my sentiments, to fight for their daughter. Instead, when the government put the pressure on, they caved in and began to make preparations to offer up Deborah as some sacrificial lamb. I couldn't believe it! It wasn't right when God asked Abraham to do it and it wasn't any more right now. My parents were willing to turn over their own flesh and blood to a bunch of strangers, for heaven only knows what purpose, without a struggle. Sure, they cried and made a big fuss, but in the end, they were still going to do it.

I probably read too many comic books or saw too many sappy movies as a kid, but I had to save my sister. We were both oops babies. Me when my parents were in high school and her after they thought they were done having kids. My sister didn't even realize what was going on. Mom told her she would be going on vacation. Meanwhile, the government would arrange a cover story: Deborah was to be studying abroad. It was a stupid cover. Deborah didn't even speak a foreign language. While "away" a freak accident would occur and all that would officially be left of my sister would be the memory. And the paperwork.

This wouldn't come to pass if I had anything to say on the matter. I talked up a storm. Calling in sick to work the next morning, I took Deborah out of school early under the guise of a doctor's appointment. We were barely out of the building before her school was surrounded by dozens of men in dark two-piece suits with guns drawn. An awful lot of trouble to go through over a ten-year-old on their part. We didn't stay to watch what happened. She was out of their clutches and that was what mattered.

We went into hiding. After four weeks underground with two close calls with agents from the Central Security Agency, we were run ragged and funds were getting low. My credit cards were useless. I had tried to use them once at a cash machine and ninety-five seconds later the bank was surrounded by helicopters. We only escaped detection because Deborah had just run into an alley and I, leaving my credit card behind in the machine, ran after her. Deborah had dashed into the alley because she saw a coffee shop throw out their day-old doughnuts and she was hungry.

Hungry was an understatement. We had found a diet plan that helped us lose four pounds a week. We joked about selling the idea to a tabloid to get enough money to afford to eat. While we hid in the alley, one of the agents found a manhole cover that was partially ajar. The lot of them took off down the sewer thinking they were chasing us. From what I heard on the news the next day all they succeeded in doing was chasing a group of homeless people out of the sewer. While they were busy down under, we grabbed some doughnuts and quietly made our way out of the front of the coffee shop and to safety.

The second time we almost got caught was at a diner in the middle of nowhere. It was a Tuesday, which meant we ate at least one good meal whether we could afford it or not. During our lunch, an overweight man dressed in a greasy white T-shirt and pants approached us from out of the kitchen. He was balding on top and had a half-smoked cigarette hanging over his left bottom lip. The scruff on his face indicated he had not seen the sharp edge of a razor for the better part of a month. The man stared first at Deborah then at me. He didn't look pleased.

"You dirty, rotten son of a ..." he began and his language became more colorful from there. Truly a brilliant conversationalist.

"Excuse me, but I thought the customers were supposed to complain to the cook about the food, not the other way around. How about laying off the rough language in front of my sister, okay?" I replied, trying to turn the sudden attention away from us.

"Sister, my ass," he growled. Turning to Deborah, he continued. "Are you okay, Honey? This bastard didn't hurt you, did he? He didn't touch you any place he shouldn't, did he?"

"What the hell are you talking about? She's my sister, I told you." I wasn't sure what was going on, but I didn't like the sound of it.

He grabbed my shirt with a huge, filthy hand. Lifting me half out of my seat, he shoved something in my face.

"This is what I'm talking about, jerk off!"

I looked closely at the object he was trying to ram down my throat. It was a carton of milk.

"What's the matter? Do you expect your customers to put the milk away?" I asked. He gave one evil laugh and turned the carton around. Deborah's picture was on it with the caption "MISSING! IF FOUND PLEASE CALL 1-800-555-LOSTKID". I began to worry and look for the exits. Stupidly, I hadn't planned an escape route when we came in. We'd pay the price for that oversight.

Deborah spoke up. "Leave my brother alone!" she said, hammering on his back with her tiny fists.

"Would you look at that? This damn molester has brainwashed the kid," he said to anyone in the diner who would listen. No one did.

I admired the principle behind what he was doing, just not who he was doing it to.

"Don't worry. I didn't call the cops yet. You're gonna wish I did when I get through with ya. Those wussy cops wouldn't even rough you up. But I will. I wanna make you pay for what you done to this little girl. Then they can come pick up the pieces."

He didn't call, so we still had some hope. If we could get away, we'd have a head start. At least two minutes if they called the moment we left, more if they delayed. It wasn't much, but it was all we had.

The flexing of the elbow continued until I was entirely out of my seat and face to face with the cook. His breath stank of onions and tobacco - quite a flavorable and unpleasant bouquet. He was at least six three and two hundred and fifty pounds; I'm only six foot and barely one ninety-five. I think he could taste my fear and it egged him on.

"I'm gonna break you into little pieces and fry your face off on my grill!" he threatened. No one in the diner seemed to care about the outcome one way or the other. Or what he cooked on his grill. We were on our own.

I hadn't struck another human being since I was in a fight in seventh grade. It's a personal thing; I believe violence is wrong. You cannot hurt another person without hurting yourself. On the other side of the coin, I don't believe in letting myself get beaten to a bloody pulp while I stand by and watch. Even Gandhi said there was a time when violence is necessary. He never found that time - I did.

While the cook held onto my shirt with his left hand, I saw him bring up his right fist to eye-level; a moment later it was rapidly moving toward my nose. My mind was at a loss for what to do when something inside I didn't even know existed instinctively took over. My left forearm sprang up, blocking the punch; I then returned the implied favor several times over with my right fist.

The bridge of his nose crumbled and blood spurted - his blood. It came pouring out of his nostrils. The assault stunned him for a moment, but he recovered and seemed angrier than ever. More profanities than I knew existed erupted forth from his mouth. Veins in his neck were bulging to the point of bursting as he rushed me. Sidestepping the charge, I added to his momentum by slamming my elbow into the back of his neck. The result was he crashed into our booth face first. The red padding cushioned the impact so he was quickly able to turn. His punches stormed out toward my head and chest. Trying to fend off his punches and land a few of my own was an uphill battle, but I was gaining ground.

The big break came when Deborah crouched down on all fours behind him. I pushed and the cook fell over Deborah, hitting his head and back on the tile floor; no padding to soften anything this time. My fists followed him to the ground and kept clobbering until his eyes fell closed. Then I clubbed him a few times for good measure. My hands hurt and my lip was bleeding, but I had to forcibly stop myself. For someone who didn't believe in violence, I was enjoying pounding someone's face into the pavement too much. All the frustrations of the past weeks poured forth into my hands and into this poor guy's skull. It was the government I wanted to hurt, not this slob. He was just a convenient substitute.

Making a swift exit, we left the diner making sure everybody saw us head north. As soon as we were out of sight, we hitched a ride going south, back in the direction of the diner. As we neared it, we saw the special agents in their sedans heading in the direction we had just come from. They hadn't had time to set up a roadblock.

Escape and freedom were ours again, but only barely. Now that Deborah's face was being plastered all over dairy products nationwide we had to alter her appearance to keep her safe. I contacted an old friend from college who was now a medical resident and he helped me arrange plastic surgery to alter Deborah's face. He even helped fake the necessary insurance forms.

Deborah was reluctant and I wasn't thrilled either, but it was the only viable option we had. It was painful for her, but less so than the alternative. She liked her new nose once she got used to it. We dyed her blond hair brown and cut it. We gave her color contacts to make her blue eyes appear hazel. For what was left of my funds and an old favor owed we acquired phony identification papers to give her a new identity. When we were done, her own mother wouldn't recognize her.

I hoped.

The next step was contacting some friends I trusted who live out in the boonies and arranging for "Sandy", Deborah's new name, to stay with them. Unbeknownst to my so-called family, they had once taken me in. No reason they should know as they were twelve hundred miles away at the time and I never told them or anyone else for that matter.

My sister was in a place where she would be loved and be safe. Then I did the most difficult thing I have ever done. With tears in my eyes and an unbearable ache in my heart, I said my goodbyes to her. The Central Security Agency was looking for a man and a girl, so she would be safer without me. Knowing that didn't make leaving her any easier.

It was time to worry about my own safety.

Staying out of sight for the next few weeks, I dyed my own hair and grew a beard, then shaved all but the mustache. I worked odd jobs to stay alive, under the table when I could because it didn't take long for someone to realize the social security number I gave was phony.

Then it happened. My conscience began bothering me. My parents must be worried sick about us. They had a right to know Deborah was safe even if they didn't have a right to know where she was. I needed to contact them. A letter would never reach them and a phone call could be traced. I needed to do the thing they expected me to do least, the stupidest thing possible. Deliver the message in person.

I wrote a detailed letter of everything I knew about the government's activities, videoed myself reading it and gave the letter and the recording to my cousin Tandy Wagner for safe keeping. She was a journalism major in her junior year of college and the closest thing to a reporter I both knew and could trust. I told her that if I didn't get in touch with her in two weeks that she should bring my letter to the press and post the video online. This was to be my insurance policy.

Walking up to the front door and yelling "I'm home!" was too direct an approach. The house was no doubt under surveillance. I needed to hide in plain sight. I stole a bible from my motel room, a nice bit of irony there, and began to preach door to door. It was a good racket too. I don't know if it was my silver tongue or the desire to get me out of their living room, but people contributed generously. My first day I cleared two hundred dollars. By my third day, I was quite well off. The Lord does provide.

I approached my parent's house near the end of the third day. I had made sure I had spent the last two nights at the home of the last family I visited that day. I hoped this would allow me to stay with my parents without detection. It also got me some interesting offers from women who believed me to be a television minister.

Slowly I made my way up the cobble walk toward the door. A car was parked across the street with two of the ever-present dark suit patrol. They were ignoring me. My plan was working. A feeling of elation swept over me as I rang the bell. I was at my childhood home, the first familiar place I had been in months. I was happy to be there even if it was just to be a short visit.

Dad opened the door and looked me straight in the eyes. He then proceeded to try and slam the door in my face, but I was prepared for this eventuality. My steel toed boot, wedged between the door and the frame, prevented the closure. Dad pulled this move on door to door religious folk and sales people who came his way. He was a religious man but he felt decent people should keep it in church where it belongs. I pushed my way inside. The gentlemen across the way made no move to stop me.

"Get out of here! This is a private residence! I don't want to hear anything and I won't give you any money. Leave before I call the police!" bellowed my father. It was very reminiscent of my adolescence.

"Come on, Dad. I'm sorry I wrecked the car. I paid for the damages. Can't you ever forgive and forget?"

"Rick?!" he said, stunned letting the door swing open.

"Yep. It's me. Your long lost prodigal son. Are you going to invite me in or what? Dad, close your mouth or something will fly in."

"Ricky!" screamed my mother as she threw her arms around me and began to kiss me all over. I swear I felt twelve years old again. I discreetly shut the door all the way.

"Where have you been, boy? You had your Ma and me worried sick."

"Where's Deborah?" Ma asked.

"Don't worry. She's safe."

"Safe! What do you mean safe? Where is she! We need to know. You don't know the hell we've been through these past months," my father yelled.

"Like I said, Dad, she's safe," I said mistaking my father's anguish as concern for Deborah. "The less people who know where she is the safer she will be."

"I'm her father, damn it! I need to know. It's the only thing that might save your Mom and me from..."

"Hush, Pa. Can't you see Ricky's tired? He needs some rest."

"But..."

"No buts. Now, Ricky how is it that you came home dressed as a preacher man no less?"

"I needed a disguise that wouldn't attract attention and I didn't think I could cut it as the Avon Lady."

I explained what I had done in the vaguest terms possible. I found out both my parents had lost their jobs after Deborah's disappearance. I gave them most of the money I had received over the last three days. After talking for several hours, I told my parents that I could only stay until morning.

"It's good to have you home Ricky. No matter for how short a time."

"It feels good to be home. I feel safe, as though I can finally let my guard down and stop running if only for a night."

"Don't worry Rick. You're safe here with us," my Dad said with a strange look on his face.

Kissing them both good night, I climbed the stairs to my old room. They hadn't touched, or for that matter cleaned, it since I moved out to go to college years ago. Dad had said he was going to make it into a den, but frankly, he was too lazy. The walls still had posters of beautiful cars and fast women I had hung up during high school. A flood of memories washed over me from a time so long ago it seemed like another lifetime.

I climbed under the covers and put on some headphones. Ma came up to check on me. She pulled the covers up to my shoulders and kissed me on the forehead. She had not done that since I was a kid.

"Good night, Ma."

"Goodbye, Ricky."

Putting my headphones back on, I turned on some music and fell asleep.

Hours later in the dead of night, I was rudely awakened by five smiling men dressed in dark suits. The reason for their smiles probably stemmed from the fact that they all had guns and I didn't.

Figuring it must be a nightmare I turned over and tried to go back to sleep but my visitors had other ideas. I started to scream, but they quickly convinced me to be quiet by letting one agent hit me in the head with the barrel of his gun until I stopped. Half dazed, I turned and saw Dad in the doorway. I pleaded for him to help me. He didn't move.

"Sorry, son. I wish I didn't have to do this, but you shouldn't have taken Deborah. She was the one they wanted, but they'll take you in her place."

"Take me? What are you talking about?"

"What daddy-dearest is trying to say, dirtbag, is you now belong to us and the United States," one of the dark suit brigade said, the one with eyebrows that met in the center of his forehead. "He called us at the C.S.A. and offered you in your sister's place."

"Damn you, Dad! How could you? Your own flesh and blood!" I reached over to my night table and grabbed some change that was lying there and threw it at him. "There's your thirty pieces of silver." He didn't respond to me. Instead, he turned to one-brow.

"It won't be painful for him, will it?"

"No, sir. Just one shot of this," said one-brow as he pushed down on the plunger of a syringe, "and he won't feel a thing." The other four held me as he leaned over me. I kicked and struggled to no avail. I was helpless beneath their onslaught.

"Why, Dad?" I pleaded again.

"Easy, kid," one-brow said. "We blackballed him from his job, framed him for crimes in his community. In short, we made his life a living, breathing horror. Your pound of flesh is his ticket out." He moved the needle closer to my throat. At that moment, I didn't care about what my father did. My whole world was centered on the shiny tip of a needle.

"You led us on a merry little chase all over the country. Too bad about that. You would have made a great operative with a little training. You made one mistake; you broke the cardinal rule. Never trust anyone. Period."

He thrust the needle into my jugular. I remember thinking the MP3 played with the headphones was still on and plugged it and I hoped it gave them one hell of an electric bill - sometimes the small, imaginary victories are the only ones we have. My next memory is of a cell much like the one Susie described. Except it definitely had rats. And no served meals. You draw the connection on what I had to eat.

Susie! I had forgotten about her. She was still holding on to my hand and we were still walking toward the light like a bunch of sheep being led to the slaughter.

The woman in front of me fainted and was shot before she hit the ground. I could feel her warm blood splatter on me. Damn them. Damn me. I was so terrified I just walked right over her.

"Are you scared, Mr. Rick?" Susie questioned in a whisper.

"Yes," I answered truthfully.

"Don't be," she said, trying to comfort me. "I said a prayer to God to take care of us."

"Thank you, Susie," I said. What I wanted to say, to scream and yell, was that God doesn't care or we wouldn't be here. He abandoned us the same way our families did. I wanted to say that but I didn't. Instead, I found myself whipping off "Our Father's" and "Hail Mary's" as fast as I could. There are no atheists in the valley of death.

I looked down again at the little girl by my side and wondered who was taking care of who. She moved on with her head held high as if she was only walking across a playground. Her courage both shamed me and strengthened me as we walked hand in hand into the light of oblivion.

MURIDAE

"GGr AKWE SQSX"

"abNBZ LdOPPQ RtWUi"

"ZxHiKLVVi pb iOZ"

"dIUOp" ...e is closed and healing. It seems to be functioning properly."

"Good. We still have 109 more implants to go on these hairless creatures."

"A waste of time if you ask me, sir."

"I did not ask."

"Yes, sir. Sorry, sir. Sir, the creature seems to be coming out of it."

"Put it back under."

"Yes, sir."

"Huh? What's going on? What are you? My neck hurts."

"Sedate it now."

"It is done."

RICK

The white light, it blinds me and becomes a rainbow. No, many rainbows. Thousands of colors. I fly and the spectrum envelops me in a cocoon of warmth. Music, beautiful music plays. I think it's Chuck Berry. I am dreaming. It's real, yet I know I'm dreaming.

I float on happily, strangely contented. It doesn't last. I slowly leave my world of dreams and awaken. I hear two people spouting gibberish and suddenly I understand them in my mind. I feel a stabbing sensation in my neck as if a giant guillotine is falling down upon me. I try to communicate but they ignore me. I open my eyes to see, but there are only two giant rats and I feel heat burn me as it flames through the sky. I should be scared, but I am still too comfortable. It's only a dream. But I'm awake? These must be the rats Susie saw. Or the ghosts of the ones I ate. Why am I seeing them in my dream? Are they haunting me? Who cares? The colors are back and I drift off to the sounds of "Johnny B. Goode".

SUSIE

"Mommy! Daddy! Don't leave me. I'm so scared. Why did you give me away? Don't you love me anymore? I can see you both, but all these shiny lights are in the way. I can't reach you and all I hear is 'Old MacDonald.' I want to wake up."

"Sir, the small creature seems to be regaining consciousness."

"The implant is in?"

"Yes"

"Rats! ARRRHHHHH!!!! Help!"

"Sedate it. Silence it. Now."

"Yes, sir."

"And make sure you double the dose for the remaining creatures. They should not awaken so soon. If another awakens while I'm here it is your hide. They are divided appropriately for storage or transport?"

"Yes, sir. I took care of it myself."

"I am not impressed."

"Sorry, sir."

RICK

"Lonso, Grillar you bastards! Let me out of here! Have the decency to give me some water, damn you."

"Are you talking to us?"

"You know damn well I'm talking to you, Lonso. First, you kidnap me then you gave me over to Grillar so the two of you could get your jollies by torturing me. Go ahead, stab me, prod me and zap me all you want, but I won't talk. Once I get loose, Grillar, I'm going to blow the lid off your whole presidential campaign. When I'm done with you, nobody in their right mind will vote for you. It's bad enough you're head of the Central Security Agency. If you ever get to be president nobody will be safe. You'll take us all to Hell."

"I think it's talking to you now, Burke."

"The drugs the Muridae gave it must be beginning to wear off. It's having a flashback to a previous recollection."

"Ah. So, it is not aware of what it is doing yet and therefore not yet responsible for its actions."

"Why are you two talking about me like I'm some thing? Is this a new plan to make me reveal where Deborah is?"

"Who is Deborah? Is it your mate?"

"You know who she is! You've been tormenting me for weeks to find out where she is! But I won't tell and it's driving you nuts that you can't break me. And stop calling me it!"

"You are right. It was improper of us. We did not want to offend you by incorrectly presuming your gender. Some beings are very insecure about having their sexuality questioned. So I'll just ask."

"Be grateful. Kerr used to look first to determine the sex of Newbes."

"Newbes?"

"New arrivals. So what are you? Male, female, uni, bi, tri, octo, auto, breeder, or drone?"

"I'm male of course, just like you two."

"I am male but we are not like you."

"What trick are you trying to pull?"

"No deception. Your thoughts are still clouded by the drugs you were given when your translator was implanted. Try inhaling deeply and focusing your ocular organs on us."

"Okay, but I've seen your ugly mugs before."

"You have seen our unsightly drinking vessels previously?"

"Kerr, it is just an interpretation error."

"And whose fault is that? I thought you would have perfected those things by now."

"Quiet. Now Newbe try and do as Kerr instructed."

I did as they asked, breathing in deeply, and my head did begin to clear. The haze that had obscured my vision lifted and I was rewarded with the view of two creatures standing before me.

Nothing in my life had equipped me for this sight. One of the creatures was over eight feet tall and almost as wide. His physique was incredible. He looked as if he had been carved out of granite. Literally. The guy seemed to be made of stone. Blue stone at that. He had two arms and legs with three digits on each. Each of his hands were equipped with two thumbs and the middle finger had four joints instead of three.

His companion was smaller in stature, being only about six feet four inches tall. He made up for the lack of height with an overabundance of limbs. He sported four upper extremities and two lower. He was covered in silver-white fur and looked amazingly like a wolf standing upright. At his side hung a sword, shaped similar to a Katana, in a golden sheath. Totally unprepared for this situation, I let my instincts take over. I jumped onto one of two cots in an otherwise barren room and screamed at the top of my lungs. They were not impressed by my act of bravery.

"Be calm, gentlebeing. We will not harm you. Allow us to introduce ourselves," said the big blue one. He cut a very intimidating figure, yet his voice was very gentle.

"I am Burke of the DeTang. My companion is Kerr of the Czarrian Empire. You have made your entrance onto the planet Liberty in the city Tore."

"I always did like to make an entrance," I muttered, wondering what he was talking about.

"Salutations o' courageous one," said Kerr as he bowed with a flourish making circles with both his right hands simultaneously.

"What are you guys? Aliens?" I asked overwhelming them with my intelligence.

"But of course. Have you not had experiences with any not of your own race? Is that the reason for your shock?" Burke asked. "I thought all Newbes were informed as to the nature of their indenture prior to their arrival."

"Well, nobody told me anything."

"You still have not introduced yourself," Kerr pointed out.

"Sorry. I'm Rick Wagner."

"And where are you from Rick Wagner?" asked Kerr.

"Oh. I'm from Earth."

"From the planet Dirt. I thought I recognized your species," said Kerr.

"Dirt? You mean you've heard of Earth?"

"Yes. The winner of the Tournament some years ago was a warrior of your world. From a place called Brook Land, I believe. Kerr, you remember Anthony Savage?"

"Tony the Terran? Of course. He was one of the best combatants this place ever had. We fought once and he clobbered me. Of course, that was early on in my career. I was just a Newbe myself. If there was a rematch I would emerge victorious."

"Of course, you would," said Burke, half patronizing, half sarcastic.

"Think you'll be able to measure up, Rick?" the wolf who walked on two legs asked.

"I don't have any idea what you are talking about."

"You really are slow, aren't you, Dirtling? It's like this. You're indentured to the Muridae for the length of your contract. You've been placed with us which means you are now, or rather will be, a warrior. You will be trained to fight, to think, to behave and to live as a warrior. You'll also be taught how to entertain the masses of the universe. Have I left anything out, Burke?"

"No, except if you become popular they merchandise you and .002 percent of the profits go into your exit account for when you contract has ended. How long did you sign on for?"

"I didn't sign on. I don't remember how I even got here."

"Then you are a Xile," informed the wolf.

"What's a Xile?" I asked.

"An indentured whose government gave them over in trade."

"The government made us go into the light...Oh my God! Susie! I've got to find her. How can I escape from here?"

"Well you can use the door," answered Kerr. A simple plan but it had merit.

"Thanks, Kerr. You're a pal," I said as I ran through the door. As I was running down the hall I realized I had no idea where I was going. I turned around and ran back in to find the two aliens laughing at me. Kerr's laugh made me nervous. His smile revealed two rows of very sharp looking teeth. I hoped he was fed well and regularly.

"Are all people from Dirt this amusing? Perhaps you should have been sent to the comedy center," smirked Kerr.

"I need to find a little girl who was with me before I came here. Do you have any idea where she might be?"

"That depends on what you Dirt beings are good for besides a good laugh," asked Kerr.

"Why do you keep calling Earth dirt?"

"The translators often have interpretation errors, don't they Burke?" the multi-limbed wolf asked in what appeared to be a sarcastic tone.

"True, but they learn from the owner's own speech patterns and will adjust accordingly with time," big blue said.

"As I was saying, in my language there is only a single word for dirt. Do not be offended. I'm sure it was not your idea to name your planet after dirt," said Kerr. Burke just looked embarrassed at the oversight.

"Wait a minute. What translator?"

"The one you just had implanted," replied Burke.

"Oh." I would have to think about that later. "I need to find Susie. Please help me," I pleaded.

"It does seem important to him," Kerr said, turning to his stony companion.

"Maybe we should help. We can check the market auction. It is nearby and she may be there," said Burke.

"But first we will take you on a grand tour of the finer taverns and drinking establishments that this poor excuse for a city has to offer," Kerr added as he placed two furry arms around my shoulders.

"First help me find Susie, then I will go wherever you want."

"Agreed," said Kerr as he shook my shoulders vigorously.

"That may not have been such a wise promise to make, Rick," Burke said.

"Why?"

"To survive bar hopping with Kerr it is usually a good idea to complete warrior training, be heavily armed, or both."

"How come?"

"Let's just say some people do not always react well to my charming personality," Kerr said as he laughed and his grin became much too wide for comfort.

NED AND BOB

Torrents poured down, as a vision and two voices boomed down from the heavens. The downpour was one of hype and had been saturating the media of Tore all week with details of the auctions. No avenue was left unexplored or unsoaked, no sentient allowed to escape dry or uninformed. Homevid and streetvid were not enough for this media blitz. The famous Skyvid was extolling the virtues of Muridae indentured labor. Two Muridae were doing the hyping. Above their faces in the sky, the phase *The best of all possible worlds* blazed brightly in six languages. In the background, between speeches by the pair, the advertisements shouted, hummed and sang the catchiest of jingles.

"That's right, Ned. Anything one could dream, create or imagine will be on the auction block today."

"Absolutely, Bob. Lifeforms from worlds too numerous to mention will be available with contracts to suit every need. Need radioactive ore mined? How about one of the durable Roserod."

"Need a nanny for your offspring? Some of the best young rearers in the universe would be offered. Famed Warriors, fully trained and fresh from the Tore Games, are obtainable and make a fine addition to any elite guard or security force."

"And Bob, did you know season tickets are still available for the Games?"

"I did, Ned. But did you know that today's auction even features an Amoropath from Ardor."

"An unbelievable opportunity, Bob."

"Completely, Ned. She is available on short term lease for the right price."

"Terms are simple. Once payment is arranged, all the contract holder needs to provide are the basics of life."

"For the mere cost of food, clothing, housing, a breathable atmosphere and a pittance of a stipend, one receives in return the perfect worker. Cheap, obedient and under contract to perform any task given provided their continued well-being is not jeopardized."

"Money cannot buy workers or happiness, but the Muridae will see to it you can rent both. Come one, come all. Bring the family, clan or tribe."

"Refreshments will be served. Easy credit terms available."

MURIDAE

The auction house was abuzz with action. A huge crowd had already gathered about the stage in anticipation of finding just what they were looking for. Veiled behind the stage, overcome with a tangible greed, stood the two highest-ranked Muridae traders on the council and therefore the planet. Neither surpassed the five-and-a-half-foot mark and bore a remarkable resemblance to rats. Both adorned themselves in brightly colored robes, jewelry, and enough dark brown fur to convince even the harshest skeptic that disco had not died, just found a new race to infest. The larger of the two, by virtue of the other's bowing and scraping, was ranting and raving over the puny size of the crowd compared with those of the past.

"It's not like the old cycles. Then there was no such thing as indenture. We sold slavery, pure and simple. None of this worry about a being's innate rights," said the Muridae superior, named Dortew, as if the words were a curse. "Those were the cycles when might made right. Live or die, rape or mutilate, the beings in our possession were ours to do with as we saw fit."

The gaily-adorned lackey, who answered to the name Smed'lee, cretin, or almost any derogatory term, groveled skillfully. "Yes, sir. Those were indeed the cycles."

"After that misbegotten creature from Dirt won the tournament we foolishly gave him his freedom," spat the larger Muridae with the accumulated bitterness of the years in his voice. As he spoke, a large, mucous filled blob flew downward from his mouth to splatter on the floor. The second took a silk cloth from a pocket and cleaned the foul spittle from the floor and replaced the soiled cloth in his pocket.

It was the law. He won the tournament, sir," Smed'lee spoke meekly, fearful of offending. It made no difference. His superior spun savagely around on him. Years of service had deadened his natural protective reflexes to the point where he did not ward off the blow which followed. He forced a smile through his repeatedly damaged bridgework in thanks for the attack.

Oblivious to the cowering, Dortew continued his rant. "Law or no law, it was the Muridae's greatest mistake. Damn primitive appealed to the Kentor for High Justice and the fools granted it. We had no time to prepare our case. The verdict came swift and was ruinous. It changed our way of life forever. The Muridae were forced to free all the people under our care and make restitution to them for their trouble. Restitution, bah." Dortew was one of the few beings in the universe who could work the word bah convincingly into a conversation.

"We took the dregs of the universe, trained them, gave them useful skills, meaningful lives of service, and then had to pay them for the privilege. The Kentor took my predecessor, Lord Dorwon's, life and those of his conclave as final payment and proclaimed their damn scales balanced. We were powerless to stop them. I barely escaped with my wealth." Escaping with his life was only a secondary concern. Without wealth, most Muridae preferred death to the horrors of an impoverished life.

"Nothing can stop a Justice, sir," the lackey offered by way of consolation.

"That did nothing to stop the immediate decrease in our profits or to reduce the shame of our people. Never before had the Muridae suffered such a crushing defeat, not even in the glory days of the Czarrian Empire. But we are adapting. We will make this indenture concept work for us. Now begin the auction," he demanded, kicking his inferior in the posterior.

"Yes, sir. Thank you, sir," he said sauntering out onto the stage. Smed'lee strutted much like a peacock would if it was covered in unkempt dark brown fur and forced to waddle on stubby legs dressed in a five-piece suit, each piece with its own neon color. The metal jewelry clanging together with each step could have kept time for a Caribbean band. "If I might have the attention of all the assembled gentlebeings, we will begin."

The crowd responded by becoming mildly hushed and taking their seats. The bidding was about to begin.

"The first item up for bidding is a Belzan nanny. The Belzans have long since perfected the telepathic art of subliminal indoctrination, so they are able to program any offspring to think and act as their parents desire. No more worries of rebellion. The contract is for five cycles. A great value. We shall open the bidding at five thousand Czarrian pounds."

As the bidding raged, three interested parties entered quietly from the rear of the auditorium. Burke and Kerr stood silently, scanning the hall. Rick, by way of comparison, was caught somewhere between fear and disbelief over what he had been witness to in the last hour. A quick tour of the free-city of Tore had altered his perceptions of the bounds of reality.

Free-city meant that no planetary or other government could lay claim to Tore, so beings of all races were welcome provided they were able to pay the immigration tax. Although Tore owed allegiance by way of treaty and charter to the Czarrian Empire, they choose to simply ignore this technicality whenever it suited their purposes. Which was always. Simply put, Tore just did not get involved in political conflicts. It was much easier to keep up trade that way. Trade was Tore's lifeblood.

No laws applied except those which the city Assembly passed, which made Tore a haven for anyone fleeing persecution or prosecution for any and all reasons. When one entered the free-city, one left all pre-existing conflicts behind. Of course, one was free to make as many new conflicts as one liked.

Being in the company of fierce looking beings like Burke and Kerr was a definite asset when walking the streets. In a city on another planet Rick expected to see floating buildings, sparkling streets and personal aircraft in use. Instead, the journey took him through gritty streets surrounded on all sides by huge skyscrapers and not so large buildings. Some were of usual construction while others appeared to be straight out of a Salvador Dali nightmare. Any and all modes of transportation imaginable were in use. Various air and hover craft could be seen in the sky and just off the street. Ground transportation used everything from wheels and treads to carts and buggies mounted on or pulled by a variety of beasts, some seemingly intelligent.

Underground lay a series of transport tubes that the trio used to reach the auction. The entire time Rick was in the tubes he was surrounded by and pressed up against lifeforms beyond the resourcefulness of his imagination. Beauty abounded. A crystalline globe floated above the crowds sparkling and speaking of peace for all. Most ignored it, having heard the message so often it became background noise. Rick was captivated by it and had to be led off the car at their next stop.

For every ying there exists a yang. On the next car, Rick stood directly across from a creature that consisted of nothing more than a variety of internal organs. He could see its food being digested before his eyes while watching its three hearts beating rhythmically.

His olfactory sense was overloaded. One moment he inhaled near a being that smelled of sweet perfume while the next greeted him with a stench that made wet dog seem like an air freshener. Rick quickly began to hope for a nose cold, which was unlikely since Kerr explained that he had been given all his shots before being allowed planetside.

The strange thing was both beings looked exactly alike. They were in fact of the same species. Each was small, eight inches in length with two pairs of oblong gossamer wings which fluttered at high speeds, keeping their tube-shaped bodies aloft.

"They are called Fragrunts. Prized by the wealthy to turn their homes into fragrance paradises. Also prized for their defensive capability of showering opponents with the foulest of stenches. They are good watchdogs. I believe that is the correct phrase in English," Rick noticed for the first time that the Elucidator did not have to translate Burke's words. The stone giant was speaking fluent American English. "A challenging race," Burke said.

"In what way?" Rick asked, trying to position himself downwind of the sweeter smelling Fragrunt.

"Their language. Languages are my avocation. The Fragrunts communicate by means of olfaction."

"You mean by smells and odors?"

"Exactly."

"Why are they such a challenge?"

"Easy," interrupted Kerr. "Burke has no sense of smell or taste so he has no baseline to begin with to quantify the language so he has to rely wholly on technology. He even was desperate enough to ask for help."

"I must have been desperate to ask from help from the likes of you, Czarrian," said Burke. Turning to Rick he asked, "Do you know what Kerr did?" Rick shook his head no. "I brought him with me on a translation secession and he is little or no help. Kerr becomes bored, so without telling me he decides to insult the Fragrunts in their own language. They stormed off in anger, ending the secession."

"Kerr, do you know their language?" asked Rick.

"Not exactly. Just a few phrases and some of their better curses."

"What did you do?" Rick questioned. Kerr smiled and chuckled to himself. Rick turned to Burke who, agitated, answered.

"Kerr released methane from his digestive tract into the immediate atmosphere."

Rick thought about the statement and burst out laughing. To Kerr he said, "You broke wind?"

"Yes. And I apparently insulted their mother in the process. But they deserved it. They had just insulted Burke's mother."

"They were demonstrating. Besides, I do not have a mother as such. It was no insult."

"That is the thanks I get for defending your family honor."

"You do not even know the language. A difference of four particles per million in the air changes the entire meaning. They could have been complimenting my parentage."

"They were not. I could see it in their eyes."

"Fragrunts do not have eyes."

"Nitpicker."

With a quiet hum, the transport tube doors opened onto the platform ending the discussion. An exit onto the platform brought the commuters into contact with a group of toughs; there was a group on almost each platform. They never seemed to use the tubes. All the other beings veered out of their way to avoid contact. When they spotted Burke and Kerr however, it was the toughs who quickly stepped aside. One even asked for their autographs but was hit upside the head by a compatriot and decided not to pursue the matter.

"Why do so many beings look similar to each other?" Rick asked, staring around him.

"Like beings such as mammals, reptiles, beings with similar numbers and types of limbs tend to congregate together here on Liberty. Living conditions are favorable for these types. On other types of worlds other forms of life dwell together," said Burke.

"But why are they so similar to each other? One would think life would evolve differently so far apart," said Rick.

"Some say the creator did not have a very vivid imagination so he used variations on the same themes. Others claim parallel evolution. Still more say worlds were seeded with life millions of years ago by the same gods or beings," answered Kerr.

"Which do you think is true?" Rick asked.

"Do not know. Do not care. Does not make a difference in my life, whatever the answer is," Kerr said sagely.

Having finally arrived at their destination, the trio chose to sit in the rear of the auditorium. It was occupied by several hundred aliens, but it was far less traumatic and claustrophobic than the tubes. Each being had his own seat.

Burke was seated on Rick's right, the chair straining under his weight. Kerr, having stopped to grab some of the snacks, was on his left. They explained what was happening on the stage.

"The Muridae running the auction is Smed'lee," said Burke.

"Smed'lee? You're kidding, right?" replied Rick.

"No. The other Muridae is Dortew. He is the Muridae high overseer. Smed'lee is his lackey," Burke said.

Rick blinked in disbelief. "You mean I've been taken prisoner by a couple of giant space rats?"

"Actually, there are thirty-six Muridae involved in the games," Burke informed precisely.

Refusing to be distracted, Rick asked, "How do we find Susie?"

"We wait. The video listing shows a Dirtling is up for auction next," Kerr said, between mouthfuls of food. He was on his third helping.

Rick stared at the characters on the screen in vain. No matter how he squinted the screen would not give up its mysteries. "How can you read that? It all looks like gibberish to me. Why doesn't my Elucidator translate it for me?"

"The Elucidator is hooked into your auditory pathways, not your optic tracts. It can only interpret what you hear. To understand the screen you must learn to read Czarrian Common, which is the most utilized language for writing."

"Has been ever since the early days of the Empire. And how it should be," said Kerr with a sense of pride in his heritage.

"Bah," uttered Burke with a sense of disgust. He did not work it into the conversation as naturally as had Dortew. "You are just afraid you will have to use your mind for something besides battle games. It is not that difficult to learn another tongue you know, Czarrian."

Kerr dismissed the notion. "Coming from the developer of the Elucidator, the best comprehensive translator on the market. Not everyone speaks thousands of languages, DeTang. How many languages are you eloquent in?"

"More than you can count. With the common usage of the Elucidator the need for a common spoken tongue was eliminated," said Burke with a certain pride tinged with sorrow. Although he accomplished his goal in the creation of the translator, he knew it meant ultimately there would be fewer languages to learn, robbing him of his favorite pastime. "I would be glad to instruct you in reading, Rick."

"I'll think about it," Rick said with half interest. With Susie in danger, his concentration for anything else was lacking. "Thanks for the history and language lessons, but what's the plan for rescuing Susie? How are we going to get her away from the rats?"

"We are not. That would be stealing. She, as well as the rest of the auctionees and yourself, are the property of the Muridae," said Burke, as if stating a well-known fact.

"So how do we save her?" asked a hopeful Rick.

"You can purchase her," suggested Kerr, preparing to trip a waiter who had ignored his request for a seventh serving and take the food from him.

"With what? I have no money," Rick said, turning out his pockets to demonstrate. The waiter flew over Kerr's leg as the wolfen warrior caught the serving tray with two of his four arms. Not a morsel was spilled. He paused only to offer Rick a sample. When Rick nodded no, his attention returned to his purloined meal.

"Then I guess they will auction her off to the highest bidder," Kerr said, wiping his mouth on a napkin which was tucked in the neck of his shirt.

"That's not fair," agonized Rick.

"Whoever said life was fair?" asked Kerr, offering by way of demonstration the now empty platter.

"But I can't let them sell her. She is only a child!" blurted Rick, on the brink of frustration. His words captured the attention that his pleas had not.

"What?!" Burke yelled, his former easy going manner fading away as an undeniable anger took its place. The DeTang surged to his feet, obscuring the stage from view. His features took on a hardness that was not present a moment before. Rick cringed in fear. Kerr ordered another plate from the now docile waiter.

"Are you telling us that she is only a fledgling of your people?"

Finding his voice Rick managed to whisper, "Yes. She's just a kid."

"By the great mountain of us all, this time they go too far. Why I'll…"

Kerr stood and, reaching up, placed a comforting hand on his friend.

"Easy, Burke. Anger won't save the child. We must come up with a plan," Kerr said thoughtfully. His roguish demeanor given way to a more solemn and devious one. As the wolfen warrior spoke, an unconscious Susie was brought out upon the stage.

"That's her!" cried Rick, causing heads and other appendages to turn his way. Burke told him to be quiet. Smed'lee called for the bidding to begin and began his sales pitch.

"The Dirtlings are a very strong people able to lift up to one hundred and twenty percent of their own weight in standard gravity. The contract is for ten cycles. Bidding will open at five hundred Czarrian pounds."

"Why is the Dirtling sedated? Is it violent? Or dangerous?" questioned a green being seated in the middle of the auditorium.

"No, it is not violent. Dirt is a planet whose general populace has not made its first contact yet. Only the governments of Dirt are aware that they are not alone in the universe. This particular specimen is having a particularly difficult time adjusting to interactions with others not of its species," replied Smed'lee by way of explanation.

"Well wake it up. I won't buy goods that are damaged," demanded the grccn buyer.

"Me neither," clamored another.

"Yes. Wake it up," yelled a third.

"Very well," Smed'lee said, caving to the pressure. The customer is always right. At least until the final payment is made. He walked toward Susie's sleeping form, snapped open a capsule and waved it under her nose. Susie began to stretch her arms slowly like a cat. Her eyes opened slowly at first, then wide in terror.

"Arrhhh! Rats! Help me!" she screamed. Laughter arose from the crowd at her fear. Three members of the crowd didn't laugh. One, without hesitation, rushed through the crowd and leaped onto the stage before either of his companions could stop him. Overjoyed at seeing the familiar face, Susie ran toward Rick throwing her arms around his neck. She held on for dear life.

"Rick! I'm so glad you are here. I'm so scared. But you'll make everything okay won't you, Rick?" Susie pleaded.

Damn, thought Rick. I promised to take care of her but what can I do? The rats may kill me for interfering. Should have thought of that before you ran up here, genius. Probably would have done the same thing anyway.

"Susie, honey, I don't know if I can make everything okay, but I'll try my best," Rick said as he carried the little girl away from the stage. His actions were far from unnoticed.

"Stand away from the auctionee now," Smed'lee demanded with a tone of voice reserved for talking to garbage and door to door vacuum cleaner salesmen.

"No. You have no right to do anything with her," Rick answered defiantly. He turned his body to shield Susie from the Muridae.

"We own her. Now, if you cannot produce prior ownership papers stand aside for unless I am greatly mistaken you also are our property," Smed'lee stated, looking fearfully over his shoulder at Dortew who was dispassionately watching the situation.

"We are no one's property. We are free people. We never agreed to any indenture," said Rick. If a soap box was handy, he would have stood atop it.

"No, but your government did," Smed'lee said, his whiskers twitching.

"They haven't the right," said Rick, as if his words alone would halt the sale.

"Ah, but under interstellar law a government has the right to sell or distribute those under its dominion any way it sees fit. Now step down off the stage or you will regret it," Smed'lee countered, with evil intent apparent in his eyes.

"No," Rick said as he protectively placed Susie behind him. Smed'lee produced a small oblong device from beneath his cloak and pressed a button. Suddenly Rick's head exploded with pain and he collapsed to the floor, dropping Susie in the process.

"Rick!" Susie screamed as she bent down to his side, trying to ease his agony with her tiny hands. "Stop it! You're hurting him," she demanded with fire coursing through her veins.

"That is the general idea. Now leave him be and come to the front of the stage so the buyers can see what they will be getting," said Smed'lee as he grabbed Susie's wrist and pulled her, kicking and screaming, away from Rick's fallen form.

"Let go of me! Stop it! You're hurting me!" yelled Susie. Smed'lee, amused at Susie's struggles, made a great effort to cause pain in the tiny body by hitting and squeezing any area that looked tender and vulnerable. He continued to drag her across the stage until a mammoth shadow covered him from behind. A huge stone hand grabbed both his shoulders, lifting him off the stage in the process. The action effectively ended his sadistic amusement. A turn of his head later Smed'lee was looking up at eight feet of angry mountain.

"Let go of the girl, now," boomed Burke's voice, shaking the rafters. Smed'lee seemed to wither in on himself, but he did not let go.

Getting up from his seat near the rear of the stage Dortew decided to take a more active role in the proceedings.

"Lord Burke, I must respectfully request that you put down my assistant," said Dortew.

"Not until he releases the girl and shuts the Nociogenerator off," replied Burke. His tone left no room for argument. Dortew nodded at Smed'lee who let go of Susie's wrist and released the button that had incapacitated Rick.

"This is most unseemly for one of your stature, Lord Burke. You know the laws," said Dortew.

"As do you which is why I am shocked and angered to find you auctioning a minor," Burke countered, bringing his body within an inch of Dortew's. The effect was not lost on the Muridae who stepped back.

"What?" Dortew exclaimed, acting shocked. "I would never willingly breach the law by doing such a thing."

"The fact remains, willingly or not, that you have done it. This girl is not recognized by her own people as a full citizen yet here you are selling her contract."

"If what you are saying is true we will most certainly buy back her contract. Now if you will just allow the auction to continue."

"No. If she is a minor she may require care that can only be given by one of her kind. I respectfully suggest that she be allowed to remain with Rick Wagner of Dirt until this matter is settled."

"Absolutely not. We will lose credits with her at the Warplex."

"If you don't let me stay with Rick I'll hold my breath until I turn blue and die," Susie threatened.

"What?" exclaimed Dortew, who previously had not even acknowledged Susie's presence.

"Holding one's breath is an expectable form of ritual suicide among our young. It is their way of protesting against what they perceive to be injustice," added Rick having recovered his wits and his voice.

Susie by way of demonstration puffed out her cheeks and began to hold her breath.

"The death of a minor by self-induced anoxia on your auction stage, Dortew. In front of hundreds of witnesses. I wonder how the Tetrarch's Court or the Kentor Justices will view that. Not too kindly, I think," said Burke. "I will also be very unhappy if anything should happen to the little human," continued Burke as his features began to darken even further. The Muridae leader was visibly shaken, his calm facade fading fast as he was overwhelmed by the pure physical presence of the DeTang.

"My Lord Burke, never have I seen you so distraught," said Dortew by way of distraction.

"Never before have you dared to involve children. I will not tolerate this."

"Easy, Burke. Diplomacy, remember," said Kerr as he stepped up alongside his rocklike friend.

"Move away now, Czarrian scum," Smed'lee hissed.

"So, the lackey finds his tongue. Is the big, bad Muridae tired of abusing little children?" countered Kerr with a mocking bow and salute. The Muridae began to shake in anger, as he gripped the pain inducing Nociogenerator tightly in his hands.

Then, to Rick's surprise, the warrior did as he was told leaving Burke alone with Dortew. Kerr did not wish to cause further torment to be inflicted. Rick and Susie were huddled together near the rear of the platform.

The crowd was beginning to get unruly. Some headed for the exits, wanting to avoid any trouble. Dortew could smell the profits slipping through his furry fingers. He would have to offer the next few contracts at cost to make up for this display.

"I respect your wishes, but you cannot prove her age. You have no documentation. All you have is her word and that of another of her species. Hardly hard evidence. We, on the other hand, hold a bill of ownership signed by her planetary rulers giving us full title for ten cycles. Until you can prove otherwise, we have full rights to her. If you can prove otherwise we will, of course, buy back her contract and make restitution. We will even stipulate this in the buyer's agreement," said Dortew.

"You will not sell her," Burke commanded.

Dortew stood his ground. "You cannot stop me, my lord. I am within my rights."

"I shall invoke Kentor High Justice," threatened the DeTang.

"Nonsense. You know full well you haven't the evidence for a case and even you don't dare invoke High Justice groundlessly. You have too much to lose," Dortew said smugly, assuming the matter was settled. It was not.

Crossing his arms in front of his chest, Burke said, "Very well. Then I shall buy her contract. I open the bidding at one cent."

"One cent? You jest. One cent for a ten-cycle contract?" Dortew sputtered, half stunned. The DeTang remained immobile. "You can't be serious."

"Do not make me repeat myself, little Muridae."

"Ahem. Very well. I am bid one cent for the Dirtling contract. Do I hear two cents?"

"Two cents," bid a purple triped in the third row. Before any more bids could be entered Kerr was alongside the triped and had twisted an upper extremity. The triped collapsed to the floor moaning.

"This noble sentient regrets he must withdraw his bid. Too rich for his blood, I'm afraid," said Kerr, a large smile draped across his jaws. In his free hand were quickly disappearing liberated appetizers.

"Only the one making the bid can withdraw it. Surely the G'morran gentleman does not wish to pass up such a bargain?" Dortew asked.

Kerr lifted the triped up but did not relax his grip on the purple arm. Or on the food. "Yes. Yes. Too rich for my blood."

"Very well then. Are there any other bids? Anyone?" begged Dortew. After looking at the towering DeTang and the grinning wolfen warrior there were no more bids.

"Here. I found this coin on the floor," Burke said.

"That contract should have sold for a thousand pounds," said Dortew.

"A pity, but I am within my rights after all. My change please," replied Burke.

RICK

"Rick, what just happened?" Susie asked.

"I think Burke just saved you from being sold." Thank you, God.

"Yay!" screamed Susie as she ran to Burke. She leaped up, hugged him, and gave him a big kiss on the cheek. The lower gravity allowed her the ability to jump higher than she would have been able to back home. "Thank you, Mr. Rockman," she said and she kissed him again. I swear he blushed.

"It was my pleasure, Susie. Call me Burke." He introduced her to Kerr.

"You are pretty, Mr. Kerr. You remind me of Champ."

Kerr ate up the compliment. "And who is this Champ? Some noble warrior?"

"No, silly. He was my Grampa's doggie."

Kerr's head tilted in confusion. The term didn't translate. "Doggie?"

"His pet," she explained.

That took him down a few notches. "A pet! I remind you of a pet? Of all the..."

"Kerr, she is only a child," said Burke, interceding. "This is a new experience for her and she is relating you to something she is familiar with. Actually, she is handling her integration into society much better than her older counterpart did."

"Or at least with more style and grace," added Kerr, with a chuckle.

"Some people. You make one mistake and they never let you live it down," I said.

Truth be told, I was learning to like these guys. Without them, I never would have been able to rescue Susie. They had no reason to help us but they did. Restored my faith in people, even if the people look like a statue and something that should be howling at a full moon.

Being in Tore was going to take some getting used to. Humans appear to be a very small minority here. Burke and Kerr said they would be helping with our integration. Susie was already beginning hers, giggling. When I asked what was so funny, she whispered in my ear.

"Mr. Burke has no clothes on," Susie said and she was right. On closer examination, he had none of the usual reasons folks wear clothes. Being built like a mountain I doubted temperature or weather changes affected him. As far as covering private parts went, he had none noticeable. Of course, for all I know he could mate with his elbow. Walking arm in arm might be considered sex.

The lot of us headed back to the Warplex where I had awakened. It was also where I would be spending most of my time from now on. Burke rated private quarters and Susie would be staying with him there. I would stay in the barrack dorms. When we arrived, Kerr reminded me I had a debt to pay. I was more than happy to go. I needed a good stiff drink. Burke said that Susie could not go because she was too young for the drinking age and he still wanted to build a case against the Muridae. Susie's presence in a bar would ruin any chance the case might have of proving her a minor. Besides, he didn't want her to get hurt. He promised to guard her against all harm which he could do much better than me anyhow. Burke's parting words to my bar hopping trip were less than encouraging, however.

"It has been nice knowing you, friend Rick."

RICK

"Hail, good tavern keep. Some ale for myself and my companion," Kerr roared as we sauntered into our fifth bar of the evening. Kerr was batting five hundred so far. We had been thrown out of two bars and he had thrown the owners out of two more. I hoped he was not looking for a tie breaker.

The barkeeper was a short, stout raspberry colored fellow with a yellow growth over his lower mouth which resembled a mustache. His upper mouth was where a forehead should have been. It was sipping from a tube that curved down to what looked like a keg mounted on his back. Four eyes adorned his head, one on either side and the other two were positioned in the front and back of his skull. Also behind the bar stood a medium-sized Muridae, much kinder looking and somberly dressed than the two I had already met. Otherwise, I couldn't really tell them apart. The bartender turned to the Muridae and whispered something. Then, after taking a large sip from his tube, appearing to almost brace himself, the bartender came over to greet us.

"Kerr! What a pleasant surprise," he said as he walked across the room to greet us. He actually appeared sincere. The bartender also sported four arms and grasped each of Kerr's hands with one of his own. Looking behind the bar I saw the Muridae quickly pulling closed iron gates in front of the glasses and bottles. These guys were no dummies.

"How's existence treating you, old warrior?" Kerr asked genuinely happy to see what I took to be his old friend.

"Not too severely. Business is good and Red wants it to stay that way, Czarrian. No messing with Red's regulars, understand?"

"You wound me, Roserod. Have I ever caused trouble in your fine establishment?" Kerr asked innocently. Without pausing for an answer, he introduced me. "I'd like you to meet someone. This is Rick. Rick, this is Red, the closest thing to a gentlebeing the planet Roserod ever produced." Red grabbed each of my hands with two of his own and shook vigorously.

"Hi," I said my flair for words peaking.

"Newbe?" Red asked as he turned toward Kerr. Kerr nodded. Red smiled and laughed. "A pleasure, Rick. You have Red's congratulations on being chosen to follow the noble path of a warrior, but many condolences on your choice of company for the evening. How did you end up tavern hopping with Kerr? You lose a bet?" Red asked as he warmly led us to the bar.

"Something like that. I made a promise before I knew any better," I said as I explained what had happened. "I should have listened to Burke."

Red laughed. He and Kerr threw several insults regarding ethnic heritage at each other. Apparently, the Czarrian Empire was never able to conquer Roserod, making it one of the few worlds to ever escape Empire influence. I wonder how their Empire fell? Lead poisoning in the water? Nah.

Despite his odd appearance, Red's easy going manner soon put me at ease. I gave him the highlights of my day. He seemed especially impressed by Burke's actions.

"Rick, considering you are new to Tore and this is your virgin trip to Red's, not to mention what will happen on the morrow, your first drink is on the house," Red said with one mouth as the other sipped slowly.

"What's happening tomorrow?" I asked.

"Hey, what about me?" Kerr chimed in effectively changing the subject. "We've known each other for years and you've never given me a freebie."

"True. But not to worry. Red charges you double what Red charges other customers so that should more than make up for it."

"Well, okay," Kerr said as he grabbed a bottle off the bar, bit off the top and drank it in a single guzzle. He put down the bottle as he realized what Red had told him. "Wait a second, you scum sucking porcine," Kerr said as he stared into Red's front eye and began to growl. Red stopped sipping. I looked around for a table to take cover under.

"You got a problem with that, you flea-ridden furball?" Red shot back. Our section of the bar was slowly emptying of customers.

"And what if I do, father of maggot spume?" asked Kerr, a chilling smile spreading across his face. They were silent as each tried to stare the other down. Then something unexpected happened. They both began to smile and then to giggle. Kerr reached up a single hand toward Red's face and slapped him gently on the cheek. Red did the same. Then they both began to laugh uncontrollably and pat each other on the back.

Confused but happy I sat back on the barstool and relaxed. The patrons gradually diffused back around us filling the gap they had left but moments earlier. It had frightened me but no one else had even put down their drink.

"Do not mind us, Rick. We just like to let off steam. Besides Red does not fight anymore. At least, not without a good reason," explained Red.

"What good reason? You fight for money," Kerr quipped.

"Money's a good reason," Red answered. Red had been a tourney winner back in the days when the warriors were all Muridae slaves and the only way to gain freedom was to defeat all comers. The losers were buried at their earliest possible convenience.

They talked about my Earthling predecessor, Tony, and how he changed the games forever even before he freed the slaves. He never took a life in the ring. Several opponents never walked again, but none ever died at his hands. He only lost a few times, including once to Burke, who was undefeated in seventy-five years of combat. No one else, even other DeTang, can match Burke's record. I later found out Red came close.

"Rick, Sally, and Red would like to propose a toast to your life as a warrior," said Red. I looked around but saw no one who looked like a Sally. "This is Sally," Red explained, patting the keg on his back.

"Naming drinking utensils just ain't normal," Kerr said with a slight slur to his words.

"Oh, and naming your weapons is I suppose?" Red asked, adding that at least he bathed regularly - apparently in beer - and didn't have to lick himself clean. Kerr countered that it was a fun way to begin a date, which shot right over my head.

"Now if the Czarrian dog will let Red finish what Red began," Red said as he refilled our glasses. The Muridae, whose name was Rod'nee, had long since gone off to serve the other patrons. "The best of luck to you, lad. May you be healthy, strong and may the gods smile down on you for the crowds sure won't. And last but certainly not least, may you survive the experience."

On that ominous note, we clinked our glasses and finished our drinks as they told me a little of the Tore Games. I tried not to worry. In the old days it was a blood sport, now it sounded a lot like professional wrestling. That I could handle or hoped I could.

Events sometimes happen that change and alter a life forever, often without warning. I do not know when or why I turned my head, but that moment was such an experience. There, at the end of the bar, she sat sipping a thick amber drink through a straw. The glass even had a little umbrella in it. "Beautiful" did not begin to describe her.

"Gorgeous" failed miserably. Shimmering and radiant merely touched the surface. Her skin was an exquisite almond color, her hourglass figure was accented by the cut of her dress. It revealed her bare shoulders and was cut low in front to reveal cleavage. She had breasts! She was a mammal! And an almost human one at that, with the right number of parts, at least those I could see. This may not seem like much you until you spent time in prison being tortured and then are stuck on an alien world among people whose appearance is nothing like yours. I'd begun to worry I'd have to take up celibacy as a way of life.

To top it off, she had blond eyes and blue hair that cascaded down to her waist. A bit reversed from the American beauty norm, but on her, it worked overtime.

My first instinct was to buy her a drink until I remembered I had no money. It was time for Plan B. As soon as I had one I would use it. My thoughts must have been obvious to my new drinking buddies.

"Red, you think he likes Sasha or does he have a drooling problem?"

"Maybe he hasn't eaten in so long that she looks like a tasty tidbit."

"Not everyone is a cannibal like you, Red."

"Those charges were never substantiated."

"It's sort of hard when you ate all the evidence."

"Tasty though."

"You two know her?" I hastily interjected, stopping their culinary discussion.

"Of course. Sasha owns the Empirical House. Great place. No pleasure too small is their motto," Red said.

"You mean she's a..."

"Amoropath. Licensed even. One of the best, too," Red answered.

"She charges a month's salary for a single session. But it's worth every cent. Makes you feel like a pup again," Kerr said. He was almost purring as he began grooming his arm with his tongue. Then he remembered he was in public and stopped. "Would you like to meet her?" he teased as he spit out a furball.

My heart almost flew out my open lips, past my dropped jaw to fly across the room and sit on the stool next to her. Luckily, I closed my mouth in time to stop a cardiac exodus and quite a messy scene. My heart responded by beating twice as fast. Either that or someone was practicing playing bongo drums inside my rib cage.

"Absolutely!" I blurted out oh so coolly. They laughed at me. I didn't care. It could be overlooked. Anything could. I was going to meet her.

She would be swept off her feet and into my arms. We would dance the night away and dawn would find us each locked in the other's embrace wearing little more than a smile. Kerr, after telling me to wipe the spittle off my chin, led me across the room to where she sat. He took her hand and kissed it. She, apparently being a liberated alien, returned the favor. Then came my big chance.

"Sasha, this is Rick of Dirt."

"A pleasure, Rick," she said her every word a sweet song sung just for me.

"!" I didn't say as my mouth opened to a symphony of silence. I tried again. "Hi," I said, barely a whisper. It was a start. This time my lips were at least moving. So were my knees. If they banged together any louder I would be able to keep time for the band. "It's nice to meet you, too," I said, my snappy repartee knowing no bounds. I ran through pick-up lines in my mind. I lacked experience using them sober and had already decided she was far too special for that. I would win her over by being myself. If that failed, I'd find out who she wanted me to be and become that person.

"So, you are new to our fair city. What brings you here?" she asked. Her solid yellow eyes glistened in the bar light.

"It was an unplanned trip actually."

"Spontaneous. I like that."

"Well not exactly spontaneous. Not even voluntary. I seem to be a Newbe," I said. Kerr chuckled behind me.

"Ah, so tonight is your first night in Tore then."

"Yes. How did you know that?"

"Elementary. I haven't seen you in the ring and you can still move under your own power."

"Well, it's been nice chatting with you, Sasha. We have to go now. Bye," Kerr said as he grabbed me by the shoulder and begin to drag me away.

"But Kerr..." I pleaded. The wolf showed no mercy.

"Say goodbye to the nice lady, Rick," he said with a smile. The teeth his smile exposed made it seem more a command than a request. Barring of teeth in other species may not be a friendly sign. With extreme reluctance, I complied.

"Goodbye, nice lady," I said. She laughed. I beamed. Kerr tugged at my shoulder and I knew the true meaning of the phrase "three's a crowd".

"Good luck, young warrior to be," she said her words caressing my ears.

Kerr led me back to our seats on the other end of the bar. He refused to give me an explanation, instead telling me to enjoy myself.

"I had been and you pulled me away."

"Ah yes, so you had. Let me get you another drink."

I downed it and two more in the space of five minutes.

"Easy there, Rick. That's strong booze you are drinking," Red cautioned. "It should be savored and appreciated, not guzzled down like it was water." He said the word water with a touch of disgust in his voice.

I spent the better part of the next hour listening to some interesting insults and old battle tales all the while sneaking glances at Sasha. The Muridae joined us. Rod'nee was an outcast among his people. No one mentioned what it was he did except that he had been one of the Muridae running the old tourney. The older warriors seemed to like him and treat him with great respect. He joined us for a few rounds and actually gave Kerr a run for his money both in quantity and quality of drinks. The unquestionable champion was Red who drank enough to put the rest of his patrons under the bar. Yet he remained totally unfazed. He claimed to have six livers. I saw no reason to doubt him.

As for myself, I was flying high and feeling no pain. I was happy and laughed at every single stupid joke told. I seem to remember telling the guys I loved them even though my speech was beginning to slur. Male bonding. Ain't it grand?

Then my alcoholic haze was interrupted. A seven-foot-tall hairless, beige humanoid was harassing Sasha. He was leering over her, tossing money at her and insulting her honor.

"Slut. Whore. Harlot," he taunted.

Sasha ignored him as best she could and continued sipping her drink. The rest of the bar turned quiet. All eyes were on the drama unfolding between the two of them. Finally, he got her attention. She turned around looked him up and then down. It took quite a while due to his height. When she was done, she looked him in the eye and yelled, "Ha!" She returned to drinking and ignoring him. He was enraged. From behind, he grasped her in a headlock.

Before I knew what was happening, someone had tapped him on the shoulder and told him to "Leave the lady alone." To my surprise, I realized it was me. He turned around. Then down. He looked me over quite quickly and laughed in my face.

I could hear Kerr yelling "Go get him, Dirtling!"

"Just leave and we won't have to resort to violence," I said. He did, in fact, let go of her neck but only so he could get a punch at me. My reflexes took over like they had in the diner. I ducked and swung. My punch connected despite the fact that my eyes were closed at the time. My opponent flew across the bar and his back was slammed into a wall. A second later, he slid down to the floor unconscious. In Tore's lighter gravity my punch had real power. I stood there shocked.

My shock soon turned into pain as something hit the back of my head. I staggered around to see the remains of a broken chair in the hands of another humanoid just like the first. He threw a punch at my face, hitting my right eye. My reflexes seemed to have taken a coffee break but that didn't mean I was out of ideas on how to defend myself. I continually pummeled his fist with my face and it felt like I was beginning to wear him down. It was obvious that his arm was getting tired. I had no time to enjoy my small victory as my legs had decided they'd done enough and knocked off for the day. I fell to the floor. I could feel the stick of spilled liquor against my face. My eye had swollen shut.

I was barely able to make out a figure take out my second opponent and lay him out next to the first. A full-fledged bar fight had broken out. I could hear Kerr howling and growling with pleasure as he joined the fray. The figure who had pulled my fat out of the fire had now lifted me up and carried me away from the fracas setting me on a bar stool in the corner. My eyes hurt too much to keep open so I didn't try.

"Thanks, Kerr," I said.

"You're mistaking me for that furbag? That blow to the head must have been harder than it looked," a familiar female voice answered. I managed to squeeze my uninjured eye open a crack.

"Sasha? So much for my daring rescue attempt to impress you. Thanks for saving my butt," I said humbly.

"You're welcome, Rick. It's been a long time since someone tried to defend my honor. A regular *Banesh*," Sasha said. "You know it was not very nice of you to pick on someone so much bigger than you."

"Huh? Why not? I was always taught that you didn't pick on someone smaller than you."

"That's okay for intraspecies relations but usually the taller the being the lower the gravity they were raised in and the weaker the being is.

Avoid fights with the short and stout cause they are usually from high gravity worlds. There are a few exceptions like the DeTang and the Kartow but it's a good general rule.

"It hurt much?" she asked referring to my eye.

"Only when I breathe," I answered.

"Well I can fix that," she said.

"But I like breathing," I cried. Before I could react, she bent over and kissed my swollen eye. Suddenly the pain was gone. I was even able to open it a bit.

"Rick, come visit my Empirical House. You can have a free secession with anyone as my gift to you, my Banesh Knight in shining battlewear. I hope you'll call on me. Have Kerr bring you by when you are able. Farewell," she said.

Sasha turned and left out the front door, wading through the thick of the fight, only pausing to throw someone blocking her path into the metal bars protecting the glassware. Red was standing there calmly polishing a mug. He put down his towel, lifted and flung that particular gentlebeing into a growing pile of bodies near the door. After pausing for a small sip, he reclaimed the towel and returned to his task.

The ruckus went on for a while and showed no signs of stopping. That is until after Red stepped up on top of his bar, carefully setting his feet on coasters so as not to ruin the finish, and offered to join in. Suddenly everyone, excepting Kerr, found something else to do. Red's Place was quiet but the silence only lasted a few minutes. Kerr picked up a beer and proposed a toast to all the brave externals, apparently a word for people who were off their native world, who had participated in the melee. Then he toasted the internals and the external who had started the whole thing. He meant me and the beige boys. They were internals or natives called the Aprahoe. Kerr made the four of us take a bow. The beige boys were triplets. I just hadn't met the third one. All who were still able raised a glass to join him. Soon laughter sounded from the rafters and loud boisterous singing was heard. Externals who moments earlier were trying to batter each other senseless were laughing and crooning together. I found myself singing *I was a freeze dried Goot until I got in heat* with an arm over the shoulders of the two beige boys I had been battling earlier.

RED

Off in the corner stood Red and Rod'nee, watching the melee with the faintest hint of a smile on their lips.

"Quiet night, eh, Red?" Rod'nee said.

"Not too bad," Red answered.

"How do you think the Newbe will fare? You being an ex-tourney winner and all."

"Too early to tell, oh former overseer. At least he's finally getting into the swing of things," Red said as he watched Rick join his Czarrian companion who was dancing atop the tables. "Red is surprised at Kerr though."

"I see what you mean. He's letting Rick lead."

BURKE

The hall shook with each step, despite the foundation's reinforcements. When he made the effort, Burke could walk soundlessly. No such effort was being made now. Occasionally he would hear someone come in the complex and his pacing would halt. It resumed soon after, unsatisfied.

Finally, sometime in the wee hours of the morning, singing rang out, stealing the silence from the night. Burke knew instantly who it was. Folding his massive arms across his equally immense chest, Burke stood immobile as a monument. Eventually, the intoxicated minstrels were able to figure out the mechanism by which the door worked and entered.

Burke stood waiting.

"I see you can still move under your own power, Rick," Burke observed.

"Barely," Rick replied. "Burke, were there always three of you?" he asked, swaying back and forth with no visible means of support save air currents. Kerr chuckled.

"And you, Czarrian, keeping the boy out until this hour and bringing him home in this condition. You know what he has in store for tomorrow; he'll be in no shape for it," said Burke, unable to hide his annoyance.

"Don't be such a dampener. You'd be surprised what he can handle. Started a rumble. In Red's, no less," Kerr said.

"And what started this fight?" Burke asked authoritatively.

"This guy was giving a woman a hard time," Rick answered. "Her name was Sasha. She was beautiful. I was just trying to help her. Turns out she didn't need it."

Burke's frown turned into a neutral expression, almost a smile. "I see. You'd better get some rest. You will need it."

"Everyone keeps saying that. What happens tomorrow?" Rick asked with almost as much interest as he had invested in watching the room spin. He barely was able to hold back from telling his companions to place their bets.

Burke looked at Kerr as if to question this. Kerr merely shrugged his shoulders. All four of them. Rick looked back and forth between the two. He could see no answers forthcoming and the movement of his head was making him dizzy, so he changed the topic for them.

"Where is Susie?"

"Sleeping," Burke answered.

"Can I see her?" Rick asked. Burke nodded and led him into the next room. He saw Susie floating three feet off the ground but her image was blurry. At first, he blamed it on the alcohol but he soon realized that she was enveloped in a cocoon of some sort, its consistency resembling translucent mercury. When the cocoon started to move in an oozing fashion Rick lost control.

"Oh my God! It's got her! Susie's been eaten by the blob!" he yelled as he began screaming and pounding at the shell. "Spit her out, you fiend." He could not understand why Burke and Kerr made no move to help him. A silver, translucent pseudopod separated itself from the shell and lifted him off his feet thereby ending the quarrel. Suddenly he saw the world from a different viewpoint, an inverted one.

Upside down, he saw the silver mass shimmer and at the same time heard it speak in his head.

"*Fiend? Now really. Talk like that could hurt my feelings,*" it said as it swung Rick back and forth in his inverted position. It was too much for his alcohol-impaired vestibular system to take. He was sick all over the floor.

"*Messy, aren't we?*" it said. A second pseudopod flowed out over the ejected contents of his stomach. The vomit glowed for a second and then vanished. The pseudopod rejoined its main body.

"*Now what am I going to do with you?*" it asked.

"If you are going to eat me get it over with. Didn't your mother tell you it was not polite to play with your food?" Rick said with all the bravado he could muster.

"*They did. But it sure is fun,*" it answered.

"At least put me down and give me a fighting chance," he yelled.

"*Okay, okay. Just stop yelling or you'll wake her,*" it said as it lowered him gently to the ground, returning him to an upright position as it did so. Rick could see Susie within. She started to move and rub her eyes.

"*Now you have done it. You woke her up. She needs her rest. She is a growing child, you know,*" it said.

"I know," a very confused Rick said.

"Hi, Mr. Rick," was heard from within the silver blob. It was Susie. Her voice was distorted, like she was speaking under water.

"Susie, are you okay in there?"

"Sure. It's neat."

"*Hush, Susie. Go back to sleep. You can talk to Mr. Rick in the morning,*" the translucent mass said.

"Okay. Good night, Rick," Susie said, her eyes already closing. A moment later, she had returned to her slumber. Burke entered the room.

"I see you have met Nanna," stated Burke. Rick nodded numbly. "She has been with me on and off for almost four hundred years. I have asked her to take care of Susie. She is very good. She even helped me take care of my children."

"You have children?" Rick asked. There was a profound silence. Nanna seemed to shrink in size and Kerr looked at the floor sheepishly.

"No. Not anymore," Burke said, sorrow coloring his voice. Sensing he had touched on a sensitive issue, Rick tried to lead the conversation elsewhere.

"Why is she in there? How can she breathe?" he asked.

"Nanna is a living fortress. Nothing can penetrate her outer shell when it is formed. I wanted to assure Susie's safety while she slept so I asked her to sleep within Nanna's whole. Nanna is a member of the Trimurti, a race consisting of three sexes. She is a Nani. The other two genders are the Insemanati and Beari. The Nani function by housing the genetic material of a mating triad until it matures. She is able to provide nourishment and the correct atmosphere for any being once she knows what that is. She also has experience rearing over seventy-two young, both her own and those of others."

"*And I rarely get even so much as a card from any of them,*" Nanna added, shimmering orange as she did so.

"So how can I hear her speak? She makes no sounds. All she does is glow," Rick said.

"I programmed all the Elucidators to be able to understand low-level energy outputs and transpose them into sounds and vice versa. More than one race communicates that way," Burke stated. "I promise you that Susie is safe. Nanna will stay with her as her custodian and bodyguard in case the Muridae try anything."

"Do you think they will?"

"Yes," said Burke, ominously.

"Oh," said a worried Rick.

"Come on, Rick. I'll show you to your cube," Kerr informed.

"Good night, Burke. I'm sorry I attacked you, Nanna," Rick said.

"*No harm was done. Get some rest of your own.*"

Kerr led him along dim hallways. Finally, they arrived at their destination. Kerr opened the door and Rick entered.

"Here is your cube."

"This is it?" said a shocked Rick. He stood in an eight by five room decorated by only a bed roll and a blanket. "I've had closet space bigger than this."

"All Newbes start out with a cube. If you do well in the Tore Games, you get benefits, including larger living space," Kerr said. "Now get some rest. You'll need it."

"So I keep getting told. Will you at least tell me what I need the rest for?" Rick asked.

"No," Kerr said with a sadistic grin. Rick decided this did not bode well for whatever it was. Exhausted, he collapsed on the bedroll and was snoring loudly before his eyes were fully closed.

RICK

"Hi ho, hi ho, it's off to warrior school I go. To fight with sword blades and hand grenades, hi ho, hi ho," I sang despite the pain it inflicted on my aching head. I was right smack in the middle of the mother of all hangovers and it felt like it was giving birth. To triplets.

"Be silent," demanded the filthy, smelly, disgusting rat pretending it was a person.

"Don't like my singing, Smed'lee?" I asked. I knew he didn't, which explains why I was willing to inflict this agony on myself. I needed aspirin badly.

"Is that what you call it? I thought you were trying to imitate the death moans of the Eclastic drone. Whatever it is will cease now," he ordered. Everyone's a critic. I knew I had talent. Not everybody is able to sing in three different keys at the same time.

"You are no fun, Smedster," I said with bravado. Oppressed heroes are always supposed to sound cocky, if for no other reason than to tick off their oppressor. It seemed to be working too well.

"You will address me as 'Sir' or another title that conveys equal or greater respect or I'll..."

"Yes, I know. You'll use the Nociogenerator to cause unbearable pain to rack through my

being. My body will go into spasms and it will fry my brain, leaving me a breathing vegetable. You've told me five times already," I said. He caressed the NG, short for Nociogenerator, like it was his lover. "Stop fondling it already or the hair will fall off your palms, your verminness."

Being culture oriented he didn't understand my insults but something I said intrigued him. His ears actually perked up as he turned to face me.

"Verminness? That did not translate. What does it mean?" he asked. Smed'lee seemed to crave respect or at least fear. From what I heard Dortew used him as a floor mat and kicking post. I guess he just wanted to pass on that special brand of love to others, particularly me.

"Its meaning is very complicated, but I assure you it conveys all the respect you deserve," I said with mock reverence. He didn't notice.

"Hmm," he said as he thought and scratched the hair on his chinny, chin, chin. Slowly his face lit up as he took his hand from his jaw and returned to stroking the NG. "I like it. Very well you may address me as such."

"Thank you, your verminness," I said as I watched him walk with a pumped up ego muttering to himself. "Yes, your verminness; no, your verminness". It was pathetic.

We continued walking through the winding tunnels under the arena in silence. My headache had finally gotten the better of me. We made so many twists and turns that I was lost. Smed'lee seemed to know where he was going. Maybe there was a piece of cheese at the end of this maze.

Not that it was hard to figure out but Smed'lee was not on my list of favorite people. It was phenomenal the amount of hatred he inspired in so short a time. Smed'lee was not the strongest or the smartest being I met, but he frightened me the most. The fact that he could torture me with the push of a button added to this fear in no small fashion. The rat thrived on the suffering and pain of others. Not even Grillar back on Earth was as sadistic as Smed'lee and believe me I had become the expert on sadism. My life was a masochist's paradise. Pity I was not of that persuasion or I would be having a grand old time. Lonso was almost at the same level of depravity as the rat. Bastards both, void of any trace of a conscience.

Smed'lee was searching frantically for any possible opportunity to use the NG, but aside from my wisecracks, I had not stepped out of line. His disappointment hung heavy in the air. So did his breath.

I wasn't feeling my best. Early this morning nature called to me quite loudly and I went to answer it. Bathrooms look quite different here, having to service a variety of shapes, none of which I recognized. Using what I took to be a toilet, I wanted to crawl under a rock somewhere when I was told I had used a sink. On top of that, whoever heard of a society who didn't use toilet paper? Well, there are a few on Earth who make sure they eat with one hand and wipe with the other, but I'd never visited them.

Here they use the more environmentally conscious sonic method. One starts by positioning a handle two inches from the appropriate area and pushing a button. An electric current runs through a crystal in the handle which vibrates in the ultrasonic range whisking away anything not a part of the person holding the handle. How was I supposed to know how it was used? A kind hearted, three-legged purple external explained the use of it but forgot to mention I had wandered in the equivalent of the ladies room until I was finished. Her name was Tarna and she was a fellow Newbe. To be honest, I had to take her world at her gender.

Under her brief tutelage, I learned the location of the men's room, what a toilet actually looked like, and how to use the showers. They also ran by sonics but used a type of soap. Tarna explained that I had to position myself two to three inches away for it to work properly. It seems many races, hers included, regard bathing in water a sacrilege. On top of that, water use is regulated and not wasted on little things like hygiene.

Muridae must view sonics as a sacrilege judging from the stench. I smelled Smed'lee coming before I saw him. His arrival ruined any chance I had of returning to blissful slumber. Smed'lee vocally expressed his disappointment about not being able to roust me from sleep. His irritation made my earlier disorientation in the bathroom well worth the embarrassment.

Adding to my list of woes, besides an agonizing hangover, I was barely able to keep my right eye open. The right side of my face was still swollen. Thankfully, my face didn't hurt. The pounding in my head and nausea in my gut was all I could handle at this hour of the morning. Whatever Sasha's kiss did, besides making my heart go pitter patter, had worked. The pain in my face was practically non-existent. Just the thought of Sasha eased my misery, making me feel tingly all over. Shivers traveled up and down my spine. When I closed my eyes, all I saw was Sasha. Her face was burned into my memory.

My feelings were bordering on obsession and all this talk about how wonderful she was sounded irrational, but did I care? Not really. I was enjoying the sensation. The only part I was uncomfortable with was how I could feel this strongly about someone I just met. Sasha was an alien, for crying out loud. Were we physically compatible? My id, already deep in the gutter, assumed yes and had some ideas of its own on how to find out. My conscience, on the other hand, was arguing that she was a lady and deserved respect. It wanted to place her atop a pedestal. My id agreed just so long as it was high enough to see up her skirt. I decided to shut them both out. Still, I found myself praying long and hard for parallel evolution.

I was still unclear as to what being an Amoropath meant. Was she a prostitute and if she was, could I deal with it? Or afford it? Prostitution never really bothered me so long as beatings and exploitation were not involved. Not that I had ever made a rendezvous with one, mind you, but it was a whole lot easier to approve of something in theory than in practice. Maybe I was jealous of the attention she might be giving her clients. How did Don Quixote deal with his relationship with Dulcinea?

A trip to the Empirical House was foremost in my plans. I wanted to take Sasha up on her offer. All my problems should be so horrible. I'm sure Kerr will show me how to get there. I got the impression that he was a regular at Sasha's.

Wonder how he's feeling this morning? He had three times as much to drink as I did and was in a dozen more fights. He must feel awful. I pity anyone who gets in his way this morning.

"We have arrived, Dirtling," Smed'lee announced. We had come to three large, simple doorways which led to a room the size of a football field. The room was round and had a dome ceiling. The floor was covered by a fine sand. "Step through the doors, please," he said. I should have known something was wrong when he started being polite.

"Door number one, two or three?" I inquired. He gave me a glare that could frost fire. Apparently, I had insulted his boss, Dortew. Quickly shutting up, I entered through door number two in the center. No sooner had my legs set down on the sand that they collapsed under me. I hit the ground. Hard. My chest told my brain it was being crushed in a vise. I couldn't breathe. My heart was pounding like it was pumping for twelve and was doing its best to push my blood out through my arteries into the outside world. My brain did the only logical thing it could. It instructed my mouth to scream. Loud. Nothing happened. My diaphragm was unable to push any air across my vocal cords. I was going to explode. The damn rat set me up. I'm going to die.

"Oops. How careless of me. I forgot the gravity field was set at the DeTang level. That's much too high for a Dirtball, isn't it? And just as you were getting used to the lower mid-grav environment here on Liberty," Smed'lee mocked. "I'm so sorry. You know I would be so saddened if any accident should befall you. Here let me adjust it," he said as he dropped the field to a more viable level.

Air rushed into my lungs. My blood pressure dropped to the point where my heartbeat no longer sounded like machine gun fire. Overwhelmed by one desire, revenge, my brain yelled, "Kill the rat." My battered body agreed. I rushed him temporarily forgetting the NG. Smed'lee quickly reminded me with sadistic glee. As my body lay crumpled up on the floor my brain quietly sent down a message saying "Never mind." My body offered no argument.

After an eternity of agony, the pain stopped. Nothing never felt so good.

"Now your training begins," he said as his fat furry body turned and walked away.

"What am I supposed to do?" I asked between gasps of air.

"Wait," was his only answer.

I was never so happy to see someone go in my life, not even after Grillar's and Lonso's tender tortures. Their pain I was able to block out partially. I never had much luck with nausea. Today was no exception. Once I had emptied the remains of my stomach onto the sand, I sat up and looked around. Just a sand filled arena. Nothing to do but wait. I noticed the sand had hardened around my regurgitated insides. I spit on the ground. The sand that was hit by the spittle became solid. Similar to certain brands of kitty litter back home. Must make cleaning all the spilt blood easier.

Time passed. Still, more time followed. The seconds ticked away turning into minutes, then hours and finally... well it is not a hard picture to get. Nothing happened. Nobody came. I explored a little. The ceilings were about seventy-five feet high and looked like it could fold back. The only doors I saw were the ones I passed when I came in and a large door on the far side which took up a good portion of that wall. A vacant stadium, complete with stands, surrounded the arena. Probably more exits up there.

Why were they making me wait so long? Do they think I had nothing better to do? Okay, so I didn't, but that's beside the point.

"Hello. Anybody home?" I yelled. A small echo was my only reply. I kicked sand and sent a shower of grains flying. I tried jumping like I had at the auction but it was nothing spectacular. The gravity level was close to that of Earth.

After twenty minutes I got tired of doing nothing. I almost walked out the door, but I remembered ratboy. I didn't want any more torment from him and his toys. Since he said "wait," I'll wait. Great. Now I am taking orders from a giant rat. Yes, but a rat with teeth, so to speak. Susie was well protected with Nanna now, but it seemed foolish to push it since Smed'lee might try to take my disobedience out on her.

I was tired, my head hurt, my mouth tasted like it was full of cotton and I needed a nap. The sand looked soft and inviting. I lay down for a snooze. If someone wants me they can wake me.

KERR

"Young fool. Now he is sleeping. Out in the open, no less. Amazing he has lived this long. I'll have to show him the error of his ways."

The sands began to shift. Subtle at first, a ripple appeared. Barely noticeable. It crept closer and closer until it was directly under Rick. All was still. Without warning four arms and a leg shot out from beneath the dune and enveloped Rick. He was helpless, unable to move and one furry hand held a knife next to his jugular. He woke quickly and silently, a gasp caught in his throat.

"Good, Dirt boy. No yell. A warrior never shows fear to a potential enemy. It can be used against him," the grim Czarrian said.

"Kerr!" Rick shouted half surprised and half relieved he was not going to die.

"Shut up, you worthless excuse for a being. A warrior would have checked this room for traps, secret entrances, food, even a bathroom," snapped Kerr knowing full well Rick had been needing to use facilities of some sort for over ten minutes. His body language had been pathetically obvious. "Then, after assessing the situation he would decide whether he should stay or go. A warrior sleeps with one eye open and is awakened by the movement of a blade of grass or a grain of sand. Only fools, after announcing their presence, lie down to sleep in a strange location without knowing what danger lurks around them. What you did was an open invitation, saying *kill me.*"

"I'm sorry, Kerr." Rick's voice cracked ever so slightly.

"A warrior does not regret mistakes he survives. He learns from them and moves on. To assure you never repeat this blunder again drop and give me fifty push-ups."

"Why should I…"

"Sixty."

"But…"

"Seventy-five."

"Kerr, can't we talk about…"

Insolence. Can't he see I am trying to save him from trouble? With that thought, Kerr grabbed Rick's ear and pressed on a nerve cluster. Rick hit the floor in agony. He quickly learned Kerr's hands could cause just as much pain as an NG. Rick started the push-ups.

Poor pup, Kerr thought. *If I whisper the microphones near the wall won't pick it up. He deserves an explanation. Besides after his drinking spree, his head must be killing him.*

"Friend Rick," Kerr whispered. "I apologize for your pain, but it is necessary. The Muridae are observing. They are a sadistic bunch. They want to see pain. Yours. Should I ever grab your ear again act as you are now and there should be no problem. But know this. I am your training master. I own you from now until I say you are a warrior. What I say you will do without question or hesitation. If you do not, I will cause you pain that will make this seem mild by comparison. Understand?" asked Kerr. Rick nodded. The wolf smiled. Rick broke out in a cold sweat and doubled his rate of push-ups.

SMED'LEE

"Out of my way, subspecies," Smed'lee yelled to the other Muridae in the control booth. Knowing it best to be nowhere near him when a mood was upon him, they quickly left. Alone, he sat and flipped on the screen.

"Heh. Kerr will make short work of him," Smed'lee cackled to himself as he watched the events in the training arena. "Ah. The pain. The agony. Life's simple pleasures. What the Dirtling will be put through. What joy."

His pleasure was cut short by a note left tapped on the console. It informed him he had half a day before he had to report to Dortew. Smed'lee's insides cringed at the thought. Even with the medic and the healer's help he had not fully recovered from the injuries he received as a result of the fiasco at the auction. The Dirtling gave his first moan of pain below. Forgetting all else he turned up the volume and waited for what was sure to follow.

Smed'lee shifted his seat as his hand journeyed downward. It stopped and rested on the NG.

"Ah, Genny, let us see what we see," he moaned to the small device. It did not respond, but he hugged it close as if it had.

RICK

"Toss me in a hole, throw dirt on me and be done with it," I moaned using my last reserves of strength. I had survived my first day of warrior school only through some divine grace. Parts of me I never knew existed were crying out in pain and exhaustion. I made it to the mess hall under my own power but just barely. Susie ran over and gave me a hug and kiss. The thought was appreciated, but I was so sore the hug hurt. I kept my pain to myself. Burke and Nanna were there also. Burke led me to the only padded chair in the room. The "man" was earning my eternal gratitude. Susie asked all sorts of questions about my day. My shirt had no sleeves and Susie pointed at my arms.

"Wow. You are getting muscles already," she said. Burke also looked. He bent down and laying a stony arm across her shoulders, he chuckled.

"Those aren't muscles my dear. Those are muscle spasms," Burke said. Our whole table, about twenty beings in all, burst out laughing. I just turned red.

The mess hall was set up cafeteria style and everyone else had already gotten their food. At Burke's suggestion, Susie and Nanna went up to fix a plate for me. Good. Despite the stretching and cool-down Kerr made me do, I think my body had fused into the chair. I would have to look into having someone carry me and the chair back to my cube after dinner. The chair should fit, albeit barely, in my spacious living quarters.

Susie came back and put the food in front of me. I didn't recognize a thing on my plate, but it smelled delicious, sort of a cross between chicken and ginger. I ate everything with gusto.

"Don't you want to know what you are eating?" Kerr asked as he scooped more protein filled foods onto my plate.

"Nope. I eat Chinese food the same way. I love the way it tastes, just don't tell me what's in it," I said. Kerr laughed as he ate his dinner, most of it raw meat. Part of his meal was trying to crawl off his plate.

"Like my food fresh," he explained. I was slightly disgusted, but Susie thought it was cool, like a snake eating a mouse in a pet store. Then, as if on cue, Nanna enveloped her "food" with some of her protoplasm and began to digest it. I later found out that she could directly convert any matter to the energy she needed, but converted food to fit in with the rest. Everyone in the mess tried to adapt to the others' customs in some way. It helped make them a community.

Burke was sipping a thick, mineral filled liquid from a full four-gallon glass. While the rest of us sat on chairs or benches he reclined on the floor at the head of the table. He was still up higher than me. I heard him promise Susie he would see if he could find any chocolate chip ice cream.

Taking me aside, he questioned me.

"Rick, what is this chocolate chip ice cream?"

"It is a frozen dairy product."

"Dairy? Mammal's milk? The child is not yet fully weaned?"

"No, she's weaned. On Earth, we raise other mammals, mostly cows, for their milk. It's used for different foods. Humans of all ages eat or drink them. Ice cream is one of the best."

"What of the chocolate chip?"

It was sad. I told him I really had no idea how chocolate was made except a plant, milk and sugar were involved. Makes me wonder how people in fiction who are transported into a foreign land or time always know how everything is put together and how to make gunpowder or the like. Who takes the time to learn these things when all you have to do is go to a store and buy them? Was I the only non-genius this ever happened to?

After the meal was finished, I felt better as long as I did not try to move. I was learning quite a bit just by listening. I was not the only unwilling warrior but far more had entered into this business of their own accord. For fame, training, or the opportunity to make money from reps and skills once the contract was up. There were different status for contracts. Mine was full; I had only the most basic rights. I could not walk away. The next step up meant the warrior could go wherever he wanted. But he fought who, where, and when the Muridae told him. Kerr's contract was the next step up. He was able to refuse a match. Burke's contract was of the highest order. He had complete control over his matches. He did basically whatever he wanted and the Muridae let him.

A Burke match was a media event. It didn't happen often. DeTang honor did not permit it. They only fought an opponent they respected. Or when they were really mad, but that was more of a slaughter. A match with a DeTang was considered the same as being bestowed with a gift. Burke was unable to even be tempted with wealth. He was already of the wealthiest beings in the galaxy because he developed the

Elucidator. And not just the technology that allowed it to be implanted in someone's nervous system. He programmed all the languages into it. He was fluent in all of them and they numbered in tens of thousands. I have difficulty ordering at a Mexican restaurant. That was one of his reasons for becoming a warrior; it was a good way for him to meet a multitude of beings and learn their languages.

Eventually, they wanted to learn about me.

"So what did you do back on Dirt?"

"I was a Physical Therapist."

"What is that?"

"A healer of sorts. We get rid of pain, make someone stronger, better. We help others to return to as normal a life as possible after an injury and give knowledge to help prevent future injury."

"So you were a physician?"

"Not exactly, but it's in the same ballpark," I answered. My analogy went over their heads. Just then my left shoulder began to throb. Grimacing, I tried to rub it with my right hand but that only caused that arm to go into spasm. I gave up, gritted my teeth and resigned myself to the pain. Kerr smiled.

"Well then, therapist, heal thyself," he said.

Smartass. I guess I won't ask him to carry me to my cube. Maybe I could just stay and sleep here. Breakfast should be starting in only ten hours.

RICK

Iwoke from the nightmare, screaming. Mercifully the dream fades back into the night but the memory of terror and pain remains. It's not a glimpse of the future but a reminder of immutable horrors past that still whisper my name just on the edge of hearing. Even if I manage to forget, each look in a mirror serves as a constant reminder of my fall from grace as my body will forever bear their signatures of depravity.

Pride calls out for vengeance, but even in my dreams is denied. My tormentors lay protected and safe untold light years away. That thought should comfort but doesn't. The fear they birthed in me, lives on. Fear because I was helpless. Fear at my impotence to stop my terror and end my pain. Fear because my torture may not be over, even on an alien world.

My bedding is drenched in frigid sweat. I wish for the nightmare to go away, but even asleep I know that wishes are useless things, bringing only hope. My torture taught me that hope is a lie, but I want to believe it anyway.

Exhausted, I reach out for Morpheus' hand,   turning a former enemy into an ally. If I don't sleep, I'll never make it through training. So I flee the waking world to take refuge in slumber, hoping to find sweet oblivion, even briefly and rest in peace while I'm still living.

The next dream denies me that. All too familiar human hands hold a flaming beacon of despair high above me in storm filled skies. From across the horizon, a brown fur coated fist reaches out toward the fire as lightning flashes and thunder strikes. The rat hand is not hurt or burned. Instead, it is passed the fiery torch. Profane laughter rains down, assaulting my ears and mind. Shivering, I wish for a quenching cloudburst to douse the searing flames, but the downpour that never comes, not even in dreams.

SMED'LEE

Through the ages, struggles have always existed between those who have and those who have not. At times the struggle is a quiet, desperate thing that follows the path of resentment and complaint. The haves may refer to it as bitching and moaning. All too often savagery and violence result from the conflict. One side reaches while the other clutches tight and defends.

Among the merchant caste of the Muridae, the struggle forms the basis for their way of life. The haves hold the right, most consider it a sacred duty, to keep the nots in line. If the means to do this must be harassment, anguish, and torment -- so much the better. Nothing is forbidden and everything allowed, as long as one has the capital to back up the deed. It embraces all Muridae who are one year past maturity. The one year is the only time allowed the young to accumulate as much wealth as possible, through any means, before their adult life begins and they officially enter society.

Honor is unheard of, honesty a lie. The only protection a Muridae relies on is an iron clad contract. Typically, they span hundreds of pages with clauses for every contingency from flash floods in a desert to Armageddon anywhere.

Fully knowing his place in the cash caste, Smed'lee stood humbly outside the office door of his superior. Dortew was of the ruling Dor class and allowed none of his underlings to address him by the title of Dor, preferring Sir instead so that familiarity didn't breed like a fungus among the nots, which encompassed every other Muridae on Liberty.

Smed'lee had been waiting silently for several hours. The message had stated a time so he was not allowed to announce his presence. The security systems had done that at his arrival. Custom demanded he stay until Dortew acknowledged his existence or five minutes after the start of Armageddon, whichever came first. Dust had begun to gather on the collar of his garish green cloak when the door slid open.

Refusing to fall for the oldest trick in the book, Smed'lee did not cross the threshold uninvited.

"Enter," was the only solicitation he received. Groveling at full force, Smed'lee did so. Within the darkened office, light shone only on Dortew. The rat was seated upon a gaudy throne which appeared to have been designed by a kindergarten class who had been given jewels and precious metals to play with instead of finger paints and uncooked pasta shells. It rested high enough that Smed'lee needed to crane his neck to see his superior. The throne was lined with implements of torment, from various whips and acids to electroprods. Smed'lee was on intimate footing with each of them.

"Waiting long?" Dortew asked.

A simple enough question, seemingly innocent. It was as far from innocent as night is from day. Each word of the reply had to be carefully chosen as not to offend. To say no would be admitting not arriving early, while answering yes would be considered an insult. Insults were repaid in pain.

"No wait could be considered long when in your service, sir," Smed'lee replied. The air around his nose seemed to take on a brown aura.

The answer was deemed non-offensive as demonstrated by Dortew's hands remaining in his lap while the whips and prods stayed in their place.

"You had a problem at the auction," condescended Dortew.

"Yes, sir," Smed'lee replied, unsure of why the same ground was being covered twice. Certainly, he had done something new to offend.

"I lost money."

"Unfortunately, sir."

"Burke has placed the human under his protection, keeping it in his quarters here. In doing so, he seeks to further increase our guilt in the case he is building."

"Guilt, sir? I thought all the papers were in order," replied Smed'lee without thought of the consequences of this indiscretion. The electroprod jumped out at him, guided by Dortew's angry hand. Sparks leapt from metal to flesh. Smoke and the stench of burning rat hide rose to fill the air. Dortew inhaled deeply, his mouth watering, satisfaction apparent at his handiwork.

Below his expanding nostrils withered Smed'lee in agony. Before he reeled back to an upright position, a feeble "thank you", one tinged with hatred, escaped his lips A second jolt consumed more of his pelt, leaving him unable to rise. A more pleasant response was spoken on hands and knees. Dortew this time found both the words and position pleasing and stayed a third shock.

Continuing as if uninterrupted, Dortew said, "It seems that there may be some strands of truth scattered among his lies. Dorwon had specifically requested Dirtling breeding stock during pickup of the shipment before last. That was after that unfortunate sterilization incident but before the fall of the slave trade and Dorwon's subsequent murder by the Kentor. The order was never changed. We received contracts on many of young Dirt females, many quite probably below the age of full citizenship. Only luck saved us from having more than one on the block that day or we would be facing this problem multiplied. If a complete case is brought to the Kentor or even the Tetrarch, we may well lose."

Inhaling deeply at the mention of "we" a small panic overcame Smed'lee. If a scapegoat was needed, Dortew would sacrifice him, without hesitation or regret. Although it stayed in its place on the throne, Smed'lee felt the noose tighten around his own throat.

"We have only one recourse. Prevent the completion of the case."

"How, sir?" a petrified Smed'lee asked. Dortew must also have felt fear in the blackened ember that beat in his chest in place of a heart, for no punishment was given for the imprudence.

"The child must be eliminated."

"Murder? I would not care to face Lord Burke's wrath if the creature is killed."

"Would you prefer mine, inferior?"

"No, sir. Shall I contact The House of Razza?"

"No. They have ties to a Dirtling Investigator. They might refuse the job and inform him. He, in turn, would feel obliged to avenge the death of one of his kind. Because of those self-same ties to those assassins, he is untouchable. At least to those who wish to remain among the living. A Razza assassin does not come cheaply. It would be far too large a fee for such a small matter. I wish you to take care of the matter, Smed'lee."

"Me, sir? Not that I object to the task but as I stated the danger is great. They would catch me. They would kill me."

"Cease this pathetic whining in my presence. Be a Muridae. Use creativity and a plan that cannot be traced back to you."

"As you wish, sir."

"Begone," Dortew spat contemptuously. "Send me your mate for my evening's pleasure." Smed'lee gritted his teeth in rage at the thought of Dortew touching his female – again - but kept silent. It was Dortew's right and nothing could be done. If Smed'lee attempted to even touch his superior's mistress it was as good as committing suicide.

He quietly replied. "Yes, sir." Smed'lee left with head bowed to tend to his wounds. Under his cloak, he pulled close the NG, his one true love, the only one who never would betray him. Comforted, he was able to continue existing for yet another day. His metal mistress endured the embrace in silence, oblivious to his tender touch.

RICK

My training went on for several weeks. Sheer torture is what it was. I even had to learn how to breathe all over again; turns out I'd been doing it wrong all these years. No matter how much I did or how good I got, Kerr always wanted more. Funny part is, I treated my patients back home the same way. Not to this extreme, of course, but I always pushed for a little bit more. Patients used to joke that PT stood for Pain and Torture. I always told them they were right. If this is what they felt like, I would like to sincerely apologize. However, it was good for me in the long run.

As I improved, Kerr decreased the amount of physical training and upped the gravity setting I worked under. I was performing in gravity forty percent higher than Earth's. It may not sound like much but I weigh close to two hundred pounds back home. With a forty percent increase, I figure I weigh about two hundred and eighty. Imagine doing an aerobics workout with eighty-pound weights on. Now imagine doing it for five to eight hours almost every day and you begin to get the picture. It was not at DeTang level, but still respectable.

Kerr failed to be impressed. His workout was in gravity sixty percent higher than Earth's and his norm was slightly lower than mine. Each workout was done slowly for a set period so as not to overtax my cardiovascular system. Kerr monitored my vital signs like a mother hen. Since they remained within safe limits, he felt free to push me further and further.

Once he considered me physically fit, the combat training began. I was taught half a dozen fighting styles from as many races. Kerr chose them by suitability to my handicaps. Basically, I had a thin hide and too few appendages. A six-limbed individual, such as himself, could launch five attacks at me simultaneously, needing only one limb to balance on. Poor handicapped me, on the other hand, could only block three, which meant two attacks were successful. Much of my training involved dodging and avoiding.

"It cannot hurt you if you are not there," Kerr repeated time and time again. He was real big on turning an opponent's force back upon itself. Minimum work, maximum effect.

"How force is used is more important than the amount of force,"

Kerr said.

"So, basically you want me to use the Force," I answered.

"Exactly."

"Yes, Obi-Wan," I replied. The joke went over his head. That happened to me a lot.

One day I asked why I had not been shown any DeTang techniques. After all, Burke was undefeated so if it was good enough for him I was willing to learn.

"I have not taught you any because it would kill you. DeTang traditional combat with other races allows the opponent one free shot. A grown DeTang is nearly indestructible so it's fine for them but you would be splattered. Burke's folk are also probably the strongest in the seven galaxies. With all that going for him Burke does not need to know how to fight. You do."

"So what do I do if I ever have to fight a DeTang?"

"Keep moving and stay out of his range."

"And?"

"Pray."

Warrior training was not all physical by any means. In each lesson, Kerr would throw in some in some tidbit of wisdom on the Warrior's Philosophy. Sometimes it was practical stuff like always respect your opponent, practice your action first in your mind, then in reality or consider a weapon an extension of yourself. Usually, it consisted of "A Warrior does this" or "doesn't do that". One day it was "A Warrior does not give in to anger in life or in battle for if he does he shall lose." I traded him "Don't get mad, get even". He pretended not to like it and even fined me a hundred and fifty push-ups on fingertips, but I overheard him using it at dinner later that night.

Despite his swashbuckling manner outside, he was dead serious during training. I wasn't, meaning I had extra work each time I stepped too far out of line. Still, Kerr needed lightening up even if he didn't always get the joke. Besides, I was becoming able to take whatever he dished out. Not that I was coming back for more, mind you. That much of a masochist I'm not. One thing, in particular, annoyed him to no end.

"Stop calling me Obi-Wan. It is not my name."

"Then call me what I asked."

"Why would you want to be called such a thing?"

"Old Earth custom."

"What a bizarre people."

"Please, Kerr," I pleaded. He sighed heavily.

"Very well. Continue with routine number twenty-four... Grasshopper," he said. With a small bow, I answered him.

"Yes, Master."

SUSIE

"What big eyes you have, Grandma."

"All the better to see you with."

"What big ears you have, Grandma."

"All the better to hear you, my dear."

"What big teeth you have."

"All the better to...what does this say?" Kerr asked incredulously, sitting up in the improvised bed and throwing the covers off.

"All the better to eat you with, my dear," Rick said, with a smirk.

"Then you jump out of bed and chase me around," informed Susie, cheerfully clearly enjoying herself.

"I will not do this. I do not eat children," Kerr announced indignantly, folding both pairs of arms across his chest.

"Kerr, it is only play," Burke offered, doing his best to encourage the Czarrian.

"That is what you said when you told me to put on this ridiculous outfit. To play dress up," Kerr said, referring to the outfit he was wearing. A makeshift, oversized nightgown covered him from neck to ankles. A baggy nightcap adorned his head. Susie wore a red cape and hood. "Besides, if it is only play, why are neither of you playing dress up?"

"Neither of us looks like the big bad wolf. You do," Rick answered, smugly. In training, Kerr was in control and Rick was out of his element. Here it was the other way around.

"And what is this with the big bad wolf? Yesterday, you three played porcine creatures..."

"Pigs," Susie corrected.

"Pigs and Nanna played three houses I had to blow down. Then I had to climb down a chimney and was cooked."

"We didn't cook you really, silly. We just pretended," Susie said, giggling at the notion.

"But I had to sit in a cauldron of water while you pretended to cook me. Cold water at that. Do you know how long it took my pelt to dry out?"

"Stop complaining Kerr. I had to play a troll last week," Burke said.

"And I had to play a billy goat gruff that you ate."

"Kerr, I played a goat too," Rick said.

"But I never get the good parts. I am always the bad guy or someone who gets eaten. Usually both.”

“That’s not true.”

“Yes, it is Rick. What are you playing this time? A woodsman? How do I die this time?”

“Actually, I kill you with my ax and then I cut you open, freeing the grandmother.”

“That is ridiculous. What did I do? Swallow her whole? Impossible! She would be dead. Cutting me open would only reveal her partial digested remains.”

“Kerr, not in front of the child,” Burke said sternly.

“It’s okay, Burke. Kerr is right if this was real life. It’s only pretend,” Susie offered, shocked that an adult could not tell the difference.

“Well, I am ready to get back to real life and so is Rick. Time to get back to training,” Kerr said tearing the nightcap off his head and throwing it on the floor to accentuate his point. Susie, seeing Rick’s reluctance to return to his workout, picked the cap up and walked over to Kerr. Baby blues working on overdrive, she looked up at Kerr’s face and handed him the cap.

“Please Kerr. Play storytime with us,” she asked.

Kerr growled, wringing the nightcap in the bottom two of his hands, looking from face to face around the room, trying to avoid the littlest one. He wanted to argue but believed a warrior should not start a fight he has no hope of winning, so he remained silent. With a grunt, he replaced the nightcap atop his head. “Fine.”

Susie pulled his face down and kissed his cheek. “Thank you, Kerr.”

“You’re welcome, little one. I would do this for no one else.”

“I know,” she said. Without hesitation, she continued. “What big teeth you have.”

“All the better to eat you with,” Kerr said, as he began chasing Susie around Burke’s quarters. Rick started to chase Kerr.

Kerr turned around and said, “Butt out, woodsman. This is between me and tiny pink driving cowl.”

“That is Little Red Riding Hood,” Rick said.

“That’s what I said. Now come here, little one,” Kerr said grinning, playing his part to the hilt. Susie refused to be taken in.

“No way!” she said, running.

Kerr continued the chase and eventually caught Susie. Then the tickling began. First Kerr tickled Susie, but soon Susie turned the tables and Kerr was flat on his back laughing uncontrollably. Once he got loose Kerr ran behind Burke and played run around, making sure he kept the stone warrior between himself and the child. Rick, watching the entire spectacle, laughed himself into a frenzy.

Kerr noticed this and headed toward his student.

"Find something funny, Rick?"

"Yes. The great warrior taken down by a kid. You have a weakness, Kerr: you are ticklish."

Kerr brought his face up to Rick so they were nose to nose.

"Tell anyone and die, Dirtboy."

"Whatever you say, Kerr," Rick said, fear winning out over a chuckle but only barely. Never one to leave well enough alone, Rick waited until Kerr turned around and began tickling him from behind. It took Kerr thirty seconds to break loose. Luckily, it only took Rick twenty-nine point five seconds to start running. He played the same run around game with Burke in the middle.

"Kerr, you are doing it wrong. The woodsman is supposed to chase the wolf," Susie instructed.

"Let us pretend this is the right way. It is much more fun."

"Speak for yourself," said Rick.

"I am," answered Kerr. Before the chase came to its conclusion, it was ended by Burke rising to his feet and draping an arm over Rick and Kerr.

"That is enough, gentlemen. It is time to try a new culinary delight. I have created chocolate chip ice cream."

"Really?" Susie said, clapping her hands together.

"Seriously?" Rick asked, taste buds tingling in anticipation.

"Oh no," Kerr said, shaking his head.

"What do you mean?" Rick asked.

"You do not want to eat any foodstuff Burke creates. Remember his problems in communicating with the Fragrunts?"

"Burke has no sense of smell."

"And no sense of taste. Sweets and lava taste the same to him."

"It is ice cream. How bad could it be?"

"Wait. You will see. I will even help you. After you get your first taste, we can return to your training, if you like."

"Nothing tastes that bad."

"Want to bet on it?"

"Sure."

"If you can finish what Burke dishes out, you get out of today's workout. If not, you do double."

Rick smiled at the easy bet. "Definite deal," The pair shook on it.

As they headed to the table Susie was already chowing down. By the time Rick sat down and had his bowl placed in front of him, Susie was looking green. As Rick began to lift the spoon to his mouth, Susie was frantically shaking her head "No" in warning. Her face was wrinkled in revulsion. It was at that point the smell of curdled milk crossed his nostrils. He looked anxiously toward Kerr, a look of "I told you so" apparent. Despite everything, Rick put the frozen concoction in his mouth. Only a sense of politeness to Burke kept him from audibly gagging.

"Rick, are you going to finish what's left in your bowl?" asked Kerr. Rick weighed his options.

"You win. Let's go," Rick said sadly, getting up to leave with Kerr.

"What do you think, Rick?" Burke asked.

"Yes, Rick. What do you think?" Kerr mockingly asked.

"Burke, honestly it needs work. A lot of work. If you will excuse me I have a very long workout ahead of me."

After hugging Susie, the warrior and the Newbe took their leave.

"Susie, did you like it?" Burke asked.

"Sorry, Burke. It was yucky. It didn't taste like ice cream. It tasted like sour cottage cheese."

"I am sorry, Susie."

"Don't be. It was really good of you to try. You'll get it right next time."

"You really think so?"

"Yep."

"So you do not want anymore?"

"No way."

"Nanna?"

With that request, silver pseudopods enveloped the frozen dairy monstrosity. It glowed and was absorbed.

"I think it tastes fine, Burke," informed Nanna, trying to raise Burke's spirits. Burke knew that, no matter how horrible others considered his recipes, Nanna would eat them.

RICK

It was night in Tore. The lights of the city bore down on us in their magnificence and tranquility, dazzling in their subtle splendor. Susie and I were on the roof of the Warrior's dorm, enjoying the night and each other's company. She sat staring up at the stars, trying to recognize constellations.

"That one up there looks like Orion, but he has too many stars in his belt. And he doesn't have a dog. Do you think it's Orion, Rick?"

"I honestly don't know, Susie. I only would recognize the Big Dipper maybe," I said. Back home I rarely looked at stars. Here, I found myself looking towards the night skies frequently. Now, staring up I thought about how much is out there, but I was no help to Susie. I never paid much attention in school when they went over astronomy. Even if I did, I doubt I could tell her the answer to her next question.

"Which one do you think is the sun?" she said. She, of course, meant Earth's. I could lie and pick one arbitrarily but I respected her too much to do that.

"Your guess is as good as mine," I said. Probably better.

"Do you think that one is Orion? It's hard to tell. My teacher told us at the planetarium that city lights make it harder to see the stars."

"Why do you keep asking?" I said. She answered my question with one of her own.

"Do you miss home?"

"Yes," I lied.

"Me too. That's why I want to know if that is Orion. One time my Daddy went all the way to Europe for a business trip. When he went to leave I wouldn't stop crying," she said, then looked a little self-conscious. "I was only five then; just a little kid, you understand."

I nodded and she continued. "Anyway, he took me out to the backyard and showed me Orion in the sky. He explained that Orion's arms were big, bigger than the whole Earth. And no matter where he went Orion's arms would be holding us both together. I stopped crying. And when I missed him, I went into the backyard and looked up at Orion's arms. I always felt better."

I stared into the heavens for a good minute.

"You know Susie, now that I look closer, I think you're right. That is Orion," I lied. I loved her too much not to. Her face lit up and she gave me a huge hug. After a minute of cuddling, I put her down and went back to my practicing. That's how we would spend our nights, up on the roof. Me practicing, both of us talking. It was the only real quality time we had together. For the first few weeks, Nanna joined us. But as my training progressed, and as Burke installed a security system, I was allowed to replace Nanna as Susie's bodyguard for a few hours.

That's right. I said I was practicing. Of my own free will. Kerr was a definite bad influence. As I was working out, Susie began giggling. Uncontrollably. She would not stop. Usually, I was able to practice with distractions, but this time I couldn't.

"All right, squirt. What's so funny?" I asked. She pointed at my bare torso. I practiced in a sleeveless shirt, pants and no shoes. Got a better feel that way.

"Kerr must really be good. You actually have muscles," she replied. She was right. My mini gut and love handles were gone. I was feeling stronger and healthier than I had ever before and I had Kerr to thank. Still, that's no reason to put up with teasing.

"Why you little..." I laughed and yelled. She took off running down what passed for stairs. It was somewhere between a ramp and a ladder. I gave chase. She ran into the mess hall and I chased her past Burke, Kerr, and Nanna. Finally, I caught her and gave her a nuggie on the top of her head. No problem. Big, bad Warrior me giving just retribution to a little girl. Then I got the surprise of my life. Tiny hands gripped my shoulder and head and pulled. Susie flipped me over her shoulder and onto my butt. The room erupted in laughter.

"Good training, Kerr. He is really ready for the arena. Who is his first opponent? An infant?"

"Rick, I told you never underestimate your opponent," mocked Kerr.

"How did you do that?" I asked Susie.

"Burke's been training me."

"Kerr, I thought you said Burke didn't know how to fight."

"I said he did not need to know how, not that he did not."

"And I'm in one point five Earth gravity."

"But I'm only in one point four."

Talk about a bubble bursting.

"Yes, but your workout is for twenty minutes. Mine is only for five," she said. "And I weigh less." Small comfort.

SUSIE

Face alight with enchantment, Susie skipped down the drab corridors of the Warplex, her blond ponytail swishing behind her, adding a splash of life to an otherwise dismal place. It was the only playground available to her for the time being. Concerned about safety, Burke had restricted Susie to the Warplex. The young girl was not upset in the least. Curiosity and imagination transformed the halls into a magical wonderland. Around every corner lay a new adventure just waiting for her to find it.

Following closer than her own shadow was the ever-present Nanna. The Trimurti was guardian, babysitter, teacher, and playmate all in one. Susie's inquisitive nature kept her busy answering a constant barrage of questions. Some were easily answered like what the purpose of a knick-knack on the wall was. Others were more difficult, such as explaining why Liberty's sky was more orange than blue at sunset. Then there were the questions that there was no easy answer for, such as why her parents had handed her over to their government and why they, in turn, had given her to the Muridae, or if she would ever see Earth again. Nanna answered each question patiently to the best of her ability, sometimes incorporating the answer into Susie's daily lessons.

Burke disappeared daily for some time alone, not used to the intensity and energy of a child. Such a long time had passed since he had lost his own that he lacked the endurance for around the clock interaction. His feelings for his ward were never in question. They ran deep and true. Burke even put aside his linguistic research to spend time with Susie, something Nanna had never seen him do in the four hundred years she had known him.

Nanna, by way of contrast, was loving every minute and had to be persuaded to spend time apart. A warm orange glow cascaded forth from Nanna's blob-like form. It had been far too long since she had a child to nurture. The world seemed new again. Susie's blue eyes revealed all of existence alive with wonder again to Nanna's sight. Nanna did not see in the traditional sense but instead sensed energy wavelengths beyond just light reflecting off surfaces. Her "vision" extended from the visible spectrum to infrared, ultraviolet, and beyond. Alert at all times, Nanna scanned the surroundings for danger. In all her life, she had lost only two charges, and although Burke forgave her, she herself never did.

Harm would come to Susie only over Nanna's dead body.

Safety was the first and foremost lesson taught to Susie. Time and time again, Susie was told to jump into Nanna's plasm whole at the first sign of trouble. Inside nothing could harm her. Burke made Susie practice every day. To Burke's ultimate dismay, she took a serious activity and made it fun. Susie transformed everything into a game. Nanna loved that ability of Susie's above all else.

Susie entered the amorphous form of her friend by running, jumping, diving, and even cannonballing. It was like having her own private swimming pool, only one step better. She could breathe under the "water" and she never got wet.

The better part of this morning Susie spent "swimming," pretending to be various fish and marine life. Burke had tried to shy away gracefully claiming he had work to do, but the greatest warrior in the history of the Tore Games was no match for Susie's innocent charm. After Nanna expanded herself, Burke entered the imaginary undersea kingdom. He played the part of blue whale to her porpoise.

Escape was only made possible by suggesting to Susie that she could watch Rick's training that day. With nary a goodbye, she and Nanna were off and running, making their way through the web of corridors that led to the arena.

The playful mood and overall progression of the pair came to an abrupt and unpleasant halt. A mass of brown fur and obnoxious fashions suddenly appeared directly in their path. With the worst of intentions, Smed'lee had been lying in wait for them. Nanna made a mental note to either reroute or disable the Muridae security cameras while leaving Burke's system intact.

Susie didn't bolt at the sight of her kidnapper. Nor did she move away. Her fear of the rodent externals had been overcome due in no small part to Nanna's presence, but her revulsion of the depraved rats remained. Anger still burned at being abducted from Earth and hatred smoldered at Smed'lee for the pain he and his pain machine hurled at Rick just for disobeying or making a joke. The pain machine glittered evilly on Smed'lee's belt. Seeing their sadism first-hand had instilled a healthy caution in her young soul, but it would not stop her from trying to protect her friends. Her tiny hands were both nimble and quick, allowing her pilfering actions to go unnoticed. The glitter vanished from the rat's belt.

The hall was silent as each of the trio stood and stared. Nanna inched even closer to her charge. Smed'lee's shrill voice broke the still.

"What a surprise. The tiny Dirtling. With the keeper of children."

Smed'lee stepped forward, bringing his evil nearer to Susie's innocence. Looking to Nanna for counsel, Susie followed Nanna's lead and body language which told her to stand tight and not leap. Yet. Susie refused to cringe at the rodent's presence but could not help crinkling her nose and eyes at the stench which rose from his putrid body. Muridae personal hygiene left much to be desired. Applying body oils and perfumes only added to the foul fragrance.

Nonchalant and slow, Smed'lee raised a hand as if to gently touch Susie's blond head. Malevolence shone clear in his eyes. With contact a fraction of an inch away, a pseudopod burst forth from Nanna's whole which harshly removed the offending arm as well as the rest of the Muridae from Susie's immediate vicinity. No effort was made to make the grip gentle. Smed'lee grimaced in pain and outrage at the affront to his person.

"Barren witch! Unhand me this instant! I was only being courteous toward the child," Smed'lee shouted, unable to bear the indignity from one with less wealth than he.

"So you admit she is a child?" Nanna questioned. When no answer was forthcoming she doubled the pain on Smed'lee's wrist. It did not go unnoticed.

"No. I admit nothing. It was a slip of the tongue. Is this how you reward my courtesy? With physical violence."

"Courtesy?" Nanna questioned, glowing red in anger. Positioned as she was between the Muridae and Susie, she could envelop the child within a protective cocoon in an instant if necessary. It was not. "Is this your idea of courtesy?" she said as a second limb shot out, tearing a ring and a good portion of hide off a furry finger.

"What of it?" he asked with a sense of bravado which he didn't feel. "It is simple jewelry."

"Then would you care to explain the microfilament needle extending from its bottom? Or why it is covered in a slow-acting poison that would kill a mammal more than a week from now?"

"I see no needle," Smed'lee said with all the outrage he could muster.

"What is invisible to you appears clear to me. You have attempted to kill my charge."

"What? This is slander of the highest magnitude!"

"Slander you say? Very well. We shall see if it was slander." With that

Nanna calmly brought the ring to Smed'lee's eye level and moved it side to side and ever closer to the fur-lined scalp. With a swift motion, the ring darted forward. Smed'lee screamed in terror, trying to free himself from the unyielding grip that held him and remove himself from the path of the golden band. The ring stopped just short of breaking skin.

"I thought as much," Nanna said. The signal was given and Susie dove to the safety within. Returning her attention to the Muridae, Nanna said, "I should kill you here and now. Instead, I spare your miserable existence. I do this for two reasons. First, is my duty to Lord Burke. As a member of his house, my actions reflect on him and your death is not worth the trouble that would cause him. Second, this child has seen far too much violence in her young life and I do not wish to expose her to more."

"A wise decision," Smed'lee said, both arrogant and smug. He felt control of the situation returning. "Now release me."

"In a moment. First, I make you a promise. Should any harm come to Susie, I shall come for you. You shall experience pain as even the greatest of Muridae torturers never dreamed. Your death will come slow and agonizingly," Nanna proclaimed, as her glow turned a dark crimson. The ring she held before Smed'lee's face took on a glow of its own. The golden band began to smoke and bubble as the metal turned molten. The pseudopod enveloped the molten mass. It was absorbed, disappearing without a trace. Sweat dripped from Smed'lee's pelt. "And there will be no body found to be used as evidence."

With that Nanna swung the Muridae high above her and across the corridor where a wall hardened his fall.

"Fool! You threatened me in front of security cameras. Your threats are now a matter of record, as is your slander since you foolishly destroyed the only evidence. I will sue."

"Cameras? What cameras?" asked Nanna with a mock innocence. It was her turn to be smug.

"This entire corridor is lined with surveillance cameras," said Smed'lee, pointing to the walls. A small squeak escaped his lips as he gazed in horror at the gaping holes which occupied the spaces where the security system used to be. He turned accusingly at Nanna.

"They were yummy," was her only comment.

Smed'lee stormed off in anger and defeat.

Once the Muridae was gone Nanna released Susie from her womb.

Perplexed, Susie asked, "Nanna, what just happened? I couldn't hear from inside you." Which did not stop her from giving Smed'lee raspberries and making antlers with her hands on the top of her head to insult the rat while within.

"Nothing you need concern yourself with, dear. Smed'lee wanted to cause trouble. Nanna took care of it."

Frowning, Susie cast a worried glance in the direction of the retreating Muridae, then turned to look again at her guardian. Nanna was again glowing orange, which seemed to allay Susie's fears. Despite her age, Susie was not as innocent as she once was. Her world had been turned upside down time and time again. Regardless of her innermost desires, she had difficulty believing in stability. She actually enjoyed Nanna, Burke, and Rick's protective smothering. They made her feel safe and gave her a new family to love. Love was the one thing she had in abundance. Blissfully unaware of the reasons behind the protectiveness, the girl continued her games. If Nanna had her way Susie would stay ignorant of the dangers so she might enjoy her young life.

Skipping and hovering they made their way to the top tiers of the arena stands where the high priced private booths overlooked the battlefield or "Pit" as it was affectionately called by the warriors. The booths were yet another way the Muridae had of fleecing the rich and the aristocracy. For several hundred times the price of a single ticket, one could obtain a private booth. For this status, many were willing to pay great amounts and the Muridae, greedy and amenable, took their money.

Entering the most elaborate of the lot, they made themselves feel at home. Laid out like a museum, sculptures of stone and light decorated the room. Most were of mountain ranges and volcanoes. Each cost more than the average citizen of Tore earned in a year. It was provided for Burke free of charge by the Muridae. Each sculpture was a gift given after a match. Burke used the room for meditation, preferring to watch the games from the stands or Pit level. Susie, oblivious to the wealth around her, plopped down in front of the wall-sized one-way viewer to watch the goings on below.

In the Pit, Newbe warriors were being worked to the brink and beyond to the realm that lays just on the other side of exhaustion. The grunting Newbes were Rick's squad. The squads consisted of five to ten warrior wannabe's, thrown together for practice and learning purposes in preparation for the Games. This was in addition to their individual instructions. Once Kerr had deemed Rick ready to join group training, he was placed with three other externals and two internals.

Currently, the sextet were all blindfolded. In addition, all limbs not needed for ambulation were securely bound down. The Newbes would have to endure the situation for two days. Amused, Susie had watched the many precursors of this activity. The Newbes had been deprived of the senses of sight, sound, and smell, prevented from using arms or the equivalent, forced to perform locomotion with only one limb, and so on. The current training began the combining of the various handicaps. Each Newbe was challenged differently by each exercise. Rick cruised through the two days without his sense of smell, which severely challenged two of his squadmates, and was in turn laid low when his world was made dark.

At the moment, he was being trounced and in turn trouncing a female of the three-legged G'morra race named Tarna. Rick had originally been wary of striking a female. Tarna, one of two females on the squad, had been instrumental in changing this view. She found it personally offensive and let Rick know this in no uncertain terms. After beating him three times, she offered a new perspective. If he did not want to initiate a fight with a female, fine. But if he was fighting a female warrior who had the intent to hurt him, he had every right to defend himself with a good offense. Finding this an acceptable compromise, he repaid her by beating her the next time they sparred. Tarna could not have been more pleased.

Tarna was constantly amazed by how males of other species treated and interacted with females. She was raised in a strict religious society that viewed women as inferior chattel, whose sole purpose in existing was to serve the male G'morra. This way of life was outlined in the Logg, the G'morran holy book. It also prohibited other things, including swearing and cursing, the eating of certain foods, but allowing maiming for missing religious services. The only advantage was that females were exempt from most public punishments, save for adultery.

Early on in life Tarna had become an outcast among her people for her outspokenness, unusual in a group traditionally not allowed to speak unless spoken to. Alone, she was unable to change the way G'morra viewed females, although it was not for lack of trying. While remaining publicly silent, other females privately expressed their admiration. They confessed to not having Tarna's courage to speak the views aloud.

Surprisingly, her mother was ashamed by her daughter while her father silently encouraged her, as he had her entire life. Secretly he had even dared teach his daughter, an unclean female by virtue of the birthing cycle, how to read. The Logg outlined the penalty for this sin in no uncertain terms. Death by stoning.

Becoming a warrior was her way of showing the G'morra that the Logg was wrong, that viewing females as weaker was not true. Tarna certainly smashed that myth. Nothing on three legs hit harder or faster.

It was an effective choice as many of her people were former slaves who viewed their race's warriors in the Games as heroes. They were free now but warriors were still heroes. She wondered if some cleric would suddenly add on a passage to the Logg that prohibited the viewing of women fighting. Since very few females read, when they were told of it, they would simply assume it had always existed. Daily she prayed to G'mor that she be proven wrong, but deep in her heart, she feared she wouldn't be.

If she advanced in the games all the written passages in the world will not be able to prevent all her people from watching her on the Skyvid.

Backing away from Rick, two of her three legs tripped over a large white tail. Twisting, Tarna landed flat on her face and frontal anatomy. The tail pressed itself over the toppled Newbe.

"I pinned somebody!" yelled the owner of the tail, a six-legged individual of the Kroc race. The sexped's name was Don. Small for his kind, a mere fourteen feet long and five high at his shoulder, he was still the largest of the squad. All trunk and tail save for small legs, stout head, and enormous jaws, he was one of the strongest Newbes, but his lack of mobility limited his effectiveness. Like Rick, he was an unwilling Newbe. His tribal leaders traded him to the Muridae for the equivalent of shiny beads. As an adolescent, he was of the least value, not even of mating age.

Only a handful of the Kroc ever left their swampy homeworld. Don was one of the unfortunate few. Chosen as a warrior, he was spared the fate of most Kroc under contract to the Muridae – a sentient of burden. The word beast was no longer used, being considered a derogatory term. Kroc served as tractors, mules, and even living taxi cabs.

Although amphibious, Kroc were more capable fighters in the water, practically unbeatable. Very few games took place in the water so the Kroc were trained on land, where they were less adept. Don, before becoming forcibly indentured, had spent most of his time alone in the marshlands of his world. This was the custom of most young Kroc as it is common practice for the large to devour the small when game becomes scarce. To the Kroc, cannibalism was just another source of food. Hatchlings survived by eating their weaker siblings. Only mates and Kroc too large for a single meal were off bounds for an entree, so Kroc avoided each other until they reached maturity, in size if nothing else.

Don enjoyed interacting with the other Newbes. It was only his second exposure to real friendship, without having to watch his back when the hunting became less than abundant. That and the two square meals he was fed each day made his life seem worry free. Because of his hermit-like existence, Don was lacking in social skills but he was both an eager learner and a quick study. On his very first day of training, he had only to be told once not to devour his opponent after the fight. The Muridae allowed it in the old battles, but not in today's games since the warriors were no longer slaves and cost more to replace. The Games were now good, clean, family fun.

Enormously pleased with himself for his accidental capture, Don was further encouraged by Rick's laughter. The string of profanity Tarna hurled his way bothered him slightly, but not as much as it intrigued him. Never having heard more than four swear words before Don was fascinated at how many she knew. Tarna's mother would have had a coronary and the clerics would be looking for a loophole that would let them punish a female if they could only hear her now.

Unwilling to take this indignity laying down, Tarna struggled to a sitting position and spit as much saliva as possible on the sandy floor. The grains solidified around the spittle. Picking up the solid mass with her teeth she flung it toward the sound of eleven legs scurrying. The projectile landed short of its intended target. Tarna repeated the maneuver. This time she scored a bullseye. The object of her intentions was a five-foot gray external that appeared to be the mutated offspring of a spider and a crab. A moment after being struck, Spike blindly rushed toward the source of the missile and straight into Don as Tarna predicted he would. Don turned his attention and his tail toward his new opponent, allowing Tarna her freedom.

Spike fended off a single blow from Don's tail and scrambled away with the speed and agility only someone with eleven legs possesses. Being of the race called Chitin, Spike had a proud history of warriors behind him. Long ago, the Chitin had a thousand-year dynasty. They ruled the twelve worlds of their system with an iron claw.

Only three hundred years of war with the Czarrian Empire ended their rule. As fighters, the two people were evenly matched. What the Czarrians lacked in limbs and numbers, they made up for in ferocity and superior firepower.

Although defeated, the Chitin never gave up or ceased their fight with the Empire. Various revolutionary groups had plagued the Empire for the past four hundred years. They were among the first worlds to leave when the Empire began its downward spiral into ruin.

In his haste to flee from the young Kroc, Spike bowled over the squad's two internals, a sister and brother team, Breeze and Runner respectively. Aprahoe were difficult for externals to tell apart. Aside from Breeze standing seven feet, four inches taller than her brother, the siblings were no exception.

Becoming warriors was a matter of pride for the siblings, for them and their people. Before the externals first came to Liberty, the Aprahoe lived at peace with nature, hunting, fishing, and farming to live. They were as content as any people ever were.

One day shadows appeared, floating in the sky between the land and the sun. The shadows grew larger and the Aprahoe did not know what to make of this development. Some believed it was an enemy approaching from the sky, but most concluded it was the sky gods descending from the heavens to visit their children as they had before.

Neither view was entirely wrong, yet neither was entirely right. The ships contained the founders of Tore, a group of various externals with one thing in common: the love of money and freedom. Within minutes of landing, they chose the site for their new city. The land was a paradise. It lay next to a huge lake fed year-round by two mountain streams at one end and formed a river which eventually led to the sea at the other. The land was level, the perfect place to build a city. Unfortunately, one was already there. Ignoring the natives, the intruders razed the existing city to the ground and the first ring of Tore was constructed.

The tall yellow people tried to fight back against the invaders, but they had no hope: metalsmithing was only a relatively recent advance in Aprahoe technology. They had no explosives to build projectile weapons. Arrows and spears proved no match for missiles and particle beams.

In an attempt to quiet the unrest, the founders showed the tribal leaders a deed they had purchased from the Czarrian Empire, granting them unlimited rights to build one city anywhere on the planet. It seemed that Liberty was a mere one hundred and twenty million miles from a nexus, a point where both Czarrian and Muridae ships emerged from infraspace. An ideal place for refueling, recreation, and trade, not to mention a free city. True, Tore had to swear allegiance to the Czarrian Empire, but this allowed them to avoid occupation. In exchange Czarrians in Tore were given privileges denied other citizens, such as the bearing of arms. All was well with the new world... from the invaders' point of view.

The deed was meaningless to the Aprahoe until they realized that the deed, by the founders' own admission, only allowed them access to the one site. The rest of Liberty, known as the Outlands, was off limits, at least in theory. In practice, it turned out otherwise. Those who tired of the city decided to make a go of it in the Outlands. Life for the Aprahoe was a choice between constant struggle or assimilation. Many chose the latter and the old ways were dying out.

Breeze and Runner were from the Outlands. Tired of the perpetual conflict and not willing to lay aside their culture, the siblings found a third option: The Tore Games. Although the Tore Games were only held at the arena, all of Liberty's western hemisphere could see the major matches on Skyvid. It was a way for the Aprahoe to face down their invaders and publicly defeat them.

They fought together since childhood, both with and against each other. Teamwork was second nature to them, which was amply demonstrated when they tag-teamed Spike, turning him over on his back, where he struggled to get up.

Kerr and a Chitin named Claw, who were acting as the instructors for the exercise, were aggravated to no end by these pitiful displays of uncoordination. The Newbes' ineptitude only made the instructors push harder. Mercy was not in their vocabulary.

Claw scrambled back and forth, side to side, and in every direction imaginable without a second glance. Swifter than the wind, he seemed everywhere at once, prodding and poking the Newbes with various appendages. He played special attention to Spike, coming down on him harder than the rest, stopping time and time again to adjust the eleven eye patches that separated Spike's eyes from the light.

Kerr moved at a slower pace, using words more than physical contact to teach, although he was not averse to using force when needed. At present, he was venting his anger at the horrible performance of the Newbes.

"Pitiful. Czarrian cubs nursing at their mother's tit could make a better showing. Forget you could ever see. Feel the air currents around you, how they are displaced by movement. Use your legs to feel vibrations through the ground. Listen for breath and life sounds. Smell where your opponents are, damn it!" he growled as Rick, Tarna, and the siblings tumbled together in one big pile up. Don was able to use his sense of smell to locate his opponents but always gave away his approach with his loud, lumbering footsteps. Stealth on land was not his strong suit.

Normally Spike could also find the others by way of olfaction, vibrations, and displaced air currents but Claw's constant badgering kept him off balance, unable to concentrate.

None of the Newbes, save Don, were enjoying the exercise. All had protested before it began until Kerr agreed to face all of them at once. He would be similarly handicapped while allowing them the use of their facilities. If they could pin him, they could forgo the exercise.

Grinning all, the Newbes agreed.

Four minutes later, the only one left grinning or standing was Kerr. The complaining stopped as they began worrying about how to survive the next two days. That was one of the beauties of Burke's Elucidator. It converted time into the units of the user. There was no techno-babble dividing a day into twenty-one point seven Earth hours. It just shortened or lengthened the time units for translation purposes. Time still passed at the same rate but everyone could converse without carrying a calculator.

Far above in the private booth, Susie was becoming restless. Waiting until Nanna was suitably distracted, she ran out the door, saying, "I'm going down to see Rick." Bounding down the stairs, Susie was able to go just fast enough so Nanna could not catch her. Or so Nanna let her believe. Reaching bottom, Susie ran across the sands of the Pit to greet the white wolf.

"Hi, Kerr," she said beaming.

"Greetings, Susie," responded Kerr, an involuntary smile coming to his lips. Susie had that effect on folks. Regaining his wits, Kerr soon remembered to scowl. "You should not be here. The Pit is off limits except for warriors and Newbes."

Unfazed, Susie countered, "But I'm bored and I want to see Rick," As if that explained everything.

"I cannot help that you are bored. If you look carefully, you can see him from here," Kerr said sarcastically, as Rick was groping blindly not fifteen feet away. Susie was not amused. "You have to leave."

Susie looked up at Kerr with sad puppy dog eyes and a tilted head. "Please, Kerr. Can I talk to Rick? Just for a minute?" The Czarrian began to falter. This is not to say he melted like butter. He was made of sterner stuff than that. His melting was more akin to that of ice - slow but steady.

Sighing heavily, Kerr said "Okay little one. Just for a minute." Of course, a Czarrian minute was only thirty-seven Earth seconds. The Elucidator was not perfect.

"Thanks, Kerr," Susie said, reaching out to plant a hug and a kiss on Kerr's furry face where it blossomed into a full-fledged smile. Running across the sands she stopped to greet each Newbe in turn before she got to Rick. They all shared common eating and recreation areas and each Newbe had come to cherish the little imp.

Once Susie was out of earshot, Kerr turned and growled at Nanna. "Are you unable to take care of your charge? Do I now have to amuse her?"

"She is no easy task, I assure you. However, if you think you can do better I will gladly turn her over to our care. Believe me, your warrior training has not prepared you to handle such a responsibility."

The wolfen warrior laughed heartily. "I'm sure you are right, but the child does not belong here."

"You are just upset that she is showing the Newbes you have a soft side," Nanna countered by flashing.

"Humph!" Kerr muttered in disgust at Nanna's radiated words. They rang too true.

Across the way, blind and without the use of arms, the squad was doing their best to play with the blond rascal. Spike and Don blocked her between them while Rick and the others took turns tickling her with their feet. Claw looked on in disgust. Kerr grudgingly admitted it was their most efficient use of auxiliary senses and teamwork that day.

Claw interrupted the fun and games.

"Return to your exercises. The time for play is over."

Moaning, the Newbes began to regroup. Susie was not so easily beaten. "C'mon, Mr. Claw. We were just about to have a tea party. You can join us too."

Standing immobile, he nodded his entire body no.

"Please?" Susie countered.

Unable to flat out refuse, Claw did what adults have done throughout history when faced with this dilemma. He deferred to the other authority figure. Since no parent was available he reluctantly said, "Ask Kerr. If it is all right with him it is all right with me."

Bouncing up, she hurtled toward where Kerr stood conversing with Nanna. Following the sound of tiny footsteps, the entire squad ran after her.

Breathlessly she blurted, "Kerr, Mr. Claw said that if it was all right with you that me, Rick, and everybody…"

Interrupting, Nanna corrected, "Rick, everyone, and I."

"Sorry. That Rick, everyone, and I could have a tea party."

"What!" Kerr roared, firing a dirty look at Claw who was intently interested in lines he was drawing in the sand. "No. Absolutely not. This is training for warriors, not socialites."

"Please, Kerr?" Susie asked, face decorated with a sad look.

"Oh, come on Kerr," Tarna said.

"Please?" Runner and Breeze begged in unison.

"Be a sport," Spike pleaded.

"Be a friend," Don tried.

"Don't think of it as a tea party. Think of it as an exercise," Rick suggested.

All faces were doing their anatomical best to imitate the sad look they knew Susie was using, all the while on their knees.

Faltering, Kerr looked to Nanna for support; none was found. Claw was acting as if sand drawing was some new kind of amazing art form.

Sensing weakness, Susie moved in for the kill. "Pretty please," she said, holding Kerr's hand against her cheek.

"Pretty please," the Newbes begged en masse, falling onto the ground to look more pathetic. Susie followed through with a pout and it was all over. The mighty glacier had melted into a meek puddle.

"Pretty please with sugar on top? You can sit next to me."

Kerr sighed softly, resolved to his fate. "Very well, little one. You shall have your tea party."

"Yea!" Susie yelled, as six cheers rose up from the ground behind her. The Newbes rose up after their cheers, leaping and dancing. Nanna and Claw were chuckling loudly.

Susie took Kerr by one hand and sat him down in the sand next to where she had taken a seat. Reaching out she led Rick to her other side. There was no need for her to guide him down. He tripped over Kerr's outstretched leg.

Claw, leaving his improvised artwork behind, attempted a quiet exit. Kerr would have nothing of it.

"Try it and die, insect. If I have to be here, so do you. Set it down,"

Kerr ordered. Reluctantly Claw complied. The Newbes plopped down in the general vicinity, most of them facing in different directions. Kerr shook his head slowly, from one side to the other and covered his eyes in disgust. It made him feel no better, nor did it make his students look any better. Dismay covered his face until a devious glint in his eyes replaced it. Only Claw saw it and he had seen it before. He got ready for the fun to begin.

"Susie, do you need anything for your party?" Kerr asked, a wide tooth grin returning to his lips.

"A table, chairs, a teapot, water, and cookies," Susie began, then added several more items to the list. Seeing Kerr's plan, Claw's eleven eyes began to twitch, the Chitin equivalent of a smile.

"Good. Listen up Newbes. Get up off your lazy keisters and bring the little lady everything on her list," Kerr ordered merrily.

"But Kerr, how will we carry it?" Rick pleaded, addressing his comments to Kerr's back.

"You'll figure out something, *Grasshopper*. After all, this is what you wanted. You have fifteen minutes. Also, find and bring Burke. He should enjoy this as much as we will. Hurry up," he snapped, adding a sarcastic "Pretty please," as an afterthought.

The Newbes rushed off arguing who was to get what, leaving a contented Kerr to play with Susie and Nanna as a disgruntled Claw watched on, twirling three limbs.

RICK

We survived Susie's tea party and the aftermath but just barely. Susie thought it would be funny to put "kick me" signs on the lot of us. Unfortunately, so did Kerr and his signs were much more imaginative. He and Claw said it was to keep us on our toes. Most warriors leave the Newbes to their training. The only worry of practical jokes is from within the Newbe pool, whether it be in squad or out. The signs were an open invitation to every warrior and Muridae who saw us coming. We were getting extremely skilled at sightless takedowns. Four hours had passed before we figured out why.

We got back at Kerr and Claw, though. The next time the pair of them went out into the city, we secretly sprayed their clothes with a perfume the Fragrunts find irresistible. The moment they hit the streets a cloud of fluttering Fragrunts was on their tail. No bar, not even Red's, would let them in. Fragrunts turn too quickly from happy to mad and with a group that size it would take a week to get out the smell if they got angry. Actually, three days as Kerr and Claw found out when they tried to leave the crowd behind. Fragrunts are sensitive to abandonment and got ticked off when Kerr and Claw tried running off without them. Even splitting up didn't save them. Kerr finally figured out it was the clothing, ditched it, and headed back to the Warplex unfollowed and unclothed. Made quite the commotion. Told the lot of us that he was with a young lady when her Fragrunt went berserk and he had to flee leaving his togs behind. Claw never figured out it was his clothes and didn't get back to the Warplex until the next day.

Neither was welcomed until the odor faded to a tolerable level. The scent lingered on for two weeks at tolerable levels. Even so, the entire squad volunteered for another olfactory deprivation secession as did many of the seasoned warriors. They never even pinned it back on us... thankfully.

The reason I let Susie off scot-free is because of what she tried to do for me, bless her little heart. After we had gotten the tea party started she came to me telling me she had a secret, but that I could not tell anybody. I agreed.

"I made sure all your pain is going to go away," she said in a conspiratorial tone. My world was darkened by the blindfold but I heard the smile in her voice. I could not imagine what she meant except perhaps something along the line of "kissing my bruises to make them go away". I was unprepared for the magnitude of her words.

"What do you mean?"

"Smed'lee can't hurt you anymore. I took care of it." Sightless, I nonetheless looked confused. Susie sought to put an end to my perplexity and guided my hands to an object she had pulled from the hidden folds of her skirt. The small item's smooth, metal surface felt cool to the skin of my palms. Unknowing, I palpated the top and sides at a loss as to what I was holding until I felt the button. Startled, more so than if my hand had been burned, I almost dropped it. The enormity of her actions struck me like a sledgehammer. I had grossly underestimated Susie. Susie had managed to take the NG from Smed'lee without him realizing it, knowing full well the danger of her actions and the possible consequences. In that one act, Susie demonstrated greater compassion, more sheer courage, and greater ingenuity than most people use in a lifetime. To say I was impressed by what she'd done for me was an understatement.

Emotions overwhelmed me. Right then I cared more for Susie than any other person I have ever known. For once I was grateful for the blindfold for it hid my warm tears. I didn't have the heart to tell her that Smed'lee undoubtedly had a spare. At that moment, it didn't matter. Having worked through my bonds I reached out and wrapped my arms around the little imp, pulled her close and hung on tight.

"I love you, Susie," I whispered.

"I love you too, Rick," she answered, hugging me back every bit as hard and with as much emotion. Claw saw what I had done and re-secured my arms so I'd be robbed of their use again. Susie rested her head on my shoulder while Claw did his tying.

That tender moment was cut short by the angry bellow that announced Smed'lee's unexpected and unwelcome arrival.

Through the ebony that clouded my vision I could almost see the little maggot running amok at the loss of his precious torture toy, shouting accusations of *thief* at Nanna. Kerr must have had a look of confusion and amusement at the rat's dismay. It all vanished as his eye caught a fleeting glint of metal from across the Pit, the source of which was Susie's hand hiding the pilfered NG beneath her skirt. Respect then took control of his lupine face as he moved to intercept Smed'lee. Kerr's goal was to prevent ratboy from getting any closer to Susie. Wordlessly, he trusted me to get her to safety. However, the sanctuary of Nanna's form was far away... across the Pit to be exact. Still ignorant, Nanna joined Kerr's block play.

Our nearest haven was slowly moving away from us. I had to get Susie there. Once Susie was inside the *whole*, Nanna would realize what was going on and "energize" the evidence. A simple plan. But was it simple enough to perform blindfolded and with my hands tied behind my back?

There were too many noises for Smed'lee to be alone so we also had to contend with an unknown number of Muridae. I tried to remove the blindfold but it was held fast by a timed adhesive not set to release until the exercise was over. Time to put my strategy lessons to work: first we needed a cavalry; can't have a decent rescue without a cavalry. Spike's blindfolds had not been sticking well and we all knew he could see out of at least two eyes. On top of that, he was probably the fastest in the squad. Having the most legs will have that effect.

"Training is over, gang. Break any rule you can, Spike. Get Burke here, now! Tell him Susie is in danger." Burke had been involved in a project and declined our offer earlier.

"Spike is gone," he said. A spray of sand showered down on us as eleven legs raced off.

"Tarna, Breeze, and Runner; get between the Muridae and Susie. Stop any that get past Kerr and Nanna. Until then act casual, as if still practicing. Don, you and I have to get her to Nanna." If we tried to get away, blind as we were, chances are we would be caught. My first assessment was still right; Nanna was the nearest and only safe port.

We were working in the dark, so we used Susie as our eyes. Made more sense than having the blind lead the seeing. At present, we were being ignored. We could not count on that lasting forever. Smed'lee still believed Nanna was the culprit. Any reckless action on our part could tip him off.

"Susie, get on Don's back. If the rats start coming toward you, give Don directions to Nanna. Have her eat the evidence."

"Got it, Rick," Susie said.

"What evidence?" Don asked, whose primary concept of evidence was being caught with a half-eaten carcass.

"You're better off not knowing," I told him. Besides I promised not to tell.

Kerr had put himself directly in Smed'lee's path and was being his most obnoxious self, hoping to get ratboy angry enough to forget what he had come for. It was working well enough that Kerr's contract was being placed in jeopardy. Kerr in response became even more insulting. Susie informed us that ten other Muridae were spreading out and moving our way. Probably intending to strip search us for the missing NG. A lot of effort. Maybe there is no spare. No, my luck couldn't change that drastically this quickly.

We had no choice but to move. At best, the rest of the squad could hold off three, leaving seven for me and Don. Unfriendly odds. I hopped on Don's back behind Susie, intending to shield her body with my own. Following Susie's instructions, Don made a beeline for Nanna. Unsure of why he was moving, the Muridae moved on an intercept course of their own. Two got close enough to make a grab. As I intended, they went for me instead of Susie. I resisted only marginally as they pulled me down, struggling just enough to keep them busy. That left five plus Smed'lee for Don; without a blindfold, he could eat them alive. I was hoping none of them would be brave enough to block his path. A half-ton Kroc bearing down on you is a terrifying experience, as anyone in the squad could attest. Especially close to mealtime.

In the distance, I heard Kerr casually say to Nanna, "Look after your charge." As there were no Muridae within thirty feet of Susie at that moment, Kerr's instructions perturbed her, but Nanna began to move closer to the girl on Krocback. I could hear her cursing herself for allowing Susie out of her safe range. Smed'lee saw this and pulled a second, smaller NG out, pressed the button and Don fell to the ground in agony. As Xiles and indentured Newbes, he and I were the only ones with the pain implants, a fact I had forgotten when devising my strategy. Just for fun, Smed'lee pushed my buttons and I keeled, joining Don both on the ground and in pain.

The race was on to see who would reach Susie first. Fortunately, not all the Muridae were up to speed, physically or mentally. Nanna would reach her in plenty of time to protect her from bodily harm, but not from detection of the stolen NG. Smed'lee held a detection device which had led him to the Pit in the first place. If he got close enough it would pinpoint the NG's location and Susie's goose was cooked. Once a lock was found on the NG, the scanner's data could be used as evidence in the Tetrarch's court whether or not the NG could be produced as evidence. Civil penalties for theft were stiff in Tore and Smed'lee would make sure each one was enforced to the max. An added bonus was the fact that charges could also be brought against Burke since Susie was now a member of his house.

Susie knew enough to run toward Nanna, but her two small legs were not built for speed. Others had legs more suited to the task. The Muridae in the know were gaining on her. Nanna was still seconds away and Smed'lee's scanner was almost in range. A furry hand grasped out, grabbing Susie's shoulder. Susie turned, screamed and bit the hand. Another, the mirror image of the first, less teeth imprints, took the place of the first on the tiny arm. Smed'lee, moving ever closer, let fly a whoop of joy in anticipation. The Muridae underling who had hold of Susie yanked her off the ground, dragging her toward Smed'lee and the scanner. All seemed lost.

Salvation came in the form of a violet blur that suddenly bowled over the Muridae, knocking him head over heels into the Pit sand. Before the little girl could hit the floor, Tarna had scooped Susie up in her untied arms and raced blindly toward Nanna with amazing accuracy. They entered Nanna's whole still in a three-legged trot. After a hurried explanation, a soft glow emanated from the whole as the NG was converted to energy. Thinking it a malfunction, Smed'lee cursed loudly, striking the scanner as it lost the NG's signal. No lock had been made. Susie was safe.

Don and I were another matter. Oblivious to our surroundings, all our perceptions focused on a haze of pain. Kerr demanded Smed'lee turn off the spare NG and release us from its thrall. Smed'lee furiously refused, until "Genny" was turned over to him. He had not realized that the lack of a signal was not an error on the part of the detection device, but the destruction of his "Genny".

Kerr ordered Nanna to envelop Don and then me. She didn't argue and had trouble with Don's size, so got the upper third of his body including the head where the implant was.

Inside her whole, the NG signal could not reach our implants and the torment ended. Smed'lee continued to press the button. We were effectively trapped, for the moment we exited our agony would begin anew. Kerr found this unacceptable and let Smed'lee know this in no uncertain terms. Smed'lee laughed in his face. Bad move. Lesson one, never tick off the wolf. Kerr pulled his sword part way out of the scabbard, exposing the gleaming upper third of the blade. He then informed Smed'lee that if the backup NG was not turned off by the count of one he would remove the blade entirely. It was all said with the famous Kerr smile, known to empty barrooms and terrify Newbes.

Smed'lee, I was told later, blanched in horror. A naked blade in the hands of a Czarrian was a challenge to a duel. One of many special privileges granted the Czarrians by Tore law allowed one to engage in the duel whether the second party agreed or not. The law enforced no penalty on the Czarrian even if he killed his opponent, while the opponent enjoyed no such protection and would be prosecuted. It was a lose-lose predicament for ratboy and he knew it. He was no match for an unarmed Kerr. Kerr with four arms and a sword meant he would be ratburger.

The switch was off long before one was reached. Kerr slid the blade back to its resting place, patting Bloodmoon gently.

Smed'lee began to make demands again but in a much more polite manner. His demands were cut short by a rumbling that shook the arena to its very foundations. Pieces of the walls and ceiling crumbled and rained down. The pounding increased in intensity until a mountain on legs burst through a wall. The intended barrier collapsed before him like it was constructed out of paper. Burke entered the area at a speed unbelievable for his bulk without the benefit of jets. Spike was hot on his heels, barely able to keep up.

The sight that greeted him was that of the four of us in Nanna's whole, her shield up. Kerr's hand was still on his sword and he stood defensibly between Smed'lee and Susie. Burke let loose a battle scream that sounded like concrete exploding from the top of an erupting volcano. One look at the thundering DeTang and every Muridae fled in terror, with Smed'lee at the forefront. Burke started to give chase until Kerr signaled everything was under control. Burke slowed to a stop that should have been impossible without hydraulic brakes. Kerr took him aside and explained the situation while the lot of us exited the whole.

Claw, the only one not to involve himself, looked to the rest of us for an explanation that never came. Burke, now bathed in the light of understanding, rushed to Susie and actually initiated a hug. Susie was all but lost in his gigantic arms. He then turned and thanked the squad as a whole and me in particular. I spoke for us all when I said no thanks were necessary. We all cared about the little imp. The others were still awed by his praise. Burke also thanked Tarna personally for her last second rescue, asking if there was anything he could do for her.

"I neither want or need a reward for helping a friend, but I would be honored if Lord Burke would consider me for a personal match." I have always thought Tarna was a little wacky, but actually asking to fight a DeTang was the purest insanity. There must be an easier way to get a Skyvid match. Or a funeral. Burke chuckled and said he would keep her in mind.

Nanna apologized for allowing the situation to even come into existence. Burke told her no apology was necessary. It did not allay Nanna's guilt at having needed help to protect her charge.

The excitement gone for the moment, we all sat down to continue the tea party. Claw rechecked Spike's eye patches, but was unable to make all eleven stick to his hard, smooth hide; he then rebound Tarna's arms. Nanna protectively made herself into a chair for Susie, unwilling to allow any distance between them. The rest of us scattered around the table. Kerr added his praise for all of us to that of Burke's which coming from him, the ultimate critic, meant more to me than any other accolade I could have received.

Burke had an announcement concerning the project he was working on. Susie and I silently hoped he was joking when he said, "I have another batch of chocolate chip ice cream ready." This would be his fourth attempt. Each one was progressively worse if such a thing was possible. Even the other members of the squad moaned. No one was immune from the taste test. Kerr found out humans here in Tore made ice cream and told Susie and offered to get some. She turned him down then begged us not to tell Burke because it was so important for him to succeed in making it himself. Despite the rumbling of my stomach and taste buds, I agreed to keep quiet. When Burke got up to get the latest batch the lot of us would figure a way to play hooky. Until then, we enjoyed ourselves.

And Burke poured the tea.

SMED'LEE

Ten Muridae were lined down before Smed'lee, on hands and knees. Their faces were buried in the floor in a bid for forgiveness. The bid was rejected outright.

Rage, betrayal, and a strange sense of loss overwhelmed any twinge of pity that may have existed in his overseer's heart. Genny, his only true companion, had been taken from him and killed as if she were just a piece of metal. The maggots postured before him could have saved her from destruction, but they had been both incompetent and derelict in their duties. No amount of pleading would save them from his rightful vengeance. He would avenge his fallen comrade.

Liking the sound of that he repeated it: Smed'lee the Avenger… Smed'lee his Verminness. Each of the ten was ordered to address him as such before he flailed their miserable hides with the neurowhip. Each body was raked first with the pain the blow brought, then as the electric current hit. Pink welts raised up from each pelt over the strike zone but no blood flowed. That was the beauty of the neurowhip; it cauterized its own wounds so there was no messy aftermath to clean.

Not satisfied with the grisly results he had thus far achieved, Smed'lee turned to his newest toy. Lifting it tenderly, he placed it on the head of the nearest inferior. At first glance, it resembled an ordinary helmet. With the simple press of a button, it generated a magnetic field which, when passed through an organic brain, activated every piece of gray and white matter in its path. This cerebral storm caused the chosen victim's body to convulse uncontrollably, often losing temporary control of autonomic functions. Once the field was off, the body returned to normal… usually. Prolonged exposure could be deadly. Stained pants were a nuisance, but the exciting possibility of stopped hearts and breathing were worth the stink to Smed'lee.

The machine could be calibrated just to stimulate pleasure centers or to promote healing, but Smed'lee preferred a wide field that hit everything in its path. Because of the risks, only licensed users were allowed to own one. Smed'lee spent two years training for his license and passed at the top of his class. Every instructor praised his ability, naively assuming he would go on to become a great healer. The blindness of the wise is often the blackest of nights.

Smed'lee had not once used or intended to use the helmet for a beneficial purpose, save his own twisted enjoyment. It did bring him much joy, as demonstrated by the torment of the ten. Forcing the nine to watch as their compatriot was put through the helmet's paces, Smed'lee's euphoria over their ensuing anxiety and fear was apparent. Their dread tasted almost as sweet to him as their future inflicted pain. Adding to the beauty, was that his new toy caused no scars after the fact, only a subtle realignment of certain electrolytes, barely discernible by medical examination. One had to know what to look for to find it. It was a divine creation and he was meant to be its prophet. The prophet of pain; him and only him.

Not even Dortew had a helmet.

He loved the helmet almost as much as his dear departed Genny. Unfortunately, it was not practical for non-Muridae use as he would have to place the helmet on the victim. No warriors would allow him that close.

In ecstasy, he fondled the backup NG. She had not the beauty of her predecessor, nor did she glisten or shine sinisterly in that way only Genny could. In her favor was the simple fact that she got the job done just as well. It was just that using it felt wrong. As if he was cheating on Genny with her sister. Guilt was not a state with which Smed'lee was familiar with; it confused him. Smed'lee knew full well that no matter how much righteous pain he imparted, nothing could change the fact that Genny was gone forever. All his efforts would not bring her back. Not that it dampened his enthusiasm one iota.

Bonding would be a long process. His heart was not a faucet that he could turn on and off at will. It would take time. Best get on with the first step. The naming... what would be appropriate? It was just so damn hard to think with all the cries of agony rising up from the ten on the floor.

"Silence!" Smed'lee ordered. "I am thinking." The noise level diminished greatly but did not fade away. Cries became whimpers, screams quieted to raspy whispers. Motion in response increased as if the thrashing was the physical incarnation of the suppressed wailing.

He considered naming her after someone he cared for but could think of no one who fell in that category. No one save Genny and her name was a derivative of Nociogenerator. Deciding it would be wrong to bestow the same name, he chose one that was close.

"You shall be called Enny, little one. Together we shall cause pain and torment like this world has never seen," Smed'lee crooned melodramatically. The need to impress was innate, even toward inanimate objects. Pulling Enny closer he embraced the tiny device passionately, nuzzling it next to his face. "Very well; the matter has been decided. Inferiors, you may resume screaming," he said magnanimously.

A chorus of thanks assailed his ears as the wailing increased to fevered tones while the bodies of the ten lay almost still from the release.

Smed'lee fastened Enny to his belt, with two separate bindings. No one would take Enny from him. Turning his attention back to the ten, he pulled his lime green cloak over the NG. With his right hand, he continued the lashings of the nine without a helmet. With his left, under cover of the cloak, he caressed Enny tenderly.

Enny remained cold and aloft through it all, taking no pleasure from the caresses of her suitor.

KERR

"No. Absolutely not!" I say to the Dirtling Rick.

"But, Kerr," he answers back

"No buts, Rick. You are not going to the Empirical House."

"Why not? I've been working my butt off."

"Must be painful to sit."

"Just one night. What will it hurt? You said you go there."

True, I do, but I know what I am getting into. Letting Rick go in there would be like sending a Fragrunt into a Muridae bidding war. He would be eaten alive... for a fee. Besides, he is going to see Sasha. How he plans to pull it off is beyond me. I tell him he cannot afford it.

The Dirtling almost snaps out the words, "Let me worry about that." I try to stare Rick down. Although intimidated, he gives up no ground. His face becomes enigmatic. Damn hard to read furless faces; they always look like they are up to something.

Rick shows too much optimism. Could be a fatal trait. Not that I have anything against Sasha, as Amoropath or as a warrior. She excels at each. I have seen the effect she has on male Dirtlings. They lose all sense of purpose around her, Savage being the perfect example.

Rick does not need the added distraction. He needs to learn enough to survive his first match and each one after that. Time spent with Sasha will lead to more time spent thinking about her and when he will see her again. Instead of spending nights thinking of the best way to take down a Kroc, his mind will be spent on thinking on how to get into Sasha's gown. Rick's skills are not at a level that will allow such diversion.

"I am not used to having my orders questioned, Newbe."

"What's your point?" Smartass needs a lesson. Faking with my topright, I expect him to dodge right into my bottomleft fist. To my surprise, he avoids both. Smiling, he decides he is not satisfied getting off easily and tries to retaliate. I drop him like a stone.

I need to channel his energies toward his training, not his mating urges. Best way is to link the two, so success in the first may lead to success in the second.

"Okay, Newbe. I have an idea. Why don't we wager?"

"Wager what?" he said, practically tripping over himself in his eagerness.

"If you can take me down, I will personally escort you to the Empirical

House to see Sasha."

"Sounds good to me. But what do you get if I can't?"

"Your confounded silence on the matter. Do not become upset when you are unable to succeed today. It will be a standing wager."

"Deal," We shook on it. "Kerr, what about if I land a blow on you?"

I chuckle. He has not been able to get closer than half an arm length. Still, it is a good idea. Prevent him from getting frustrated.

"Trip to Red's if you can touch my chin. Agreed?"

"Agreed." Again we shook. When we break our grasp, he makes a try for my chin. I lash out at that arm's brachial plexus, deadening everything below Rick's shoulder. Diving away from me he uses his other arm to restore movement. Impressive how fast he took to that. Faster than any other Newbe I have trained. Now if he could learn the rest of his training half as quick we would be in business.

Coming at me, he tried everything I taught him in an attempt to land a chin punch or take me down. Even showed some promise by improvising. All unsuccessful, of course.

The wager was working. Rick's attacks were becoming more enthusiastic, less like drudgery. Each onslaught was planned out in advance, trying to use foresight on how he has seen me move before and how I might move this time. The boy may have a chance to survive yet.

After a solid hour, he calls a "Timeout." Dirt phrase. Time out of what? Why he does not just say he needs a rest is beyond my meager understanding. Human skin is too fragile, particularly if Rick is any example. More scars decorate his hide than even the most veteran Czarrian campaigner. Shuts up every time I try to find out where they came from. Right now, he is bleeding from four different places. He keeps a first aid kit in his cube; needs to use it after almost every secession.

Breathing heavy, he comes up to me.

"Kerr, I'm sorry. I bled all over your tunic."

"Damn inconsiderate of you bleeding on someone who was pounding on you," I answer. Rick carries politeness too far sometimes. "Perhaps next you would like to apologize for breathing so heavy and loud, disturbing my quiet."

"Maybe," he answers with a laugh. "Let me wipe that off you," he says picking up some sand from the floor of the Pit. It absorbs the spilt crimson, solidifies and falls to the floor.

Rick whispers "Time in." I look at him confused. Time in what?

"Kerr, I'm sorry. This will leave a stain. Look at it."

Complying without thinking, I look down at my stained tunic and my chin meets Rick's ascending hand.

"Gotcha," he says, running away like a teasing child.

Suckered like a cub. He got me good. Used deceit over force. I taught him well.

"Not bad, Rick. A deal is a deal. Go get changed; we are going drinking tonight."

"All right!" he cheered, dashing off to his cube to get ready. By his enthusiasm, I gather he has hopes of Sasha being at Red's. Does not know the first time he went was her night off. Tonight is a work night. No chance of her stepping out.

I head toward Burke's suites to invite him along. He has been cooped up here too long, worried over the little one. He needs a night out. Just have to convince him of that and to just leave the child protected in Nanna's whole. Even the Muridae are not stupid enough to make another attempt so soon after the last two failures. Smed'lee knows we are on to him. If Nanna's threats did not do the trick, I am sure Burke's threats to tear down the entire Warplex around their ears will ensure their best behavior. For at least a day or two.

I debate whether or not to change my tunic. I decide not. Why bother? Going out drinking, I'm just bound to get more blood on it.

RICK

The doors flew open at our approach. The portal swung wide, hurling two externals out of the bowels of the bar. Their heel-over-head mode of locomotion was swift and without great poise. The sounds of the two screaming, mostly to themselves, took away any trace of dignity that might have lingered. In the doorway stood Red, brushing off his hands with a dishrag. Great, it must be bowling-with-patrons' night. As the three of us were left untouched by Red's throw, this frame was a gutter ball.

Literally, as that is where the pair landed, with a plop and a splash. Into what, I can't rightly say; it hadn't rained in over a week. I was the only one who paid the spectacle any mind, except for a passing Muridae, whose clothes they splattered on touchdown. Judging from the rat's reaction, the liquid was not water. I chuckled softly. Leaving that drama for our own, we headed into Red's.

Kerr took up the forward position, Burke the rear. Despite all my weeks of training, they still didn't trust me to be out in the streets of Tore solo. All my pleading meant naught as I was entering the bar with not one, but two babysitters and an insulted ego. Susie only needed one. Burke said one was all she needed because she listened to reason easier than I did. The fact that I turned down his reading lessons was still bothering him. I argued that I could already read and write. Burke countered it was next to useless if nobody knew what it meant.

We took up a table in the center, probably to assure that any fight started would somehow have us in the middle. Aside from the two bowlers, the body pile by the exit only boasted a five count... must be a slow night. Then again, the night was still young.

In spite of my escort, I was feeling good. It was Saturday night and I just got paid. One hundred and fifty Tore francs. At present, the currency meant no more than a handful of metal monopoly money, since I had no idea of its relative value. There was one quick way to find out: spend some of it. I ordered the first round; Red was quick to oblige. The tab came to half of my money. The stipend the rats were dishing out wasn't going to go far. Kerr informed me that tipping a Roserod was considered disrespectful, which was fortunate because I was sure the amount I had left would definitely be an insult. Kerr also informed me that Rod'nee expected a tip, so to always order from Red.

If luck was with me, things here would run the same as an Earth bar. By buying the first set of drinks, I would ensure a nightful of libations without having to spend another franc as my drinking buddies would be buying. Cash flow was just another line on my constantly growing list of worries. At present, I had no prospects of increasing my paltry income. Tore apparently has no welfare system and my contract didn't permit moonlighting. Before the evening was over, I would again be broke. Reminded me of college.

Most of the warriors I'd met did well for themselves money wise. Burke, Red, Sasha, and even Kerr seemed financially well off. None needed to fight to survive, physically or financially. Yet they didn't retire. I, on the other hand, would jump at the chance to retire and I have not yet begun to fight.

"Kerr, why do you and the others still do the warrior thing?" I asked.

"Each warrior has reasons all their own. With Burke, it is a matter of honor. Your Sasha…" he said sarcastically, "…does it for the publicity for her and the Empirical House. Claw does it because it was what he was born and bred for. Red, over there," he said, pointing a furry finger toward the bar, "does it for fun and profit." Nothing I didn't already guess. That still left one warrior unaccounted for, the one I really wanted to know about.

"What about you, Kerr? Why do you still fight?" I asked. Taken aback by the question, Kerr became uncharacteristically silent. Raising his mug, he took a long sip of his drink, savoring every drop as if each was a barrier between him and something unpleasant. Lupine eyes blankly scanned the wall for a full minute before an answer came.

"It makes the pain go away for a while," he said softly, finishing the drink in a single gulp. Kerr completed the motion by pounding the glass on the table, which shook in response. He motioned to Red for a second. Red pointed at me and I nodded no. Burke was having a slow go at a glass barrel of the darkened mineral gook he survives on. Looked like cooled magma in a cup. I much preferred the amber liquid and foamy head that was in my mug. It was good beer.

Yes, beer. Red had gone into a partnership with a fellow Earther named Samuel Troubell to make the native Earth brew and it did well for both of them. Red had a dozen such partnerships and supplied liquor to most of the bars in the city as well as much of the Outlands.

In the wake of Kerr's answer, silence shouted at me for asking the question. The noiseless void was almost deafening until the drink was brought. Red placed it down in front of Kerr. The simple thump was magnified a hundred times. Red placed a seven-digit hand on Kerr's shoulder. Kerr placed his hand on top. Their touch conveyed more than words could ever hope to. They shared a moment out of time. When the moment had passed, both hands returned to their respective sides leaving the silver, fur-covered shoulder to fend for itself. Kerr himself was not left to the same fate. Red pulled up a chair and joined us, sitting so his front rested against the back of the chair. He didn't like to sit normal because it left no room for Sally. All the while, his lady keg supplied her suitor with all his imbibing needs.

Kerr took an ample mouthful of the liquor and a deep breath to steady himself as he found the strength to continue his tale.

"Life is not always an adventure; at times it is more desolation than anything else. Especially in the depths of the night. A heaviness settles around the heart, a cloud of gray, a dark mist that refuses to disperse. It stays and casts its black shadow over all that you do. Attempts to alleviate it all useless. Soon all is done in a half-hearted manner. Apathy is how you deal with the world.

"Your mind knows something is wrong, but it is not logic that wins the day. It is action, danger, and adventure that finally lifts the gray veil. With your heart pounding and your blood racing, there is no time to think; you merely act. Worry, self-doubt, and insecurity all fall by the wayside. Instinct takes over. And the gray is gone, banished. You feel again. You enjoy the air you breathe, the food you eat, the music you hear, and the people you love. You know you are truly alive."

Kerr's was a disturbingly familiar story that reminded me of a horrible night in a place now so far away it seems a dream. It began with a knock on my old apartment's door which I answered. A crimson apparition greeted me covered in tears and blood. A horrible act of self-mutilation had just taken place next door and its result stood before me. I barely recognized my friend, Nina, hovering on my doorstep, her pale white face and hands blanketed in the blood that bubbled from her wrists. Her hair and yellow robe were matted down by a mixture of soapy bath water and crimson fluid.

Barely able to remain upright, Nina's raspy voice matching perfectly her wraithlike appearance she begged, "Help me!" Wide eyes looked back at me, whether in horror or hope I couldn't tell. I tried to stop the bleeding.

Already in the know, I asked what had happened. Calmly, as if talking about someone else, Nina told her tale of desperation. A final feast, good music, a warm bubble bath and some contemplation on her life preceded two deep gashes into her wrists with a sharp kitchen knife. She couldn't find a razor. The final deed done, she lay back in the warm waters to die, thinking the misery that hounded her every waking and dreaming moment was finally beaten. She'd taken the only way to escape her despair.

Instead of being a means to her end, the act of wooing death brought her back to the land of the living. The pain of her wounds made the anguish of her soul depart. Somehow the physical hurting made her feel alive again. Death was not her intention. She only wanted to lift the gray veil over her heart, to make the agony of her life leave her. She wanted to live again, but her gray would not let her so she struck back at it in the only way she knew how. Death had seemed her only solution.

Embarrassed, Nina refused to go to the emergency room despite my pleading. Unable to outlast her stubbornness and unwilling to let her bleed to death, I reluctantly sewed her wrists closed with a needle and thread.

Pent-up frustrations, buried hopes and dreams from the renovated graveyard of Nina's heart, everything that led her into a bathtub coffin which almost became a watery grave, poured forth. Laughter and tears mixed freely. We talked through the night and greeted the dawn together. With the light of a new day shining bright and warm on our faces, she agreed to seek therapy. The sunrise only lasts a moment, but the beauty of that moment seems enough to get one through the day.

Unfortunately, a day is not a lifetime. Before the week had passed, the Grey had returned, crushing the bright hope of that morning mercilessly. She told me neither therapy nor life was working. The world was screwing her over and nothing could stop it. In retaliation, she would strike back against the world by driving her car into a tree. That would show life. When she was gone, everyone would be sorry. Then they would care and blame themselves.

She was right, but for the wrong reasons. Reasoning with her was useless. My pleas fell on deaf ears. Nina would not be stopped. Bolting out into the parking lot, she ran into something other than a tree... difficulty. It seems she was unable to open the car door without a key. The keys were no longer in her purse; somehow they had ended up in my jeans pocket. Sometimes the hobbies of a well and misspent youth came in handy. She was furious and let me know this in no uncertain terms demanding I let her end her life. I refused. Her fury gained momentum when she found out I had called the local suicide helpline and they sent a professional out. An hour later, Nina was deemed a danger to herself and committed for a twenty-four-hour evaluation. That began her treatment. Medication was able to stop her mood swings. Unfortunately, she didn't talk to me again for years.

Out of the blue, I received a wedding invitation from Nina. Inside was a thank you note asking for my forgiveness. I called and told her there was nothing to forgive and offered my congratulations. I love happy endings. Be nice if I was in one. Her wedding is next week. I should RSVP but I'm fairly certain knowing her phone number won't do me any good here. Instead, I'll just have to drink a toast to her happiness. And to Kerr's.

This was the first time in all the time I'd known Kerr that I'd seen him anything other than dead serious or wildly enjoying himself. It made him seem less perfect but more human, if that term can be applied to a four-armed wolf-like being from another world.

The wolf continued his story.

"Rick, let me try and explain the history of the Czarrian Empire. In the process, perhaps I shall answer all the questions you have asked and I have ignored," Kerr said.

"You mean you'll tell me where the Empirical House is?" I asked with a grin.

My smile was quickly mirrored by his own razor-sharp one. "Except that one."

Kerr began, "My people, once the greatest warriors in the universe..." Across the table, both Burke and Red coughed, raising what passed for eyebrows on each of them. Kerr winked and kept talking, ignoring their subtle challenge to his claim. "...are now reduced to a race of old women. Not without reason, mind you, but we have accepted this fate far too easily."

"For the last three thousand years, we ruled the seven galaxies with iron hands. Hundreds of worlds fell before our assault and were brought civilization. Each world learned our language, used our measurement systems, and our currency. Technology was advanced and people of different worlds were able to communicate with each other easily for the first time. Without our strength, much good would have never come to pass; civilization would not have grown."

A familiar speech, I thought to myself. Many history teachers and fanatics spout similar rantings to justify certain actions. Grillar himself tried to convince the lot of us that what he was doing was for the good of the United States. What bothered me more than Grillar trying was that some of the other prisoners believed him.

Red exploded. "And the universe was happy... Bah! Don't you be preaching fleabag propaganda in Red's. Excrement ain't true. Don't be warping the Newbe's mind. Fleabags are butchers, murderers, and prohibitionists," Red spat, a curse on the last word. Burke mutely nodded agreement.

Surprisingly, Kerr merely shrugged his multiple shoulders. "It's a free city. Everyone's entitled to an opinion, even a wrong one." No more was said by the others as wordlessly they agreed to disagree.

After irrigating his muzzle via his mug, Kerr continued. "Each world the Empire conquered further increased its appetite. As borders expanded, new prospects for conquest were explored. I believe one of our scouts even visited your world over two thousand years ago, Rick. She set up some of the locals to conquer the place so that when we arrived we would have just one world government to conquer instead of a hundred little ones. I believe her Dirtling underlings' names were Romulus and Remus."

I guess the legend of the two of them being raised by a she-wolf was based in fact. Kerr cut short my historical musing. "It was a common practice. The Empire gave the process a few thousand years to work since your world is on the very outer border of known space and they planned to conquer the worlds in between first. My people were great planners and did not believe in rushing things. Worlds were conquered on a timetable, so we did not overextend ourselves and so each generation of youth was not deprived of the honor of battle. I believe the invasion was planned for this century. How would your world's government be able to defend itself at this time?"

"My people would put up a fight," I answered truthfully. I trusted Kerr, but I didn't want to give him any inkling of our possible defenses. Not that I knew enough to be useful. Still, the thought of someone putting Grillar out of power gave me the warm fuzzies. "As far as a world government goes, we have none. Romulus and his brother both raised armies which fought over the possession of a city. Romulus won and the city was named Rome after him. Years later, Rome was the center of an empire which ruled much of the world for hundreds of years."

"The Roman Empire? He named it after himself? How vain," Kerr said, muttering the words "Kerran Empire," quietly to himself. "I take it they no longer rule?"

"No. The Roman Empire fell many centuries ago."

"How?"

"Historians are not really positive, but most seem to suspect that lead water pipes poisoned and weakened them to the point that barbarians were able to conquer them," I said. A burr of scarlet rushed me from my left. Red grabbed the mug from my hands and carried it to the bar. He poured out the contents and filled another one from the tap. He gave me the new drink.

"Sorry. Did not know humans were sensitive to lead vessels. They make the drinks sweeter," Red apologized.

"Don't worry about it," I said dumbfounded, wondering if I had drunk enough for it to affect me; I hoped not. "What is this one made from?"

"Silver," Red said. I nodded okay. If I could eat with it, I could drink from it.

"So, if invaded there would be multiple governments to conquer?" Kerr asked.

"Hundreds," I said.

"Ah. A challenge. Pity it does not matter now. The Empire is not conquering anyone these days," Kerr said wistfully.

"I was under the impression that the Empire was no more."

"It still exists, but as only a shadow of what it was."

"What happened?"

"It is a long story."

"Yours always are," Burke quipped. Kerr threw a knifey stare at him; it shattered on impact.

"My people spent years developing the perfect weapon. It was named Razza in honor of one of the Pantheon, a god of destruction and death. For years, it remained inactive, untried in battle, tested only on uninhabited moons and asteroids. My people have a saying, 'What good is a sword that remains in its sheath?' And so it was with the Razza. We were in the process of conquering a system with five inhabited worlds. They were putting up too much resistance and Command decided a lesson was in order. The ultimate weapon was dusted off and brought to bear. The most powerful of the five, a world called Wandum, was given a choice: bow down or suffer the consequences. They chose the consequences."

"Even the scientists who built the Razza were unaware of the effect it would have on a planet with an atmosphere. The planetary gases, mixed with the cascading energy output increased the devastation of the Razza a hundredfold; billions died that day. Wandum and its people were reduced to a cloud of space dust. Their only crime was resisting the Empire. Not surprisingly, the rest of the system surrendered within the hour."

"Killing in battle was almost second nature to us, but never before had we committed genocide. Individually and collectively, my people have done things too heinous to mention. As Burke knows well," he said. Burke nodded grimly.

"They murdered my children," Burke said. Sadness was palpable in the timbre of his voice. Burke had broached the matter before, but it was obvious he didn't wish to talk about it any more than merely mentioning it.

"No world, except Roserod, failed to fall before us."

"Strata was not conquered," Burke stated irately.

"But it was occupied for almost two years."

"Occupied?" Burke snorted through a flinty mouth. "Your ships were in orbit and a handful of troops were planetside. We ignored you until the horror began. The detachment you sent was reduced to amino acids. Then we made certain your kind would never come back."

"True," Kerr admitted.

"I loathed all Czarrians for a century after that. My hate was one of the things that led me to develop the Elucidator, to stop externals reliance on Czarrian Common. In fact, when Kerr and I first met it was all I could do not to beat the life from his bones." Burke looked thoughtfully across the table at his furry friend.

"And don't think I did not appreciate it," Kerr said with a smile and slight bow.

"Once I knew him better, I realized my hatred of the entire race was not entirely justified. But in his case, it was," Burke joked sarcastically.

"Thanks for nothing!" Kerr spat back, at a loss for a better comeback.

"Actually for a mammal, he made a decent warrior. In time, I granted him the gift. By gift, I mean personal combat with myself."

"Kerr fought you?" I said like a wide-eyed child. "How'd he do?"

"I lost," said Kerr, head bowed.

"No, you survived," Red said with pride. Kerr sat a little taller at the praise. Burke just drank his mineral gook quietly, nodding in agreement.

He did that a lot. It got more attention than I would if I got up naked on the table and sang. I learned my lesson last time... never again.

The DeTang was one of the richest externals and possibly the mightiest being on the planet, but for all that power he was very unassuming. Burke didn't flaunt his strength. He exuded something beyond confidence, something more akin to the attitude of a con man who has all the pieces for his greatest scam in place and was merely waiting for the score to fall in his lap. Except Burke's integrity was so far above question, anyone trying to search its boundaries would wind up with a nosebleed. The dependability of Burke's word was so legendary that the Muridae didn't require a written contract. Burke was not so trusting with them. He differed from the Muridae in many ways. Tearing down others to build himself up, the Muridae credo, was an alien concept to Burke. Instead, he raised up the people around him. It was as if he realized others viewed him as being somehow above them so he treated those he was close to as an equal, building their self-esteem in the process. At least, that is what he had done for me.

Kerr brought the conversation back to its beginning. "That holocaust did what no army had ever done; it broke the spirit of my people. In mourning for the slain, all battles were halted. A full week passed. The Emperor and Command discussed what to do when the Justices appeared."

Burke threatened Dortew with invoking Kentor Justice. It scared him.

"What is Justice?" I interrupted. Somewhat of a rhetorical question since I'd asked before and been ignored, except being told I'd be more dangerous with the answer than without. Burke and Kerr did that a lot. Apparently, I'd become a much safer person now because Burke answered.

"The Kentor are an ancient race. Practically immortal if the legends are to be believed. They are also one of three races that have unlimited access to space travel, excluding certain individuals and groups," Burke explained.

"The other two being the Czarrians and Muridae?"

"Exactly. Except Kentor have no need of ships. They need only think of a place and there they be. The secrets of here and there, the wonders of teleportation are an open book to them, as well as many other secrets. Centuries ago, they set themselves up as a court of last resort for the entire universe. They made many rulings, but since sometimes the verdict was harsh it was difficult to enforce; often it was ignored. To ensure that their will was done they chose Justices, one from each sentient race, to carry out sentencing. Each Justice was given jurisdiction to judge any injustice save one involving a native of their own race. The logic was that this would help them remain impartial."

"But how can one being enforce a verdict on a group of people?" I asked.

"With the mantle of Justice, each being is given the power of teleportation. Imagine if you will someone refusing to pay a judgment. If the money is physically available, a Justice just transports it or anything of value away. A being refusing a death penalty suddenly winds up in a vacuum, insides exploding or frying in the heart of a sun. Or perhaps one finds their body solidifying inside a solid object. The Justices are safe from retribution; enacting revenge on a being that can be anywhere in the blink of an eye is impossible," Burke said.

"Not to mention unhealthy for the would-be revenger," Red added, apparently with the voice of experience.

"What laws do they enforce?" I asked. I better learn them and make sure jaywalking is not a capital offense.

"They do not go by laws so much as by a scale. An offense is measured by the amount of harm it brought. The verdict is rendered in such a way as to balance the scale. A death for a death, money for injuries. Justices are not all-powerful. Once each cycle every Justice is brought before the Kentor themselves and is judged in turn. If the Kentor decide a decision was in error the Justice must endure the same punishment given, up to and including death."

"So why wouldn't a planet being invaded call on Kentor Justice to stop the attack?"

"They take into account cultural mores. Since war is present in some form in most races the Kentor do not interfere."

"How is Justice invoked?"

"Any sentient may invoke High Justice, merely by contacting the Kentor."

"Then why don't we invoke it against the Muridae? I'm sure kidnapping is considered a major crime."

"True, but in this case, they are not guilty of it. They recognize a native government's right to do what it wishes with its citizens. This right *now* stops just short of death. If High Justice is invoked without adequate reason or evidence a penalty is invoked on the accuser at the discretion of the Justice. Including death."

"Oh," I said numbly, my hopes of freedom smashed in tiny pieces at my feet. I now understood why Burke was taking his time building the case for Susie and why they didn't tell me. I might have invoked it prematurely and paid too great a price for it.

"I can understand why your people were made nervous by them, Kerr," I said.

"Nervous? We were defecating in our undergarments terrified. Dozens of Justices were standing in judgment. Prior to our crime, the greatest number of Justices deciding a case was five."

"Six," corrected Burke.

"In sheer terror, the Emperor and the High Command ordered all conquest to halt permanently, before stepping down from their posts. In a society where power was valued more than life, these positions remained unfilled for almost a full turn of the seasons. The Justices left without saying a word."

"That was good, then?"

"No, just the opposite; no verdict was given. My people believe they can return at any time. And if the penalty for a single death is death, then the penalty for genocide is..." Kerr left the sentence unfinished, but the same could not be said for his drink. "Worlds left the Empire by the score, each testing how far they could go. Our fleets did nothing to stop them. The new Command issued a policy ordering ships and warriors not to engage in battle without being first attacked. Our military might is now just a sword in its sheath. I was only a cub, barely on the brink of manhood, when this happened."

"I grew up in a world very different from that of my ancestors, trained as a warrior, but not allowed to fight. A warrior who knows not battle is considered a child by my people. It was then the Grey first found me and I had no way to fight it until the Games. It was here on Liberty that I was made a warrior. My father, no longer ashamed of his youngest, traveled here for my first battle. After we performed the Bakda ceremony, I was made an adult in the eyes of the Empire. And in doing so, I won my first battle against my greatest foe. That day the Grey fell. Although it and I have done battle many time since, each time I emerge victorious, stronger than before."

Beats slashing your wrists, I thought with grim amusement. I'd never seen him depressed; I never pictured Kerr as anything less than in full control of every situation he was in. It seems a natural assumption about someone who can walk into a pub, start a fight with a dozen externals and be the only one left standing. All that without ever having to draw his sword out of its sheath. I wonder if he realizes that or if he thinks of Bloodmoon as useless.

The conversation drifted off to warrior tales. Not one fight was started, probably owing more to Burke's presence than anything else. Having told my two battle tales, I had nothing more to contribute. One was the episode in the diner and the other was about me standing up to a bully in junior high school who tried to take lunch money and getting a black eye for my trouble. It was not even my lunch money. I actually believed my father when he told me bullies were cowards who backed down from anyone who stood up to them. He lied to me even then.

After several more drinks, Kerr and Burke began singing, at the table so I pulled Red aside at the bar.

RED

Kerr's Newbe approached me, a troubled look on his face. He kept a careful eye on Kerr and Burke. If Red's time as a barkeep had taught Red anything, he's got mischief on his mind.

"Red, can you give me directions to the Empirical House?" he asked, in a quiet whisper. Kerr's ears twitched but the song continued, against the wishes of music lovers everywhere. Newbe has not learned that nothing calls attention to one's self more than whispering in a bar.

"Why not ask Kerr again?" Red asked, knowing full well the answer. Good to see Kerr putting someone else through the paces Red put him through.

"Kerr does not want me to break training, but I have to get out or I'll go crazy."

"What? Red's place not good enough for you?" Red said, adding a touch of harshness to Red's tone. Mammals sweat so easily.

"No, Red. Nothing like that. It's just that all my life has been since I came to Tore is training, fighting, philosophy. I need a night out."

"You're out here."

"That is not what I mean. You see, Sasha..."

"Ah, Sasha. The ultimate mammal's fantasy. Red has seen your credit roll and it would not buy thirty seconds of her time."

"I'm not buying. She's giving. Last time I was here she said for me to come down for a free session."

"Free? That is indeed a rare and different story. Red will help you. Besides, it will really get under the fur of that flea-bitten, lice-ridden, worthless mongrel."

"Hey!" Rick blurted out reflexively.

"You have a problem with that, Dirtling?" Red asked. He swallowed hard and his shoulder muscles tightened, but he did not back down even as Red brought Red's face in front of his, close enough that we shared air.

"Well, yes. You should not say that about him. Especially not behind his back. He is one of the best beings I've ever met."

"And would you still defend him even if it meant Red breaking some bones?" Rick flinched only barely.

"Are you threatening?"

"Perhaps. Answer. Would you?"

"Yes," he answered. Lifting four arms Red made four quick feigns toward him. He did well for his level, better than expected. He blocked three.

"Relax, Rick. Red is playing with you. Red would not harm you. Kerr regards you too highly. I'm just glad to see you are just as loyal." Red gripped his limbs in salutation. He was lacking the proper number so Red made do putting two on each of his. Never let it be said that Red has no sympathy for the genetically handicapped. "Kerr is like a son to Red. Red cares deeply for him, although Red will deny ever having admitted it. We insult each other because our feelings run too deep for us to admit them comfortably."

Rick nodded slowly, never breaking eye contact. Damn Dirtling was turning the barkeep trick against me. Beings revealed secrets to Red, not the reverse.

"Your courage is commendable but foolhardy. Had we battled you would have lost."

"I know."

"Then why not back down?"

"Kerr and Burke have helped me, stood up for me when no one else would. Not even my people. I could do nothing less for them. Sounds corny, huh?"

"Not corny." Why would he sound like vegetable matter? "Honorable. A rare and noble quality. It should be rewarded." Since Red is not in the business of giving medals Red poured him a shot. Rick has a lot of potential, but that nobility complex will get him into trouble. Kerr and Red will have to discuss ways of toning it down.

Red gave him the directions. Rick wrote them on a napkin which he quickly hid in his pocket. His thanks were profuse.

"Rick, Red will not lie for you. If Kerr asks Red will tell him where you have gone."

"I understand. Can you at least give me a five-minute head start?"

"Yes." Again with the thanks. "Be cautious."

"Hey, I'm almost a warrior. I can take care of myself."

"Confidence killed the Curel." Rick stared dumbly. Wisdom is so wasted on the young. Newbe did not even break stride. No sooner was he out the door when the fleabag and the pebble stopped their song. It had been mostly for the Dirtling's benefit.

"You promised him a head start?" Kerr asked, slightly annoyed. Tough. If Red had a pound for each time Kerr snuck out on Red would not have needed the winnings to open the bar. Nice to see the tables turned. Red did wish on him a student like he was to Red. Glad the polymorphic deities have not lost their sense of humor.

"Yep," Red answered.

"How much?"

"Only five."

"Good. Plenty of time for another drink," Kerr said. "And make it a deep one, *Father*," Kerr added with a chuckle.

Froggen eavesdropper. "Red should rip those ears off, mongrel."

"But, Papa, I thought you loved me. Does this mean I don't get my allowance?" Kerr mocked.

Red moved slowly across the floor toward him. Patrons scattered except the pebble. Burke just lifted his mug off the table. Pebble should. I have to import that plop halfway across the universe for a mere three customers.

Fleabag and I crossed arms. He got the drop on me first but I recovered quickly. Sitting down in a chair I spread the furball across my lap.

"Sorry, Sonny, but this is for Kerr's own good. Spare the spanking and spoil the child."

"Isn't this the part where you tell me it hurts you more than me?"

"What and lie to you, Sonny boy?"

"No wonder Mom left you for Uncle Scarlet." The pebble smiled as did the fleabag. Two palms on the posterior ended that and began the howling. Justice and retribution were served swiftly in the end.

SAVAGE

Draped in shadow, the black vehicle hovered silently and sinisterly. Tinted windows obstructed the view from the street side of the glass. Inside, infrared filters displayed the night with the clarity of a summer's day. Those within could see all of the night's secrets. They watched carefully.

Vaulting down the otherwise deserted street, Rick Wagner wandered into the skyster's sights unaware of his hidden audience. Inside, voices spoke in quiet, practiced tones as if they feared their quarry hearing them.

"Careless," hissed a sunken mouth set beneath two deep set eyes. Both were surrounded by a gray face, which had once been purple and looked as if it had never known a single day of simple joy. The face alone would not merit a second glance, save perhaps one of pity. It was the eyes that captured one's attention, releasing it only reluctantly: the red orbs shone with a life all their own, separate from that of their owner. These eyes set this face apart and all who suffered their glance knew them for what they were: zealot's eyes, whose depths spoke of danger and death to any who impeded his holy mission.

In the abyss of his soul, all missions were grouped in that category. Mercy was not the way of these eyes. Not a stray thought was spared for what he did. Rip the wings off fragrunts? Sure. Tear the limbs from screaming infants? Without hesitation. Horror required no justification. He cared not, for his actions earned his rightful place in paradise. Those who did not share his beliefs were not worthy of consideration. For that matter, he had yet to be convinced regarding many who shared his convictions.

"Probably the first time they let him out on his own. He's testing his limits in the lower gravity," said the second voice calmly, talking to himself, confident that all within earshot hung on his every sound. The confidence was justified. Before translators became commonplace, he had almost inadvertently ordered a ritual suicide of a hundred externals. It seems the command and the sound of a belch were amazingly alike.

Even within the skyster, the darkness conspired to hide his features. The other voice grumbled to itself, disturbed by this defense of the unworthy outsider, even as half-hearted as the comment was. Acting casual yet quite purposeful, the figure on the street entered a comm booth and took out a piece of paper, which resembled a napkin, and proceeded to study it intently.

"What is he doing?" asked the gray-skinned member of the G'morra, barely concealing his distaste for the young warrior. Only the company he kept maintained a civil tongue when he spoke.

"He's lost; obviously checking his directions. Probably can't read the street signs yet, although I'll bet Burke offered to teach him. Doesn't know the landmarks."

Rick walked out of the booth, fresh resolve and optimism apparent, acting as if his actions were all part of a master plan. After progressing a disoriented several hundred yards, the resolve faltered and died a quiet death; its passing was marked only by a heavy sigh.

The paper was again removed from the comfort of Rick's pocket to face the cruel night air unaided and alone. It was treated as if a great secret was written on its face. Rick didn't look at it long without scrutinizing his surroundings as if he was fearful others would realize he was utterly lost. Unaware that what he thought hidden was as plain as the glare of headlights to a panicked deer, he journeyed on, muttering something about there never being a gas station around when you need one. Adjusting his course one hundred and eighty degrees, he marched back the way he had just come.

"Pull alongside and invite him for a ride, Santo. I think it's time I met Rick Wagner of Earth."

"As you wish," the gray external replied from beneath his Fedora hat. He tried to look menacing and succeeded quite well. Looking in the rear-view mirror, he almost frightened himself. Santo signaled the driver who in turn followed the order. The skyster halted, obstructing Rick's path. Scanning the street, he came to the realization that he was quite alone. What meager external population had been on the street mere moments before scattered to the four winds at the skyster's approach. With nowhere to run, Rick immediately dropped back to a defensive position. As if to dramatize the affair, the piece of paper fell from his pocket and was borne away on a gentle breeze; it wandered over his foot and continued on its way, perhaps looking for a new pocket to occupy. Ominously, yet keeping with the general mood of the moment, the darkened window nearest him rolled open lethargically. A fierce pair of red orbs greeted him.

"Salutations," Santo said, attempting to exhibit a friendly facial expression. He was not up to the task.

"Howdy," Rick replied, eyes narrowed to slits.

"Allow us to offer you a ride," Santo offered, doing his level best to be gracious. That it was not in his nature was apparent.

"No thanks. My mother told me never to take rides or candy from strangers."

"Obviously, a wise woman," Santo replied. Rick grimaced slightly.

"Not when it counted," Rick replied, a touch of bitterness coloring his voice.

"Be that as it may, this section of Tore is very treacherous. Were you not to accept my very gracious offer, only G'mor knows what fate might befall you," he said, his soft words failing to hide the threat veiled behind them.

"Thanks, but I'll walk," Rick said, slowly backing away. His eyes never left Santo's features although their desire to do so were clear.

"I tried to do this the nice way, but you force my hand," Santo said with mock sorrow. His eyes displayed the joy he felt at being allowed to coerce in his natural manner, a violent one.

The ebony door opened upward as a leg, the first of a triad, slid out onto the pebble covered pavement. Grabbing hold of the door, Rick smashed it down quickly. Wasting no time in blazing his retreat, Rick took off running and leaping down the street. In a matter of seconds, he was on the next block and around the corner.

Meanwhile, the mouth that was connected via various neural pathways to the crushed leg began to shout. When that failed to alleviate the torment and pain, it began to curse.

"Procreation!" Santo shrieked. The sound of his own voice, of the forbidden oath he had uttered, rendered him numbingly silent. A sudden shame overwhelmed him. What scant color lay in his cheeks departed for parts unknown. He bowed his head as if asking for forgiveness; it was not long in coming. A deep voice, cloaked in the veil of the night, spoke softly.

"Rejoice, for thus I absolve you of your sin."

"Gratuities," he said, turning to give chase, any deviant behavior forgotten as soon as forgiveness was granted.

"No," the voice snapped, hard as a whip. It stopped Santo cold. It was as if a brick wall suddenly sprouted in his path.

"But the Dirtlin..." Santo said, barely repressing the last syllable of the hated term. His world abruptly transformed into an arctic wasteland covered in icy fear.

"He is a Terran," the voice whispered with a quiet rage. "Remember that." Santo nodded solemn and meek. Even through the darkness, he could feel those eyes upon him, those eyes he must never offend. "Let him go. For the moment. We'll find him later." Santo meekly and without comment climbed into the rear of the skyster, shutting the open door behind him.

A piece of paper rolled back across the barren street in the direction of rapidly fading footsteps. It would spend the rest of the night tumbling alone.

The shaded window rolled slowly closed.

RICK

The journey of a thousand miles begins with a single step and bad directions. Overcoming many obstacles and an attempted mugging, I managed to find the Empirical House. That or this city has two neon castles. It was an unusual setup, but it had a boisterous beauty about it, a cross between Buckingham Palace and the Las Vegas strip. I was expecting an area akin to Times Square, but the neighborhood was quite nice, almost classy.

Tore itself was laid out like a circle with a cross down the center. At the very middle was the Tetrarch's palace and the homes of the older aristocratic families. When the city was first settled, five hundred or so years ago, they were the hub from which the rest of Tore sprang. As time passed, the city grew and that which was first built became outdated as the more modern structures were erected around their predecessors. The poor and downtrodden were allowed into the older neighborhoods as the more affluent moved into the outer rings. The inner rings became slums except for the center city palaces and four safe roads protected by the Guardsmen, Tore's police force and army. Guardsmen also safeguarded the underground transport tubes that covered the same route. On all other streets and tubes, you were on your own.

At present, Tore had nine rings, each one worse off than the other. Every ring had its own name and charm. Or so Kerr tells me. The safe roads divide each ring into quarters. There are some quarters even Kerr won't enter, even with Burke or Red. Luckily Sasha's place was on a safe road, Eastway. Red's was somewhat off the same road, in the sixth ring. The Warplex was in the seventh, off Northway. I had lost my way somewhere in between.

Like I said, the Empirical House was a sight to see. It put Broadway to shame. Light sculptures lined the perimeter of the castle, or perhaps fortress would describe it more appropriately. Each sculpture depicted different races performing various activities. None looked very suggestive, although I was quite certain the nuances of alien reproduction were beyond my grasp at this point. I spent several minutes trying to figure out one of the more interesting holograms but it turned out to be a drink advertisement.

Gathering my nerve, I walked into the front door. Literally. It was transparent and didn't open automatically; I smashed my face right into it. My nose was going to hurt for days. Giving the rest of me the once over, I decided nothing else other than my pride had been damaged. They should put up some sort of sticker to prevent that from happening. Or perhaps the architect has a sadistic sense of humor. Maybe Smed'lee designed doors in his spare time.

The lobby put Kubla Khan's pleasure dome to shame; elegant was a gross understatement. Putting on the Ritz barely made the dress code: chandeliers carved from white and blue quartz floated below the ceiling, each refracting ordinary light into a chromatic pageant of illumination; flawless and smooth white marble lined the floors and walls; exotic plants were placed strategically around the room, although for all that I knew some of them may actually have been patrons.

Feeling and looking extremely out of place, I found myself wishing I had a tuxedo on instead of my warrior togs. At least they were my clean ones. Choosing retreat as the better part of valor, I made for the door, hoping I could open it without hurting myself.

In short, I chickened out. I'd call Sasha to meet me for a drink at Red's. Like she would come. What had I been thinking? Sasha's out of my league. What would she want with someone like me? I'd only embarrass myself.

Moving so quickly that it seemingly materialized out of the air behind me, a violet limb grabbed hold of my arm. Strong, it prevented me from completing the one hundred and eighty degrees necessary to reach the door. A G'morran hostess, in a glimmering evening gown, had taken me in hand. Other than the three legs, she and Tarna looked little alike. Tarna preferred simple clothes while this lady was decked out in enough finery to put a Muridae to shame. She led me toward the reception area. It was set up similar to a Beverly Hills hotel. I was even asked to sign the register. I used the name John Smith. It seemed appropriate. Too bad no one but me would get the joke.

"What is your pleasure?" asked a mass of violet limbs attached to a bulbous center core; the receptionist was the member of a race known as the Calamari. None were involved in the Games, so I knew nothing more than their name.

The extremities moved fluently as if underwater. It was both strangely beautiful and revolting. I had no idea what, if any, sex it was nor did I think Kerr's method of looking was appropriate. Besides, I had no idea where to look. The idea of sexes other than male and female was still extremely foreign and hard to accept. Burke and I had not even decided on an English neuter pronoun for the Elucidator. I suggested hem or hir, combining him and her into a single word. Burke wasn't convinced it was a valid word. Despite my best efforts, I still thought of everyone I met in terms of boy or girl. The receptionist's voice was high pitched and somewhat feminine so I labeled her a she. I addressed the center mass, assuming it was the face.

"I'm here to see Sasha," I replied. Brushing a tendril over a ledger, she appeared to be reading. Several of the as yet undetermined number of limbs shook side to side while her vocal apparatus, in the same limbs, made a "tisk-tisk" kind of sound. She was an alien with an attitude. I got the feeling I was not the type of client she felt the Empirical House should have. Tough.

"I'm sorry, but the Mistress has no openings for the evening. Can I interest you in something else?" the Calamari said. Her tone made it clear she had the exit in mind.

"That's too bad; I was hoping to see her. Sasha told me to stop by anytime. It was weeks ago, but I've been unavoidably detained," Pretty much the story of my life. "She may have left something for me. Please check. The name is Wagner. Rick Wagner." Not quite as catchy as Bond but I had to make do with what I had. She leafed through some metal plates, her tendrils reading the bumps.

"Yes, she left something for a Rick of Dirt," she said as another limb scanned the ledger. "But you signed in as John Smith."

"Stage name," I explained while trying to figure out how she was able to read English. With her "hands" no less.

"I see," she said, obviously not believing a word. She pressed a button on the side of the counter. Almost instantly, the lights to my rear became very dim. A huge shadow fell across my back, almost knocking me over. I hoped it was someone moving a wall. No such luck. With a disconcerting lack of sound, a DeTang had arisen behind me. I fought my bowel and bladder for control. I won, but it was close.

"Trouble, Boopsie?" he asked. He wore an external translator around his neck and a short burgundy silk robe, barely covering his equivalent of hips. He addressed his comments toward her limbs. I had guessed wrong in talking to her center and probably made a large social blunder in the process.

"Perhaps BoBo. This gentleman is trying to get in to see the Mistress using a false identity."

"Possible lawbreaker?" the DeTang asked, pounding a boulder-like fist into his other mountainous hand. It made a sound like thunder... a literal thunder clap. My bladder indicated it was ready for a rematch.

"Perhaps," she said, as the mammoth bouncer advanced toward me. My back was against the reception desk. I was trapped between a rock and a hard place.

"Wait a second, Boopsie and BoBo." Nice names. "Sasha and I really know each other. We met during a bar fight in Red's. I'm sure she'll remember me." I hope. "We met only once but it was special," I babbled.

"It always is with an Amoropath; at least for the customer," said Boopsie. "Show him the door."

"Thanks, but I have already seen it... well, kind of couldn't see it but nevertheless it's wonderful. Love what you've done with it. You might want to consider making it visible in the future," I said, backing away from the desk.

BoBo moved slowly toward me. His granite hands hovered between us as they opened and closed with a sadistic glee all their own. They seemed to be arguing in some perverse sign language over which one would be given the honor of shattering my skull into microscopic fragments first. The one on the right won and made a grab for my head. Neurons and synapses were working at double and triple time. Ducking below his wide swing, I dove beneath him. Not one to let a perfectly whole skull get away, BoBo bent forward and reached after me between his legs. Twisting, I saw his face coming after me upside down beneath his rear end and I had to fight the impulse to sing "Blue Moon." He looked ridiculous... and off balance.

Coming up, I placed both my hands on his blue butt and pushed. Hard. The floor came rushing up to greet him. It was a short greeting and not a very friendly one. The floor was wondering if gravity was really worth all that bother as it caved in beneath BoBo's tonnage.

Like some grim statue of an angry god of death and destruction, BoBo rose up from the white marble crater his fall had created. The floor almost sighed with relief. I let out a sigh of my own but it was so high pitched only a dog or maybe Kerr would have heard it. With him towering over me, we stood, each staring the other down. BoBo advanced toward me. Without flinching I stood my ground. It was not because of any misplaced sense of bravery. My mind, realizing what my body just did, had paralyzed it with fear to prevent it from causing any more trouble. I found myself unable to even blink. Seeing my immobile state, the DeTang stopped short. Probably trying to figure out why I was not running away screaming in terror. A damn good question.

The attention of all the externals in the immediate area was fixated on us. There was actual awe on faces or what passed for them. By knocking down a DeTang, I had upped my social standing. My funeral would probably be attended by all the right people.

Taking advantage of the situation I used my command voice, somewhere between demand and request. "I would like to see Sasha. Tell her Rick is here." Boopsie made no move to comply with my request. "Now, please." Might as well go out with a bang.

It worked. Boopsie reached for an intercom. "Mistress, you had best come down," she said, relaying the rest of my message. No one moved. They all wanted to see what would happen next. Me too. No time and an eternity passed before she appeared at the top of a staircase. With the arrival of my vision of beauty, I lost all sense of reality. I longed to rush to her, to embrace her, but I couldn't. My mind still had not forgiven my body for what it did the last time it had freedom of movement. So instead I stood and watched. And longed.

"Well, my Banesh Knight in shining armor has finally come to take me up on my offer. Did you have to wreck my place to do so?" she said looking at the DeTang-sized depression in her marble floor. Her presence made all else fade into the background. It was a dangerous reaction. Kerr would have been upset, but I didn't care.

"It wasn't my intention, I assure you," I said.

"Good. Come on up," she said. It was an offer I couldn't refuse. Sasha was adorned in a golden gown, which hugged her in all the right places. I was actually jealous. Never in my life had I wanted to be an item of clothing more. Actually, I never had the desire before. Generally, clothing spends too much time in closets. In this case, the advantages would more than make up for it.

"Wait," said Boopsie, ever the snob. She refused to lose gracefully. "There is still one more matter that needs to be settled. How will you be paying? Cash or credit line?"

"Neither," I said. Boopsie turned almost white and BoBo tensed up.

"It is okay, Boopsie. This one is on the house," Sasha said. What little conversation had restarted ground to a rapid halt with a startled group exhalation. Boopsie's body forgot to resist gravity for a moment, but she caught herself before hitting the floor. The floor was probably relieved; it had enough trouble for one evening.

Kerr had lectured me on the importance of showmanship, so I

bowed deeply to BoBo as a sign of respect. It also gave him less reason to ambush me on the way out. I gave a smaller bow to Boopsie while waving my hand with a flourish in imitation of my master. She didn't react. I wasn't sure if she was still conscious.

I made my way to the top of the stairs. Once there I took Sasha's hand and slowly kissed it. She took my hand and touched it with her lips. It felt wonderful, like my face had in the bar only better for there was no pain to block the pleasure. I had one happy hand; the rest of me longed for the same joy.

From inside my sleeve, I produced a red flower or "blossom" as it translated. It was the closest thing to a rose I could find. I'm sure nobody at the park will even know it is missing.

Sasha smiled as she took it from me, putting her nose to it and inhaling deeply. Locking her arm in mine, she led me away toward the stairway to heaven.

SANTO

Neon reflected eerily in the nebulous surface of the floating skyster. In trying to act inconspicuously, it stood out clearer than the light sculptures. Were it not a floating car the act never would have gotten on the road. Exiting the Empirical House, Santo straightened his suit. The interval within was far too long to merely be asking questions. Santo's time was no doubt spent in the Observatory, a viewing room of sorts where the secrets of the universe unfolded in all their passionate glory. Santo denied enjoyment or curiosity in the proceedings, choosing instead to denounce those within for their sins of the flesh. Condemnation was not given before the act in order to save the participants from their iniquity. Comment was instead saved until completion. If Santo remained silent, it was generally agreed the customer had not gotten his money's worth.

Cold and sweaty, Santo climbed in the back seat.

"What happened in there?" queried the voice.

"Apparently, they attempted to throw him out," Santo said. The voice chuckled knowingly.

"I hope BoBo didn't hurt him too badly," declared the voice. Santo shifted uneasily knowing the treatment messengers historically received.

"Um... actually, Boss, from what I heard he took BoBo."

"What!?!" the figure screamed from the shadows, his serenity lost. "No human can beat a DeTang. It is impossible. If it weren't, I'd have done it."

"I remember, Boss. I'm just repeating what everyone is saying," Santo spoke meekly, wringing his hat in his hands as if it were a wet rag. No response from the voice; only a low hum filled the air.

"I am slowly becoming impressed by the newest Terran. He is full of surprises. Make sure I meet him," the voice said. Santo nodded, exited the skyster and returned to the Empirical House. Despite his intention to do otherwise, once inside the transparent door Santo found his feet carrying him back to the Observatory. Rationalizing that the Terran might be an exhibitionist, he waited and watched.

RICK

"Come into my parlor," said the Amoropath to the man, no double meaning intended... unfortunately. Light sculptures of candles covered the room in a hazy luminescence. Dark drapes hung from all corners at peculiar angles, folding over on themselves.

Sasha's eyes sparkled and her gown glistened as if made of liquid metal. She motioned me to sit on a couch that was without back or sides. I expected a bed of some sort. None was present. The couch was only wide enough for one.

I had trouble remaining seated. My feet were barely able to suppress the urge to pace. Sasha didn't seem to notice my nervousness or was polite enough to ignore it. What was going to happen behind these closed doors was still a mystery. At least they were not transparent.

Kerr could have at least helped me out but no, all he could do was smile and make snide comments about my finding out when I was old enough. Burke was equally mum on the subject. He seemed embarrassed whenever sexuality is discussed. What it boiled down to is I was on my own. At the moment, I would not have it any other way.

Now I had to decide what happens next. I don't even know how this goes down in a house of ill repute on Earth. Shows you what clean living got me. Sasha's heavenly form sat next to me. A fog rolled in, veiling all my thoughts. My heavy breathing took the place of a fog horn. Her face shone as a beckoning lighthouse. Her voice called to me like a siren to a sailor.

"How are you adjusting to life here in Tore?" Sasha asked smiling.

"Fine," I replied, letting my talent for small talk shine through.

"Good. It can be rough. How is your training coming along?"

I almost said fine but stopped myself.

"Depends on who you ask. Kerr says I couldn't fight my way out of a room full of Tads. I'm sure I would be insulted if I knew what a Tad was."

Sasha chuckled. It was a wonderful sound, like the purest silver chimes. "A Tad is an insect. Loud, annoying, but harmless." Joy. I can't even cut it as a fly swatter. "I wouldn't worry if Kerr insults you. It means he likes you."

"So I've been told. He must be crazy about me. If I'm lucky, I'll survive the experience."

"I take it you were not a warrior on your homeworld?"

"Far from it. I was in the healing arts. I'm having a lot of personal problems justifying fighting for the sake of violence."

"You prefer a cause to do battle for?"

"Yes... no... I prefer not to fight at all. But I can't sit idly by when I see an injustice being done."

"If it doesn't affect you, why bother?"

"It's my nature, I guess. On my planet many years ago a leader killed off millions of people because they didn't fit his idea of a master race. I once read a poem that spoke of a man who said nothing as they took away different groups of people to concentration camps. He didn't speak up because it didn't affect him directly. One by one, each group vanished yet he kept silent. Eventually, they came for him and there was no one left to speak up for him."

"What happened to the people?"

"Too many died because the leaders of my world turned a blind eye to the genocides. This was seen as approval."

"What happened?"

"Eventually the madman was stopped and the survivors freed. Too late for millions. Before I was taken from Earth, decades after this happened, another group started up new camps. The world governments remained silent again, even one made up of a people that was hit hardest by the first set of exterminations. I didn't expect them to send their armies in. They have too many border disputes of their own to be able to do that. But they didn't even raise a diplomatic protest. Nobody did until the press showed what was going on. The people of the world were so enraged that the governments had to protest. Conditions of the prisoners improved but then it was forgotten again,

"Then it came time for my own personal trial by fire. My government demanded a member of my family, my sister, for some unknown purpose. All we knew is we would never see her again. I disagreed and did something about it. I lost. It's how I ended up here."

"Did they get your sister?"

"No."

"Then you won. You took on a superior force and stopped them from achieving their objective. It is an obvious victory," she said. What she said made sense. It only made me feel a little bit better.

"Why did they choose you for a warrior I wonder? Take off your shirt," she demanded. Surprised by the sudden return to the original nature of my visit, I complied. She looked me over and motioned for me to turn in a circle. I felt like a side of beef and enjoyed every minute of it. I suppressed the urge to moo.

Trying to look sexy but feeling rather silly I let my shirt drop to the floor. Sasha sighed out loud at the sight that greeted her. It was not a sigh of passion but of dismay.

"I know why you were chosen. All those scars. Only a being with a true fighting spirit could survive them. Take off your trousers," she asked. Again I complied, this time meekly with no attempt at being alluring. I stood wearing only a pair of boxer shorts.

She sighed again. I could not blame her really. There was barely a patch of my skin left without a wound of some kind. Much of my skin would never be smooth again. Only my face was untouched.

Her eyes were alight with curiosity. I'd been through this before with Kerr. I gave him some cocky answer. He let it slide. Susie never mentioned it except to ask if they hurt. I think somehow she knew.

"How did you get so many scars?" she asked, not with pity as I expected but with a sense of empathy.

"My government. Two representatives in particular. M. Herman Grillar and Lonso Hobbes. They run the 'exchange program' with the Muridae. They wanted to give my sister over. I wouldn't tell them where I'd hidden her. They tried to convince me otherwise and were very creative in their persuasion," I said unable to hide the bitterness in my heart.

"So you spoke up for your sister, but nobody spoke up for you?" Sasha asked.

"Basically," I replied, unable to keep eye contact. I gazed at the thick rug as if it was the most interesting thing I had ever seen.

"Why did they not use truth drugs to get the answers they needed?"

"They tried after the first round in the torture zone. It didn't work. I babbled incoherently. Try as they might; my tormentors weren't able to keep me on a single subject long enough to get the answers they wanted. I ended up singing songs. The one thing they were able to learn was about my insurance policy. I had left a letter and a video with my cousin, with the intent of her sending it to the newspapers if I didn't contact her. Under the beatings, I gave up her name. Now I don't know if she's alive or dead."

I curse myself at night for that moment of weakness. Sorry, Tandy, so very sorry.

"How did you survive?"

"At the time, I thought it was force of will. Looking back, I can see it was because I was worth more alive. The Muridae would have no use for a dead human."

"You would be surprised."

Sasha came closer and her hands traced the patterns of the wounds down my chest. She bent to pull down my shorts.

"No," I said sharply. My hands grabbed and stopped her, something I had never pictured them doing.

"Even your genitals?" Her blond eyes opened wide in horror. I nodded numbly, fighting back recollections of horror. "Bastards!" she said, fury in her voice. I offered no argument. I could barely speak, choosing to not even try. Instead, I froze up, stood as stiff as a board, refusing even to breathe. Memories that had been blocked out engulfed me. Many of my scars were still as fresh and painful as the day they were inflicted. Unable to debride the mental scar tissue, I buried those memories in the deepest, darkest hole of my mind. Sasha's touch was acting like a shovel, bringing those memories to the surface.

Unable to return those thoughts to their pit, I began to tremble and shake. My vision became clouded over by watery eyes. I wasn't strong enough to hold back the tears. Floodgates behind my eyes opened and let loose a torrent. I tried to stop them, to prevent the emotional dam from bursting, but Sasha would not let me. Tenderly she put her arms around my shoulders and held me tight. At first, I recoiled from her gentle touch, acting as if in a flashback of terror past but her embrace held no threat. Surrendering my horror to her compassion, I collapsed into a fetal position, sobbing and shivering like a babe in her arms.

SASHA

The cruelty of lifekind never ceases to astound me. How any being is able to inflict so much emotional and corporeal torment is beyond comprehension. If all were Amoropaths, this would be at an end. None would be able to bare the giving of pain. At least not beyond what the being finds enjoyment in.

Myself, I prefer inflicting pleasure. Pure and unadulterated. Sometimes it can ease pain caused by others. Rick's pain runs deep. Even he does not know its full extent. He fights it, he submerges it, laughs at it. Yet, he refuses to look at it. After what was done to him, many beings would go inside themselves never to emerge. Yet he fights on. Rick's body was broken and his spirit violated, yet his soul was not conquered. A spark remained that they were unable to extinguish. I have only rarely encountered a spark so strong and willing. It glows beautifully within him. A pity only I and my people can see it. His aura inspires rapture in an Amoropath. It is the one time I feel as good as a patron.

Rick begins to regain his composure and I let him. Terran male pride wounds easily. Apparently, it's a humiliation to manifest signs of weakness or sorrow, let alone the violations of his body that Rick suffered. A flaw they are not alone in. A display is made as if nothing has occurred. Body language displays shame, not at his emotions, but his words. Shoulders slumped, head down, Rick avoids my eyes. I know his secret and his shame. He believes it makes him less in my gaze.

"Rick, it was not your fault," He turns to face me, ready to defend his tormentors. A victim ready to accept blame for occurrences beyond his control. Typical and tragic. His thoughts are crystal. Grabbing his head, I make him look at me. "I would not lie to you."

"I should have been able to stop them. To escape. Something. Anything. I let them do those things to me."

"No. You did not. You had no choice." He pulls away. Realizing his lack of clothes and the accompanying vulnerability, he reaches for the togs.

"Don't. Your body is too beautiful to cover," He looks at me as if I were mad. "The scars are a part of you. Think of them not as symbols of shame but badges of strength and honor. They are an acclamation of all that has happened to you and your will to survive. You travel through life still able to laugh and to care. That night in Red's you impressed me.

Not with your fighting ability, mind you." He smiles. "Your heart. I was unknown to you. But you rose to defend my honor. Most folk accept the misassociation between whore and Amoropath." My life is spent ignoring the snide comments and lack of respect in social standing. My profession is one of the few barred from buying into the aristocracy. I earn more in a year than most of the Aristos earn in a life. It makes no difference. I am not respectable by their standards. Rick does not see me that way. Or as an organic means of pleasure. Naiveté can be very attractive.

Some of his fallen confidence had risen again. As had other things. Thankfully, he was not damaged beyond repair. We embraced, he caressing my back as we hugged.

"Sasha, I..." he said stumbling over his words. Regaining his verbal footing he proceeded on. "I really like you. I realize this sounds stupid," It did not. "Love at first sight was always a euphemism to me. Something to hear about but never experience. Until I looked across a bar, on a planet God only knows how many light years from home, and saw you. All the stories of romance I had ever heard and dismissed as sappy became real. My soul has been laid bare before you. I have no idea why I did it," Easy. He could hold it inside no longer. The pain is still there but it has been lessened in the sharing. "It just seemed right. Just being around you seems right. It makes me feel good."

"You make me feel the same way," Disbelief shone in his eyes. "Why do you not believe me?"

"The whole city falls at your feet. Princes and Dukes must court you," Actually I have a strict policy on Aristos. Most of them anyway. "What could someone like me offer you? I'm only two steps up from a slave."

"No. You are several steps removed. Be thankful." Not all of us can be.

"What can I give you?"

"Rick, I'm richer than sin. Anything I want, I buy. Offers I do not need. I am with you because that is what I want."

"Thank you."

"You have awakened things in me that have slept too long. It is I who should thank you," Damn my weakness for Terrans. "And I shall. I shall grant you what you came here for." Cute. He is nervous.

"I can't believe I'm saying this but I don't think we should."

"Should what?" I forget. Terrans think of sex as limited to physical pleasures. They have so much to discover.

"Make love." Always with the euphemisms. Cannot say what they mean.

"How can you stop love? It is made naturally."

"Perhaps I used the wrong words. During my torture, they did things to me. I'm not sure I can… I mean I'm sure I can, but maybe we should wait before we…procreate."

"Procreate? That is not what an Amoropath does although if that is what you want I employ many who will be happy to oblige you."

"Sasha, I don't want to sleep with someone else." Again with the euphemisms. Must be something instilled in them at a young age. "I have feelings for you. Deeper, more intense emotions than I imagined possible."

I hear that selfsame speech hundreds of times in a week. Usually, I nod my head and smile. Rick's profession of passion came before the rapture. His words are truth, not a pleasure-induced confession. I swore never again to become emotionally involved with a Terran after Savage. Yet despite my better judgment, I invited Rick here. It was very thoughtful of him to bring blossoms. So very few of my clients do. At least before. After they are willing to give me anything and everything. Pity I can't take some of them up on it. Damn licensing board cuts into my profit margin.

"You did not offend me," His spark grows hotter within him, blazing resplendently. I feel giddy. I know what I'm going to do. I have known all along. After all, promises were made to be broken. "Let me show you what an Amoropath does do."

RICK

I don't have a clue about what's happening. Sasha's parlor spins around me at warp speed. Lights, colors, tastes, smell, sight, and sound merge together in jubilation. An azure haired vision guides me to her couch. My every nerve is tingling, axons firing like it was Independence Day. Sasha places me on my back, her nimble fingers guiding my head to Siesta in her lap. The ceiling had seen so ordinary before. Now each nook and cranny is alive and moving, dramatizing existence. Watching, I suddenly understand the meaning of life. Leaving the couch behind, I fly away to ecstasy, passing through suns and seas, fireworks and waterfalls. I reach a place that watches me intently with dazzling eyes that hold all existence in their thrall. I bow my head in reverence, awaiting judgment.

It never comes. All I am offered is acceptance of all that I am which I accept gratefully. In thanks, I reach out to kiss the hand of God. My lips touch Sasha's flesh instead. I am not disappointed as a squadron of angels, all blessed with Sasha's face, surge over and envelope me within their confines. Pulsing and throbbing my body, my very essence, detonates and explodes, shattering me into a million glimmering fragments.

Then it gets good.

SASHA

Rapture with Rick was particularly intense. The after-effects lingered beyond the typical. Wobbling side to side, the Terran is unable to find the door. He does not understand why he has to get dressed. I have to coerce him to clean himself up after his body's joyous ejaculations, a side effect of the rapture.

Rick showers me with rapid-fire kisses. I hate to make him leave, but I am already five clients behind. Once he is sober enough to face BoBo, I bring him downstairs.

Poor BoBo. Floored by a half-trained Newbe. His pride may never recover. I will have to let him know I would be most displeased if Rick was harmed in any way. It should help keep him intact. That and Savage's decree safeguarding Terran lives. Still, it may not be enough to get him through two circles back to the Warplex. I cannot spare BoBo to escort him though.

"Boopsie, is Samuel here?"

"Yes, Mistress. Visiting Peri."

"Get him. I have a job for him."

"And if he will not come?"

"Remind him of his tab."

Soon he came, hat in hand, trademark raincoat over his right arm. Set a Terran to catch a Terran. Or protect one.

SAMUEL

Everyone loves a parade; it's one of the few things the many and myriad races all have in common. Most parades are eye-catching, trying to attract attention; however, ours was aiming at being inconspicuous and falling far short of the mark. Still, young and old enjoy watching as the participants go by. That can be the only reason the Sentinels are letting us pass unchallenged. That or the Guardsmen are hiring blind flatfoots, which I doubt since I am the only one holding a cane. Being oblivious is bad enough, but do they have to smile at each of us as we go by?

First to pass their reviewing stand was the fellow Earther, Rick, who Sasha bulldozed me into babysitting. Next, Savage's goon Santo strolled by followed by yours truly. No doubt by the time Savage, his driver Wheels, the moving mountain Burke, the fleabag Kerr, and whoever it is who is hanging back far enough behind them that I can't ID him, pass they'll all be hugged by the Sentinels and bought a beer. The more beer they buy, the more money that floats my way, so I shouldn't complain. A pity, complaining is so ingrained in my nature.

I owe the Guardsmen a debt that I have paid back hundreds of times, yet it can never be fully erased. I arrived on Liberty as a slave, my past life forever unreachable. Led upon a cold stage in a foreign world wearing nothing but a scowl and chains. Creatures of fairy tales and nightmares argued over my future in languages I had no hope of understanding, save that of pain. I saw grown men reduced to babbling infants and a half-grown woman spit in the eye of the Muridae auctioneer after she kneed him in the groin. I loved Peri from that moment on.

Furnished with some rudimentary information on our past lives, the Muridae tried to up the asking price. Peri's last job was the kind where you walked on street corners and got into dark cars with strange men flashing a little green. A bidding war between the brothels broke out. Unfortunately, the nastiest madam, name of Mamma, won. I didn't see her for years after that, just before Sasha took Mamma down for the last time.

My resume, on the other hand, listed law enforcement as my specialty. I went cheap, fifty times less than Peri. Only one bid, only one bidder; The Guardsman. By the end of the day, I was a free man, although I didn't know it. By the close of the week, I was speaking pigeon Czarrian

Common, Common for short. By the finish of the month, I was semi-fluent and pounding the pavement as a flatfoot Sentinel, same as these two.

This duo's incompetence embarrasses my sense of pride in the outfit. If only they'd at least ask for a parade permit, I'd feel better, but no, they just stare dumbly, like a Kroc in headlights. Maybe I should be impressed that their patrol takes them this far off the safe roads. Not that it'll do any good if they have no street smarts; some quarters are deadly, especially for Guardsmen.

Time clouds memory with a pleasant haze. Way back when I was probably just as naive, but it went away. I lived and learned my way up through the rank and file through promotions and a well-earned retirement. So, what do I do? Retire and buy a small ranch in the treaty protected Outlands? Nope, that'd make sense. It would also contain a modicum of safety which would never do. Instead, I go freelance for less money than a street cleaner makes, sticking my head out more often than not without benefit of backup. Not a good way to live.

I probably won't see the other side of fifty, only two years to –forty-five now; with luck, I might make that. I hope these flatfoots do. Better than dying for the Tetrarch. Or a city that, on those rare occasions when it is shown who maintains order, says thank you for the service with a spit in the eye. This would be followed by an evil smile after which they expected a thank you as we came back for more. Why we did, I'll never know.

That's not entirely true. I do know one reason: the outfit, love 'em or hate 'em, bug eyes or two-leggers, is family. You protect your own because if you don't, nobody else will. Which explains Burke and Kerr's parts in this little promenade and maybe mine... but why Savage? I can't buy Terran unity. He treats most of our people like crap, even if his proclamation forbidding harm to us Earthers on pain of death has worked in my favor more than once.

From the looks of things, it shouldn't be long before I find out the answers to these questions and more. Santo is moving in; sleaze doesn't see me. Behind me, Savage and Wheels think I'm as oblivious to them as they are to the two warriors to their posterior. The stranger in the shadows is barely a whisper, almost invisible. Too good for anyone from Tore save four people. In all due modesty, I know I'm here so it can't be me. My ex-partner is still in blissful oblivion back at Sasha's so he'll be out of it for the better part of tonight. Next on the list is our friendly neighborhood assassin. I can cross him off. Razza is kind enough to let me know when he is working so I can stay far out of his way.

That leaves only my fellow Earther Jake: best set of ears on the street; better moves than me. Not bad for a seventy-five-year-old human. Pity the KGB frowned on recruiting Jews. Lost a great agent when they sent him here to "Siberia" for "crimes" against the state. Must have been one hell of a bar mitzvah.

No time for idle contemplation. This soup is almost at its boiling point. Time to choose up teams with the kid and Tony as captains. Savage has his goons, but the kid's got me and the wolfhound. On top of that lineup, Burke gives the kid's team the ultimate advantage. Even with his DeTang tendency to refrain from non-honorable fighting, his mere presence will prevent Savage from doing anything stupid. Of course, there may be plenty of time for acts of stupidity between now and the time Savage learns who's behind him.

The team I'm on would win the battle but a war might follow. Tony is not well known for his forgiving nature; vengeance is more his speed. That could be a problem down the road. Lord knows he has enough reason to want to cause me pain. I'm the one who brought him in, red-handed, to Grillar.

Kid's obviously more of Grillar's handiwork. Think he would at least do the decent thing and stop the damn exchange. Right, and I'm the new Tetrarch. Couldn't he send more women? Or better yet, not send any. Ignoring the fact that Peri has helped me keep my sanity more times than I care to recall, I could kill him for "exporting" her. And she would kill me for wishing for other women. What she don't know won't hurt me.

Sasha was over-worried. The kid knew he was being followed and he lost his first tail. Gave him the slip and Santo's steaming. If he keeps raving like that, he'll need absolution real soon. Santo's the biggest hypocrite going. Holds out his G'morran religion as if its customs were law. Condemns those who stray from *The Path* but doesn't think twice about sinning himself because Savage will forgive him. Dates back to when they were in the Pit together. I was walking a beat, so all my info is third hand.

As the story goes, Savage convinced a group of G'morra that he was some sort of savior. Exactly how is unclear. A prophet claimed he was destined to free them from their slavery and in the process, the G'morra became his own personal army. I know from experience that there is nothing divine about Savage. Funny part is, he came through, although the prophet didn't live to see that day. Despite his many sins and crimes, Savage will go down in history as the external who ended Muridae slavery.

At this point, the parade could have ended and everyone gone home none the worse for wear. The kid couldn't just leave well enough alone. He doubled back behind the goon.

Stupid! Kid should have stayed lost. He'll live longer that way. Newbe is still too wet behind the ears to know about Savage's proclamation. They would have kept that info from him to prevent him from getting cocky. Too late for that. He is young and immortality is the curse of the young; it's a shame death lifts that particular curse so easily.

Got to admit, the kid's got style. Crept up behind Santo without a sound and yelled "Boo." The goon must have jumped three feet straight up. What goes up must eventually spiral downwards. Santo did. Right on the kid. It started out a battle of wits and words. Santo lost in the first round. He doesn't like a fight where his is not the upper hand. The triped kept shouting for Rick to "go for a ride". Typical Savage gangster cliché. Like my private dick act is original... but at least it's honest.

Things got physical; not surprising. Guess Santo got permission to touch a Terran. Not that it did him any good; the kid blocked everything thrown at him. Santo's been out of the arena too long. He's become lazy, gotten in the habit of letting Savage's name do the work instead of his muscle. It shows.

Kid acts odd for a warrior. He tries to reason with his opponent, talk his way out of the fight. Does him no good, as Santo wants nothing to do with peace, argues to give violence a chance. Kid's rebuttal is short and sweet. Before Santo knows what hit him, he's lying on the ground holding his dislocated shoulder. Kid has the hands of a surgeon; they'll love him in the Games.

Savage's chauffeur, Wheels, slinked in behind and out of sight. He's a small, high-grav, ex-warrior who does not need any practice. The kid was in trouble. He doesn't see Wheels coming in from the rear for the kill. Just as I think he's going to get creamed, he ducks at the last second and gets a glancing blow instead of a concussion. I remember when I had reflexes like that. The lower gravity has me spoiled, making me think I'm still hot stuff. Rick is good, but he's outclassed. Wheels was in when they still allowed killing; his boss still does. Rick's warrior buddies are still a block away and he is going to need help real soon. Time for me to earn my keep. Damn. I just finished paying off my medical bills.

"Back off, Wheels! The kid's under my protection," I say in my best tough-guy voice. It always worked for Clint Eastwood. It never does for me. Someday it will. Pity the bad guys will win that day. It's too easy to knock off a man passed out from shock. I can see the fear my threat has inspired in Wheels by the smirk he sends my way. Figures his protection by Savage beats any threat I pose; I hate it when the bad guys are right. Instead of backing off, I'm inspired to wipe the smirk off his face. Not the healthiest reaction, but it's not my fault. Nature forgot to give both lemmings and Mama Troubell's first-born a real strong survival instinct.

Wheels turns, looking full of menace and death. I get ready to bust his head. The kid beats me to it by side-swiping him in the chest with a kick. I hear the snaps. So does Wheels, who grabs his side as much out of shock as of pain. In retaliation, he knocks me down. The kid does the damage and I get the lumps... life just ain't fair. I give him the old one-two upside the head with a pair of nightsticks I always carry.

In the more dangerous quarters, you can carry any weapon you like. Checks are a joke: always on the same day of the month. Unfortunately, work takes me to more upscale quarters where they do random spot checks and being caught with a blaster or blade would get me a cycle of time, ex-Guardsmen with an Aristo title or no. The sticks are legal everywhere because of their ability to combine into my walking stick. In emergencies, they have even been known to work as projectile stunners. Thankfully, weapon checks do not involve detailed scans of walking sticks.

Wheels doesn't rate discharging a fire-stick. During the struggle, he bolts away from me toward the kid, charging into him like a wounded Rhino. The kid hits the ground still fighting. Using a flying tackle, I knock him off Rick and roll to my feet. He does the same. He looks back and forth between the two of us, unsure of his next move. Unable to deal with an attack on two fronts, he got dizzy when a third party leaped into the fray. A white blur soars over my head, landing between the downed Newbe and Wheels.

"Back off," the great white wolf growled. Of course, Wheels listens to Kerr. I bet Kerr never even once practiced saying that line in front of a mirror in order to get the maximum effect. I bet he can't say it fourteen different ways with five different facial expressions. All he does is smile and ad lib. I hate amateurs; especially when they show me up.

Kerr goes to help the kid up. But does he stop to ask how I am? No.

Don't know what Red sees in the fleabag.

"You all right, Sam?" Kerr asked, once the kid was on his feet.

"Yep." Okay, maybe I spoke too soon and judged too harshly. It's a long-standing habit. I actually like Kerr, even if he does cheat at cards.

Not one to let a moment of compassion go unabused, Wheels decided to assault Kerr. Wonder if he ever hits someone who is actually watching him. Without looking, Kerr lands a back punch with each left hand, one in the face, the other in the gut. Wheels fell. Down but undaunted, he wastes time on looking mean. Wheels was about to renew his attack when someone else joined us.

"Stop," Savage whispered. Another of my favorite lines to be grouped in the same category as "back off," with the same rate of success. Of course, Wheels stopped. Maybe I should whisper. No... It's very embarrassing when the bad guys have to ask you to repeat yourself.

Tony moved toward the kid. The wolf tried to stare Savage down. It was a stalemate which was broken by the arrival of our next contestant. I should open a concession stand and maybe charge admission to the alley.

"Stop," Burke said. There was nothing special in the way he said it. He could have been asking for a loaf of bread or discussing the weather. Did Savage stop? Of course. I give up.

Savage's eyes opened wide before he regained his composure and that glintly look in his eyes that inspires fear. For one full week, I tried to imitate that look. No one made an extra effort to avoid me out of terror, but I did inspire many questions as to why I was squinting.

"Check and Mate, Tony." He hates it when I call him Tony. I do it often.

"Stay out of it. This ain't your concern, Troubell," Tony snarled, not even bothering to turn toward me. All his concern was focused on Burke. It was the only sane thing to do. After all, the mountain had come to him and despite his rep, he was no Mohammed. Savage was fighting off a sweat. Burke may be the only thing Savage fears and when he does something he goes all out. Burke could physically destroy Savage and has the financial resources to bring his "mob" down around his knees. This goes beyond that into the realm of terror. He stands his ground so as not to lose face. Determined not to be left out of the fun, I join in the snappy repartee.

"Actually, the kid's a client... indirectly. I was hired to keep an eye on him. Make sure he got home in one piece."

Kerr was watching Wheels and Santo as if they were raw meat and he was just coming off a fast. The kid was staring, splitting his attention between Savage and me. My guess is he has not seen a human since his entrance and now he was confronting two.

That, or he's trying to figure out our outfits. On Tore, human fashion is whatever you want it to be. Most people indulge their fantasies by dressing however they want. Being partial to the P.I. tradition myself, I tend to wear a trench coat and very often a matching hat. I have the same style in seven different colors. Savage fancies himself a gentleman gangster and dresses like someone out of the roaring twenties. Pinstripe suits, fedora hats, and the occasional violin case with a blaster inside are his stock in trade. Makes the help wear similar outfits. He even went so far as to wear spats one time. We looked more like time travelers than exiles.

"Who's your client?" he said to me, still looking ominously at Burke.

"Sasha." Normally I don't reveal my clients but knowing their history I figured I might get a bonus. Maybe even get my tab down into the triple digits.

Savage spun on me, his fear forgotten and replaced by rage; his face afire with fury. Obliviously he's not over her. Pity. It's his own fault. You can't treat a woman of her caliber that way and expect her to take it. Savage just wasn't used to defiance. I wasn't used to subservience. We didn't get along particularly well, but we tolerated each other. There are reasons, not the least of which is sometimes you just need to talk to someone who has been through what you have and comes from the same place you do. Liking them would just be a bonus.

"Appears she has taken quite an interest in Rick. Who would have thought it?" I jibed, hitting him where it hurts. Truth be told, I don't like Savage or what he stands for. I make no secret of that. Nor do I pull any punches. Santo has wondered for years why he has not "put me to death." Savage's reasons are his own. He also knows if I died he would join me before the next sunset. It pays to have the House of Razza in your debt.

"So, has the little cub become a man tonight?" Kerr asked Rick. A river of blood rushed to his face, painting his cheeks a shade of pink that would do a flamingo proud.

"No comment," Rick gentlemanly replied with a smile. Smart kid. Make them wonder. Kerr seemed pleased and was patting Rick's shoulder knowingly. Probably proud of his bad influence.

"Where did you steal the money?" Kerr inquired half sarcastic, half serious. Amoropaths do not come cheap and Sasha is the best of the best.

"Didn't need to. It was a gift," Rick said.

Savage's jaw dropped to the floor and his eyes bulged out as if they were being inflated with a hyperactive air pump. Disbelief was scribbled all over his face. Rumor has it that even when they were an item, Sasha still sent him the bill. Savage looked degraded somehow. His whole body language had changed. Shoulders slumped, head bowed. He looked like a hurt puppy versus the angry pit bull image he thrives on. Despite all his delusions of grandeur, he is still human and any man can have his heart broken.

Burke interrupted, his quiet voice halting everything short of breathing in the alley.

"What were you doing here, warrior?" His address was formal but respectful. Savage was once again composed, any signs of emotion hidden beneath the mask that is his face.

"I had heard that one of my people was newly arrived and I wanted to meet him," Tony replied, falling just short of indignant.

"What else?" Burke demanded, unconvinced by the act of ignorance. Savage always had the talent to sway people, angry mobs and juries alike. Comes across innocent as an angel. Could even persuade the Devil into going to church. Burke, fortunately, had dealt with Savage before and knew better.

"What do you mean?" Burke replied, unwilling to concede any hint of wrongdoing.

Burke watched Santo writhing on the ground in pain and added, "Rick, kindly reset your opponent's shoulder." Santo looked to Savage for guidance; his boss nodded affirmatively. Kerr went nose to nose with Santo, who blanched. Suitably distracted, Rick popped the shoulder back into place. From the look on Kerr's face, I could not shake the feeling that Rick had just passed a test on practical external anatomy. Meanwhile, Burke continued his questioning of Savage.

"Introductions could have been arranged at the Warplex. Why use a dark, deserted alley if you had no other purpose in mind?"

"It is a private matter."

"Please feel free to share it with me."

"No, as I said, it is a private matter... a Terran matter."

The fecal material was getting deep. I would need hip boots soon.

Burke didn't buy it, but he was willing to let it go. Savage wouldn't try anything further. In fact, he may even grant the kid added protection because if he was to be harmed Burke would come looking for him. Burke doesn't take prisoners.

"Very well: Anthony Savage meet Rick Wagner," Burke offered by the way of introductions.

Fingers met and hands shook. Savage tried to intimidate by squeezing to the point just shy of crushing. Rick unfazed, met grip for grip. Then the name sunk in.

"Tony Savage? The Tony Savage? You and Jimmy Hoffa are supposed to be buried in the same unmarked grave."

"I don't know about Hoffa, but I'm still kicking."

"Grillar?" Rick asked, knowing the answer.

"Grillar." Something in common already... mutual hate for a man. Good for traditional male bonding. However.... mutual love for a woman... not healthy when the competition plays rough.

"And..." continued Burke, "this is Samuel Troubell."

Our hands crossed in friendly greeting. No intimidation on either part. Secure in our own identities, I guess.

"Pleased to meet you," said Rick.

"Likewise," I answered.

"Thanks for your help back there. Did Sasha really send you?" he asked. Easy, kid; that is dangerous territory and you don't even know you've entered it. That's not a safe subject. With my insurance policy, I can get away with tweaking his nose. You may not be so lucky.

"Yes. Have you heard of me?" I said quickly changing the stream of conversation to one without rapids.

"Sorry; can't say I have," he replied. Savage snickered; let him. I may never be famous or rich. I may never see my home or family again, but after fifteen years I've accepted that. But my life, no matter how miserable, is mine. I own it free and clear. Except for a few tabs.

"Old Sam here used to work for Grillar," Savage added sadistically.

The kid stood back, a look of disgust on his face. "You worked for him?"

Now I end up looking like the villain. Never let it be said that Savage gives any less than he gets. I just have a few hundred less skeletons in my closet to choose ammunition from.

"Not exactly. I worked for the CSA; Grillar was my supervisor. I've done a lot of things I am not proud of. Working under him was one of them. "

"If you worked for the government, how'd you end up here?" asked Rick.

"I disagreed with Grillar's exportation policies to the Muridae. I tried to stop the shipment of prisoners Tony boy here was on. I told Grillar it was wrong at gunpoint. Grillar disagreed, stated free trade was not a bad thing. It was our God-given right as Americans. He won that argument by virtue of a bigger gun. Several of them in fact. One was being held by my partner, name of Lonso Hobbes," The kid cringed at the name. Guess I know who got my old job. "I still didn't believe Grillar's argument so he sent me along to prove it and made me a Xile. So much for job security with the CSA." I was going to quit anyway.

"Sam is okay, Rick. Red vouches for him. Even if he does make that swill," Kerr added.

"You can say what you want about me, fleabag, but leave my beer out of it."

"Ladies, this is all nice and good," Savage said interrupting our friendly bickering. "But I still have the private matter to discuss with Rick."

"That will have to wait for another day; Rick and I must return to the compound to check on Susie," Burke said.

"Who is Susie?" I asked.

"Susie is a human girlchild who, at present, is a ward of my house. Dortew attempted to auction her; we prevented it," Burke said.

"A little girl? Here?" I asked stunned. Rick nodded.

"Dortew tried to sell her?" Tony inquired so calmly I could see murder for the Muridae in his eyes. Again Rick nodded.

From the darkness of the alley, a shadow spoke. Everyone but me jumped in surprise. Had he remained silent nobody would have known of his presence. Goes in and out of the security areas of the prime ring as easily as I do my office, usually with a lot less trouble.

"Honorable Lord,
I ask your most gracious personage for a boon.
If you would suffer
       the requests of a loon.
May we,
who are of the same ancestry as she,
be allowed
in her presence to be?" asked Mad Jake. He was a little-known poet

in his younger days and felt the need to speak in poetic verse. Not necessarily good verse, but he does speak off the top of his head. He has been in his rhyming phase for the better part of a year. I've just about given up hope that he'll grow out of it.

"What he said," I added.

"I do not know," Burke answered.

A human child is reason for celebrations.
It causes my old heart palpitations.
We seek only joy in her presence.
Surely you would not refuse us in essence?"

Mad Jake and his poems get on people's nerves, but he does grow on you. Not a human birth has gone by without him planning a celebration. The birth of one of our own is one of the few and far between times the human community gathers together. It has been far too long between gatherings. Jake always writes something for the occasion. His written work is much better than his spoken, even if it does lose something in translation from Yiddish.

Burke was debating the danger we might pose to his ward. Deciding we were nothing he could not handle, he agreed to the request.

"My thanks to you
for this that you do," rhymed Jake.

"Burke, would it be okay if I bring Peri?" I questioned.

"Yes," replied the mountain of few words.

"Great. I'll run back to Sasha's and get her," I said.

"I'll go with you," offered Rick. A silver hand and a grin of white convinced him otherwise. "Um, maybe I'll just meet you back at the Warplex."

"Good idea," Kerr answered, as he led Rick out the alley and back down the street, with Burke a few steps in front of them. My tailing job was done. Rick would be seen home safe. Poor Kid. Looks like he thinks he is about to get grounded. Doubtlessly right too.

Jake had already been swallowed up by the night. It would regurgitate him out at the Warplex. Tony and company summoned the ebony skyster and piled in. Santo held the door for Savage. The door shut and they sped off with no mention of offering me a ride. Nothing liked being popular.

As I left the alley, I stopped and waved toward the rooftops. Without thinking, the two Sentinels waved back. They had doubled back and observed us from a safe vantage point. I had underestimated them.

By way of apology, I gave the unit salute which they returned before getting back to their patrol. The Tetrarch must have been serious about decreasing crime. Will wonders never cease? His father, the former Tetrarch, would never approve. Probably why he's doing it.

My pride in the Guardsmen was redeemed. My tab at the Empirical House was reduced. I was on my way to meet a child of my people and I would get to spend an evening with Peri without paying Sasha. To top it all off, I had no lasting injuries. All and all, it was shaping up to be a beautiful evening.

RICK

Blissful dreaming often leads to rude awakenings. This time I tried to make the return to the waking world as gentle as possible for Susie, even going so far as to climb inside Nanna's whole. I was honored that she allowed me inside, but being enveloped in her liquid plasm gave me the creeps. I still had no working concept of how we could breathe inside. Nanna's explanations of molecular conversions left me in the dark.

"Wake up, sleepyhead. There are some people here to see you," I said, gently touching her shoulder. With a lazy turn, she was facing me, her small hands wiping the sleep from her eyes. The yellow specks floated away sluggishly, only to be enveloped by a soft glow and then vanish. Calming my fears over the fact that Nanna could just as easily do the same to my flesh and bones, I picked up Susie in my arms.

"Rick? Who's here? Is it Mommy and Daddy? I was just dreaming about them," she asked with the hope that is born in dreams. A hope that I crushed and killed using only my words as murder weapons.

"I'm sorry, honey. You know that's not going to happen, no matter how much we wish and pray for it," I said, despising two people I had never met except through the wide-eyed stories of a little girl. I did my best to hide my feelings but my best was far from good enough.

"I know, Rick. But sometimes wishes and prayers come true. Please don't hate them. They must have had a good reason for what they did," Susie said, her loving eyes staring into mine. I nodded silently. She had known my true feelings on the matter ever since she overheard me venting my frustrations on the subject to Kerr. Wordlessly, we agreed to disagree as we pulled each other close in a bear hug. I continue to wonder which of us was the adult and which was the child. I kept my question to myself knowing the sarcastic answer that would ensue from Burke and Kerr.

With Susie cradled in my arms, I gave two frog kicks and we climbed out of Nanna into real air. I was told the air outside was not as pure as the atmosphere Nanna provided, but it smelled sweeter and definitely safer.

Now that we were out, I could make out the sounds of two separate and distinct arguments. One was between Nanna and Burke.

"She needs her rest. These are her growing years."

"These are her people. They have not seen a new child her age in many years. It will do both her and them good," Burke said. Reluctantly, Nanna acquiesced.

The other was between Tony Savage and anyone who would listen to him.

"She should not be in that thing. Is it even safe?"

"That is a Nani of the Trimurti, Savage. A person, not a thing. As for safety, she is safer inside there than Fort Knox or even the Empirical House," Peri countered, a stunning ebony beauty who was the object of quite a few of Samuel's affections judging by the way he looked at her. His gaze was somewhere between that of a big brother and a wild-eyed lover. He tells me Peri is one of the few humans in Sasha's employ.

Upon seeing me emerge carrying the object of everyone's attention the bickering ceased. As if on cue the crowd merged into a receiving line of smiling human faces. Interest in her visitors had banished thoughts of sleep from Susie's mind as I lowered her to the floor.

Tony Savage was the first to step forward, acting as if it was his inalienable right to be dominant in all that was done. He was still upset that Burke demanded Wheels and Santo remain outside the Warplex. Tarna had been at the gate when we entered. Santo stared unbelievingly at the female of his people, standing on warrior ground, dressed in the traditional togs. Turning to Burke, he demanded to know what the lady G'morra was doing there, purposefully ignoring Tarna in the process as if she were somehow inferior. This was the kind of thing she had been fighting a battle against her whole life. She was not about to let Santo's snubbing go unchallenged.

"If you have a problem, take it up with me, Santo," Tarna demanded. Santo gasped in shock that a female G'morran would address him by his name. The traditional greeting was something along the lines of "honored sir" or "master" and lasted thirty seconds or better. Eyes were to remain on the ground which makes me wonder how they were supposed to know who they were greeting. Tarna met Santo's shocked look with a steely gaze, tainted by just the slightest hint of mischief. She enjoyed getting under people's skin and punching their buttons with a closed fist. She claimed to be teaching, but truth be told she loved shock value... that value was high at present.

"Infidel! How dare you!"

"I dare a lot, old man. I plan to surpass even your record."

"You cannot mean to imply you are a warrior?"

"Newbe at present. Tourney winner in the future." Tarna returned with a smile.

"This is an outrage! You shall be disciplined."

"By who? You are not being enough to pull it off."

"I shall inform your husband."

"Not married."

"But you are past the age of pairing! Very well, then I shall inform your sire of your transgressions. I shall include the shameful way you clothe yourself," Santo threatened. Tarna was wearing a triple of shorts (two leggers wear a pair, tripeds a triple) which exposed violet flesh above her knees. Traditional garb covered all but the hands, forehead, and eyes. Tarna's present outfit was self-tailored and exposed her arms and midriff. Must have been scandalous.

"Be my guest."

"I shall bring you up before the clerics."

"You cannot. I am excised, banished. By their very actions, the clerics have lost jurisdiction over me. While you still must follow the Logg. You have seen the forbidden flesh of a woman not your wife? I believe the Logg demands you put out your eyes, does it not?"

Terrified, Santo backed off, realizing her words were true. He turned to Savage for spiritual guidance, falling to his knees in the process. Savage whispered something about absolution and Santo stood again triumphantly, glaring at Tarna. Knowing any argument would be futile, she retaliated in a different matter. She hiked up her shorts to the mid-thigh. Santo, outraged yet fascinated, could not take his eyes from her legs.

Burke, tired of the games, spoke up. "Tarna, would you mind returning to your quarters, as your presence seems to be causing a commotion."

"Certainly, Burke. I need to rest up for my upcoming match," she said, unable to resist the chance for another jibe. She walked to my side before leaving and gave my cheek a small peck. Santo looked like a volcano about to erupt. Contact with externals, especially male externals, was extremely forbidden. Just to add to the fun, she slapped my bottom. I returned the favor. Tarna walked away slowly, moving each leg individually instead of her usual gait in which she advanced her two front legs followed by her rear limb. Apparently, this was a seductive walk, judging by Santo's stare as she receded into the building.

"Savage, have Santo and Wheels remain outside," Burke said,

unwilling to bring trouble into the Warplex. Reluctantly, after a nod from Savage, the pin stripped externals stayed with the ebony skyster.

Now inside, Savage was marching toward Susie as if no one else was present. Ignoring Savage's haughty ways, Jake, dressed in white pants and tunic, vaulted ahead, springing into a cartwheel in the process, which ended with him on his knees in front of Susie. The entire action made Nanna extremely nervous. Only Burke's insistence kept her from blocking Jake's path.

Susie's feelings were a different matter. Delighted by the acrobatics she laughed and clapped loudly. He bowed before her and began speaking in rhyme.

"My greetings to you, child,
so beautiful and mild,
your very presence turns dismal night
into bright day,
Welcome to Tore,
I hope you enjoy your stay."

Susie returned his greeting by reciting a passage from *Green Eggs and Ham*. It was Jake's turn to be delighted. Apparently, he had never heard Dr. Seuss before. He eased himself to the floor and sat by Susie's right side. Nanna casually eased herself closer. Jake, thinking no one was watching, was rubbing his knees.

Hiding his annoyance at being made to wait, Savage came forward, hands behind his back.

"Hello, Susie. My name is Anthony Savage," he said, taking his right hand from behind his back and extending it to Susie, who took it and shook it. A wafer thin transparent appendage was snaking its way along the ground toward the pair, generally unnoticed.

"Nice to meet you, Mr. Savage," Susie answered.

"Please, call me Uncle Tony," Savage insisted, smiling brightly.

"I'll think about it," Susie replied. Her honest answer was met with guffaws from Samuel and Peri, amused at Savage being shot down by an eight-year-old. Savage's smile was beginning to look strained as he attempted to ignore the snickers. In response, Savage whipped his left hand to the front only to have the object he was holding snatched away, seemingly by the floor itself.

"What the?" he said, dropping back into a defensive stance I recognized as having excellent backward mobility, especially in terms of retreat. Nanna was holding the object up before her and examining it.

It looked like a giant lollipop. Apparently it was, because she returned it to Savage who in turn gave it to Susie.

"Thank you, Mr. Savage," she said, giving him a small kiss on the cheek. Savage insisted on her calling him Tony and she agreed.

The receiving line continued with Samuel. He had insisted but lost his request that Peri go next. He introduced himself sans last name, thinking to avoid the "mister" moniker, but he was called Mr. Samuel anyway before convincing Susie to call him Samuel. When he shook her hand, he made a show of it, shaking both arms in their entirety as well as most of his body. Susie joined in the fun until she got so dizzy she had to stop.

Pretending to also be overcome with vertigo, Samuel fell down to the floor in a spinning fashion coming to a stop with his hands and feet in the air. Laughing, Susie joined him. Together, they gyrated on the floor until a subtle "ahem" from Nanna encouraged Susie to return to an upright position. Nanna did not deem it proper for a young lady to be wiggling around on the floor with a strange man she only just met. Normally I would agree, unless of course the young lady was my date for the evening. This was just plain silly fun. Susie didn't complain, but Samuel looked as if his feelings had been hurt. He carried on.

"How do you like it here, Susie?" Samuel asked.

"I like it."

"What about all the different kinds of people here?" he asked, meaning externals.

"They're great. Especially Nanna, Burke, and Kerr. It is sort of like being at Disneyland except everyone is real. I still miss home, though."

"I figured you would and I knew the Muridae didn't let you bring any of your toys, so I thought you might like this," he said, reaching into an inside pocket of his trenchcoat in an exaggerated manner for Nanna's benefit. She watched intensely as a doll emerged from its inner folds. I recognized it as Aprahoe by the make of the dress it was wearing and the yellow skin tone. Breeze had told me the tribes had once used certain dolls in fertility rituals and other religious ceremonies. Now the dolls were sold to tourists to make a quick franc.

Susie's expression exploded with joy, putting firework displays to shame. Susie took the rag doll and hugged it close. Somehow the lot of us had neglected to give her any toys. Samuel was rewarded with a big wet one on his cheek for his trouble; Savage looked jealous.

Last came Peri. She greeted Susie.

"You have a pretty accent. Are you from England?"

"No, South Africa," Peri answered with a smile. Susie took to her quickly. Maybe it was because Peri was the first human woman Susie has met since our arrival. Peri was among the most beautiful women I have ever seen. Her dark skin looked as smooth as marble. A figure that was hourglass in design but not overbearingly so. Each movement seemed choreographed for a dancer, but with an ease that many ballerinas strive a lifetime for and never achieve. Braids tied up in a bun and worthy of a princess adorned her head. Peri was definitely in Sasha's class although my blue-haired beauty was easily the valedictorian.

Introductions accomplished, Burke herded the lot of us out, caving to Nanna's demands that Susie get some sleep. Burke told everyone they were welcome to visit as long as they made an appointment first. At Susie's request, Peri was allowed to go with her and Nanna to help her brush her hair before she returned to bed.

Savage motioned me over to him, using a minimum of movement with a maximum effect. I went. He asked me if there was anywhere we could talk. Alone. I ushered him to the mess hall. Anything to avoid a confrontation with Kerr. I couldn't run, but I could hide in a crowd of two for a while.

Savage was an enigma; I knew his history. I watched the mini-series on his life and disappearance. He was compared to Jimmy Hoffa. Grillar was his Robert Kennedy. Amazing how the media can get something so wrong. Grillar, the so-called hero, secretly sold his people into bondage while the villain of the piece turns out to be their savior. Racketeering, gambling, shakedowns, prostitution, weapons smuggling; he did it all. Except the drug scene. The story has it he had some code of honor that would not allow him to make money off of the degradation of innocents. Interesting code considering his other activities. People can justify anything to anyone, themselves included.

Yet here on a world called Liberty, where slavery was ironically legal, a criminal became a hero. In the games, by refusing to ever kill an opponent he made the warriors question their Muridae masters. Then the ultimate accomplishment, at least for my peer group. A win in the tournament and with victory came freedom. A freebeing, he didn't turn his back on those still in bondage. Eventually, he brought freedom to Liberty.

A villain, a warrior, and a messiah. And now a gangster again, from what I have gathered; the pinstripes and Fedora spelling it out for all who can read the language. Savage walked with a slight limp, a memento from his time at the games. Legend has it he refused Muridae medical care, preferring to let his body heal itself. Imperfectly at that. I may be able to fix that. Might as well put my old Earth skills to work.

Savage opened something that looked like a cigarette lighter. It dimmed the sounds around us. I could barely hear him as he spoke.

"Rick, I hope you can forgive Mr. Santo's enthusiasm from earlier this evening. When I asked him to arrange introductions between us, I am afraid he got carried away," Savage explained, feigning an innocence that even Susie would see through. Most people who claim to be innocent at length are not. A true innocent doesn't realize their own innocence, therefore wouldn't lay claim to it.

Still, he expected me to believe this story so I humored him by nodding my head.

"Why did you want introductions, Mr. Savage?"

"Please call me Tony. I have a business proposition for you."

"An offer I can't refuse?" I asked. He laughed. Soft and short. Not the laugh of an innocent. It was tinged by pain and blood. Still, I finally found someone who understands my jokes.

"To put it bluntly, yes. Together we can make lots of money. We just need to confer before your matches to determine who the winner will be."

"You mean, you want me to throw a fight." Talk about cliché.

"Not always. Sometimes you'll win."

"Sorry, not interested."

"I'm talking enough money to buy out your contract."

Money, the root of all evil. Not exactly true. Once when I was six, I planted a dollar bill in the backyard, with hopes of growing a money tree. No tree sprouted, but neither did any roots of evil and I watered it every day.

Savage was offering me not only money but the chance for freedom. At the cost of my honor. Honor was my only source of wealth. In the end, his price was not high enough.

"I am tempted, but I can't."

"Why? You don't owe the rats anything."

"As sappy as this sounds, honor. I have no desire to fight in the rat's games but I won't take a dive. To lose a fight on purpose would be like betraying Kerr and disappointing Burke. Not to mention my squad. To them, the way of the warrior is the way of life. Besides once I got out, where would I go? How would I earn a living then?"

He nodded thoughtfully. "Working for me." I could almost hear the part where I would be groomed to take over the business. Keep it in the family. The human family.

"No."

"I could make you," he said in a tone that said even though it was in his power he would not.

"I don't think so. Perhaps under other circumstances, I might not be able to get away with a no but considering who my friends are I think we can leave it at that." He nodded again, not angered or intimidated by my threat in the least.

"I'd suspected as much but I had to try. Perhaps even help a fellow Terran in the process. There is one more matter I wish to discuss with you. A more serious matter whose name is Sasha."

SAMUEL

Jake and I waited outside for Savage and Rick to finish their talk. We caught up on new times. Seems the Tetrarch was stepping up Guardsmen patrols throughout Tore and it made Jake nervous because there was no ulterior motive. The Tetrarch genuinely seemed to be cracking down on crime while not turning the city into a police state as some of his predecessors had. Most people would be pleased to see their tax and tribute dollars hard at work, but not Jake. Not that he's paid a cent to Tore, ever.

Jake still considers himself a fugitive, but he's the only one left who does. Jake was a runaway slave from a time before I even came to Liberty. He formed an underground railroad of sorts, smuggling other runaways to the Outlands to live with the Aprahoe tribes or to make it on their own. He also found many of them passage on outbound ships to worlds that didn't recognize slavery.

He was one of the five prime who formed the Web, a group who operated in the city itself for its own purposes, most of which were beneficial. In its own way, the Web does as much good as the Guardsmen, since their hands aren't bound by red tape. Jake still has a position of some influence even if he has turned the day to day running over to a younger external.

Jake remains convinced that he's wanted because of his status as a runaway, despite the amnesty given to all the other runaways who came forward. Hell, some even got restitution depending on how long they were in servitude. But not Mad Jake. He refuses to trust any government again... ever. The last government body he trusted was the KGB and look where that got him. The one before that was Hitler's SS. And his own parents had trusted Stalin. Not a good family track record; he had every right to be gunshy.

Out walked Savage, a man who wouldn't know the meaning of gunshy, alongside Rick, a man so young that, in comparison, he was just a boy. Savage was doing things I'd never seen him do: one, he was laughing. Not his evil "I'm going to get you laugh" either. The kid must really be a comedian to have that effect on Savage, especially with what was going on with Sasha.

Secondly, Savage was barely limping. Savage wore that limp with the same pride most men wore medals. Any man who goes one-on-one with Burke and survives with only a limp has every right to be proud. Refused all Muridae care after the fact; sometimes pride follows a fall as well as preceding it.

I heard the tail end of their conversation.

"Do the exercises like I told you and it will help your walking. Unfortunately, there is too much damage that has gone untreated for too long for me to be able to fix you entirely. But that should help the pain."

"Thanks, Rick. Appreciate the help. Feels better already," Savage said in a genuinely grateful tone. Personally, I was thinking he was an impostor. In a more serious tone, he added "You treat her right, understand? Or you'll have me to deal with."

"I'd treat her like a queen even without the threats."

"I know," Savage said. This time his voice was tinged with sadness. Love does strange things, even making Savage into a human. It sounds like he's letting Sasha finally go. Surprising. Savage is the type that if someone he loves does not come back after he let them go, he would go out after them with a shotgun. Then again, maybe he's just agreeing not to go after the kid. He'd view Rick as an innocent and Sasha as guilty. Wonder how long that arrangement will last? I give it until he actually sees them together.

Savage exited quietly into the shadows, almost silently with his new and improved mode of ambulation. I made a mental note, with this new stealth, Savage could mean trouble. I always knew when Savage was approaching by the shuffling steps. Almost worked as well as a clock in his belly.

The kid glanced around nervously, expecting the wolf to jump out of the woodwork. Will never happen; the kid embarrassed him privately, so the matter of discipline will be handled in the same manner. Kerr's got a good sense of justice that way. He prays the Kentor never find out. Doesn't want to be drafted for their holy, never-ending war for balance. Despite popular opinion, they do take no for an answer.

Jake spouted some lame poetry at the kid, praising the girl to no end. She seemed like one hell of a youngster. Damn good to see a human child again. Youngest next to her was a group of seven between twelve and thirteen; a few were a little older than that, not counting those who escaped to the Outlands.

It was almost time for the young generation to start having kids of their own, those that still could. Two Tetrarchs ago, they started a sterilization "cleansing" program of all the slaves and a good portion of the poor downsiders, save certain breeding stock. The rich and aristocratic lived on the hill that comprised the prime ring, in towers that may as well be made of ivory. The downsiders were the needy that lived in their shadow, which could encompass the rest of the city. The Aristos were exempt from the cleansing, others were not.

Humans were included in the first wave. And the second, not to mention the third and fourth. The powers on the Hill thought it would cure the overpopulation problem downside. It certainly slowed it, but the Muridae and many owners hid slaves or gave them false scars to mimic the ones the operation left. As a freebeing, I escaped. Most of my fellow Earthers did not. It kills Peri that she can never have kids. Mamma wouldn't go the scar route cause it might displease the clients so most of her girls, boys, and others went under the knife followed by cosmetic replication to make sure nary a scar was left. At least on the outside.

The Tetrarch got his, though. Downsiders, slaves, and even a few Muridae, upset at the loss of free baby slaves, pooled their resources and, led by the Web, put an end to the problem. Jake himself contacted The House. The House of Razza, that is. The Razza, which was the current one's father, took the contract. The next day, throngs of the common folk gathered up on the hill at the Palace entrance before sunrise.

As the red and violet rays of first light drifted lazily across the land, they revealed the Tetrarch, lifelessly impaled on his own palace gate. A huge cheer arose from the assembled throngs at the sight. He had his own sex organs removed and placed in his mouth. Not a pretty sight. Still, it raised the spirits of the downtrodden. The ruler's public death gave the masses a feeling of power and control which had been long absent from their lives. On that day, it was better to have been a slave than a king.

Most folk had brought their meals and made a day of it. The celebration, an undeclared and unofficial holiday, lasted until nightfall. Jake led a conga line around the palace with a delicate part of the Tetrarch's anatomy, still moistened by all the folks who spit on it, high on a pole. A good portion of the Hill was trashed that day in the revelry, which rolled over Center City and the Prime Ring like a wave over sand. Even the Guardsmen dared not go near the body to remove it until after nightfall. Children were shown what happens to the truly evil and many beliefs of a higher power were strengthened that day.

The House of Razza got immeasurable goodwill and PR. The successor to the throne, the former Tetrarch's brother, learned from past mistakes and publicly banned forced sterilization. And so, a grievous wrong was put right and the cleansing ended. Too late for thousands, but many who were to be included in the fifth wave were saved.

I later learned that the whole sorry thing started because the Tetrarch's chief wife, the Lady of the City, was barren. She saw no reason why slaves should enjoy something she could not, so she ordered her henpecked husband to do the dirty deeds. The Web, in the form of Jake, handled that loose end, all the while spouting verse expounding on her evil and all the suffering she caused. Unmoved by any emotion save fear, she begged for mercy, but in the process expressed that someone of her station should not have to listen to such drivel. Bad move. Jake never did like critics or anyone of her station, so he gave an encore performance. It was the last thing she heard before her eyes closed forever. Poetic justice at its very best, pun intended.

Jake was making ready to do a swift exit. His body tone changed from that of a relaxed old man to that of a jungle cat. He could not resist imparting some of his own brand of wisdom in his parting words.

"In the morning I walked as a child,
in the day, alone I travel the road.
At twilight, the children came and lightened my journey.
Behind, followed those who would extinguish that light.
Beware, laugh, and play."

Rick looked lost. Jake continued.

"Eat your vegetables,
wear clean underwear,
and enjoy the rest of your stay on planet Liberty.
Call on me if you are in need,
stand before the temple of enlightenment;
strip down to a smile, covered with gooseflesh.
Turn twice and scream thrice
and sacrifice a small waterfowl with a secondhand skyhook."

The kid looks stunned and worried. They don't call him Mad Jake because of his temper.

"Or leave a message at Red's," I offered.

"That will work, too. But it is not nearly as much fun," Jake said with a giggle. He snapped his neck to the right and threw his eyes open wide in silent shock. Surprised by the sudden movement, Rick followed his gaze and fell for the trick. Jake's expressions are completely under his control. Once I saw him smile while removing a chunk of shrapnel from his gut.

By the time Rick turned back, Jake had disappeared into the same shadows that Savage did. They both love to make a good exit, almost as much as a good entrance. When we entered, the building was fully lit. Now, the corners and doors were dark. I wonder which of them took out the lights so they could play their games? They both think I'm odd for using the main doors. Being cesarean born, I used to do the window thing, but it got old after a few decades. Everyone who knows them expects them to disappear and is waiting for it to happen. No one expects it from me so I get away with it in times of dire need. Incompetence is a great smoke screen. They buy it as much as I buy their acts, which means there is a natural basis on which exaggeration is built up to staggering proportions.

Jake's exodus leaves the kid and me alone. I decided to indulge my curiosity.

"What'd you do to Savage's knee?"

"What I used to do for a living. Physical Therapy stuff. Simple thing actually. His patella doesn't track right so I used a little trick called patella taping."

"Huh? What's that mean in layman's terms?"

"I fixed his knee. His kneecap was moving wrong. I rearranged it so it moved right, causing him less pain."

"Surprising. He has refused medical care on it for years."

"He told me. Says he'd only let a Terran work on him. I'm the first to come along."

Not really, I thought.

"You must be pretty good."

"Yes. I was," he said, looking sadly at his hands. "Problem is my hands are limited these days in what they can do."

"Why? They look like typical warrior hands." Gnarled, twisted, and hard.

"They are now. Been molded so they make good weapons. Every striking surface is covered with self-induced calluses. They hurt like hell most of the time from hitting something five hundred times in a row, twice a day. I've had a dozen hairline fractures, but I can smash through stone. My hands will probably be crippled by arthritis by the time I'm forty."

Kid says it like it's old. To him it probably is. "Makes it harder to use them for healing. I'm reminded of that with every blow and it makes the hurt just a tiny bit worse. Don't get much chance for therapy anymore, except the occasional training injury. Used to be the highlight of my day when I took away someone's pain, kind of a warm fuzzy glow. Now I'm happy if I can avoid additional pain of my own for a few hours."

"Life's rough that way. By the looks of your last patient there, you still have the knack, despite the condition of your hands."

"Thanks."

"No need to thank me for telling the truth. Not to change the subject, but what did he say about Sasha?"

"How did you know about that?"

"Deductive reasoning. It's what I still do for a living"

"He told me to stay away from her. I said no. We talked a bit more. Finally, he said okay but treat her nice. I said, no problem."

"You got lucky. He isn't usually so reasonable."

"So I've gathered."

"Do you plan to continue seeing everyone's favorite amoropath?"

"Absolutely! It just may be quite some time before I get the chance. I have a feeling Kerr's going to ground my butt."

"Yes, into hamburger." The kid's face turned pale. He shouldn't worry about the Czarrian. Pound for pound humans are stronger. Kerr is just an exceptional fighter, even among a race of trained warriors. Most of them use the same fighting style. Makes them easier to get around. Although the law says otherwise, Kerr's one of the few Czarrians allowed to carry a warblade in the city limits. Truth is, no one would be able to take it from him, save Red or Burke and perhaps BoBo. Since he doesn't abuse the privilege by racking up a body count in duels, the Guardsman let him enjoy his legal rights. "Don't worry about the furbag. His bark is worse than his bite."

"Obviously, he has never bitten you."

"True enough. If you are worried, I could bring Sasha a message for you."

"That might be best. I do not relish the thought of returning to the Empirical House and facing down BoBo anytime soon."

"You're safe on that account. Sasha has forbidden BoBo to harm you in any way."

"Will he listen to her?"

"He would sooner climb into a fusion reactor than disobey his mistress."

"That is a relief. One less external I have to keep watch over my shoulder for." Kid's an amateur in that respect. On a good day, I have only several dozen shadows to watch out for. On a bad day, it can number in the hundreds. On my worst day, almost everyone in the damn city was out to get me. Oh, to be young and unwanted again.

"What kind of name is BoBo for a guy that size anyway?"

"Actually, BoBo is Czarrian for 'Destroyer of Worlds'."

"You have got to be kidding!"

"Nope. It's his taken name, so translates as the sound rather than the definition." Modesty was never one of BoBo's faults. Vanity is. Only DeTang I ever met who wears clothes for everyday life. "Many words that don't make sense in translation are Czarrian. Our fair city of Tore, for instance, means mosaic. But if you wanted a language lesson, you would have asked Burke. What's the message?"

"Tell Sasha that she is great and wonderful. Tell her I had a fantastic time and..."

"Kid, keep it twenty-five words or less. Or learn Czarrian Common and write her a letter." If that works, it should get me some brownie points with Burke.

"Okay. My message is this: I had a wonderful time. She is constantly in my thoughts. As I will be unable to visit her, I would be honored if she could visit me. That's twenty-eight words."

"I'll let it slide this time. If the situation arises, make sure you protect yourself," I said tossing him a small metal circlet. He caught it turning it over in his hands trying to figure it out.

"State of the art. Called a circlet. It' a force field condom," I said. He looked at me, eyes agape.

"How does it work?"

"The ring expands to fit any appendage. As soon as the body part is inserted, hit the switch and the field activates and stays on until you take it off. Make sure the light-colored side is facing out otherwise the field will cover the rest of your body and cut off your air supply." It happens. Most folks get them off in time.

Razza used the concept on a hit once. He reversed the colors and placed an adhesive on the inside to prevent it from ever coming off. The mark put it on and instantly realized his mistake. With the circlet stuck fast, he had very few options. In desperation, he tried to hack off his privates, but the force field prevented that so he did the only thing he could do: finished what he had started. Lasted a full five minutes before he ran out of air, but he died with a smile on his face. Rick looked apprehensive. "Go ahead. Try it out." The kid gave me a worried look. "No. Use your finger."

He did and a light blue luminescence lit up his fingers. He took it off and the glow did a fade. "I take it they are reusable?"

"Yes."

"I could see them having other uses," he said. I asked him what and he just smiled. "I'll tell you if it works." Good. Hope he figures it out. Will give him that extra protection, in more ways than one.

It was getting late. Actually, it was getting early. I would have to hustle to be in bed before sunrise and with any luck, I wouldn't be alone if I can take Peri on a detour by way of my place. No matter how hard I try, she never does anything more than cuddle outside of the Empirical House. Peri feels she would be being disloyal to Sasha to do anymore. We never had this problem when she worked for Mamma, but she hated Mamma. Most sane folks did. Sasha took herself and Peri away from that life so I can understand the loyalty. I don't have to like it. So cuddling it will have to be, but with some women, that's enough.

Kerr was also standing in the shadows opposite me, but behind Rick, signaling that I should go. Doesn't want to embarrass the kid in front of me. Something I can appreciate.

"Rick, it has been a pleasure. Best of luck with your upcoming match."

"What match?" Oops. Let the Curel out of the bag.

I pointed to a list on the wall. "It's written up there in black and white."

"I've got to learn to read this stuff," he said staring hopelessly at the symbols. "Who do I go up against?"

"Looks like a Kroc name of Davv."

"A Kroc?! Oh great. It had to be a Kroc, couldn't be an Aprahoe." As upset as the kid was, Kerr looked more so. I shrugged my shoulders by way of apology and got ready to make my exit.

"You'll take him. Don't worry about it. I have to go. If you need to get in touch with me, you can do the same way as with Jake."

"What kind of waterfowl would you prefer I dismember in my birthday suit?"

I laughed. "No, the other way. Leave a message at Red's." I'm in the book too but for that, he would need to read. "Or if you get out before you have gray hair, come by and I'll buy you a beer."

"You got a deal." We shook hands and I made a hasty retreat. I would pick up Peri and say goodnight to the smaller kid. Then, it's off to slumberland. At least there will be someone else to help warm up the sheets.

As I rounded the corner, I heard the show start behind me.

"Kerr, I can explain everything."

He is answered by a ferocious growl. "No, you cannot, Dirtboy. Drop and give me two hundred. Then you can begin your ten-mile run. After that, you will clean my quarters until they shine."

"But Kerr, you have all hardwood walls."

I thanked the powers that be that I went to the Guardsmen on the auction block instead of the Games. The last thing I heard was the sound of fading wolfen laughter.

RICK

Twilight was approaching swiftly, as were two of Kerr's fists, each in rapid-fire succession. If one connected, night would be upon me faster than any sun ever set. Rolling under the blows, I attempted a leg sweep in the process. A face full of kicked sand was all I got for my troubles.

No matter how good I got, Kerr was still better. I was holding my own with the other Newbes in my squad, winning more often than I lost. Kerr couldn't care less. I was his student and I fear he expects more than I'm able to give. Every other word out of his mouth criticized my technique.

"Sloppy, dirtboy. The arc of the roll left your back unprotected for a full three seconds," Kerr reprimanded. "Your blocks go too wide. You have no reason to protect the air alongside you. Be aware of where your body begins and ends. Do not waste effort."

"Waste not, want not," I quipped.

"Take this seriously, damn it! Tomorrow your life will depend on what you learn here," Kerr yelled with real anger. My joking was a source of constant contention between us, but he had never exploded like this. Usually, he would roll his eyes back, shake his head, or hit me upside the head. Kerr did none of the above. He seemed more worried about my first match than I did.

"Relax, Kerr. There is no killing in the Tore Games anymore."

"Not officially, no. But those in the arena are fair game. Warriors still take the final fall. Others are maimed or crippled. It is against the rules and the warrior who inflicted the damage is given a mild reprimand. This does not prevent it from happening... often. The light punishment is the Muridae way of encouraging it. Muridae and the crowds love it. If you survive to become a famous warrior, you will be a mark for every street punk looking to make a name. Those fights will be no blows barred. On top of that, your contract has a mercenary clause which allows them to drop you in the middle of a warzone if they damn well feel like it."

"Sounds pleasant."

"It's not. It's deadly, so stop antagonizing Smed'lee. Yes, he is a defecating bodily orifice and a sadistic bastard, but he holds your life in his grasp. Do not give him any more reason than he needs to hurt you or you may have many new scars added to your collection," Kerr said, referring to the many souvenirs left on my hide by my imprisonment on Earth. "Now, defend yourself."

"Why are you criticizing me for fooling around when I'm fighting? You treat every fight as a game."

"No. I do that to keep my opponents off balance. I know exactly what I am doing. One has to be good enough to get away with goofing around. That is a lesson for life."

"What makes you think I'm not good enough?" I questioned indignantly. No sooner had the words passed over my lips than five consecutive blows struck five nerve plexuses. Limp, unable to move, and in terrible agony, I plummeted faster than a falling star.

"I think that answers your question," Kerr replied, his dread smile returning for a brief moment.

Aside from fighting, Kerr instructed me in the anatomy and physiology of all beings I might face in the arena and some I might meet in the street. With my background, I excelled in these areas to the point where he was unable to answer all my questions and had pawned me off on Burke for that part of my training. I knew the vulnerable sites, nerve cluster locations, and killpoints of almost two dozen externals and the Aprahoe. I knew which caused pain and which stopped movement. I knew where to strike to cause permanent damage and how to kill. I only learned the killpoints under threats of pain but I knew them just the same. I could, theoretically, take a life.

I found this utterly terrifying and sickening. I prayed that I never had reason to use a killpoint. I prayed to the God who never answered, the same God who allows children to be sold or killed and innocents tortured. I prayed partly because I didn't know if I could, but mostly because I feared that I was capable of the deed. If Susie was threatened I might do anything. In fear for my own life, I would strike out.

There had grown a hardness in me forged in pain. It had been with me since my first captivity and had grown steadily with each conflict I faced. I barely recognized the face that stared back from the mirror these days: the eyes were cold, blue pools; the face was hard and worn. Not to mention the beard. Kerr had insisted I keep my hair cut short, just long of a buzz cut... one less handhold for the enemy. In compensation for the many inches of hair I lost, I grew a beard. I kept it well trimmed, cutting away most of the stubble along the cheeks and neck, emphasizing the hair along the mustache and chin, giving the effect of a goatee while keeping a full beard. I thought I looked distinguished yet daring with a touch of darkness... the type of beard an Errol Flynn type character or the devil might wear.

Susie liked it, even going so far as to pet my face as if I were a puppy. Kerr was very impressed, even proud, of my "pelt". He seemed to think I traded my skin for fur as a tribute to him; I've never said anything to the contrary. If I'd known it would have meant that much to him, I would have done it gladly and kept it even if I didn't like it. Kerr, Burke, Susie, my squad, and even Nanna were like family. The only family I was ever likely to have again. Despite my dislike for violence, I would gladly fight for any of them. Kerr was first and foremost among the lot, save Susie. Which brought me back to the lessons at hand.

Striking a plexus caused maximum pain with minimal harm. I preferred it that way. I still felt a twinge of emotion for every successful blow I landed. As if to justify in my mind this knowledge of the destructive arts, I persuaded Burke to teach me beneficial, healing techniques. Kerr doesn't know about that aspect of my training and I have no immediate plans to tell him; he would not approve.

To facilitate learning, Burke translates most of the text into English, but I am slowly learning Czarrian Common. Language was never my strong suit and, frankly, my time is at a premium. I want to survive. Burke finally understands this and is tailoring the lessons accordingly. So far, I can read a menu as well as street signs and the markings on restroom doors. Turns out that physically I qualify to go into two different kinds. Susie, on the other hand, is reading short stories and books. But I can still do more push-ups... a minor triumph, but my hungry pride always searches for crumbs.

Reviewing my lessons mentally helped me focus past the torment my axons were inflicting on my brain. Nothing had been permanently damaged and if I were able to move, I could have excised the pain and eased my gasping for air. My solar plexus was one of the five struck, making each breath a struggle. My body had endured enough agony in the past few months to last three lifetimes. I would have been satisfied with just one to myself. Little chance of that until my ten-year contract ends.

After letting me writhe in agony, Kerr used his magic fingers and returned me to my former pain-free and mobile state. Kerr never lets me suffer long because of the remote risk of permanent harm if the nerves were blocked too long; Kerr just did it to make his point. There was no vindictiveness in his actions, only a strange form of caring. He gave me a hand up, shaking his head as if disappointed.

Leaving me standing, he walked to the far side of the Pit, lost in thought, muttering to himself in disgust. I considered rushing him while his back was turned, but thought better of it; seventeen attempts in one day were enough to convince me to quit. After many moments lost in the recesses of his mind, Kerr returned to where I stood.

"Why do you hold back when you face an opponent?"

"I don't hold back...that much."

"You should not hold back at all. A moment's hesitation could spell defeat or death."

"Kerr, I told you before; I don't like violence. I don't like hurting anyone."

"Excrement. You initiated a fight with a DeTang. Sheer suicide."

"It was pure reflex."

"Only Sasha's intervention prevented you from being pulverized into a puddle of amino acids. That same night you had eluded Santo, yet you circled around and engaged an unknown in combat in an unfamiliar territory. You could have kept going."

"No, I couldn't. He'd been following me all evening. For all I knew he'd be hiding in wait outside the Warplex ready to ambush me. Better to confront him when I controlled it."

"Then instead of running, you stayed and faced off against Wheels."

"I couldn't just leave Samuel alone there."

"He was then a stranger."

"He was a fellow Earther who had jumped in to help me. How could I not do the same?"

"He could have been one of your attackers, preying on your better nature."

"He wasn't."

"But had he been, and Burke and I not been following, you would be on the other side of the veil. And before you blame any of this on your reflexes and training, remember your first night here. In Red's you laid into that Aprahoe. He was not bothering you at all."

"I was drunk." And he was harassing Sasha.

"Then do it sober. Hit me!" he said, baring his abdomen to me. I hesitated, but he insisted so I punched him after making a fist in such a way to minimize the risk of injury to my hand.

"Ha! My dead ancestors roll in their graves with more force. Hit me again."

I did. The blow was received with biting laughter.

"Again!" he shouted. "Harder!" With each command, I complied and each one was followed by guffaws. I tried open and knife handed blows. Kerr didn't even raise a hand to block me. A mocking smile adorned his face through it all.

"Not good enough by far, Dirtling," he said beginning at last to block my blows. "What an insignificant piece of life from an unimportant planet you are. How worthless you are; your own parents thought you were worthless. You are so inconsequential that you were unable to even protect your own sister."

"Liar!" I screamed, pounding furiously away at his defenses. "I saved Deborah's life."

"It is true and you know it, scum. Susie would be better off without you. Sasha was with you only out of misguided pity. She has no desire to see a lowlife like you again. She told me herself. Hell, neither do I. What good are you to me? I'll never make you a warrior or earn a cent off your worthless hide. I'll turn you back over to Smed'lee. Tell him our little plan did not work. You won't last a minute in the Games tomorrow against a Kroc, but you might survive the experience... as a cripple. A financial burden to society. Best to just not feed Davv before the match, so he will make a meal of your hide. Better yet, we drop you in a battlezone in one of the Outland border wars. Then the lot of us can get back on with our lives," Kerr said venomously, spitting in my face to accentuate his treachery.

"Damn you, Kerr! You're no better than the stinking rats. Worse, letting me believe you were my friend."

"You must have me confused with a being who cares. Go off and cry about it somewhere else."

My body was slipping into a state of shock. Once more betrayed by someone I cared about. Never again. I will never open up and allow someone to get close to me. People, no matter what their species, are nothing but pain. Screw them all! I never had the chance to confront my parents after their act of Judas loyalty. Kerr, the bastard, was not going to be that lucky.

After a moment standing in stunned silence, something deep and primeval, something I had fought against for all my recent life, erupted with more force than a thousand volcanoes. Anger replaced the blood in my arteries. Fury flowed through my veins with the force of a tidal wave. Crimson rage blinded my eyes as I lashed out at anything white with fur. Instinct and ire seized me as a demon possessed.

Physically I attacked Kerr, but emotionally I lashed out at all who'd hurt me. Mentally I saw the faces of betrayal laid out before me. I struck first and I struck hard, taking no prisoners. My mother and father, Lonso and Grillar, Smed'lee, and all the damn Muridae and even God were the objects of my wrath. Impotence at the events that directed my life was momentarily blasted to smithereens as the frustrations came pouring out in one progressive act of violence and brutality. Flesh rended beneath my hands. I spat torn fur and red plasma from between teeth that had gotten close enough to taste warm blood. I fought like an animal with the calculating mind of a man.

The heat of betrayal burned in every pore of my being, blazing in glory beneath my skin. The pain and scars that were inflicted on me by all my torturers didn't compare to the sorrow of this single betrayal. To be betrayed, I had trusted each Judas with a part of my soul. Otherwise, they wouldn't have any power over me.

I trusted my government to put its citizens first and foremost. I believed that my parents loved me more than life itself and would choose their children over the unreasonable demands of an evil world. I had confidence in my friends to stand by me against the evil of a second world. Most of all I had faith in my God to make a world somewhere in the universe that was just and safe for children, where he would protect all his creatures from atrocity - all of it just the delusions of a fool. A fool whose heart has been broken, ripped apart, and stomped on for the last time. Forget about what Lonso and Grillar did to my body. I stopped caring if I lived or died. Nothing mattered except revenge.

The part of my essence that knew compassion seemingly ceased to exist. Mercy became a stranger to me. I reveled in my savagery. Clutched by the berserker's rage, I wanted to annihilate, to ravage, to destroy. To kill. To drink the blood of my enemies. My mind made ready the killpoints for my battle trained and battered body to finally make use of.

I raised my right hand high for the deathstroke at the base of Kerr's throat. It fell with a terrible swiftness. Not all of Kerr's skill could stop it. Instead of the intended target, it struck the side of the wolf's skull. The final safeguard against my becoming a murderer had kicked in. My soul. The very thing that gave my betrayers power over me saved them. I might know hundreds of killpoints but I wouldn't use them. At least not on someone I had once called friend, no matter what his crime. Pain

I would gladly inflict; Death I could not.

Silently, I thanked and cursed God in the same breath.

My rage was not a bottomless pit. The crimson soon turned to light. I collapsed from utter and total, physical, and spiritual exhaustion. Mentally debating the benefits of becoming comatose, I was brought back to reality by the voice of a bruised and bloody Czarrian wolf speaking from beneath me. The voice called softly, rasping between heavy gasps for air.

"Not bad, Rick. Undisciplined but with great potential. Keep that up and you may be ready for tomorrow's match yet," Kerr remarked, blood staining his face, tunic and just about everything else. He braced an arm against his bruised side.

Looking at the amount of injuries he had sustained in my brief attack, I felt twinges of guilt over what I'd done, but one thought was foremost in my mind.

"I did that? To you?" I asked somewhere between shock and exhaustion.

"Yes, you did," he said with an odd amount of pride for someone who had just had his butt and most of his body kicked, punched, bitten, and chewed to within six inches of his life. "You just required the proper motivation, which I gave to you in abundance. Now you have to learn how to do that under a controlled situation."

It took a while but the meaning behind his words sunk in.

"It was all a trick?" I asked, incredulously. Kerr smiled affirmatively. "You son of a bitch! I almost killed you!" He was unfazed by the insult as that is exactly what he was in his own language. I opted for a series of stinging curses, some I learned from Tarna, which I let sail his way. Curiously, most of them translated as "Procreation" and questioned his heritage. Two of them were in his native tongue. Burke would be pleased.

Surprisingly, he didn't counter with any curses of his own. Instead, he threw all four arms around me, lifted me up and gave me a wolf hug. Still, in a daze, I hugged back sobbing tearlessly. He grimaced only slightly under my embrace. As my anger faded away, my guilt grew at Kerr's injuries. He tried to convince me they were nothing, but the subtle changes in how he moved told me a different story. Reaching out, I massaged a pressure point located over his sternum. He let out a small sigh as his pain vanished.

"Thank you," said Kerr. After a moment of pain-free thought had passed, he asked suspiciously "Where did you learn to do that? Do humans have the same pressure point?"

"No. Not exactly," I answered. Actually, we have several. One in each big toe, another in the web space near the thumb, several in the head and two in the neck to name a few. The Czarrians had just as many, but I only learned four, the best of which I had used. I remained silent, avoiding the question. Kerr decided to drop the matter but I think he knew, especially after he saw how easily I set the shoulder of Tony's G'morran goon. Perhaps now that he has experienced the benefits, he will not be so opposed to me "cluttering" my warrior's mind with healing knowledge. Still, he was in a gracious mood and I was not about to let such a rare opportunity go unused.

"Kerr, let's put this whole sordid business behind us. I know the perfect place to go to do just that."

Kerr's eyes narrowed marginally, as he glared at me suspiciously. My act of innocence, learned from acts of experience, seemed to be working. Perhaps I might pull the wool over his eyes yet. An interesting idea, would that make Kerr a wolf in sheep's clothing?

"Where might that be?" he asked.

"The Empirical House, of course." I don't know what reaction I was expecting but the one I got was not it.

"No," he said softly before turning and walking away. I ran after him in a subdued yet frantic trot.

"Why not? We had a deal."

"Which you broke by sneaking out of Red's that night."

"Our deal had no conditions and I paid for that in spades. Besides, Burke tells me you used to do the same thing to Red all the time."

"Burke has a big mouth."

"Perhaps I can help settle this," said a heavenly voice behind me. I turned and my two favorite faces were smiling back at me. Susie was holding Sasha's hand and pulling her in tow. Nanna and Peri were close behind. Kerr looked up shaking his head in disgust. The only two people he had trouble saying no to were about to tag team him and he knew it.

"Rick, I met your girlfriend. She is every bit as nice and pretty as you said."

"Susie, she is not my girlfriend." Unfortunately.

"Yes, she is," Susie said. As if to add fuel to the fire, Sasha came forward and kissed me on the cheek. Susie could not let that go by. "See! She is," Then she broke into song. "Rick and Sasha sitting in a tree, K-I-

S-S-I-N-G. First comes love then comes marriage, then comes Ricky in a baby carriage," I responded in my usual fashion. I tickled her until she collapsed on the floor laughing.

"Rick, I got your message. Interested in having dinner with me?" Sasha asked.

"Absolutely"

"Wait a second. Rick has his first match tomorrow. He needs to spend tonight practicing," said Kerr.

"Kerr, have some confidence in your student and yourself," Sasha said. "Besides if he hasn't learned enough to survive, one more night will not make the difference."

"I disagree. Especially based on the breakthrough I just witnessed." Great. My mind snapping is considered a breakthrough. If I go mad, will the job be complete? Then I realized I don't know how long Susie and Sasha had been there. They might have seen me go berserk.

"How long have you been watching?" I ask.

"Just long enough to see you and the fleabag locked in an embrace. Should I be jealous?" Sasha asked.

"Not in the least," I said with relief. Sasha jealous of me? Fantastic. Dreams do come true. I had to go out with her tonight and I had an idea. Kerr is a sucker for tradition.

"Kerr, you told me that in the old games the night before a slave's first match he got a request. Although I'm not a slave I didn't volunteer to be a warrior. I have a request."

"As if I did not know what it is."

"Kerr, I did earn it by your own agreement."

"I suppose you did."

"Come on, Kerr. Let Rick go out with his girlfriend. Then Peri, Nanna, and I can play," Susie said in her teasing tone. She was using her natural talents of persuasion to help me. What a great kid. Kerr began to falter.

"Does that mean you'll turn Rick over to my tender mercies?" Sasha asked with a smile that could melt ice. Kerr looked to me expecting me to add my appeal to theirs. Kerr didn't get what he expected. I did not plead with my words or my face. I had earned this. I would not beg for what was rightfully mine. Standing tall, I met his iron gaze with a stainless steel one. My eyes told him I was going, with or without his say so. There was no disrespect for him in my actions, just a deepened esteem for myself. It was what a warrior would do and soon I would be one. After tomorrow, provided I won, I would be a Newbe no more

Kerr approached me, bringing himself to his full height at an attempt at intimidation. It worked but I didn't let him see that. My stance remained proud but relaxed. Our eyes remained locked for what seemed an eternity. Never before had I been able to out-stare the master: this time was different. A smile, patterned after the wolf's own, engulfed my lips. It radiated confidence. I wouldn't lose this contest. Kerr returned it with a smile of his own, breaking eye contact in the process. Four lupine hands gripped my shoulders as his grin radiated pride.

Unconsciously, I stood even prouder.

"I'll tell you what. Give Rick and me another hour to fine tune our breakthrough and I will grant him the battle's eve request," Kerr said. "Acceptable, Rick?"

"Yes."

"Mind if we watch?" Sasha asked, directing her question toward Kerr. He didn't answer. Instead, he turned toward me. I answered it.

"Not at all."

DREG

The night before the opening games: last chance to practice. Last night of innocence for some; another eve of decadence for others.

In the Pit below battled two male G'morra and a man. Although technically a last practice, it was more of a slaughter. The human showed no compassion toward his opponents. He addressed himself as Dreg. Not his real name, but it was all he let himself be called. To his face, at least.

From above the arena, deep in the shadow that was his closest friend and dearest enemy, Savage watched the Newbes below. It was the second training session he witnessed this night. The first was between Rick and Kerr. Rick was young, strong, and had good instincts. A fighter born, albeit late in life, as demonstrated by him taking down the Czarrian. Still, he lacked the ruthless edge which made a truly great warrior.

Dreg was a direct contrast: his skill was minimal and he lacked instincts other than those that caused pain. He possessed something else that served him in their stead: sheer savagery, ferocity, and a love for causing pain unmatched even by a Muridae. His fighting style brought to mind the image of a butcher. Each blow carried the force and subtlety of a battering ram as they rained down upon even unconscious opponents. Dreg was a throwback to the original games where he would have been the ultimate crowd pleaser. If the reactions of his squad mates were any judge, he hadn't made a friend in the bunch. It appeared Dreg lived as he fought, without honor. He was just the type Savage needed if his plan was to work.

The match ended and the participants were dismissed, two of them limping toward the medic's office. A second match between an Aprahoe and a Chitin began. Dreg made to leave but was stopped by a living shadow which maneuvered directly into his path. Without thought or hesitation, Dreg punched the midsection of the darkness. It in turn not only blocked the blow but added to its force, carrying the body behind it into an arc which ended with Dreg floored on his back, a blow aimed at his throat. Fear in Dreg's eyes lit up the darkness. It slowly transformed into the light of recognition.

"Hey, you're a man!"

"Are you always this observant?"

"Yeah, it's a gift. Nice to meet ya. You're the only other human I've seen on this hellhole planet. Except the wimp and the girl."

"Wimp? You mean Rick?"

"That's the one. Creep won't hang with the man. Actually likes these hellspawn creatures."

"You don't?"

"No way! If they ain't white, they ain't right."

"The Kroc are white."

"But they ain't human and that makes all the difference. God don't like that."

"Then why did he create them?"

"To test his chosen race."

"Of which you are one, I assume."

"Of course. You are, too."

"Afraid not. I'm Catholic."

"Bummer! Nobody's perfect. Besides, you can always convert."

"To groups like you belonged to back on Terra?" As if he had to ask. Savage already had a pretty good idea before he asked the question.

"Terra?"

"Earth."

"Oh." Dreg appeared slightly confused but quickly recovered as he enthusiastically replied. "Hell, yes! I belonged to plenty of the best.... let's see.... the White Riders Biker Club. Gang actually, but the cops react better if you say you are a club. The Neo-Nazis too, but I never was into the do... liked my hair too much," he proudly bragged. "I was third down from the grand wizard in the triple K. I was even a card-carrying member of the Young Republicans for a time in my younger days. And I was Born Again, but they threw me out. Amazing how some people who claim to be God-fearing will react to a few burning crosses."

"People are funny that way," Savage said, trying and only barely succeeding in hiding his disgust. Savage didn't believe in judging any man or being by things they had no control over. Judging someone by the choices they made was another matter, however. Prejudice against the prejudiced was fully acceptable.

Savage was pragmatic, believing it was best not to mix personal feelings with business. Things would be fine so long as Dreg didn't cross the line that Savage would draw for him.

Savage introduced himself; after Dreg returned the favor, Savage sprung his plan.

"I have a proposal for you, Dreg."

"What's in it for me?"

"Money."

"Money won't do me no good here. No place to spend it."

"You could buy your contract and freedom from the rats."

"What about the damn pain button?"

"You buy the NG frequency with your contract."

"I'm in!"

"But you have no idea what I am offering."

"Don't matter; for the right price, I'd sell my mama to the niggers." Savage winced at the use of the term. Biting his tongue, Savage let it go by without comment. Savage thought about the rest of the statement and decided Dreg meant every word of it. He pitied Dreg's mother, half-wondering if she got the type of son she deserved. Not for the first time, he doubted the wisdom of involving such a man. Trust would never be an asset of their relationship.

However, ultimately Dreg was still a Terran and deserved respect for that if nothing else. Besides, this way Savage would have some control over his actions and might be able to prevent him from embarrassing their people. The only thing a man like Dreg respected was superior force which is why Savage had engineered their first meeting to happen as it did.

Dreg continued. "Besides, I'd love the chance to screw the rats over."

"I'm sure you would." Having acquired Dreg's history from the Muridae files for a small price, he wondered in what respect Dreg meant the comment. Dreg had a long list of alleged crimes against him ranging from racial attacks to sexual deviancy, both of which led to murder. Which is why the crimes were alleged: no witnesses, no conviction. Had the Exodus Project ever become public knowledge, he was the type of man Grillar would use to justify his actions. Most of the public would agree that they were better off with this scum light years away, as opposed to cruising down America's highways on a bike.

Savage outlined his plans specifically for the next day's match.

"No problem, as long as I get to win."

"You'll win when I say you win. You will lose when I say you lose."

"Up yours, man! No way am I going to lose on your say so."

Savage silently responded by applying pressure to a nerve cluster in Dreg's left ear, followed by a knee to his breadbasket. Dreg folded in two.

"I'm sorry. I don't think I heard you correctly."

"Screw you, douchebag!"

Savage doubled the pressure, doubling the pain.

"Care to try again?"

"You the man. Whatever you say is the word," Dreg gasped. With that, Savage helped him up from the floor and brushed him off.

"I thought you'd see it my way. I brought you a little sign-on bonus," Savage said, pointing to a silver keg glittering silently in the corner.

"What is it?"

"Beer."

"You're shitting me!"

"Nope. Enjoy. Just make sure you win tomorrow."

"No problem," Dreg replied hefting the keg onto his shoulder.

Savage turned to leave, his back to Dreg. "I'll be in touch after the match."

Unable to resist a shot in the back, Dreg, lifted the keg high over his head with both hands.

"You do that," he growled, preparing to heave the keg into the back of Savage's unprotected head.

Halfway through the movement, before the keg could become airborne, with nary a backward glance, Savage shot a back kick into the center of Dreg's solar plexus. Shocked by the sudden pain, Dreg forgot about the keg and grabbed his gut. Gravity had no such memory lapse and dropped the keg on his right foot. At the sounds of the snaps, Savage smiled and Dreg winced. They both knew two toes were broken.

"There should be more than enough brew to make the pain go away. Or go to the medic if you like. Just be sure to win," Savage said, without turning toward the figure on the floor who had one hand holding his stomach, the other his foot. Dreg looked down at the fractured toes to assess the damage and decided they hurt like hell.

Looking up, he yelled, "Bastard!" but no one was there. Only a broken light and shadows greeted him.

RICK

The evening was warm, but a cool breeze was puffing its way around the streets, brushing over us in a gentle caress. Sasha's arm was locked in mine, her head rested softly on my shoulder. The clouds seemed to be floating low this evening or perhaps it was my head that was soaring with the mists of the sky. Sasha described it much more simply, but just as accurately.

"It is a beautiful night."

"Yes, it is. But nowhere near as beautiful as you, Sasha," I said, not believing the words as they escaped my mouth. They sounded so corny. I mean every one of them but I didn't want her to think I was being insincere by using lines that were old when the world was new.

Her golden eyes gently sought mine. Perhaps she was thinking the same thing. Maybe not, but what did it matter when she looked my way with a smile that lit up my night.

"Thank you, Rick," Sasha said, then kissed me gently on the cheek.

"I should be thanking you for taking me to dinner in New Terra."

"I still cannot believe that neither Kerr nor Burke thought to take you to the quarter that your own people have settled."

"Kerr doesn't seem to want me out of the Warplex."

"He just worries about your safety."

"True, but now he's going to have to let me. I have two good reasons to venture out: I'm definitely coming back to New Terra. I haven't had that much fun in a long time."

New Terra was an incredible jumble of Earth traditions. Back home, no one would have thought of combining Irish and Russian folk dancing with the hustle. I didn't have the heart to tell my fellow Americans that disco was dead, although some folks were trying to revive it when I left. Hard to believe they'd been here that long.

Earlier, we stopped briefly in another restaurant, after I was drawn by the sounds of rock and roll and the familiar image of a man in black leather and sideburns. He had lost quite a bit of weight. For a supposedly dead man, he put on one hell of a show, much like the footage of his earlier days. As this was not the restaurant Sasha had made reservations at, she dragged me out after a few moments and we went to dinner.

"What did you think of the food?"

"I'm glad I listened to Luigi's recommendation; the lasagna was absolutely delicious once I got past the blue sauce. The vegetable they made it from tasted just like tomatoes. The hamburgers and hot dogs smelled out of this world, no pun intended. Real corn on the cob, French fries and baked potatoes," In addition to its people the government also sent certain foods that could grow off world. "I have to bring Susie here." I had a doggie box with a hamburger and hot dog for her. I had tried to pay, but Luigi said that since I was buying for Susie my money was no good here. Hard to call a red-headed man with a face full of freckles and an Irish brogue "Luigi", but it's his restaurant.

Here, Earthers can dress and be whoever they want to be. So far, I'd seen cowboys, a fireman, ballerina, medieval lords and ladies, and samurai, not to mention every major movie hero and heroine ever to grace the big or small screen. Most folk dressed for what passed for normal here, but enough play dress up to make New Terra look like Mardi Gras in New Orleans, less the floats and flying beads. The partying put Red's to shame, mainly because none of the participants required medical attention afterward.

"Bring her and you won't have to pay for a thing, at least for the initial visit. Was that the first time you have spent time with your people since your entrance?"

"There is another human Newbe named Dreg, although I avoid him whenever possible. I see Susie every day."

"Yes, the girlchild has made quite an impression on your people here it seems."

"I noticed. The reason why is so horrible. It's unbelievable that so many people have been sterilized. At least the older children who escaped back then will be ready to start the next generation." Puts a lot of pressure on them though.

"That's the result of better living through government."

"I am glad you asked them to send all the gifts they wanted to give her directly to the Warplex. I would never have been able to carry all of them."

"A Kroc pulling a wagon would have trouble."

"True," I said, then got back to her original question. "I also spent the latter part of the evening I visited you with Samuel, Peri, Jake, and Savage."

At the mention of the name, Sasha's grip on my arm tightened reflexively, then relaxed.

"From what he told me, you and he used to have a thing going."

Her head snapped up. "He told you that?"

"Yes. Is it true?"

"Yes."

"What happened? Why did it end?"

"Personal question, isn't it?"

"It is. You don't have to answer."

"True, but I will. When I first met Tony, we were both slaves. I had not yet fought in the Pit. He had snuck into Mamma's where I was laboring. It was interest at first sight. He had a beautiful spark, not unlike yours. But he also had a vast darkness that the spark had to contend with. It had been fading before he was brought to Liberty, but once here it began to burn brighter. Every time he refused to kill in the games, it became brighter. Each time he defended another slave against a bully or an overseer, the spark grew. I later found out it was his suggestion to Mamma that was the reason I was sent to the games on a part-time basis. Mamma thought if I won enough she could increase the fee she charged for me. She was right."

"Tony and I became close as his inner beauty fought back his inner darkness. His life as a villain on Earth was left behind. Then he won the Tourney and instead of enjoying his freedom, he risked his life building a case against slavery. He called down Kentor Justice and won. All we slaves were freed. It was a great day. Unfortunately, without an enemy to struggle against, Tony grew restless. His worship by the G'morra as their savior warped him until he believed it. With that sense of power, Tony reverted to the role of the villain. Slowly at first, but increasingly the darkness took control. We went our separate ways. That was quite some time ago."

"Are you over him?"

"You never stop caring for someone you once loved, but I have no desire to restart our relationship. Are you worried?"

"Not if you tell me there is no reason to be."

"Did he do anything else?"

"Like what?"

"Threaten you."

"Yes, at first. But then we talked a bit. He asked me how I felt about you. I told him. Then I fixed up his knee."

"What did you tell him?"

"To do the exercises I gave him three times a day, tape his knee like I told him to, and to work on strengthening his vastus medialis muscle to help his patella track better."

"Not about his knee, silly man. About how you feel toward me?"

"Never figured you the type to have to fish for a compliment."

"I am not; I am just curious."

"Everything I told you the other night is still very much true. I think about you all the time and when I do, I smile. You make me feel good. Now, how about returning the favor?"

"You do not seem the type to fish for compliments."

"Oh, but I am. I'm very insecure in certain areas."

"Is love one of those areas?"

"Sometimes."

"I cannot believe that."

"Why not? I'm not that great looking."

"I would not say that. But appearance only means so much. What is inside means much more; your insides are beautiful."

"My heart is pure and I have the strength of ten men," I grinned.

"What?"

"Literary reference from back home about a knight."

"Then you must have the strength of ten men."

"I wish!"

"So why are you insecure about relationships?"

"Past experience, I guess. I have had plenty of relationships before my exile. Many of them were special, but none were right. Not for long anyway."

"What about this?"

"This is different."

"How can you tell?"

"I don't know. I just can."

"That is good enough for me. What do Terrans typically do on a date?"

"Anything the couple wants: dinner, dancing, maybe a show or movie."

"Well, if you count the spectacle you made of yourself while dancing as a show we have done everything typical."

"Time with you is never typical. My dancing isn't that bad. Besides, I was having fun. I never step danced before. It was nice to spend time with just humans, present company included. But I didn't get to dance with you."

"Sure you did; I was there with you. We did the 'bump'. And you showed them break dancing and moonwalking."

"A leftover of my youth. It's almost as out of date as disco, but it was new to them. It was easier than trying to explain grunge and slam-dancing. That's not what I meant. We didn't get to slow dance."

"What is that?"

"Slow music is played and the partners wrap their arms around each other and hold on tightly, swaying until the music stops. Sometimes longer."

"Next time."

"What is wrong with now? Would you care to dance?"

"There is no music."

"Sure there is. Just listen to the night sing."

She smiled and took my hands. We pulled each other close, swaying to a very special kind of music. The kind only two people can hear. The kind that involves ringing bells.

As we danced together, so did my mind and body pair off of their own accord, carrying the rest of me along as an all too willing passenger. My heart beat and my feet stepped, keeping perfect time. I looked into the eyes of my otherworldly angel and as she looked back, I was overwhelmed by her beauty.

I remembered not very long ago when I thought Tore was the abyss, a cruel punishment by an unjust God. They say you meet the nicest people in hell; that certainly has proved true, especially in this case.

I still wouldn't call Tore a paradise. Yet here I was, standing in yesterday's hell that has somehow been transformed into tomorrow's purgatory because tonight I was holding heaven in my arms.

We kissed, soft and magically. Heaven and the world faded away. Thoughts of tomorrow's match were so much wisps of smoke. All of creation was soft, warm, and held in my arms.

RICK

"Rick, I cannot believe you stayed out all night."

"I was back in time to get eight hours of sleep which is an hour more than I usually get. Don't worry, Kerr. I'll be fine."

"You better be. Your match is after next."

Tarna was up first. She was pacing in anticipation. It was the first time a female G'morran was allowed in the games as a Newbe Warrior. The arena was two-thirds filled. Most of the matches were between Newbes. Unknown before today, some soon to be famous. Sasha told me last night that I was the biggest crowd puller in the bunch. Turns out, a great many people want to see a human who willingly took down a DeTang. The story has been exaggerated to the point where I mopped up the floor with BoBo, stopping only when he begged me for mercy. That rep was going to get me in trouble one day.

There was a large G'morran contingent in the stands, mostly veiled ladies, but several males. In deference to custom, Tarna was covered in togs from ankle to neck so the males would not all have to run to the clerics for absolution after her match for the sin of viewing female flesh not of their lodge. Ever the rebel, she refused the veil, but that was a sin on her part, not theirs, so it wouldn't affect G'morran viewing enjoyment.

The most important G'morran, from Tarna's point of view, was seated in the first row. It was her father and he beamed with pride at his daughter's accomplishment. Her mother would not attend, but all five of her sisters and three of her six brothers were there. Not to mention a dozen clerics, ready to condemn her as soon as the match was over. They worried her more than her opponent.

She was set to face off against the scumbag Dreg. I disliked him from the moment we met but decided to give him the benefit of the doubt. That doubt vanished when he made a pass at Susie. The man, and I use the term loosely, is sick! He asked eight-year-old Susie for a kiss... and not the kind on the cheek. Susie kneed him in the groin instead. Dreg lunged after her but his attack was cut short by Nanna, who almost ate him. His salvation came from a very unusual source: Smed'lee intervened and saved him. Ratboy claimed he was property and should Nanna destroy him he would consider it theft and prosecute to the fullest. Nanna offered to buy him, but his verminness would not sell.

So Nanna threatened to break both his legs and deep fry his privates if he ever came within fifty feet of Susie. Next on her list would then be Smed'lee. They never told Burke, because Smed'lee's threats would not detour Burke from ending Dreg's existence. No great loss to the universe, but a world of legal trouble for Burke. Susie only told me after I promised not to tell or go after Dreg. I have never been so tempted to break a promise in my life, but I kept it. I just added an addendum that I would behave provided he did.

I hoped Tarna would make him hurt and told her as much. My bloodthirsty attitude surprised her, but she agreed to oblige. The squad was standing by to wish her luck. She hugged each of us in turn for luck. Don even licked her face for luck, an old Kroc custom. The idea was one could not get much luckier than to be licked by a Kroc and walk away uneaten. Susie was standing with us and wasn't one to miss out on a hug.

"Kick his butt," Susie said darkly. Tarna laughed.

"I will, little one," Tarna promised before turning to me. "Wish me luck, Rick."

"You won't need it. You can take me half the time and even Kerr says that jerk isn't as good as me."

"Only half?"

"Lately at any rate. Good luck, anyway." We hugged and it lasted just a little bit longer than the others. As we separated, I whispered, "Your Dad, Drello, looks real proud."

"He is. He defied the Clerics and snuck in this morning to wish me luck personally."

"Couldn't they excommunicate him for that?"

"Yes. Still would not stop Drello. To him family comes first, then the Logg. He would not let harm come to any of his children. If he had not spoken up for me, I would have been stoned instead of Xiled."

"You'll do him proud."

"Yes, I will," she beamed, throwing him a loving glance. Turning then to Kerr, she embraced her trainer. Together they walked out onto the sandy Pit as Dreg and his trainer, a Chitin named Spear, did the same. It was a Game tradition that all Newbes were presented by their trainers prior to first fight.

High atop a simple metal throne sat Dortew, acting as if he was lord of all he surveyed. With any luck, he was incredibly nearsighted. Five feet down and to the right sat Smed'lee. To his right sat three more Muridae, each lower than the next. I half expected them to be wearing crowns of olive leaves. Dortew, acting like a minister at a wedding, asked, "Who gives these two in combat?"

"I, Kerr Silverfurr of the House of Honor, loyal subject of the Czarrian Empire, present Tarna, first among equals, of the mighty G'morra," Kerr announced proudly. The words were chosen carefully by the pair. The statement was to present Tarna as an equal of the males and at the same time build up the G'morra. Judging by the reaction, it worked. Few males jeered although their stares stopped the cheers of the females in mid-yell. The only G'morra jeering were the clerics, but the cheers of Tarna's family drowned them out.

Next spoke the Chitin. "I, Spear, drone and hivebrother of warlords and heroes, loyal servant of the Chitin Republic, present Dreg of the Planet Terra, of the white race."

Kerr winked at Tarna, saluted her and turned toward the dais. Spear just turned. The two instructors then saluted the Muridae. Kerr's salute was negligible in comparison to his earlier one.

"Newbes, salute us," Dortew ordered.

Dreg shot the rats a Nazi seig heil. Tarna made a fist over her heart and extended her arm outward. "Salute your opponent." They did.

"Begin!"

Thus, the match began. Above the Muridae, announcers Bob'ber and Ned'soo, Bob and Ned for short, were beginning their descriptions of the pair and what could be expected from the match.

No weapons were allowed. It was warrior to warrior, pure and complex. Tarna circled her opponent cautiously, scoping out his strong and weak points. Dreg didn't feel the need. He just rushed forward and leapt into a flying kick. Stupid move: first, he was limping; he seemed to have injured his foot. Second, the move was poorly chosen. Although it looks good, it's not practical in a real fight. Too easy to dodge, plus it leaves the kicker vulnerable to a counterattack.

Tarna dove under it, coming up beneath him with a shot that caught the outside of his right knee. Dreg landed in a heap. Tarna ran toward and over him, hitting him seven times before he could react. Swinging out blindly, he got lucky and landed a punch on Tarna's left rib cage. She was only winded, while the scumbag was hurting... badly. He spit two teeth and dragged himself to his feet by sheer force of will. Bracing himself, he motioned toward her with his fingers, daring her to attack.

"C'mon bitch! You want a piece of me? Come and get it!" Dreg taunted, taking a step forward and almost landing on his face in the process. Tarna smiled to herself, overconfident of her victory. Tarna's good, but not good enough to underestimate her opponent. Since the first running charge worked so well, she did it again. Mistake number two: like a magician, a warrior should never repeat the same trick twice. The limp had been a feign.

As she charged, Dreg sidestepped and climbed on her back as she passed. With one arm around her throat, he began pummeling her head and back with his fist and elbow. Violet blood spurted from three different wounds and Dreg kept beating her mercilessly. The neck grip was so tight Tarna couldn't breathe. He was out of reach of her arms. Tarna ran in circles and zig zags, speeding up and stopping, trying to throw her opponent, but Dreg held on and kept on battering her. Without thinking, I started to run out to help her, but Kerr and Breeze were ready for me. They gently restrained me.

"Rick," Kerr said. "Win or lose, Tarna has to do this on her own."

"Yes," Breeze added. "If you try to go out there and help her, she will take it as an insult." They were right of course, but it didn't make it any easier to stay on the sidelines. Tarna's father was having the same problem; it was taking all five daughters to stop him from leaping from the stands into the arena.

Tarna became a warrior to prove something to herself and her people: that she as a woman could do anything a male could and do it better. To help her would be to prove her wrong; Tarna would rather die. Personally, I'd rather have the help, but it wasn't about me. I would respect my friend. Or avenge her.

Tarna's right front leg had collapsed and was on its knee. Her other two legs were looking wobbly. I could see Kerr debating on throwing in the towel. As her mentor, he was the only one who could stop the match without dishonoring her. Kerr stood fast, confident in his student. She fell to her back knee. The veins in her face were bulging and she was an even deeper shade of purple, almost black.

Tarna would not surrender. With her last reserve of strength, she broke two of the fingers Dreg had around her throat while dropping her rear leg completely. Then, she pushed back with both front legs. The result was a semi back-flip in which she landed hard on Dreg, while simultaneously pulling his arm free of her windpipe, putting her elbow in his gut, and her rear foot in his groin. Quickly rolling so she was atop and facing Dreg, she placed one calf over his throat and began repaying him in triplicate for every blow he had given her. His face turned pink, although it was hard to tell with all the blood flowing down it. The crowd was going wild, including more than half of the female G'morra.

Tarna didn't wish to kill him, but he wouldn't yield. The Muridae weren't about to halt such a crowd pleaser, so Tarna looked to Spear, who met her eyes and did a full body nod. He tossed a white cloth onto the field, officially ending the match. Releasing Dreg, she skipped the customary salute to the opponent, since by using the choke hold for so long he violated the rules of honor that governed the present games. She then saluted Kerr, followed by the Muridae. Finally, she turned toward the crowd and saluted them, but her eyes were only on her father. He was on his feet, wildly applauding.

In the glory of the moment, Dreg was forgotten by everyone save Susie. He had reached into his boot and removed a blade. Concealing it, he snuck up behind Tarna. She was oblivious to him, as tears of joy showered her face.

Susie yelled to me. "Rick, Dreg has a knife!"

"What?!" I shouted. Looking, I only saw Dreg hiding his hand, but Susie's word was good enough for me. "Tarna! Behind you! He has a blade!" I yelled as I ran out onto the Pit. Kerr and the rest of the squad were hot on my heels, but it was clear we wouldn't get there in time.

At my words, Tarna turned her head and back-kicked the knife from Dreg's hand; changing direction, she landed successive blows in his groin and head. He went down hard. I was the first one there, so I made like a referee and lifted her hand above her head. I looked down at Dreg. Through dilated pupils, he stared up at me.

"Traitor! God made you one of the master race and it was your words that betrayed me to that alien cow," he whispered, spitting blood and teeth.

"Tarna is worth a hundred of you."

"God will avenge me," he muttered as he lost consciousness in a pool of his own vomit, so it made no sense to rebuff him. Frightening that his view of God makes this kind of existence seem right. The medics carried him off.

Runner, Spike, and I lifted Tarna onto our shoulders - or whatever it is that Spike has above his limbs - and carried her around the stadium. The crowd went wild. The female G'morra were unstoppable in their standing ovation. Some of the males, caught up in the excitement, were joining them. Regardless of gender, it was a G'morran victory. The only ones who sat unmoving were the G'morran Clerics, save one who broke from his fellows; he didn't stand but he did applaud. Tarna was in her glory. Her mission had new hope.

We carried her back to the sidelines. The hugging began anew. As we embraced, she leaned and whispered in my ear, "Thanks."

"You're welcome." I knew she meant for both my action and inaction. The squad's mad dash happened after the match was done, so it didn't dishonor her.

"Good luck. You are up next," she said louder. In all the excitement, it had slipped my mind. That was for the best; I would've paced a furrow into the ground worrying. Before I could start my round of hugging we were overshadowed by the entrance of Burke.

"Good match, Tarna," he said. She beamed at the praise. "I have decided to grant you your request."

Tarna stood stunned, neither moving or breathing. For her, this was a dream come true. Burke had never honored any G'morran with the gift of personal combat. To top it off, every Burke match was on Skyvid. She would reach all of her people on the planet. Even some off-world. She leaped up and down in joy. "I will announce it to the crowd after the last match of the day."

"Thank you, Lord Burke," she said, bowing before him. He insisted she stand upright.

"Please, address me as Burke. You have more than earned the right by saving my ward; the entire squad has. I also wanted to wish you luck for your first fight, Rick," Burke said.

He extended a hand as if to shake; it could have enveloped my entire arm. He had seen our squad's one match old tradition of embracing for luck and was attempting to join in. Burke was usually uncomfortable by physical contact. Susie said he wanted to, but was afraid of breaking us "fleshies".

I figured, what-the-hell, and hugged the stone man. My arm span barely covered a third of him. He very gently hugged back.

"Thanks, Burke. I'll make you and the fleabag proud."

"You already have." I felt like a kid being praised by his parents. Except this is the first time I've had that experience.

I hugged each of the squad in turn: Breeze. Runner. Spike. Tarna. Don even licked me for luck. He needed a breath mint, but I'd take any luck I could get. Susie was next. Even Nanna got in on the fun. Last came the master.

"Ready, dirtboy?"

"Ready as I'll ever be, furball. Let's do it!"

Walking out into the arena, I was strangely detached, as if everything was happening to someone else. I watched as my opponent and his trainer, an Aprahoe named Storm, marched out to meet us. Davv was a good five feet longer than Don. His jaw span was wider and he seemed to lack Don's good humor.

One of the reasons I was so calm was a precaution I had taken earlier. The entire squad – along with Sasha, Susie, and me – took all the food we could carry to Davv's cube. It had taken my entire month's stipend to buy the meal, but it was worth the peace of mind. As I've said before, the Muridae do not serve breakfast. A well-fed Kroc was easier to face than a hungry one. Don had told me what foods made him sluggish and I bought those in abundance.

I told Davv it was an old Earth custom to make sure an opponent that considered you one of the basic food groups was well fed before a battle - ask any stuntman or diver who has gotten in a tank with sharks. Thanking me for the food, Davv pigged out. There was even some left over. All is fair in love and war. Kerr was a little upset but calmed down when I assured him I had not drugged the foodstuffs. I claimed I had him to thank. He was the one always lecturing that the mind was the best weapon. That made the break from Game tradition easier to accept.

I had made a study of vids of matches involving Krocs and of how Don moved and fought. I had boned up on their anatomy. I was confident and ready. One thing from the vids gnawed at the back of my mind, though. Often Kroc warriors wore a muzzle in matches that were not to the death. Many were unable to control their hunger and took chunks out of their opponents. Although sentient, the Krocs are not considered to be among the most intelligent of species. Don is exceptionally bright for his people. Action for them was ruled primarily by instinct and secondarily by intellect. Benefit of the doubt was given in all cases. One nip and a Kroc was forever muzzled in the new Games. Davv was a Newbe and this was his first match. No one knew if he'd be able to control himself. If he couldn't, I'd be the first to find out, which explained my gift of breakfast.

Kerr presented me as "The noble Rick Wagner of the proud planet Terra." Storm presented Davv. The trainers saluted their students, then the Muridae. Before we could do the same, a single figure vaulted from the stands onto the Pit and came straight at me. I smiled at the approach of my blue-haired beauty. I was at a loss as to what she was doing, but where she was concerned, I didn't worry. She turned toward the Muridae on the dais and addressed them.

"Gamemasters, I beg your pardon for my intrusion onto these sacred fighting fields, but I had to wish Rick Wagner luck personally."

The crowd cheered, some because it was Sasha - she was one of the most popular warriors. Some of the thrill-seekers cheered because they knew BoBo worked for her. Some just liked to yell. Since the crowd was enjoying the show, the Muridae let Sasha continue.

Sasha took a perfumed scarf out of her cleavage and, with all the considerable sex appeal she could muster, she tied it around my neck. The males in the crowd went wild.

"What's this for?"

"In your mythology, a fair damsel would give her knight a token of esteem to carry into battle. Especially when facing a dragon," she said. Actually, if Krocs were green, they would resemble the fire-breathing beasts. "Is this not true?"

"Yes, it is. Where did you learn about that?"

"From a story Samuel told me. Good luck, my Banesh knight in gleaming armor," With that, she kissed me on the cheek.

"Is that all I get?" I joked.

"Win and I will give you all you can handle." Maybe it was a sad illustration of my priorities, but that motivated me much more than the thought of mere survival. Poor Davv didn't stand a chance. But I had to know what would happen if the match didn't go my way.

"And if I lose?"

"I will give you all you can handle." I toyed with the idea of conceding the match and leaving with Sasha right then and there. Unfortunately, I couldn't bring myself to do it. If the match was going badly and Davv was still hungry, I would have no problem running away, screaming in terror, but I had to give it my best shot.

"I look forward to it," I said with my most dashing smile. I untied the scarf and slipped in the right front pocket of my battle togs. "I hope you don't mind, but I see no reason to give my opponent a handhold around my throat."

"Of course. Now 'kick his butt'," Sasha said in English. I laughed. She must have learned that from Susie. She turned and ran with the grace of a gazelle to the sidelines where the squad was.

Dortew retook control of the match. "Newbes, salute us," Davv gave a traditional Kroc salute by lifting his head up and exposing his vulnerable throat. I had a salute of my own in mind. I had watched Tony's matches and he gave what is now considered by most externals the typical Terran salute. Personally, I call it the bird. Middle finger raised high, I saluted Dortew and Smed'lee separately. Smed'lee puffed up his chest like he was receiving some sort of special honor. I then flipped off Davv and the match began.

Having six legs, a Kroc is generally faster than a man but they do have some weaknesses: for one, sharp turns are impossible. Keep up a serpentine running pattern and avoid corners and a Kroc can't catch you. Which is exactly what I did as Davv began his onslaught. Out of water, they are so large that their endurance is low. Krocs tire easily. Easily meaning upwards of five minutes, which would tire me out as well but I had an advantage.

The gravity field was set at Tore normal, which was about the norm for my opponent. For me it was low. I took to the air and came down hard on a pressure point on the Kroc's back with both booted feet. Pushing off again, I leapt down, traveling toward the large white tail. A Kroc's tail is long and very sensitive; it acts as an early warning system. When swimming, it sways side to side under the water propelling them forward. It makes such swift, wide arcs that nothing can get near a swimming Kroc from behind unannounced or untouched by the tail. The nerve endings are so sensitive they sense changes in water temperature and vibration.

So it was quite understandable why Davv shrieked when I stomped on that appendage. It was like a human male taking a knee to an unprotected groin. It hurt like hell. As I hit the ground running serpentine, I hoped it was enough pain to incapacitate him. Truth be told, the Kroc outweighed me by more than half a ton and was strong enough to break me in two like a brittle ragdoll. In a fair fight, I had no chance. I had only my agility, speed, and mind. In short, I fought dirty. By my standards at least. By the Tore Games Code of Honor, I was well within my rights.

Davv's roar shook the stadium as he clutched his injured tail to himself. I began to doubt the wisdom of my plan of attack. With any luck, the anger would make him sloppy. Instead of rushing me again, Davv stood his ground. Turning to face me, he reared on his back four legs, lifting his upper body vertically so he stood eight feet tall and looked something like a dinosaur. He was leaving his back unguarded. Not that it mattered. This was a solo, not tag team match.

My options were few: serpentine was useless, unless he chased me. I couldn't jump over him without risking being caught by his jaws. A natural armor covered his belly as well as his back and had less pressure points and nerve plexuses to attack. His eyes and throat were out of reach, but I'd only use them in dire straits anyway, for any blow I struck there would seriously injure him. If I went for the belly or legs, all he'd have to do is fall down and I'd be trapped like a man underneath a Volkswagen. My defenses were all against a moving Kroc; I needed to make him mobile before I could press an attack.

I faked forward to the right, waited until Davv began a lunge, then cut left, backwards and fast. Teeth, long and sharp, missed me by inches. My elbow hit its intended target on the left side of Davv's skull, directly above his vestibular organs. Wobbling as if drunk, Davv moved toward me. The blow was only hard enough to disorient him for a couple, three minutes tops. Enough time for me to finish him off. It was then I fell prey to the same mistake as Tarna... overconfidence.

Intending to hit a nerve cluster in the back of Davv's neck, which would knock him out cold, I initiated an attack. I was counting on the vertigo I induced to lay waste to Davv's defenses. With my hand a mere two inches from the mark, I found myself staring down Davv's gullet. Instinct yanked me back like a giant hand as tremendous jaws slammed closed with a terrifying snap. Davv had gone primitive. I only lost the front of my sleeveless tunic and a dozen chest hairs, but I finally felt true terror. But I'd felt terror before.

Terror... I was jostled awake in the middle of the night to betrayal carried on the tip of a needle. I was lying helpless and bound in the C.S.A.'s dungeons, having my skin flailed and my insides fried and violated. I was standing on the empty field with the masses waiting for death. My head was exploding with the pain of the NG. I was waking from nightmares, shaking and drenched in sweat... all that had gone before was a mere prequel, an hors d'oeuvres for the bloody banquet before me.

The match was no longer a game. It was real. I finally saw what Kerr had been trying to tell me but I had been too pigheaded to hear. One crucial difference separated this time of terror from the rest: I was no longer helpless. Already Burke, Kerr, Sasha, and the rest of the squad were moving in to help muzzle the berserk Kroc before the match could continue.

"No! I'll do it," I yelled, the part of me that felt fear unbelieving that it was my mouth that was refusing help. The part of me in control told it to shut up and go sit in the corner of my mind. I was a victim no more... a Newbe no more. Willing or no, for better or worse, I had been forged into a warrior and I would fight my own battle. More by instinct than by plan, I pulled Sasha's scarf from my pocket, holding one end in each hand. Dodging under the jaws I leapt onto the back of the Kroc, wrapping my legs around his neck like a rodeo cowboy would a bucking bronco. My knees were directly beneath his jaw. His stubby legs were made for running and swimming, not scratching the back of his neck where I held fast. Unable to reach me with tooth or claw, he opted for throwing me off. Slamming his upper body from side to side like a sledgehammer did him more damage than it did me. Still dizzy, he struck his head against the ground trying to smash me - in vain.

All the while, I was working the scarf over his head and beneath his lower jaw. Davv paused for a second to regain his equilibrium and I pulled the scarf taunt and knotted it closed, effectively locking his jaws. Feeling the pressure, Davv realized what I had done and snapped his neck forward like a bullwhip. Like a rock out of a catapult, I soared through the air and landed spinning in the sand.

Turning, I saw Davv hadn't waited until I landed to press his attack. He was bearing down on me like a runaway locomotive. Standing my ground, I waited until he was almost on top of me. Then I threw a handful of sand in his eyes, sidestepped the charge, and put my left elbow into the left side of his skull, right where his temple would be if he had one. No temple... I guess Krocs are not a very religious species. The mental pun helped me focus.

Half blind, his world reeling, Davv didn't know up from left but he could still smell me. Making sure I was downwind of the environmental unit, I waited. Davv was moving, unsteady and sluggish. I guess breakfast was finally kicking in. I waited until he was five feet away, took to the air and cuffed him in the back of the neck. My aim was off and I missed the nerve cluster. Second time was a charm. I hit it dead center and Davv was in la la land. Come morning and a couple of painkillers, he'd be none the worse for wear. Neither would I.

I saluted my opponent and the rats in the good seats with the bird but when I turned to the crowd and gave them a polite salute they booed. So I flipped them off. The lot was so happy at getting the finger that they rose as one on their collective feet and cheered. Those with digits flipped me back. I caught a glimpse of Peri and Samuel in the stands, folded over in laughter.

Last and foremost, I saluted Kerr and my personal cheering section. Kerr, Burke, Breeze, and Runner mimicked my salute. Sasha and Tarna gave the same salute as Tarna had earlier. Don bared his throat while Spike and Claw lifted six limbs and waved them in the air. Nanna glowed a bright orange while Susie, smiling, crossed the index finger of one hand over the index finger of the other and mouthed "Tisk Tisk" at my use of "bad language." The lot of them came out onto the Pit as a dozen medics carried Davv off. Hugs were exchanged as Tarna, Don, and Runner carried me for my laps around the Pit. They put me down next to Sasha, who I kissed passionately on the lips to the catcalls of the crowd.

"I will see you later to make good on my promise. I have to get back to the Empirical House," Sasha whispered. With a wave to the applauding masses, she walked off with a flare through the warriors' door. That done, I lifted Susie to my shoulders and started to carry her back to the sidelines so the siblings' match could begin. That's when the ground quake hit.

It wasn't a true quake, but the ground did shake at the impact of another figure leaving the stands in a leap and a bound. BoBo the destroyer had entered the arena and was heading my way. Cheers rose forth from the crowd. This was what the thrill seekers were hoping for. Personally, I could have lived without it. I hoped to live with it. The logical thing was to run away screaming and yelling. Problem was, if he wanted me, he would catch me. Only two externals have beaten him in the games. I checked but only could find out who one of them was: Burke's first match in the games was against BoBo. Half the stadium was destroyed in the three-day battle, but the profits from the ticket sales could have bought three stadiums.

The only person BoBo listens to is Sasha. Hiding behind her skirts seemed but a prudent and pleasurable idea at first glance, but it had a few bugs in it. Basically, she told him to stay away from me and here he was. Another order might work for a short period, but he would come after me again. Next time it might not be in front of witnesses. My body might never be identified then - no dental records here. Better to face him down here and now.

Putting Susie down, I started to amble toward the approaching

DeTang. She didn't know what was going on but she had enough sense to know it was bad news. Grabbing my pant leg, she said, "Rick, what does he want?"

"He has some business to settle with me."

"Why? What did you do?"

"I knocked him down," I answered. Susie's eyes bugged out in disbelief at me. She looked at the eight feet of stone across the Pit and looked back at me confused.

"How did you do that?" she asked. Despite the incredibility of what I said, she didn't doubt a word. She just wanted to know how. "Did you throw a banana peel in front of him?"

Despite myself, I smiled at the wisdom of a generation raised on cartoons. "No. He started a fight with me. I got lucky and pushed him. He was off balance and fell down," I said honestly. I had no reason to exaggerate for Susie. "Unfortunately, it happened in front of people and he was embarrassed."

"And now he wants to get even?"

"Yes."

"Why did he wait so long?"

"Sasha told him to behave."

"I knew she was a nice lady. Rick, just talk to him. Apologize. It is what my Mommy would say to do."

"I'll think about it. I don't think he's in a talking mood.

Susie's were wide and she was shivering. The poor girl was frightened. I wanted to reassure her but she would see through the lie. Turning around, she ran through the warriors' door like the building was on fire. Nanna followed behind "yelling" for her to stop. I guess she didn't want to see what was going to happen next. Hey, neither did I, but I was staying against my better judgment. It hurt, her leaving like that but I understood. There was nothing she could do but watch.

I resumed walking toward the pink-gowned DeTang. Every fiber in my body was trying to run away. My brain argued this was an unnatural act. Remember survival of the species? Can't do that if you're dead. Somehow I ignored it all and kept going. A morbid thought crossed my mind as I looked through the open dome at the bright sky and felt the warm sun on my face: it would be as good a day as any to die.

Kerr intercepted my path and grabbed my arm, stopping me short.

"Rick, remember when I told you the best thing to do when facing a DeTang was to keep moving?"

"Yes."

"I meant in the opposite direction."

"What do you suggest I do?" I asked hopefully. Kerr's face held no smile, only a frown.

"Run away?" he suggested half-heartedly. "No shame in doing that when faced with this superior a foe."

"I could run but I can't hide," I said. Kerr nodded slowly. "Any last-minute advice, master?"

"Confuse him with one of your bad jokes and hope for a meteor to hit him." Susie's plan had more merit.

Our paths came closer. The crowd grew silent. My not backing down had confused him last time. No such luck this time. Must have figured me for someone with a death wish. He may be right. Half-bowing with a circular flourish of the hand, I spoke.

"Greetings, Master BoBo. Welcome to the Arena. How kind of you to attend my first fight. I hoped you enjoyed it."

Like gravel grinding, he responded, "I hope you are ready for your second fight."

"Well, not really."

"Too bad," he said. The crowd watched with anticipation. The Muridae watched with smiles. Kerr watched in disbelief. I would have loved to be watching fifty miles away in the Outlands.

"Would it help if I apologized for what happened?"

"No."

"You did start it for no good reason."

"I will finish it for the same no good reason."

"I was a guest, invited by your mistress. I believe she had spoken to you regarding this?" BoBo stopped for a minute and seemed deep in thought. It was actually quite shallow, as it only lasted thirty seconds. As he started toward me again, a second gravelly voice boomed out. The crowd rose to its feet and began chanting the name of my savior. "Burke!"

"Stop, deviant," Burke ordered. BoBo was shaken. The Muridae looked scared. A DeTang vs. a human was a crowd pleaser. Messy, but a crowd-pleaser nonetheless. Two DeTang could literally bring the house down. The ticket sales for the Newbe matches were a mere fraction of that of a single DeTang match, let alone a double. Any property damage would come out of their profits. They stood as if to intervene, however, seeing the determination on both stone faces, they decided to wait for a better moment.

"Burke," BoBo said simply.

"You no longer have the right to address me by name. You who dishonor our people's way by doing battle with any who ask for a mere profit."

"We cannot all be wealthy like you."

"I earned my wealth. With honor by my efforts. It was not given to me. You will not harm Rick Wagner. I will not permit it."

Thank you, God. "Thank you, Burke," I said. Burke nodded curtly in return, never taking his eyes off BoBo.

BoBo seemed to have lost the urge to fight a fair fight.

"But I am here on a matter of honor," BoBo insisted. Burke laughed, unbelieving. "Rick Wagner has dishonored me."

"Impossible to do something that had been done for some time now."

"Exactly. By defeating me in combat, he has gained my respect. One who has gained my respect is worthy of the gift. Combat may be initiated. Is that not the way of the DeTang?"

"Yes," Burke said, suspiciously.

"Really, I am not worthy of such respect," I said. I was ignored by BoBo. Burke didn't do the same.

"Actually you are, Rick which is why I am facing off against one of my own people for your sake. Had I thought you wished it, I would have chosen you instead for my next combat. If what this miserable creature says is true, I am honor bound not to stop it. Even such as he deserves the chance to be brought back to the fold."

'I speak with the utmost sincerity," BoBo added.

"Very well. The gift shall be granted."

"Burke!" I screamed. My earlier bravado was fading faster than a puddle of blood in the Pit sand. He winked at me.

"The gift shall be granted only if certain provisions are made. The Terran is a warrior of the new games. Therefore, the rules of these games shall be followed by both combatants: it shall not be a match to the death. No permanent injuries shall be given. The result of the battle shall be the end of this matter, never to be brought up again. The training master may end the fight if he deems necessary. Kerr shall act as such for Rick. Does the opponent wish a training master appointed for him?"

"No."

"Very well. I shall enforce these rules on both parties by inflicting any violations on the violator."

BoBo seemed shocked at this. "You would kill your sibling over this bag of flesh?"

"Without hesitation."

Burke had done his best. For him, I knew honor meant more than life, mine or his. He had manipulated events so I would survive the experience and be able to be mended by the medics. Not as good as shaking hands and forgetting the matter, but a whole lot better than before.

"If I might make a request, honored Warriors," Dortew interrupted from his throne. "The human Rick Wagner must be exhausted from first fight. Might it not be best to schedule the match for another time so he might be rested and at his best?" This might seem like a break from the Muridae's sadistic nature but it wasn't. The only thing the Muridae like more than causing pain is making a profit. If the fight was postponed, they could charge for it, probably get the city to pay for the Skyvid. They would get no argument from me. BoBo was another matter.

"No. The battle will be now," he said, emphasizing the words by clapping his hands together. Lacking a better alternative, I dropped back into a fighting stance. Before events could progress, a white blur interceded itself between BoBo and me. Don was facing off against BoBo with his teeth bared and hissing.

"Don, what are you doing?" I asked incredulously.

"You stood up for me against bully. I do the same for you," he responded. This was not the same. Dreg had been putting down Don at dinner one evening, insulting his intelligence. Don had very limited experience with verbal sparring. I had it down to an art form, so I ripped into Dreg. Left eventually without a comeback, Dreg stormed off. Don said he was grateful. We were fast friends after that. Especially with our shared history as Xiles and forced indentured Newbes. Kerr even made sure we were assigned to the same squad.

On his homeworld, only one being had ever stuck up for him. Here, there was no reason for anyone to defend him because of his size and strength. I never expected this. His survival instincts were too strong. But there he was trying to protect me from harm. I was almost speechless. I would rather take the blows and as I stood in front of him I told him so.

"Thank you, my friend, but this is my fight. I cannot let you be harmed protecting me."

"You cannot stop me," Don responded. He had a point there. "DeTang BoBo, why do you not let Rick rest so he may face you fresh?"

"Because I want him now."

"No, because he is afraid," Tarna said, bringing herself out so she was between us and BoBo.

"Lies! I fear no one," he bellowed, but he was aware of the murmurs of the crowds who had heard Tarna's words and of Bob and Ned discussing the possibility for all to hear.

The remaining three members of our squad, not wishing to be left out of our suicide pact, took up places in front of Tarna.

"I'm glad to hear that," Breeze said. "That means you will not mind giving Rick adequate time to rest."

"Or if you do, you realize you will be facing all of us instead of just Rick," Runner added. Each of the siblings brought themselves up to their full seven foot plus height and each stared into a separate stone eye. The team match allowed weapons without an edge, so they each held a battle staff in front of them. Spike looked with menace at the DeTang but remained silent.

"Fine. I will take on all of you and win."

"Don't bet on it," came a voice from behind the blue man mountain. He spun to find Kerr's smiling face waiting.

"Kerr, I am surprised. Newbes cannot be expected to know any better. But an experienced Warrior like yourself violating battle etiquette like this is surprising."

"A reasonable request has been made of you. I suggest you follow it," Kerr said curtly.

"If I choose not to?"

"Then you will have a real fight on your hands," Kerr added, with a grin.

"Yes, you will," Burke added. "If you decide to fight these Newbes and Warriors, I will join them against you."

"What?" BoBo asked.

"I may believe you respect Rick, and possibly even Kerr, but you do not know these others. Therefore, you could have no respect for them and you are again back to your deviant ways."

When Burke finished talking, the lot of us encircled BoBo, wordlessly and in perfect coordination. Kerr looked on with pride at the good technique we used as he joined the circle. BoBo looked nervously around, his glance lingering overly long on Burke. He could hear the whispers of "coward" emanating from the stands and the announcers. With a sigh, he conceded.

"Very well. Rick, you may have your rest."

The squad roared in triumph, but the Muridae on the dais let out whoops that made our yells seem like they came from church mice. With this kind of buildup in their commercials for the match, profit should be phenomenal.

Just then, Susie broke through our circle, with Sasha in tow. Running up to BoBo, Susie looked him right in the kneecap and demanded, "Don't you dare hurt Rick!" Susie had a fierceness in her eyes that was terrible to behold. She had not run away. She had gone for help.

"Or what?" BoBo asked, bending over so he was looking her straight in the eye in a threatening manner. The lot of us tensed up. We had been through this before. No one but no one threatens or hurts our Susie. Turns out yet another shared our sentiment.

"Or you'll be out on the street," Sasha said. BoBo had not backed down from even Burke. At Sasha's words, he cringed. "And don't you dare touch that child."

"Mistress, I did not think you would be here."

"Obviously that is why you waited for me to leave the arena before you issued your challenge. Why did you disobey me?"

"Mistress, you said I was not to harm Rick in the Empirical House or on the streets. You said nothing of challenging him to a game."

"Well, I am saying it now."

"Mistress, it is too late. A match has been agreed upon."

"BoBo, it's okay. I don't want to get you in trouble. We can call off the match," I graciously offered.

With an evil look, touched with jealousy, he turned on me and said, "No."

"If the match is already arranged, then it must go on." BoBo smiled at Sasha's words. "But BoBo, I am disappointed in you. Instead of listening to the spirit of my words, you took them literally in order to find a loophole. Will I have to make all my words literal from now on?"

"No, Mistress. It will not happen again."

"It better not. You best get back to the Empirical House."

"Yes, mistress," BoBo groveled. With nary a backward glance, he turned and left through the warrior's door, his head hung low in shame.

"Sorry about that, Rick. BoBo has too much pride sometimes but he is a good person. He just acts without thinking more often than not. Underneath all that gruff he is soft-hearted. He would do anything for a friend."

"Guess I don't fall in that category." I thought about saying more but decided against it. Sasha was nothing if not loyal. She would defend BoBo against any criticism, even mine. I respected her for that.

"As far as BoBo goes, no. But more than a few people here seem more than proud to call you friend."

Looking around at the smiling faces, I knew she was right. The air was thick with emotion. Every person in the bunch had just risked their life for me. Money could not buy such dedication. Nothing could. It had to be freely given. I was the luckiest man I knew. What does one say at such a moment? Flowery words filled my heart but when I opened my mouth to share them, all I could whisper was "Thanks" through misty vision.

Wordlessly, they let me know I was welcome. Don licked my face and I hugged his thick neck. Tarna and Breeze fell, each in the folds of a separate arm and held me tight. Susie squeezed my leg in a bear hug. Runner came up behind me and wrapped his arms around all of us. Spike did the same but used six arms. Still, on the inside of the group, Don snaked his tail out and wrapped it around Runner and Spike. The lot of us just stood there, holding on tight, making the outside world fade away for just a little while. Sasha, Kerr, Burke, and Nanna looked on as did the audience, many of whom gave us a standing ovation. Goes to show that not every game-goer is a bloodthirsty maniac out to get his kicks vicariously. Some have a heart that can be touched.

Dortew, unfamiliar with the concepts being displayed below, stood and addressed the assembled.

"Disperse and clear the playing field immediately," he demanded. We stood unmoving, ignoring his order. He repeated it but was cut short by Burke.

"Leave them be."

"This is a battlefield, not a love nest. I will have it cleared," Dortew countered.

Burke smiled, then turned to Kerr and placed an arm around his friend's shoulder. Kerr returned the favor by putting two arms around Burke's waist and the other two around Sasha's. Burke placed his free arm atop Nanna's plasm. A limb sprang forth from her whole and folded itself around Burke and Kerr. Together they walked forward and joined our group embrace. We gladly made room.

Many of those in the audience ceased their applause and instead turned their limbs to a better use. Holding on tight to their loved ones.

Friends held friends. Strangers embraced strangers and were strangers no more. Tarna's father held each of his children close to him and told each how special they were and how much he cared although he did not need to. Love shone from his eyes, even through his tears. Even the Muridae announcers, Bob and Ned, embraced and stopped their bantering. Their Muridae in the field, Stan'noo, tried to interview us unsuccessfully.

At the edge of hearing, Dortew continuing his yelling, none of it making a bit of difference except to make us hold on tighter. That may be the meaning of life or at least the secret to surviving it. When life screams at you and tries to take you down, grab hold of your friends and hold on as tight as you can. For that moment, life cannot harm you, safe in the arms and limbs of those who love you. Dortew's voice became an annoying buzz. It and all other noise faded to silence as plasm surrounded us. Nanna had embraced the lot of us and taken us into her whole. We stayed that way for an eternity. No matter what happened in the future, for that brief moment in eternity all was right with our world.

DREG

"Death to the enemies of the Aryan race!"

The infirmary still held the aroma of dried blood, pain, and the telltale odor of antiseptic. Hours earlier it had been filled with the end results of the Newbe matches. Victor and defeated alike had need of the medics' attention. The majority were treated and sent on their way, most to join in the reveling and celebrations abounding throughout the Warplex.

"The Man will escape and he will triumph over you godless creatures. Jesus will see to that."

The sounds that rung loud in these halls were not those of celebration. Three Newbes' wounds required overnight healing. Nothing life threatening, but Muridae do not let their investments wander about in less than premium condition. A female Aprahoe and a male G'morran were sleeping soundly, nutrient and protein flowtubes pouring into their injured areas as carefully controlled UV radiation was shined upon the wounds. The UV speeded the healing by doubling the rate of mitosis in the healing tissue while the harmful, potentially cell mutating rays were filtered out as much as possible. Their sound slumber was surprising, considering the screaming and cursing of the infirmary's third patient.

"Hellspawn! Demons! Liberals! Untie me, scumbags!" bellowed Dreg as he struggled helplessly at his bonds. His yells and curses had been flying fast and furious for so many hours that the sound faded into the background. Nobody in earshot was left unaware of his views on externals and internals or of the fact that because he continually had pulled out his flowtubes that he was restrained forcibly to his bed. Using their professional judgment, the medics decided he had sustained a mild concussion so he needed to be kept awake for the next day, so to their ultimate dismay they were unable to sedate him.

When insults failed, he switched to threats every ten minutes like clockwork.

"I'll burn this place to the ground. I'll slice off your heads and piss down your throats," Dreg informed the uninterested what he would do. Finally, to his surprise, he got some attention. The infirmary was white wall-to-wall, save one darkened area. From that dark, a pinstriped shadow flowed forth from the wall to stand by his bedside. In addition to a dark two-piece suit, dark shirt, and white tie, the shade wore a severe frown which silently radiated disdain for the piece of trash he looked down upon.

"Quit your whining and act like a man," the shade hissed.

"I'm more of a man than you'll ever be, Savage," Dreg shot back to his bedside visitor. His words and tone of voice didn't sit well with their intended target. Savage grabbed Dreg's hand, the one that Tarna's back kick had shattered while separating Dreg from his knife, in a viselike grip and squeezed.

"That hit to your head must have been harder than it looked if you think you can get away with talking to me like that," Savage answered, gripping the hand tighter as he spoke. Dreg's face reddened and contorted in agony until it looked like it would fold in on itself. Dreg knew what he had to do to stop the pain, but he would not say the word. Pride fought pain. Pride lost.

Dreg whispered "Sorry" and the new pain faded as quickly as it had begun. The old pain rushed back in to take its place. The medics had been so impressed by Dreg's kind words that they had only given him a fraction of the painkillers he was allowed.

Savage looked down silently in judgment on his fellow Terran and found him wanting. Dreg, despite initial displays to the contrary, was intimated and withered under his glance. Fidgeting, Dreg turned away, quietly speaking.

"I'm sorry about the fight, Savage."

"Mr. Savage."

"Sorry, Mr. Savage... but the bitch cheated."

"Cheated? If anyone cheated, it was you. You who broke from the code of honor. You who brought a weapon into a hand to hand fight. You who lost miserably despite your promise that you'd win."

"I apologized. What more do you want? Blood?"

Savage smiled. Dreg, feeling his impotence at the ties that bound him, gave an involuntary shiver. Matching his glare against that of Savage was a battle he couldn't win, so he switched tactics and gave his best look of abject pity. He did his best to imitate the look of a scared puppy. It was a look he knew well. It was the look his victims had always given him before he ended their life. Savage was unmoved by the display.

"Blood would be too easy on you; I have something worse in mind.

We are no longer partners. You have no way to get out of your contract now. You will be the servant of a race of rats for the next ten years."

"Wait! Today was a fluke. We can still do business."

"No, we cannot."

"Sure, we can. I'll even throw a fight. Please don't leave me to these creatures."

"Pity. That's how life goes down. Some I win, some you lose. Goodbye."

"Wait, don't leave me like this! Anything would be better, even death."

"Okay, if that is the way you feel," Savage replied, raising his hand into a knife blow position. Dreg saw the blow, realized what Savage intended to do and screamed in abject terror.

"You wouldn't!" Savage remained silent, towering over the reclined figure. "We aren't alone. The others will stop you. Medic...anyone... Help!"

"Scream all you want. Nobody cares. You've made no friends here. Nobody will save you. They are too used to your screams to pay them any attention. In fact, I would be willing to wager that some of them would pay me just to end your caterwauling."

Dreg began to tremble and shake because he knew Savage's words were true. He would die here so far from home, friendless and alone. No one would mourn his passing; some might even celebrate it. Fear gripped him in the pit of his gut. His mouth was as dry as a desert wind. The hand loomed over his head like the angel of death. Savage pulled back his hand to chamber; Dreg had not learned much from Spear, but he knew that was the position used before a blow was struck. Pulling against his bonds until his arms felt like they were going to break availed him not. Screaming, Dreg closed his eyes and turned his head waiting for the blow.

The screams lasted for minutes and the echoes even longer but no blow came. He heard a whisper. "You're not even worth the effort."

When he opened his eyes, only shades of dark on white walls threatened him. Savage was gone.

The fear lasted for a little while longer than slowly it transformed from wounded pride to embarrassment which begot a slow, burning anger. The familiar feeling of hate soon followed, bringing Dreg back to his own brand of reality. Dreg's little mind, cluttered as it was with petty hatreds, made room for this big one. Only one thought possessed him: to make Savage pay for this humiliation. Him and the traitor Rick. The method would come to him later, but for now, the thought would do. Besides, there was something that needed to be taken care of first.

"Medic, I need a bedpan. And some wet towels. Now, damn it! If you alien bastards are going to keep me tied down, the least you can do is keep me clean."

No one listened. Nor cared. Nor came.

RICK

The boulder masquerading as a fist arced through the air, missing my head by inches. As I tucked and rolled, I tried a body sweep. I would have more luck pushing down the Warplex. Nothing else so far had worked, so I tried begging.

"Burke, please."

"No, Rick. I am truly sorry, but I cannot," Burke said, lunging toward me again. I backed away quickly. Burke missed me by almost two feet. His heart was not in the attack.

"But you have been training me for almost two weeks now."

"Yes. I have been training you on how to face a superior opponent, a stronger foe. You have won your last two matches."

"Yea, against a G'morran and an Aprahoe. A male Aprahoe at that. They're much weaker than the females. Neither was in the class of a DeTang. Why can't you train me to fight BoBo?"

"Honor forbids me from training an outsider to face a child of the great mountain, even that deviant. I have taught you techniques that will aid you. I will personally monitor the match and make sure BoBo does not kill you. I can do no more. My actions thus far have been questionable, but they have been done because of friendship - that can never be considered dishonorable."

"Is there anything I could say or do that could change your mind?" I asked. Burke nodded in the negative. I was doomed. No two ways about it. I tried one last plea. "Burke, you are my last hope."

"You give Pebble too much credit. Will erode his face. Make him smooth, looking old before his time."

"Red!" I said turning to face the front eye of the smiling, crimson barkeep.

"Burke, you have done all you could for the boy. Time for a real warrior to take over," Red said. I resented the boy comment, but it was accurate in this company. My quarter of a century didn't measure up to Red's ninety-three years or Burke's six hundred plus. From their point of view, Susie and I were almost the same age. "Fleabag said Rick needed help against the molehill."

"Absolutely! Where is Kerr, anyway?"

"Fleabag is watching Red's Place so Red can be here. Damn Czarrian is going to imbibe every last cent of profit from the day." Probably an understatement. "Rick better be appreciative."

"I am, believe me. Do you have experience fighting DeTang?" My question brought thirty seconds of laughter.

"Ask the Pebble."

"Burke?"

"He does, Rick. He and I fought to a standstill. Twice. Once in the Games and once…"

"Elsewhere," interrupted Red.

"Did you ever face BoBo?"

"Yes. For the longer part of an afternoon."

"And?"

"Red was the victor. BoBo does not care for Red much now. Can't figure out why." Red laughed. Red was the warrior whose record of victory against BoBo I couldn't find. Wonder what happened to it?

"Do you think you can teach me to beat him?" I asked.

"No."

"Oh."

"But what Red thinks is not important. What Rick thinks is. Does Rick think he can beat BoBo?"

"No."

"Then Rick has not got the chance of water passing Red's lips. Does Rick think Rick can fight BoBo to a draw?"

"If he doesn't show up."

"Ah. Planning on surviving?"

"Definitely."

"That is a start. Gives us something to build on. Now if Pebble will excuse us, can't have Pebble learning all Red's secrets. Might be a number three."

"Anytime, warrior," Burke said with a genuine, friendly smile. For him, a fight is a gift to be granted, a bonding experience. Kerr and he have a special relationship which resulted in no small part from their match. For him to have fought Red twice is amazing. Red placed his two left hands on my right shoulder and led me out of the Pit.

"Where are you going with Rick?" asked Burke.

"The Terran has enough handicaps so I'm taking Rick out of this playground to a real fighting arena."

"Where is that?" Burke asked indignantly, as the Pit had been more than adequate for his purposes.

"To Red's Place, of course. One hour of tending bar will teach Terran more fighting skills than two days here. Besides, someone has to watch Kerr to make sure he does not drink poor Red out of bar and home," said Red. "Would Rick's squadmates be willing to come also? The lunch rush is almost over and we will not have enough patrons to practice on until after sunset falls."

"I'm sure they would."

"Good. Red plans to take the lot of you through Abbandon on the way."

"Abbandon is in the third ring," I said with great apprehension.

"Exactly. Even DeTang think twice before wallowing in Abbandon."

"I don't think that is such a good idea, Red."

"Nonsense. It is a technique I used in training the fleabag. Look where he is today."

"Tending bar."

"Exactly," Red answered patting me on my back for my intuitiveness. Truth be told, I didn't see the point. Red sensed my hesitation. This observation was aided greatly by another observation. I had stopped dead in my tracks. "What is the matter? Does Rick not trust Red?" Actually, I did. Kerr and Burke both trusted him. I trusted them. Ipso-facto, I trusted Red by association. Sighing, I picked up the pace and, with some reservation, headed toward Abbandon.

RICK

Midday and the street was deserted. We were just three blocks off of Northway, one of the four safe roads. The change was dramatic. Northway had hustle and bustle. Abbandon seemed, well, abandoned. Buildings were boarded up. Not a soul on the street in plain sight save the squad and Red. I waited for the tumbleweeds to roll by. They never came; probably got mugged on the way over. Appearances aside, we weren't alone. The alleys were occupied as were the lower rooftops. I mentioned this to Red, but he was unconcerned.

"Pretend to ignore them. Otherwise, they may let a group of this size travel unmolested."

"Sounds good to me."

Red stared at me with his rear eye, a sort of hindsight, then looked down to check on Lady Sally. The keg was unchanged, save perhaps being a few quarts lighter than when we began this quest. "Quiet. Take note of their numbers and positions but do not react. Most likely they will wait until we reach the clearing."

The clearing was the only part of the street without a ruin or rubble. The lesson for the unwary traveler to learn from this seemed obvious to me so I decided to share my wisdom. "Beware of wreckless Abbandon." Red glared, and I turned my attention to census taking.

Runner and I made out four, Don and Spike five. Tarna and Breeze saw eight. Red told us there were no less than ten. Ten to seven odds. Not bad odds, but not good ones. We were unarmed. Were they? Red was going to ensure we learned the answer. How this would help me against a DeTang was an answer that eluded me. Of the squad, only Don was not apprehensive. Abbandon apparently was a field trip compared to a Kroc swamp. I made a mental note never to visit Don's home.

The stalkers were being too cautious for Red's sensibilities.

"Stagger, act drunk. They think we are out looking for trouble."

"We are."

"Convince them otherwise."

Like, good little warriors, we did as we were told. Spike and Don reeled into separate walls, shaking loose some mortar in the process. The siblings did a rain dance. Tarna joined me in a few chorus' of "I was a freeze dried Goot until I got in heat." She taught me three rowdy verses I hadn't heard before. Red winced at the sound. My voice I understood...

I could not carry a tune if it had handles, but Tarna's voice was good. She often sang Susie to sleep at night, albeit with a different song. At least when Nanna was in hearing distance.

The stalkers must have enjoyed the show because they came out of the shadows and into the daylight. Forming a semicircle which, had we let it, would herd us toward a wall too tall for even Spike to climb.

"Drunken travelers having lost their way. Pity," muttered one of them. I didn't recognize his race. Actually, of the eleven – Red had missed one – I only recognized the species of three: Two Muridae and a male of the same race as Wheels, Savage's driver. I expected banter, threats, and demands. Instead, there was only quiet as they moved on most of us one to one: Spike and Red rated two attackers, while Don had a whopping three opponents.

We all maintained the drunken act until they were in striking distance. Then the predators became our prey. Red was the first to engage the foe. One minute his two were standing upright, the next, they were resting uncomfortably in a single hole in the wall that was not there previously. The siblings didn't even slow down but instead switched the mode of their dance from rain to war. Without missing a step, they took out their pair. Tarna and I made our victories quick and simple. Don and Spike had each knocked out one opponent and were playing catch with the remaining three like a couple of jugglers. Moves like that would go over big in a match. Claw would probably chastise Spike for having fun. The juggling went on longer than it should have. The jugglees got loose from the patterns and each pulled a blade. Two were laid low the instant the glint of metal flashed in the sunlight; the third was quicker than his comrades and moved out of range. The advantage of surprise was lost and no amount of searching would ever find it again.

Despite the infrequency of matches involving weapons, I was well trained in their use. This external held the shiv correctly. We were not dealing with an amateur. I didn't want anyone to be seriously hurt, so I took out my surprise weapon. Kerr had familiarized me with the weapons code of the city... almost everything was banned. That didn't stop weapons from being bought or made. It just increased the price so the common criminal had to make do with a homemade knife. Being homemade didn't make it any less deadly. Still, my weapon, entirely legal, would neutralize the effectiveness of the blade. I took the circlet, which Samuel had given me, out of my pocket. Tarna gave me a strange look.

"Rick, I did not know you cared. But now is not the time or the place," she joked, referring to the force field condom I was holding.

"Sorry to disappoint you Tarna, but it's not for you. It's for him," I said, referring to the knife-wielding attacker. At this, everyone else, Red included, looked at me as if I had two heads. Not that two-headed beings were an uncommon site. One of the fallen foes was literally two-faced.

"Trust me," I said with a smile.

"My father told me never to trust a man who said that," Tarna said.

"My mother said the same thing about a woman who told me to trust her," Runner added.

Ignoring them, I expanded the circlet until its diameter was wider than that of my head. Making sure it was facing the right way, I lowered it down until I was wearing it as a necklace. The field, once activated, bathed my body from the neck down in a soft glow, barely noticeable in the sunlight.

"Damn Terrans don't even know how to use sex toys right," Red grumbled to no one in particular.

I approached the external holding the knife cautiously. He looked at me as if I were mad. Why should he think of me any differently than my friends? As soon as I was in striking distance, he lunged toward my midsection. I made no move to stop him. A collective scream rose up from the squad. Red gave a slight smile as he realized what I was doing. The knife hit the glow around my abdomen and slid harmlessly off. All I felt was a soft pressure. The attacker looked first at his knife then at me. There was fear in his eyes. Doing my best to feed his fear, I gave my best Kerr smile and disarmed him with my right hand. Holding the blade and the hilt I squeezed and it bent in half. Poor quality. Probably made out of a metal can. A strong child could have folded it. This was lost on the attacker as he looked up at me in awe. As I raised my hand up, I half hoped he would faint away. No such luck. I had to hit him twice. He would have a headache and a story to tell when he woke.

I turned around, expecting praise and accolades. Instead, I got knocked on my butt by Tarna. I bounced twice.

"How could you pull a stunt like that, you idiot! You could have been killed!" Tarna yelled.

"I wasn't," I responded with a smile. Infuriated, Tarna gave me a swift kick in the leg. It tickled. Her concern was touching in a brutal sort of way.

"Tarna is right, Rick," Red said. "It was a stupid stunt. What if the field did not hold? Fleabag would never forgive Red."

"I knew it would hold. I tested it against a sword and it held."

"Fleabag let you use his warblade?"

"No, not his warblade. A sparring sword he has in his quarters. He was teaching me how to fence. I borrowed it for an hour. If it held against a Czarrian sword there is no way a two-bit tin knife going to hurt it."

"How did you know the increased field size would not diminish the strength?" Breeze asked. Spike was looking on in confusion. As a drone, he had never been exposed to the concept of birth control.

"If I expanded the field much more it could be partially penetrated. I'd tried positioning it higher up under my chin to up around the sides and top of my head. The field covered all of my body, except my face. It lost too much potency. Like that it was not safe to use."

"It is safe to use now?" Red asked, with a smile.

"Of course. Why do you ask?" I said. Just then the glow flickered and faded to nothing.

"No reason," Red said smugly. "Better make sure you carry fresh batteries. Increasing the size of the field increases the power drain exponentially. At normal size, the power supply lasts for years. At body size, it lasts a matter of hours. Ask Samuel, whom Red is sure gave it to you. He has pulled that stunt before. You got off much luckier than he did. Samuel's died in the middle of a firefight."

Having seen the field fade, Tarna kicked me again.

"Ow!" I yelled. Smiling, Tarna nodded her head once and she and Breeze started walking back toward Northway. Runner laughed. Don asked where he could get a field but I explained it barely had enough power to protect his tail. Red ordered us back into formation, catching up with the ladies.

"Fighting is thirsty work. Sally needs a refill."

We headed back to Red's place, unmolested. At least until we walked in the door and I got behind the bar. Being a Newbe barkeep was much more challenging and dangerous than being a Newbe warrior. No rules or code of honor apply and the battles seemed nonstop. Only two patrons even tipped me the entire evening, one quite literally. By the time the night was over, I would almost have preferred to face BoBo than spend another hour tending bar. Maybe that was Red's purpose. Maybe not. Only time would tell.

DREG

Dreg stood silently outside the chamber door, revulsion battling hatred, aided by the specter of greed. The decision had already been made before his arrival. He was just using the heat of his inner battle to warm his cold feet. The plan he had was nothing new back on Earth. In fact, it was one of the older scams. Dreg hoped that perhaps it was new on Tore. It wasn't, but his angle offered possibilities that had not existed previously, at least for him and the Muridae he hoped to make his partner. Vengeance had allowed him justification for trying to ally himself with his tormentor. The question remained: would Smed'lee reward his initiative by meeting his demands or with unending pain. There was but one way to find out. Dreg knocked loudly on the chamber door.

It remained closed, ignoring him completely. Retaliating against the slight he knocked again, louder this time. The door stood unmoving, mocking him in its stillness. Clenching both hands into fists, Dreg pounded hard and furious until he could hear the echoes sounding within. Stilling battering the door, he began to shout.

"Open up, rat face."

At his words, the door slid open swifter than if he had said *open sesame*. The space where the door had been was now filled with Smed'lee, a pink polka dot and striped cloak hanging from his rounded shoulders. His hand held the NG. Without a word, the Muridae pointed the device at Dreg and pushed the button. He watched smiling as the Dirtling fell to the ground, convulsing. Smed'lee savored the simple pleasure that raking the human's body with pain gave. Having his fill, Smed'lee turned his back and returned to his sanctum, leaving the NG in the on position. The door swiftly reappeared to fill the space it had been but moments earlier.

Dreg fought the agony long enough to whisper, "Have way to make money." The door again disappeared. Smed'lee stepped out and helped Dreg to his feet, turning the NG off only as an afterthought.

"Why didn't you just say so?" Smed'lee asked with a predatory grin as he led the disoriented human into his quarters, barely allowing him enough time to avoid being hit by the door returning to its post.

SUSIE

Susie sat in the common room of Burke's suites and worried. Three of her friends would be fighting in the rats' stupid game in the morning, two of them against each other. For some unknown reason, Tarna and Burke were both happy about it. Why did they have to fight at all? Mommy and Daddy always said fighting was wrong. So did Rick, but he and everyone in her new family did it. Susie wanted to blame it all on the rats, but she knew that wasn't the only reason. All she knew is she could do nothing to stop it. Her one try hadn't worked. Smed'lee could still hurt Rick. Burke, Nanna, and even Rick had told her in no uncertain terms not to try anything like that again.

Reluctantly, Susie agreed, but Smed'lee still hurt Rick. Don too, but not as often because he listened better than Rick. Why should either of them have to? It was wrong, but nobody but Rick even questioned it. Burke, with all his strength, didn't lift a finger to stop it unless it got "excessive," whatever that meant. Burke said he had to respect the law. Susie said the law was wrong but Burke only shrugged. The only change Susie noticed was that Smed'lee never used the NG on Rick or Don when Kerr was around or the wolf put his hand on his sword. That stopped the rat and made him leave every time.

To top off everything else, she was restricted to quarters. Burke and Nanna were busy with each other and Susie was left to her own devices. Usually, that was enough. Not tonight. As if in answer to her loneliness, the door chime rang. Susie ran to the door, excited. Before opening it, she was careful to check the view screen. After seeing who it was she hit the door open switch.

"Rick!" she yelled, wrapping her arms around his neck. Rick, in turn, hugged back, lifting her off the floor and swung her in circles. Faster and faster they spun until her giggles and his laughter filled the empty room. Finally, they collapsed in a heap. Moments later, her brief rest done, Susie grabbed hold of both of Rick's ankles and tried to return the favor. Rick never left the ground although he was spun on his back for the better part of a minute.

After several more minutes of play, Rick noticed the distinct absence of Susie's guardian and babysitter.

"Susie, where are Burke and Nanna? They didn't know I'd be stopping by. I've never seen them leave you alone without anybody."

"They do it all the time when they are having sex," Susie said as if it was common knowledge. Rick's jaw, on the other hand, dropped so low it almost hit the floor.

"Huh?" was all the stunned Rick was able to mutter.

"It's okay. They turn on the security system so nobody can come in without permission."

"Susie, they can't have sex. Not with each other. They are two different species. Neither one of them is male or female."

"Sure, they can, silly. Just not like humans."

"You know how people make love?"

"Sure. Nanna explained it to me. Maybe you are right though. They are making love more than having sex."

Curiosity was stronger than embarrassment. Rick asked, "How?"

Susie began lecturing as she had often seen Nanna do. "Well, normally the Trimurti mate as a triad. The Insemanati and the Beari do the actual mating inside the whole of a Nani. When they are done, the genetic material is left in the Nani to grow and become three babies, one of each type. A Nani can even bear the young of some other races."

"Okay. That much I understand. But a DeTang mates only with itself."

"True. They lie down in a pool of magma and sleep for years until a fledgling is able to survive outside the lava. During that time, the parent teaches the child."

"There you go. They are incompatible."

"No, they're not. Let me show you." With that, Susie took Rick by the hand and led him, hesitantly at first, to Burke's night chamber. Susie bypassed the controls and manually pushed open the door just slightly. A warm fluorescent pink light shone from the heart of the darkness. The source of the glow was Nanna. She shone beautifully. Lights, sparkles, and colors danced wildly within her whole. Each one was a work of splendor. Rick literally forgot to breathe.

At the center of the kaleidoscope lay Burke, curled up in a fetal position, asleep. The part of the whole surrounding him moved and flowed like molten lava. In fact, that's what it was. It was the source of the pink light that shone forth. Rick could feel the heat and the passion which, while different than his own, was undeniable. The two humans each took the other's hand and held it tightly. Unlike their first time holding hands, they felt no fear, no terror, only joy and wonder. Together the two stood basking in the splendor laid out before them, unable to keep their eyes from their friends. Slowly, with almost palpable sorrow for leaving such wonder, they turned away shutting the door behind them.

"Wow." With a single word, Rick described what they had just witnessed. Rick pulled Susie close in a hug and they sat in silence for several minutes.

"Beautiful, isn't it?" Susie asked.

"Very," Rick answered. "Susie, when you first told me Burke and Nanna were having sex I sort of freaked out."

"I noticed," Susie said.

"I always knew I'd have to talk to you about this but I thought it would be many years from now and it would be about the birds and the bees, not Nani and DeTang."

"What's the difference?"

"Birds and bees have males and females. Only birds do it in midair and only some bees mate. There is one Queen bee who a bunch of drones fly out after. The first one who reaches her becomes her mate. Only problem is they only do it once and then parts fall off."

"Ouch."

"Definitely. To tell the truth, I never saw what that had to do with anything," The only time people mate in midair is in an airplane restroom. "But after witnessing that, I think you knowing is a good thing. You'll always think of making love as something beautiful."

"Don't you?"

No need to share what happened when I was a prisoner. "Yes, as long as it is with someone I care about. I'm a bit old-fashioned that way. But I was not always so open. I grew up half-Catholic, half-Baptist. Sex was never talked about openly, except in derogatory terms. It was dirty, it was a conquest. I had years of guilt to overcome. I was never told about love and that made all the difference. Now, I don't think you're old enough for sex."

"I understand. I don't want to. It is just interesting to know about. How old do I have to be?'

"Forty-five."

"Rick!"

"Okay... thirty-five. For my sake at least. Actually, there's no age for sex although most states back home tried to legislate one. I have never heard of two people in the heat of passion stopping and saying 'We can't do this. It is illegal.' It should happen when a person is ready, emotionally and physically. Back home, some children were having sex at ten years old. I think that's too young. I wouldn't have been able to handle it at that age. Meanwhile, there are people who chose to remain a virgin until they are thirty-five or older. A noble endeavor but again not one that I could handle. Many people believe two people should wait until they are married. I think each person has to decide for themselves when they are ready."

"How will I know when I am ready?"

"When the time and the person comes, you'll know. Just promise me you'll talk to someone when it does. It doesn't have to be me. I just want to make sure nothing bad happens to you."

"You mean like getting pregnant or getting AIDS?"

"Exactly. How do you know about that?"

"Teacher showed us a film about it at school. Mommy had to sign a permission slip so I could watch it."

"That's good. We don't know if anyone who came away from Earth is infected, so everyone has to be careful."

"Rick, have you and Sasha made love yet?"

"Getting a little personal there aren't you, squirt?"

"You don't have to answer if you do not want to."

"I know. I don't know why we're even having this conversation. An hour ago, I would've been too embarrassed. No, we haven't. But don't think I'm going to come running to you to tell you if and when we do."

'Okay. Don't expect me to, either. You be careful, too. I don't want anything to happen to you."

"Fair enough."

"Rick, does it bother you that she's not human?"

"A little."

"Dreg said it was unnatural. But he's an idiot. What do you think, Rick?"

"I think there are going to be problems with any interspecies romance. But there is something more important than species and that's love. I love you and you're human. But I love Kerr and Tarna and the rest of the squad."

"Me too. And Burke and Nanna."

"As do I. Could you love them more if they were human?"

"No."

"Me neither. So, what difference does it make? Love may not conquer all but it can put up one heck of a fight."

"If you get married, will you be able to have babies?"

"I honestly don't know. Now it's about time you went to sleep."

"But I don't want to."

"You need your rest."

"I will if you tell me a story."

"No can do, kiddo. I need my sleep too. It's past my bedtime."

Rick tucked Susie in and kissed her goodnight on her forehead.

"Are you sure you won't tell me a story. You and Breeze tell the best stories."

"It's too late. If I don't get some rest Kerr will have my hide. Tomorrow after the match."

"And a tea party too?"

"And a tea party too."

"Promise?"

"Cross my heart."

"Rick, BoBo won't hurt you, will he? And don't say something nice because I'm a kid. I turn nine in two weeks you know."

"I know. Susie, BoBo will try to hurt me but I'll be trying harder to make sure he doesn't succeed. Burke will be watching to make sure things don't get out of hand so the worst that could happen are several broken bones."

"I hate it when you get hurt."

"Me too. Not a lot we can do about it, though."

"I'd fight him for you if it would help."

"I know. I'd rather get hurt than let anything happen to you."

"Good luck tomorrow, Rick."

"Thanks, Susie. I'll take all the help I can get."

Rick went to leave but no matter how many times he hit the switch the door remained locked. Seeing this, Susie jumped out of bed and ran to the switch and hit it with her tiny hand. The door obediently slid open.

"When the security system is on only Nanna, Burke, and me can open the door," Susie offered by way of explanation.

Goodnights were exchanged and the door locked behind Rick. Susie snuggled back under the still warm covers of her bed. Seconds later the door chimes rang. Susie rushed to the door and hit the open switch saying "Did you change your mind about reading me a story, Rick?"

The man facing her wasn't Rick. Susie started to run and scream but Dreg was upon her, forcing a chemically treated cloth over her nose and mouth. Susie's last thought before losing consciousness was that Burke was going to kill her for not looking at the view screen. Susie's struggles soon ceased.

Lifting her tiny body, Dreg ran off like a bat out of hell. In his wake, a klaxon of alarms were sounding in response to Susie leaving without Burke or Nanna present. The pursuit soon followed but it was too late. Dreg and his unwilling passenger had disappeared and no trace would be found.

BURKE

The mood in Burke's quarters was frantic. A search of the Warplex revealed nothing. No trace of Susie was found. The outer security system cameras had been disabled, so it was useless in trying to figure out where the kidnapper had gone. The Muridae system was also conveniently off-line along a path to the nearest exit. Burke would have been tearing down every block of the Muridae living quarters, for they were his first suspects, save for the playback on his quarters' internal cameras. The kidnapper was no Muridae. It was the human Dreg who the cameras showed as the culprit. Burke still did not eliminate the Muridae as suspects but they were less likely. Dreg's disdain for all things not human was no secret. The thought of him working with the Muridae was far-fetched.

A puddle of blue plasm littered the center floor. Nanna had collapsed into this state upon seeing the captured images. She revealed what Dreg had tried to do to Susie and her part in hiding the truth from Burke. Burke's fury was already terrible to behold but after hearing this it intensified. Burke trembled with anger and his tremblings shook the very foundations on which he stood. His anger was not directed at Nanna however, for he knew she was correct in what she did. He would have killed Dreg and the Muridae would have leverage against him.

The fury was directed at one source... Dreg. The human would not survive his next meeting with the DeTang. The chances of that meeting seemed slim and as time passed the odds became smaller. Burke was at his sanity's end. He knew of no way to trace Dreg. Nanna was in a worse state, having withdrawn almost completely. Only habit kept her limp form in a solid state.

Knowing he needed a clear mind to call on, he had summoned Kerr. The Czarrian had come quickly and added his efforts to the search with no greater success than Burke had. Kerr had however thought to check the warrior dorms for Dreg but he found no trace. One thing about the whole situation nagged at Kerr.

"It makes no sense, Burke. Why would he do such a thing? There is no clear motive or way to profit from this."

Burke was not so fortunate. He explained to Kerr the incident of perversion that Nanna had relayed to him. Kerr's anger almost matched Burke's own.

"Do you think that is why?"

"I do not know," Burke said sadly. "I pray to the great mountain that it is not."

The communications center in the corner of the room chose that moment to beep, signaling an incoming message. It was scrambled and because Burke was unprepared he was unable to use his security system to trace it.

Burke looked at the message and his trembling slowed, although it did not cease. Burke seemed almost relieved in a way. Kerr noticed this.

"What is it? Good news?" asked Kerr.

"In a way. It says if I ever want to see Susie alive again I have to lose my match with Tarna tomorrow."

"How is that good news? For you to purposefully throw a match would be the greatest sin against honor that a DeTang could commit. You would be a greater deviant than your fallen sibling, BoBo," said Kerr. Burke glared at the reminder of his own relationship with the deviant. The glare did not last long. It seemed unimportant now.

"Yes, but it means greed, not depravity, was the reason for the taking," Burke said. Kerr nodded understandingly.

"What will you do?" asked Kerr.

"Whatever is necessary," Burke answered, his head bowed in shame at his admission that something was more important to him than his honor. Kerr laid a pair of consoling hands on Burke's stony shoulder.

"Burke, we are in over our heads. We need help."

"I agree. The message specifically states we are not to call the Guardsmen."

"Shall I contact Troubell? It is the type of thing he does and Susie is one of his people."

"Yes."

"I'll go to Red's and leave a message," Kerr said. Going to Red's was the only way to leave a message. Red did not believe in or own a communications board. The Roserod belief was if the message is not important enough to deliver in person it was not important enough to spend the time listening to. "You try to call his office and contact him that way. I will also leave one for Jake," Burke frowned at this. "I realize you do not approve of what he stands for but he cares for the child and he has more resources than the Guardsmen."

Jake and the Web stood for the common man against government, business, and any other overwhelming force. DeTang traditionally believed the will of a government to be a law immutable save by the same body that made it. Burke bought into the aristocracy of Tore for that reason. As one of only three Tore Lords, he ranked only below the Tetrarch himself and was in a position to change injustice as a member of the government. Jake, by way of contrast, fought everything government stood for. His entire existence was subverting the laws because that is what he judged to be important. Their views were miles apart and showed no signs of ever meeting on common ground.

Still, Kerr was right. They needed Mad Jake. To add to that admission was another. By not reporting the crime to the Guardsmen he was guilty of breaking the law. It didn't matter, nothing did except Susie's safe return.

"Do it," Burke said quietly. "Would you tell Rick? He deserves to know."

"No," answered Kerr after a moment of silent contemplation.

"Why?"

"Tomorrow is the biggest match of his career. He has a chance of surviving unharmed, but that chance will greatly diminish without a good night's rest. There is nothing he can do to aid us and he would insist on helping. I will search the city for anything that may lead us to her. I will return before morning. I will decide then whether to tell him before or after the match."

Burke nodded agreement and looked toward Nanna with concern as Kerr left the room. Tenderly he laid a hand on the blue mass of plasm.

"Everything will be all right, my friend. We will find her and bring her back safe and sound," Burke spoke. Nanna remained lifeless and unmoving at his words. She may not even have heard them. It did not matter. The words were not entirely for her benefit, anyhow.

SAMUEL

I sat at my desk, the list of all my current jobs laid out before me on my desk screen. After several moments, I flipped the screen off. After all, there is only so long I can stare at a blank screen.

I hit the comm screen. My receptionist's violet visage greeted me.

"Sylvia, hold all my calls," I asked, half joking. My communications board has seen busier days. Weeks for that matter. I could draw pictures in the dust on the screen.

"I'll do what I can. I only have so many limbs, Samuel," Sylvia's limbs replied musically, each note matching my sarcasm. By way of demonstration, she waved her many purple limbs in unison and as a Calamari she had quite a few to wave. They gave a great massage though.

"Thanks," I said sincerely, ending the call. Sylvia was better than I deserved. If this business drought keeps up I may not be able to pay her. It would not be the first time nor probably the last. Yet she stays on. Luckily, she is independently wealthy and doesn't need the income. Truth be told, she's a Countess in the aristocracy and outranks my mere knighthood. Actually, I'm not a knight; I just hold the title of Sir, the lowest notch on the aristocracy. It was my fee for a job I performed for one of the Tore Lords. It's come in handy more than once.

Anyway, Sylvia doesn't let her title go to her head. Good thing too, because fifty-five percent of a Calamari is head, the rest is limbs. In her eyes, I outrank even the Tetrarch...the last one ignored her plea for help a few years back. I didn't. In the process, I saved her entire brood and a large part of her fortune. She then gave me one of the biggest bonuses of my career and showed up at my office the next day acting like she belonged there.

Truth is, she did. More than I did and certainly more than my four previous receptionists. If it wasn't for Sylvia, I wouldn't be in business today. In the old days, I had some mighty lean times. Savage was always willing to offer me money but I'd sooner starve than be under anyone's thumb, especially his. Just when my financial times looked darkest, a donation appeared on my desk from a mysterious benefactor. Sylvia always denied any connection. It was the only time she would actually act Aristo and insulted when I tried to give her the money back. When times get tough now, I have my beer royalties to fall back on. The cash would be more of a cushion if more folks drank the beer. Only Aprahoe and Earthers like the stuff; most other races consider it swill. How they can talk that way about the nectar of the gods is beyond me.

Still, I had plenty to keep me busy. At present, I have sunk seventy-three out of the last one hundred and eleven shots into my wastebasket. Rolling up another piece of paper, I aimed my next shot. Three seconds left in the last quarter... down by two... Samuel Troubell shoots a three-pointer! The wad of paper flew through the air with the greatest of ease, then rolls around the rim twice. Much harder to do than a swish. In defiance of the laws of physics and good taste, instead of falling in it goes up over the rim and rolls off the basket onto the floor. Guess that makes it seventy-three out of one-twelve. I had a good excuse. Being a southpaw those righty shots are more difficult.

Before I could try number one-thirteen, the comm rang. It was Sylvia. No surprise there.

"Boss, you have a call on line one," Sylvia informed me musically.

"Sylvia, I thought I said hold my calls," I said with a smile. Sylvia only listens to me when it is for my own good. Then I realized what she sang. "Wait a second. I have more than one line?"

"Yes, you have three."

"Why, pray tell?

"It came with the office."

"Oh. Now about this call."

"I think you'll want to take it. It's Lord Burke."

The stone man himself and the richest external on the planet. He could definitely throw some business my way. I may even have to raise my fee. Before I used my new found wealth to move to a bigger office I needed to answer the call. I flipped on the communications board screen.

"Top of the morning, Burke. What can I do you for?"

"I need your professional help."

"I didn't figure this for a social call. What's up?"

"Is this a secure line?"

"The securest."

"Are you certain? Your picture is a little cloudy," Damn dust. I did not have time to clean the screen. Too busy playing. As casually as possible I wiped the screen with a handkerchief. Burke was too polite to notice.

"I'm certain."

"Susie has been kidnapped."

Shock lasted a minute before instinct and training kicked in. "When?

How long ago? Who did it? Was there a ransom demand? I assume they stipulated not to contact the Guardsmen."

"Yes, they did. How did you know?"

I held back the wisecracks. "Simple. If they didn't you wouldn't have called me."

Burke nodded. "She was taken about eight hours ago. We have been trying to reach you all evening," Good thing I didn't choose today to sleep in. "Kerr even left a message at Red's."

"I usually stop in at lunch to get my messages," Breaks up the monotony of the day.

"The deed was done by a Terran. His name is Dreg."

"The Newbe who pulled the blade on Tarna?"

"The same. There was not any ransom as such," Burke hesitated a moment. "All information I share is confidential?"

"Absolutely."

"He wants me to throw today's match."

"Sounds like a betting scam."

"That is what Kerr and I concluded also."

"One problem with that scenario: there's no way a Newbe Warrior would have the stake to make the scam worthwhile. He has to have a backer. If we can figure out who that is, it may lead us to her. My next question is how did he bypass your security system?"

"I do not know."

"The fact that he got past it adds credence to my partner theory. That system is the best on the market. I should know; I was a consultant on its development."

"Could you bypass it?"

"Yes. But the question is - how could he? As a new arrival, all the technology would be alien to him." No pun intended.

"I do not know."

"That's my department. Anything else I should know?"

"Yes, but I prefer to explain it in person."

"I'll be at the Warplex in twenty. I want to check out the scene of the crime." Corny, but a necessity.

"Make it five. I have sent a Hoversine for you. It should be at your office momentarily. It will be at your disposal."

"Thanks, Burke."

"It is I who should thank you. You have not mentioned your fee."

"No need. Susie is one of us and Earthers take care of our own.

Expenses will cover it."

"No. I can well afford it."

"Well, if you insist."

"I insist."

Burke looked despondent.

"It'll be okay, Burke. We will get her back. But just in case it's not before the match are you willing to take a dive?"

"Yes."

"I'm a fan. I'll do my best to make sure it doesn't come to that. Can't ruin the only perfect record in the games. See you in five."

We said our goodbyes. Sylvia wobbled in.

"Boss, you're too soft-hearted. You almost turned down a paying client."

"It wasn't the client I almost turned down. It was the pay."

"My point exactly." When I made no comeback, Sylvia gave me that worried tentacle look. "You're worried about the child."

"Very. She's a sweet kid. I can't let anything happen to her."

"It's not your fault."

"Doesn't make it any easier."

"This is not the Anda case." Anda was another kidnap victim. I knew him. He was a neighborhood G'morra kid whose dad happened to be rich. Anda fell in between a revenge play. I was hired to deliver the ransom. Afterwards, the kidnappers delivered Anda... in pieces. Razza and I later returned the favor. That was before he became *The* Razza. Now, he can't do freebies, but for an assassin, his heart's always been in the right place.

The revenge didn't make the loss easier to take. It just made it easier to sleep at night.

"I won't let that happen to Susie."

"I know."

"Call Jake. He'll want a piece of this."

"Already got a call into the Web. Jake has been doing what he can since early this AM."

"You were listening in?"

"Of course. Don't I always? I was even using all three lines at once."

"Three? Who was on the third line?"

"Sorry. That call was personal," she joked. Calamari can hold as many conversations as they have limbs. They move them about so much I'm unable to get an accurate count. I understand why we had three lines.

What I don't understand is why we didn't have more. Sylvia helped me into my gray trench coat and hat, then handed me my "walking stick".

"Bring her home safe, boss."

"Thanks, Sylvia. What would I do without you?"

"Well, for a start you'd have to answer your own phone. And clean your own office. Make your own meals. Solve your own cases."

"Okay, I get the idea. I have a better question. What am I going to do with you?"

"Anything you want. After you find the girl."

"Temptress. Be careful what you offer, I might take you up on it." "Boss, don't make a girl promises you won't keep. You stick exclusively to humanoids."

I didn't argue with the truth. Besides my Hoversine awaited as did an alone and frightened Susie. I would find her or drop trying.

SMED'LEE

While above the city was being torn apart, below there was calm. The dimness of a hidden chamber half hid Susie as she lay unconscious, dreaming drug-induced visions and dramas. Unpleasant was just the beginning. Tossing and turning, Susie tried to escape from the horrors of her mind. It was best she could not. The dreams were safer than her reality. Watching over her sleeping form were two creatures on the low end of their respective evolutionary scales.

Anticipation oozed from every pore on both of them. Smed'lee had sunk every last cent he could coerce, borrow or steal into this scheme. The odds against a DeTang being defeated were astronomical. The odds against Burke losing were higher than that. When Burke lost, the payoff would put him into and past the Dor class of wealth. He would be able to buy and sell Dortew. When that glorious day arrived, scant hours from now, Dortew would learn the true meaning of pain. Every insult, every injury that Smed'lee had ever suffered at the hands of his superior would be paid back in triplicate. Life would finally be good.

The other was the more foul of the pair. In this company that was saying something. Dreg's life had three bright spots he saw when looking toward the future. The first glow on the horizon was his impending freedom followed by the small cut of the winnings that would be his, but these were not the foremost thoughts in his mind. Those thoughts embodied the very essence of depravity and involved the sleeping child. Dreg was awaiting her awakening before turning those thoughts to actions. Susie's head was positioned on Dreg's lap, while hands shaking in expectation were stroking her blond hair gently. Even unconscious, his vulgar touch made Susie's skin crawl. The act appeared tender and caring but it did not even fool Smed'lee. Muridae have raised depravity to a way of life, but this was too much for even Smed'lee...at least for a brief moment. He had young of his own. Pain was one thing, this obscenity was another.

"What are you doing, Dirtling?"

"None of your business, rat."

"I think it is," Smed'lee answered, emphasizing his point with a jolt from the NG. Dreg decided not to argue the matter.

"Preparing for a mating ritual."

"Mating ritual?"

"She is the only white human female I have met in this cesspool, so she's the only choice for me. The Man has needs, you know."

"I was under the impression that she was but a child. That would make her too young for your needs."

"If they are old enough to pee, they are old enough for me."

"You are not to leave any visible scars on the child. We may need to show her to Burke before the match. Move away from her and do not touch her."

Dreg looked as if he was about to argue the command, but after Smed'lee pointed the NG his way Dreg swallowed the protest. Dreg left Susie alone on the cot and walked across the room.

"No problem. I was waiting for her to wake up so she could enjoy it too."

Smed'lee did not need to ask what "it" was. Instead, while Dreg's back was to them, he gave the unconscious child a second dose of sedative to ensure she did not awaken.

"Burke has called in a Dirtling Investigator. He was in the Warplex earlier."

"Did he find anything?"

"If he did, would we be standing here?"

"Guess not. So is the freak going to throw the fight or what?"

"He will have no choice."

"Good! So, are we really going to turn her back over to them?"

"I thought she was to be your mate."

"Not my mate. Just someone to mate with. She has been corrupted by exposure to all the freaks. If it weren't for her age, she would have no purity left and I wouldn't touch her with your weasel. Of course, after being with me, she won't want to go back. But she can't stay with the Man. Might finger me."

"So you have no objections against our disposing of the body when this matter is completed?"

"None, provided we have our fun first." Smed'lee was not one of the "we". Smed'lee did not mind. He had not shared with Dreg the fact that the internal security system had identified him. Nor had he shared his plan to keep the child unconscious for her entire captivity. That way she would be unable to identify her captors and could safely be returned. The child was worth far more alive than dead for if she was eliminated, so would Burke's one weakness. Then Smed'lee, or rather Dorlee, would have nothing to extort favors from Burke with if the need should again arise.

It was strange to be scheming to save the child as opposed to killing her. A one-hundred-eighty degree switch of mindset. Dorlee might just provide Burke with the evidence he needed for Kentor Justice. He would have the power to hand Dortew out to hang in that hurricane. That possibility in and of itself would grant him power over Dortew.

Of course, Dreg would have to be put out of the picture in a permanent and painful way. Left alive, he would be found and he would tell of Smed'lee's part before he was killed. Then Smed'lee's life would be worthless regardless of how much wealth he possessed. It would be a race to see who ended his life first, Burke or Savage. Despite his finesse in the art of torture, Smed'lee had never killed before. He could never afford to. The best his financial status allowed him was the occasional maiming.

Susie was to have been his first taste of murder, but Dreg would substitute just fine. Shivers of anticipation traveled up and down his spine, exciting him nearly as much as his pending wealth. With the smell of death hanging like a stale wind in the distance, the old thrills were no longer enough. Enny lay neglected and untouched at his side.

"Very well. I must go to the match. My absence would be noticed. Leave the child untouched until my return. Then you can spend your new wealth on her."

"Spend cash on this tramp? No way. Just the Man is more than she deserves."

"So you can control your carnal urges until then?"

"Waiting makes it better in the end. It is just a form of foreplay." It was the only kind Dreg knew of.

"Until my return, wait in this outer chamber. If you enter the same one as our captive, an alarm will sound and I will know. I can cause you pain even from a distance."

"All right," Dreg grumbled. Smed'lee used his Enny – after only a brief fondle – and exploded Dreg's world. Eventually, the pain ended. Dreg answered in the prescribed manner. "Yes, your verminess."

Smed'lee nodded, smiled and left. Dreg did as he was told, but turned his mind and hand to other matters.

SAMUEL

Evil filled the room like a raging river. Anyone unaccustomed to the current would be swept away to a watery grave wearing new shoes. Cement, size twenty. Sitting tall in the center was Savage, unaffected by the black undertow. The wave of darkness had long ago washed over him, dragging him out to an ebony sea.

Savage didn't look happy to see me. The fact that I had entered his sanctuary unmolested did nothing to lighten his mood. None of the sentries even thought to stop a dark Hoversine entering the area. Figured it belonged along with the five others parked outside. I got the rest of the way on natural talent.

"Morning, Tony. Didn't know this would be a party. I would have brought a cheesecake to add to the potluck breakfast."

"Troubell, even you aren't this stupid," Savage said. At his nod a dozen externals, mostly his G'morran followers encircled me. I knew from past experience none were trigger happy, at least when dealing with an Earther or Terran as Savage prefers. None of them are exempt from the proclamation. That didn't stop them from breaking bits and pieces, including some of my favorites, if their boss gave the say so.

So, there we stood in a face off. Actually, Savage sat through the whole thing. He waited for me to say something. I would have preferred to keep him waiting longer but finding Susie was too important.

"Susie has been kidnapped by Dreg," I blurted out. It was the quickest way.

"What?" Savage yelled, jumping to his feet. All hostilities ceased in that moment. I was transformed from enemy to ally. Us Earthers stick together regardless of what we think of each other. Only trouble was this time it was one of us that was the problem. I explained what went down so far to the best of my knowledge.

"You did right by coming to me," Savage informed. I was not so sure about that, but he had resources that would be useful in the search. "I'll get my people right on it."

"Good," I said. There was no need for thanks. If the positions were reversed I would have done the same. It is all a matter of priorities. Our only priority was Susie's safety. "I need something else from you." I refused to use the term favor. "I could do the legwork myself but it would take the better part of the day and I can't spare the time. Has anyone been placing a large bet or a lot of little ones on today's match for Burke to lose? With you or any of the others in town." Savage's eyebrows raised at the concept of a DeTang losing, especially to a G'morran female. Would undermine his power base with the purple people. Savage nodded to Santo who left the room in a hurry. Five minutes later he was back with the information.

"More than twenty wagers have been placed around the city and at least three in the Outlands. It amasses to a small fortune. A large one if he wins," Santo hissed.

"Who placed the bets?" I asked. Santo ignored me, refusing even eye contact. No great loss there.

"Who?" Savage asked.

"The Muridae chief overseer, Smed'lee."

"Fine, he's at the game. We'll kill him there."

"Wait a second, Tony. Don't be going off half-cocked."

"What the hell are you talking about, Troubell?"

"First, today's match is on Skyvid. The entire city and half the Outlands will see you kill him."

"Good. He'll set an example."

"But if he's dead, he can't lead us to Susie. Her safety is paramount. He may have given Dreg orders to harm or kill Susie if he doesn't check in at a certain time with a certain phrase. Even if he didn't, he'll be smart enough to make it up on the spot. There is no way to beat or force her location out of him. You know better than I that there is no torture or pain you can devise that would match what he has suffered through as a member of the Muridae cash caste. Your tender mercies would be a joke in comparison."

Savage's temper cooled. "Agreed. I will watch him myself. Sooner or later, he will have to go to where she is. I'll be one step behind."

"Good. Unfortunately, that method may be too late. Have the rest of your people search the city," I said. I made no suggestions on how they should go about it. They have their methods, I have mine. Never the twain shall meet.

"What will you be doing?"

"After I check in with Mad Jake, I'll be doing the same."

"Agreed. Take a Hoversine. The search will go faster."

"No need. I already have one." Savage shot me a quizzical look. "Courtesy of my client." Savage nodded sagely.

I turned to leave. The mass of mobsters that barred my path remained unmoving, then as one, they parted quicker than the Red Sea did for Moses. I could almost hear Savage's nod behind me. I played deaf.

"Samuel," he whispered. I stopped.

"Yes?"

"We will get her back. This won't be another Anda, I promise." Savage has two weaknesses in terms of decency – kids and Terrans.

"Savage, I didn't know you cared."

"I don't," he replied with an honest smile. He was lying. He really did care and that scared me.

"Thanks," I said, with actual gratitude. He nodded again. It got annoying. I wished neck cramps on him and hit the streets hoping they didn't hit back. I prayed we found a scared little girl before it was too late.

RICK

The day of doom was upon me. Melodrama becomes me. Despite all my moaning, Kerr refused me the last wish of a condemned man. Besides pizza delivery hadn't reached Tore yet. I'll have to suggest it to Luigi. Through luck and friendship, I had gotten an extra few weeks to prepare for my showdown and today at high noon my luck runs out. In between, I won eight matches.

Now, that may sound great and it was much better than losing eight matches, but I didn't emerge unscarred. Over the course of those matches, I'd suffered five broken bones, two concussions, and after my match with a female Czarrian, I was laid up in the infirmary for three days. Of all the warriors I've met, I'm the only one who goes out of my way to minimize the harm to my opponent. It would be nice to see even one of them return the favor.

Take the Czarrian – Mangrel was her name. I was her first match. A break from the tradition of having Newbes only facing Newbes, but the Czarrians still have a great deal of pull. To earn the right for the Bakda ceremony, a Czarrian must defeat an accomplished warrior. In days of yor that happened on the battlefield. Since Wandum, there have been no battlefields, save places like the Tore Games. However, the Muridae are no dummies; they will let a Czarrian fight in the Games, but there is a price... a five-year contract. It weeds out all but the truly dedicated.

Mangrel was among them. Since I was undefeated and trained by the ranking Czarrian warrior, I was the lucky opponent. Kerr is a celebrity among his people as the premier practicing warrior. Mangrel was my toughest opponent, not counting today's match. She had me on the ropes several times, but I was used to Kerr and frankly, she wasn't in his class. Eventually, I triumphed, Mangrel laying unconscious at my feet. I gave my endmatch salute and joined my collapsed foe on the floor.

I spent three days recovering; Mangrel was out in three hours. My knee still twinges when it rains. So do most of my other joints. I know the weather before I even go outside. Something as simple as a change in barometric pressure plays havoc with my body. Many of my patients had often complained of this, but I never imagined how profoundly it affected one's life. I did my best to rehabilitate myself using my training as a Physical Therapist and the medic's technology, but my poor body is not given the time it needs to heal.

Meanwhile, my opponents are no worse off than before they faced me. Being a nice guy sometimes just does not seem fair, but they finish last. In a match that means victory. Of course, Tarna has another meaning for the same line. That woman has the most sexually overactive mind of anyone I have ever met. Makes half the patrons of the Empirical House pale in comparison.

More than one warrior has suggested I change my fighting philosophy. Stubborn, I've refused, proud that I can look myself in the eye each morning unashamed. With the help of a mirror, of course. They can take me from my home, they can make me fight against my will but they can't make me a monster. Only I can do that. For the most part, I've been able to keep the beast within locked up tight. Every so often I feel him rattling the bars of his cage, but, save for that one time, he hasn't escaped. Bars do not a prison make. Red still does not understand that one. Says he would never let the criminal element in his place. Unless they paid cash.

Mangrel did win her next match, however. The Bakda ceremony was performed right there in the Pit. It helped explain the anatomical difference between Mangrel and Kerr. It was not in terms of male-female difference as is the case with humans. Mangrel's breasts were no bigger than Kerr's. Czarrian females do have permanent mammalian protuberances but they develop only after childbirth. For the interested, Czarrian females have six breasts lined up in pairs.

No female is permitted to bear young until she has proved herself in battle. The same goes for mating for the male. At present, the Czarrians are having a population growth slow down, almost an implosion. Czarrians give birth to four to eight young at a time, an obvious reason for their history of expansionism. Before they discovered space travel and infraspace, the young of each litter fought death matches until only one remained alive. With the finding of other worlds, this barbaric ritual was halted. No move has been made to jump-start the population or to change the custom of who is eligible to mate because with more and more worlds seceding, the Empire would have nowhere to send the young.

As I was saying, the Bakda ceremony explained the anatomical difference between the two Czarrians, which is Mangrel had a tail, Kerr did not. The ceremony began with Mangrel's mother and father holding her warblade in the heart of a burning flame, lit upon an altar. When the blade was so hot it glowed it was handed to Mangrel. Bowing, she received the blade. Tail in one hand, blade held in two others, Mangrel raised the warblade high above her head. Silent and without flinching, Mangrel brought the blade down, amputating her own tail.

The hot blade was then held over the wound to cauterize it. That bit of wound care out of the way, she approached the altar, tail in hand. Again bowing, she laid the tail across the ceremonial fires and let it roast until only ashes remained. She offered prayers to a variety of Czarrian deities in their pantheon, the only one of which I recognized was Razza. The ashes were then gathered by Mangrel and mixed with Czarrian bloodwine in a large goblet. Mangrel offered the chalice to both her parents, who drank deeply. The cup was then offered in turn to all other Czarrians present, Kerr included. When all had their fill, Mangrel raised the goblet to her own lips and drained it.

It was a symbolic sharing of her strength and ferocity. A tad barbaric, but no more so than some Earth customs, where in order to become a man, a boy has to perform a do it yourself circumcision.

Still, I had beat her and seven others. With all this success came perks. I have a bigger cube. My stipend has tripled, which puts it up to only fifty percent below the poverty level. Folks I have never met beforehand me pictures of myself, asking for my autograph. The pictures are of me topless and smiling. Susie has one hanging in her room. So does Sasha. Never knew so many women were into scars.

The entire squad has their own trading cards including a group picture. There is even one of Kerr whipping my butt early on in my training. I have a complete set. So does the rest of the squad except Don. He ate his. Don't feel too bad for the eating machine. Don's eyes are on opposite sides of his head and he has trouble making sense of two-dimensional images.

On top of everything else, I've been propositioned by more lifeforms than I'm able to recognize to perform acts that would confound even Don Juan. Admittedly, it's due more to my public association with Sasha than any irresistibly on my part. Her reputation is legend and people want to touch a piece of the legend. That and the fact that before my fourth match she publicly announced to the crowd that I was the greatest lover on Tore. No one was more shocked than I, considering the noncarnal nature of our relationship. Sasha explained there was more to "making love" than sex. She seems to like that phrase. She laughs every time she uses it.

Now I have a reputation that is nothing short of impossible to live up to. Sasha said it would keep me on my toes. In addition to fighting off admirers, I've become a better warrior than I ever thought possible. None of that means a single thing today... if I make it to tomorrow it will mean quite a bit.

From my Newbe squad, Tarna and I are the biggest draws. Look where it got us. Facing off against two DeTang. Tarna is psyched; she should be. My day of doom is her day of triumph. Today her dream becomes a reality. As does my nightmare. Burke would never kill Tarna. All she has to do is minimize her broken bones. Despite Burke's assurances, I have no such guarantees with BoBo. Burke will be too far away to prevent a deathblow. The fact that he has promised to avenge me is of little comfort.

I explained all this to Sasha, who's decided to spend what could be some of my last moments with me. Of course, she denies this was her intention but it would be impolite for her to actually admit it so I let it go. She listened intently and said all the right things, avoiding the traditional "Don't worry, you'll be fine" line. None of it makes a difference. I'm looking death in the face and praying he turns away first. The last few days I have prayed more than I have in the last few months. All my doubts have been put aside in hopes that some divine solution will present itself. So far, no burning bush. Not even an unlit match has presented itself. I'm still waiting.

Sasha tries to instill some added confidence to my sagging ego.

"Rick, BoBo will not be trying to kill you."

"Easy for you to say. I'm the one who has to bet my life on it."

"I ordered him not to."

"He has disobeyed you before."

"Only once out of years of service."

"Frankly, I think he's jealous."

"BoBo?" Sasha asks, shocked.

"He loves you. Trust me. I can tell." And relate.

"True, but not like that. DeTang are androgynous. They tend to assume a sexual identity based on who they are around. Burke has assumed a male role. BoBo has assumed the female, although he still prefers to be addressed in the male gender." I hadn't known that. It explains the outfits while Burke goes au naturel.

"After the games today, I am holding a party in your and BoBo's honor at the Empirical House."

"Sounds great, but I have only one problem. I promised Susie a tea party tonight." If I survived.

"No problem; bring her along. We will combine the two. Besides, Peri would love to see her again."

"Sounds good to me. I'll run it by Susie and Nanna." Speaking of which, where were they? I haven't seen either since last night.

"Rick, you understand I cannot wish you luck publicly in the Pit today? I cannot show favoritism. Toward either of you."

I nodded. She refused to betray old or new friends. I respect that. Sasha smiled and whispered, "Good luck, my Banesh in gleaming armor." Bending her head forward, her lips touched mine. All panic and fear left me as my brain exploded in pleasure. There has got to be a way to bottle that. Sasha sauntered off to the warrior area, her hips swaying like seductive clockwork. A pendulum in the Pit, so to speak. I enjoyed the view and the euphoria while it lasted.

Today was only a two-match card: Burke and Tarna, BoBo and me. As Burke was the more popular of we four, his match went last. My match was the warm-up act. I suggested a band or comedian instead, to no avail.

Red no longer attends the Games since he won the Tourney and his freedom: personal reasons. He had wished me luck last night, telling me he believed I was good enough to survive. From him, it was an overwhelming vote of confidence. Red promised me a free drink if I survived, two if I won.

Burke had seemed beside himself earlier when he wished me luck. It was truly unlike him. Now that I'd entered the Pit, Kerr was acting the same way. I hope it's not out of concern for me. If they were that worried, I was in bigger trouble than I thought.

I was still concerned about by one absence.

"Kerr, have you seen Susie?" I asked. Kerr looked taken aback by the question. "Kerr, is something wrong with Susie?"

"Rick, Susie will not be at the match today."

"Why not? And where is Nanna?"

"Nanna is not here for the same reason Susie is not. Put it out of your mind. Concentrate on the upcoming battle."

"Kerr, will I do it?"

"I have every confidence in you. Reluctant you may be, but you are a true warrior. Just lose this lack of confidence. Right now, it is your greatest foe, not the DeTang."

He was right. Worry was giving a big thing a bigger shadow, to paraphrase one of Kerr's warrior sayings. If I wasn't ready, worry wasn't going to make me a better fighter. It will only slow me down, making me question my own decisions. Terror would actually help me. The fear and adrenaline will heighten my reflexes and make me faster, stronger. I could do this. I didn't want to, but I could.

The squad and I went through our prematch ritual. Don even licked me twice. Turning, I walked out onto the Pit. The journey of a thousand deaths starts with a single step... melodrama is my life.

No longer a Newbe, I walked alone. BoBo did the same from the opposite direction. We met midway. I readied my first salute but the crowd let loose a sound midway between a cheer and a question. Before I could complete the flying finger, footsteps shifted the sand behind me. Turning, I saw Kerr coming up behind me. Smiling, the wolf gave me a wink and turned toward the Muridae dais.

"Gamemasters, pardon the interruption. Rick Wagner of Terra has impressed me both as student, warrior, and friend. He has reminded me what nobility and honor truly mean. I would, therefore, like to publicly present him with an honor that has never before been granted another warrior." Turning to me, Kerr unbuckled his sword belt. With all four hands and the care usually reserved for fine crystal, he lifted the warblade high above his head, then lowered it to waist level.

"Kneel," he whispered and I complied. He then touched each of my shoulders with the hilt. "I hereby grant you Bloodmoon, my warblade, to carry into this battle with you."

Shock, both the crowd's and mine, filled the stadium to capacity. Kerr has never let another, save Red and his own father, touch his warblade. Never has he let another carry it. For him to give it to me was an honor unmatched. At his prompt, I took the blade gingerly.

"This is one of the single greatest warblades ever forged. It has cleaved through battle armor and steel, flesh, and bone. Its age is measured in centuries. It won't break if you grip it tightly, Rick," Kerr whispered so the crowd couldn't hear. "Don't let that speech go to your head. It was for the crowd's benefit," he lied with a wink. "Well, most of it anyway."

"Thank you, master," I managed to get out past the choke in my throat and the tear in my eye.

"You are welcome, jumper of weeds."

"That's grasshopper."

"Whatever."

"I'll make you proud."

"Make yourself proud, Dirtboy."

"I will, fleabag."

"Now put aside that toy," Kerr said, referring to the Bo staff I was carrying. Custom permitted the opponent of a DeTang to bring three weapons onto the battlefield. The Bo was one of the three.

Kerr moved to fasten the belt around my waist.

"Wait. Let me put this on first," I said, pulling the first of two circlets out of my pocket. The first I placed on the sandy floor. Kerr shook his head in mild disagreement. Those in the audience who recognized the birth control device snickered.

"I wish you would not use that. It is most unwarriorlike."

"It is my best bet. I'm sticking to my decision. There was no specification as to what the weapons could be except that they must not be projectile." The fields qualified provided I didn't throw them.

"But the crowd is laughing."

"Let them. I'm bigger than that." It was clear that Kerr wasn't. He cared what they thought of me.

"It is your match."

That it was. I placed the circlet around my neck and hit the switch. My body below the circle was enveloped in a warm glow. I had spare batteries in my pockets. At the moment, I couldn't reach them because they were inside the field, but if it ran out of juice they would be again accessible. That was the reason I had waited before donning the warblade. Otherwise, I'd be unable to use it as it'd be inside the field.

As I strapped the sword belt around my glowing waist, a thought struck me.

"Kerr, If I pull the warblade, am I bound by the same rules as a Czarrian?"

"No, Rick," Kerr said with a chuckle. "You do not have to kill him."

Picking the other circlet up, I placed it so it encircled my face from behind my neck to the top of my forehead. Once activated, the only part of my body unprotected would be my face. I would cover that too, but I've grown quite accustomed to breathing and didn't feel I could give it up on such short notice.

Kerr, his job done, returned to the sidelines. Me, I headed back to the middle of the Pit where BoBo was waiting restlessly. As far as I was concerned the mountain of doom could wait forever. Alas, as with most of reality it wasn't my decision to make. One day that would change. Soon. Just not today.

Got to keep the attitude at maximum cocky.

"Howdy, BoBo. Come here often?"

BoBo did not return the greeting. No manners, these all-powerful warriors. "Ignorant Dirtling. That is not the proper use for that equipment."

"How would you know? You don't have the proper equipment to know the proper use." Knowing how sensitive he was to his sexuality, or lack thereof, it was a low blow. Not that a low blow was more effective than any other. It did nothing to lighten his mood. He still had no sense of humor.

We did the salutes and turned to salute each other. I gave him a double. He didn't deem me worthy of a salute. Burke stepped forward onto the field. If I was not worthy of a salute, I was not worthy of the gift of combat. Burke would not allow the match to proceed.

Unfortunately, BoBo decided to salute and the match proceeded. I activated the second circlet. Lacking the personal tradition of Burke to allow one free shot, BoBo wasted no time and pressed an attack. I leaped away. As the challenged, I chose the gravity level as Tore normal. Kerr questioned this as it increased BoBo's strength advantage, but it also upped my mobility and agility. I wanted to stay as far out of the reach of those boulder-sized fists as possible.

Today, the dome of the arena was opened to the sky. Looking up, I saw a two-hundred-foot version of myself poised in the heavens, looking confident. How deceiving these appearances be, even on Skyvid. I briefly wished I could switch places with my giant doppelganger. That wish lost most of its appeal and was quickly retracted as I realized the Skyvid BoBo was two hundred forty feet tall. We towered over the city like a couple of beasts from a Japanese monster movie. One of us should probably climb a building holding a screaming woman. I wouldn't mind having a dozen biplanes on my side about now. They wouldn't be able to beat BoBo, but they could airlift me out of here.

BoBo was getting wise to my avoidance strategy and was closing the gap and narrowing my escape margin. I had a trick up my sleeve. It was a long shot, extremely silly and would only work once.

"Look," I shouted, pointing to the ground at BoBo's feet. "Your shoes are untied."

Confused, BoBo did exactly what I said. His lowered head threw off his center of gravity. I leapt on the back of his neck with all the force I could muster. It was enough. BoBo plunged face first into the sand as I made my way across the stadium with speed undreamt of by mortal men. It was a speed born of fear and desperation. I was also laughing uncontrollably. A bizarre thing to do but it was that or babble incoherently. The crowd loved it, some adding their laughter to my own. Others cheered at the confirmation of the rumors that I had actually downed a DeTang, however briefly. BoBo was already on his feet and giving chase.

Yelling over my shoulder as I ran, I said "How silly of me. You don't wear shoes. Never mind."

BoBo roared and picked up speed. I put on the brakes and sidestepped at the speed of hope. BoBo, as full of inertia and anger as anyone I have ever met, was easy prey to a technique that added to his momentum and sent him spinning out of control. His stone form plowed into the sands belly first, hydroplaning waves of sand into the air as he traveled a good twenty feet. Red was right: if he made me come to him, I didn't stand a chance of a Muridae keeping a vow of poverty. I simply had to refrain from initiating an attack, opting instead to let him come to me. Anger would cloud his mind and his thoughts. He was an untrained fighter. With his strength, it never mattered. In a real battle, I'd be eventually reduced to protoplasm. In a match, rules enforced by the only external stronger than BoBo, hope still burned, flickered, and refused to die. So did I. If this were best two of three falls, I would have won already. It wasn't. The match is timed to last thirty minutes or until Kerr decides to throw in the towel.

BoBo, covered in grit and grains of sand, rose from where he had fallen. This time it was done slowly, with thought. A bad sign. I needed to keep him worked up and this time he wouldn't be distracted by false tales of shoelaces.

"I never realized DeTang were so clumsy. First Sasha's marble floor, now the ground of the Pit. You must have one hell of a liability policy. Maybe you should change your name from BoBo, destroyer of worlds, to DiBo, the destroyer of floors."

That did the trick. BoBo threw caution to the wind. As there was no breeze present to catch caution, it fell soundlessly to the ground. BoBo more than made up for the lack of sound in pressing his next attack. At least I'd didn't have to worry about him trying to sneak up on me. Adding my own version of a Czarrian battle howl to the DeTang's roar of rage, the battle was rejoined. The attack was avoided. I was unscarred.

Only twenty-six minutes to go.

SAMUEL

I was at my wit's end. Mind you it wasn't that long of a trip, but I still had high hopes of finding my way back. I had torn Tore inside out, upside down, and six ways from Tuesday. Every rock had been overturned, X-rayed and dusted for fingerprints. I found myself searching in rings and quarters that normally a million pounds could not get me near. In desperation, I even unofficially notified some old friends still in the Guardsmen. The city is not tremendous by American standards, at least the standards of about fifteen years ago. Only two hundred thousand folks or so, but it's a tremendous area to scour blindly, without the aid of a seeing-eye bloodhound.

So far, my search path had crisscrossed three Web agents, two of Savage's men, and Kerr. Their luck had been no better than mine. If Susie is in the city, we'll eventually find her. At least that what I keep telling myself. Eventually, I might even believe it. Nobody knows nothing, so we are reduced to a randomized search of Muridae hangouts, safe houses, and hideouts. The other possibility is that Dreg has somehow gotten her to the Outlands.

Judging by past experience, I know the type of help I'd get with a search there. Most Outlanders are there for a reason, varied though it may be. The end result is they hate city dwellers and all city things. Not without reason, mind you. The city treats them like refuse. Personally, I think it is a dumb move. Only half our food is supplied by space traffic; the other half comes to us by way of Outland farms. It must be hell having to test each batch for poison. Outlanders traditionally ignore or harass we urbanites, especially if they smell an official investigation. If she's outside of the city, there is nothing I can do for her, so I have to behave as if she is still in the city. And pray.

Hey, God, it's Samuel Troubell. Yes, me again. I know I only tend to talk to you when I want something and this time is no exception. Help us find Susie safe and sound, untouched in any way. I don't want to say you owe me or anything like that, but I don't think I could handle another Anda. I will owe you big time. I'll even remember to say thank you.

My pleas go unanswered. Not a big surprise, but I put in the request anyway. I hope it's enough. I climb back into the Hoversine after another lead fails to pan out. I refuse to use the term dead end under the circumstances. I checked back in with Sylvia three times in the last twenty minutes for some good news, but none was forthcoming. My efforts are becoming too scattered. Sylvia told me I needed to rest, regroup my thoughts. As usual, she's right. I recline the seat and open the moonroof. Spread out above me is Rick's match against BoBo. I don't envy the kid. After the fight of his life, Kerr is going to break it to him about Susie. He'll be frantic. Smart move to keep it from him until after the match. Telling him would blow any chance he had of emerging unscarred. Hope the kid understands.

Every time I watch the Skyvid, I'3m completely amazed at how the entire horizon turns into a giant television screen. Skyvid by day is an incredible spectacle but Skyvid night matches are a sight unmatched by any other. It is as if the gods have left the heavens to do battle in the skies. At night, half the planet can see the show.

By no means am I a scientist, but I do understand how the process works. Red and Sylvia had explained it to me often enough. It works much like a tube in a TV set or perhaps a better example would be a neon light. The Muridae have satellites set up complete with electron guns. When the show starts, the so-called guns are aimed and fired by electric and magnetic fields. The electrons penetrate Tore's atmosphere to within sixty miles of the surface. They collide with the molecules of various gases and emit different colors of light depending on which gas gets hit. Oxygen burns green or white. Nitrogen, when ionized, emits purple and blue while neutral nitrogen turns pink. By mixing the colors they can get the rest of the spectrum. A computer coordinates the picture.

Basically, Skyvid is a high-tech version of the aurora borealis on the pay-per-view concept. In this case, the city is dishing out the cash. Entertainment for the masses and all that. The Outlands enjoy the show for free, although they are in the figuratively cheap seats. Sound can be paid for on an individual basis. If there is a way to make money off a situation, the Muridae will find it. I bitch about that. Most folks figure it's because the Muridae are responsible for my exile from Earth. Sylvia claims it is because I'm jealous of their financial talent since my talent lies in the opposite direction. If there is a way to lose money, I will find it. Money does not just burn a hole in my pocket, it incinerates the entire outfit. Luckily, I wear asbestos underwear.

A pity that my first time in the lap of luxury with a custom Hoversine at my disposable, that I can't relax enough to enjoy it. Stress is mucking up my mind, filling my thoughts with concrete cotton. The details of the kidnapping leapt unbidden across my mental landscape, hopping over my optimism like sheep over a fence. No matter how many times I count them, realization eludes my grasp. I feel as if one small detail doesn't fit and that detail is the key to finding Susie. I'll be damned if I can figure out what that detail is.

Meanwhile, I watch the skies. Rick is surviving. The Hoversine is wired for any frequency so it is just a matter of fiddling with the controls until I pick up the match.

"Your mother wears combat boots," Rick informs BoBo. Insulting his opponent, an interesting strategy. It explains why BoBo has been charging him blindly. The rock was always too sensitive to what others said about him. The last words mean nothing to a creature who had no mother, only a parent, and is one of the few of his kind to ever wear boots himself. BoBo's attack this time is well thought out and, unable to avoid the punch, Rick goes airborne, slamming into a wall. That had to hurt. If it wasn't for the circlets, he'd be hamburger now. Rick was still moving, albeit very slowly.

I don't mind him using the circlets for protection, in every sense of the word. That is why I gave them to him, hoping he would figure out what he has, but did he have to do it on Skyvid? My protective edge has just become public knowledge. A secret weapon loses its edge when anybody who has eyes and the ability to look up knows all about it. Probably hock up the price, too.

As Rick takes a few seconds to recover, the Skyvid pans the stands and the Muridae dais. Smed'lee is still sitting and watching. No luck there. Seeing the smug look on the rat's face, I half regretted stopping Savage. Although I couldn't see him, I knew Savage was there in the shadows, waiting. Must be driving him crazy.

The view returns to the match. Bob and Ned's faces light the corners of the sky with their constant commentary. Rick has called BoBo a blockhead. No insult there. That's exactly what he is. He must have used all his good material before I tuned in. BoBo's next offensive ends with Rick soaring through the air yet again, this time landing hard on the sidelines at Kerr's feet. Kerr visibly restrains himself from helping Rick rise, although he lets the kid pull himself upright using the wolf's legs.

Rick is barely able to stand. His hold on Kerr is the only thing keeping him upright. The nonsense he is spouting must sound like babbling to a non-Earther.

"I could have been a contender, Kerr," Rick says.

"Do you want me to stop the Match?" Kerr said, examining Rick's eyes for signs of a concussion. The kid considers the option seriously before making his decision.

"How much time left?"

"Nine minutes. Shall I stop it?"

"No," he says simply and meanders back onto the Pit. No sooner had he done so than BoBo put him down again but the DeTang didn't stop there. Rick's left shoulder was pulled, twisted, and hit, dislocating it even through the field. I could hear the sickening pop. Rick fell, gripping the shoulder. BoBo debates about pressing the attack but is detoured by Burke's sudden presence on the field. Instead, BoBo turns and plays to the crowds, basking in the adoration. The view moves to Kerr, his arm raised high, white flag in hand. With a toss, Kerr lets the flag fly. Zooming in, the Skyvid version is the size of a jumbo jet as it soars through the heavens. Out of the clouds comes a hand, catching the flag. The view fades back. Rick is standing, lifeless left arm hanging on one side, the white flag held defiantly in the other.

"It ain't over yet," Rick growls, tossing the flag back to a smiling Kerr. Why the fleabag is happy over that is beyond me. Then Rick does something unexpected. By me at least. He shuts down the field. Using his good right arm, he takes his left shoulder in hand, twists, and pushes. The kid reset his own damn shoulder. Now he's pulling a Czarrian warblade from around his waist, tosses it into the air and reactivates the field. Catching the warblade, he refastens it. Where did he get a warblade from? They are still considered contraband. Kerr is the only one he knows legally entitled to one and the fleabag would not let it out of his sight. Red says he even sleeps with the thing.

Rick looks like hell warmed over with an attitude. The kid is major angry. Angry enough to press an attack. BoBo just sidesteps him.

"Deviant, honorless, sexless piece of trash, bullying your way through life. You would be unable to survive as a normal being without your strength. You are ugly and your parent dresses you funny. You have the fashion sense of a Muridae. You expect me to just lay down and die? I half expected to do that, but I will not. You know damn well a fleshie has no chance against you, so what do you do? Bully me, threaten me, hang like a huge specter of terror over my life. The terror is no more. No matter what the outcome of the match, I have won. I won the moment I refused to bow down to you. Now I have lasted twenty-four minutes."

"Twenty-five!" yells Kerr from the sidelines, one eye on the clock.

"I stand corrected. Twenty-five. The fact that I am still standing ensures that you have lost. You and all the bullies that mess with the lives of the little people. It is David and Goliath revisited, big boy, and you are going down."

The speech was good, but it was more than that. The kid was standing on a soapbox for his health. BoBo wasted two minutes listening to him instead of fighting. If Rick is still standing at the end of the thirty minutes, the match is a draw: the first for an Earther against a DeTang. Pretty good for a kid who claims he doesn't even like to fight.

The commentators give their opinions of the speech, none of them realizing what it really did.

Rick draws the warblade. The crowd falls as silent as an Abbandon street after dark. Surprised, BoBo takes a step back. Attention focused on the sword, he fails to notice Rick deactivating and removing the circlet that covers his head. Rick lunges forward with the tip of the blade at BoBo's face. BoBo ducked his head down right where Rick was holding the circlet open. The kid clamped the circlet, inside out, around the rocky neck and turned it on. The stone warrior was enveloped in a glowing cocoon. Brilliant move. BoBo hit Rick's midsection full force. Rick shrugged it off. Full force just is not what it used to be. The inverted field surrounding BoBo absorbed the force of his blows even as he struck. Rick's field took care of the rest. As long as the power lasted he was facing his opponent on an almost even footing. All Rick needed was three minutes.

BoBo actually sprinted away from Rick, trying to remove the circlet. Rick was not about to give up that advantage.

"No way, coward. You won't get away that easily," Rick said. Coward did the trick. Forgetting about the circlet, BoBo began a new onslaught.

Wait! *Won't get away that easily.* That's what's been nagging me at the back of my mind. The time frame for Dreg to get Susie out of the Warplex was all wrong. I fell for the decoys, but the wool is off my eyes.

As I move the Hoversine into overdrive I phone Sylvia with the news. I know where Susie is. I tell her to alert the good Rabbi, Mad Jake. Anyone seeing my driving would think the devil himself was at my heels. Not to worry. The only Hoversine that gets stopped is a stolen one and those only rarely. With luck and a good tailwind, it may not be too late to both save Susie and Burke's career. It's like the answer to a prayer. Oh yeah. It was.

Thanks, God.

Now just let me get her out of there safe and sound and I'll promise you double or nothing on anything I owe you.

DREG

Unable to amuse himself alone any longer, Dreg began contemplation of how to access the chamber. Susie had slept long enough. It was time, rat or no rat. The question was how to get in. Not being prone to long thought processes, Dreg decided the rat was lying. There was no way he would be able to tell if he joined the girl. Once he believed this to be the truth, it wasn't long before he put the thought to the test. Slowly and with great caution, Dreg opened the closed door, inch by steady inch, until the open space was just large enough for him to squeeze through. The door was shut behind him just as gingerly.

Dreg waited, afraid of breaking the silence with even the sound of his heavy breathing. Eventually, Dreg's confidence grew and he inched up on the still form of the child which was curled up in a fetal position.

"Stinking vermin lied. Thought he could fool the Man. No rat has ever been so wrong," Dreg boasted, which despite his bravado was said in whispered tones. "Now, little girl, prepare to become a woman. Boy, are you going to enjoy this wake-up call."

At the words and the sounds of cloth sliding off along skin, Susie's muscles tensed up, her eyes lids squeezed tighter together and her breathing stopped. Her tiny hands desperately tightened into fists, ready to strike rather than submit. Dreg was oblivious to these small changes in movement.

The whispers became screams as Dreg doubled over holding his anguished head. Smed'lee had not been bluffing, just slow on the NG trigger. Grabbing his fallen clothes, Dreg crawled out of the tiny chamber slamming the door behind him. Minutes later, the pain ceased. Dreg cursed the rat in shouts that shook the room, but within a darkened chamber a little girl loosened her fists, opened her eyes, and began breathing again. She was ready to feign unconsciousness at a moment's notice. Susie had already searched the room for a means of escape or a way to call for help. The search came up empty, so she lay silent, hoping a friend would be the next to come through that door. That or a miracle were her only hope.

Luckily, she believed in both.

RICK

Sheathed in the field, BoBo was trying furiously to exhaust the power by slamming his hands together. Over and over, again and again, he struck one fist against the other. Clap hands, clap hands till BoBo comes home. It was a great strategy. The field began to flicker. I decided the opposite side of the Pit would be the safest place for me to be, so I headed that way. It was a good thing because the next blow blew the batteries and with a flash of light the field faded out entirely.

His applause complete, BoBo turned his attention to other matters, namely where had I gone. Being he and I were the only ones in the Pit, he had no trouble locating me. Before he could make his way to join me on the far side, the buzzer rang. The time was up and thirty minutes of eternity had fallen by the wayside. My left shoulder hurt like the devil, but I was alive. I was standing on unfractured limbs. Disbelief on disbelief – the match was a draw. Only one problem: BoBo had not stopped. He was still coming at me with the intent of extending our match. I wanted to explain that it was over between us and that was that. How to get across my point?

I tried the subtle approach.

"Good match, BoBo."

I tried the logical.

"Thirty minutes is up. The match is over."

When that failed, I tried the direct.

"Stop!"

In desperation, I went the emotional route.

"Remember what Sasha said."

That one worked. He stopped, looking as if he was fighting an inner battle between his emotions and Sasha's orders. Rage lost to loyalty. BoBo extended his hand. I considered shutting down the field before I shook his hand in return and decided against it. The handshake was without incident.

"Good match, Rick."

"Thank you, BoBo. It was by far the most difficult of my career." Long, many week-spanning career that it was.

"Kerr certainly has improved his training methods, even to include unorthodox methods."

Time to pay the piper. Red asked only for only one price for his training. This was it.

"Actually, Kerr had some help. Red handled a large part of my training," BoBo froze up at the mention of the name. It was some time before he regained his composure. As the crimson barkeep himself put it, Red is not BoBo's favorite person. To know Red had a hand or four in this must not help matters. BoBo hides it well. His civility is unexpected but welcome. I half expected Burke having to come to my rescue, but I guess Sasha was right. BoBo will listen to her.

With the endmatch, the feud is over. With the closing salutes, the vengeance of BoBo has come to its end, as ridiculous as that sounds. I enjoyed my go around as the squad carried me round the Pit to the cheers of the crowd. I will never admit it out loud, but I actually enjoy the feeling of victory and the roar of the crowd. It thrills me even more than it worries me. I only wish Susie could have been here to see it.

Kerr takes me aside to congratulate me. I return Bloodmoon to him, again thanking him. He barely acknowledges my words. For someone whose student just fought a DeTang to a draw, he seems rather somber, unhappy even.

"What's wrong?"

"Rick, there is something I need to tell you and I hope you can forgive me for not telling you earlier. It was for your own good. You never would have survived the match without Burke's aid otherwise."

Icy fingers gripped my insides in a vice grip and my heartbeat began to sound like gunfire. "Kerr, did something happen to Susie?"

He nodded, the Grey attacking him. "Dreg has taken her."

The icy fingers tightened their hold on my heart. Turmoil attacked my soul. First and foremost in my mind was fear for my Susie. "Dreg!? Do you know what that scumbag tried to do to her?"

"Yes."

"How did he get past the security system?"

"Susie let him in thinking it was you returning. She forgot to check the view screen."

"This happened right after I left Burke's quarters last night and you waited until now to tell me?"

"Yes. I searched the city all night until just before match time. Burke hired Samuel and I alerted Red and Mad Jake to join in the search. Even Savage is out there looking. You would not have been able to add anything but worry."

"I could have helped search."

"Where? You only know the city around the Warplex and between it, Red's and the Empirical House. You would be more a danger to yourself than a help to us."

Though loathe to admit it, Kerr made sense. But that didn't mean I wasn't going to help search now. Kerr explained that Burke was going to throw the match and how the kidnapping was pulled off.

It didn't make sense. Kerr's point was more valid for Dreg. The scumbag has never been off the Warplex grounds. In the dark of night, he would be lost hopelessly within minutes. That combined with carrying an unconscious Susie would make escape difficult. Add a rampaging Burke to the equation and getting away was made impossible. The downed camera trail was a decoy.

"Kerr, I know why the search of the city is coming up empty. Dreg never left the grounds." I explained my reasoning.

Kerr's smile and a glint of danger in his eye vanquished the Grey. "That would explain why I could not pick up their scent. There was none to be found."

"Kerr, you know the Warplex better than me. Where would you hide?"

Kerr thought about it. "The warrior dorms are out. So are the Pit and the mess hall. The Muridae quarters are a possibility. The best place would be the dungeon."

"We have a dungeon?"

"Left over from the slave days. Has not been used for more than storage since. Immediately after you give Tarna your pregame hugs, grab Don and meet me outside Burke's quarters. We can use his nose in the search."

"What about the others?"

"Leave them. The three of us can search the dungeons alone. We are not convinced that the Muridae are not tied up in this. We do not want to arouse suspicion by having all of the squad suddenly vanish during one of their own's bout. If you are right but I am wrong about where they have taken her, I do not want them to have a second chance to move her. Before you ask, you are the only one who knows. Otherwise, there is no way any of them would stay put."

"So you're asking me to keep them in the dark, same as you did me?"

"Yes. It is for the best. In your mind, you know that."

"But my heart disagrees. Still, I'll do it." May they forgive me. "Still, we should tell someone where we are going."

"Agreed. Burke is out. Reason would leave him if he thought Susie was so close; if he did not show for the match Razza knows what they would do to her."

"How about Breeze?"

"She would never be able to keep it from her sibling. Runner would never be able to be silent on it and not only would your squad vanish from the sidelines, so would an informed Tarna and Burke."

"Claw?" I asked.

"I would not trust him with his own life."

"Nanna?"

"Not likely. She had regressed to a puddle of plasm, oblivious to the outer world."

"Perhaps this news would pull her out of it. Nanna's whole could protect the lot of us if things got rough."

"That is not warrior-like," Kerr said.

"That is what you said about the circlets, but they worked. What it comes down to is I don't give a damn. I want Susie safe and I'll do anything to ensure that."

"For a cub, you show wisdom."

"I had a good teacher."

"I will try to awaken Nanna. I will also call Troubell's office and leave a message there with instructions to get Red in one hour if I don't call back. I can also leave Burke a message on his comm board letting him in on it if we do not get her back before the end of the match. We rendezvous in five minutes," Kerr ordered, stopping only to wish Tarna luck.

Tarna radiated, beautiful three-legged purple lady that she was. Today she achieves her life's goal. New goals are already coming into creation. Her trading cards are banned among the G'morra by the clerics. Therefore, they are worth a small fortune, which helps Tarna supplement her income and her goals by selling them to her own people, autographs slightly extra.

I hugged her tight. She knew me too well.

"What's wrong, cutey? You did good," she asked me. Looking in her eyes, I knew that if she found out about Susie, nothing would stop her from helping, even giving up her dream. I could not take that away from her. I could not lie to one of my best friends in the world. Two worlds in fact. At least not with her arms wrapped around me.

"I'll tell you later. Right now, you need to concentrate on your match." Where have I heard that before?

I backed off and Spike took my place.

"Don, make sure you're next."

"Why?"

"Trust me," I suggested. A large leap of faith for the average Kroc. Usually impairs survival. Don trusted me without reservation.

After his last lick for luck, Don joined me in a subtle exit. As subtle as a fourteen-foot body allows. I explained the situation en route. Don's anger matched my own. Once we were out of sight of the arena he turned that anger into speed. I leapt onto his back and held on as we sped toward Burke's quarters.

KERR

"Nanna, it is Kerr. We need you."

No response. The blue puddle remains inert as if no words were spoken. I will not be ignored.

"Pull yourself together. Susie needs you."

As the mention of the little one's name, I sense a ripple in the whole. Nanna is not completely gone...a spark still exists in the plasm. I do not have time to be gentle. The little one has even less time.

"We may know where Susie is. We need your help to find her."

The puddle tightens its borders. Still no response.

"Never pictured you for a coward, Nanna. Shows you how wrong one can be about another person. I always figured you had more strength than this. Hiding from life, sticking what passes for your head in the ground."

Plasm takes shape, rounding out shapeless edges. A flicker flashes and translates as a moan. Finally, a sign of life.

"Susie needs you and here you lay, a mass of self-pity. I am amazed that you would abandon your charge."

That did it. Plasm explodes, showering fire upward until I am facing a tower of flame, spouting rage at impotence. All of it focusing on me... Joy.

"Leave me be, damn you, or be destroyed," she radiates.

Something well within her power. Not within her spirit, even gripped by the Grey as it is. It is only her second battle with my old foe. She needs an ally. I will aid her and pray I have judged her spirit correctly. If not, I am deep fried.

"You won't kill me."

Nanna does not argue the point.

"You are needed, Nani. A child is in danger and you may be able to save her."

"It is my fault she needs to be saved. My failure that endangered her. I lost Lord Burke's two children."

"To a nuclear attack launched by the Empire. The fledgling's shells were not fully hardened, but even that would have been no guarantee."

"I could have saved them."

"You do not know that. You could have just as easily perished. Two adult DeTang perished in the blast. Burke only survived because he was out of the blast range. The radiation left him sterile."

"Exactly. And now I lost his adopted child."

"You did not lose her. She was taken. Take her back."

"How do you even know she is even alive?"

"I do not. Susie may be dead. But I do not believe it. Would not matter if I did. I love the child and I will not stop searching until I see her body. The Pantheon willing it will still be breathing."

"I cannot. I may fail."

"That is the Grey talking. Do not let it win. Fight it. Defeat it."

"How?"

"You must try. That is the key. Resist the temptation to go inside yourself. I know it is hard; I have been there myself. Give in and you may never come out again. The Grey wins."

"You go through this periodically?"

"Yes."

"My apologies for thinking you were a whining bag of flesh."

"Those who have not battled the Grey can never understand, those who have can never forget."

"I do not know if I have the strength."

"Do you have the strength to lay back and do nothing, then live with yourself for the rest of your existence knowing you may have been able to save her?"

The flames flickered and died. Nanna's whole had returned to its resting state.

"Let's go."

Nanna deactivated the door lock. Good thing, too. If she had not come out of the Grey, I would be stuck in here. Burke gave me an emergency access code but it is good only once and that was the way in.

Rick and Don were waiting outside.

The dungeon entrances were blocked up. I was planning on having to break through them. With Nanna that is no longer a problem. I explain my plan to locate the entrance.

"Rick, Don, start at the doorway and run all out for thirty-four seconds." That was how long the internal system said it was before Burke hit the door.

They do as I say. Kroc are many times faster than Dirtlings, so Don covers more distance. After marking the spots, Don and I begin searching the area between for scents. I start the search working back from Don's mark. Dreg would have traveled faster than a battle-weary

Rick. Maybe even as far as Don. Dreg was running for his life after all.

Don's nose is much more sensitive than mine. The price of evolution. He finds the scent first. Even with him pointing it out, I barely scent it. It is so faint it is no wonder I missed it. It is almost a body length up along a wall where Dreg must have brushed her body against. We find no trace of Dreg's odor. Must have treated his body to eliminate his scent or blend it in with the smell of the walls. Rick and I search the wall, banging and listening for the echoes that would indicate a hollow chamber. We find it, but before we can even search for an opening latch, Nanna dissolves the wall revealing a stairwell full of dust, save the steps. They had been cleaned so as not to leave us with a trail.

At the bottom, we split into two groups. The dungeons spanned the entire area below the Warplex and then some, so we had a lot of area to cover. Safest to do it in pairs. Wish I had thought of this before the match. Would have gotten every warrior I could get my hands on down here and searched. That and a franc will get me a shot at Red's.

Hold on, little one. We are coming.

NED AND BOB

"What a day for upsets, wouldn't you say, Bob?"

"Yes, indeed, Ned. First, the Dirtling Rick Wagner battles BoBo the destroyer to a draw."

"That he did, even if his methods were unorthodox."

"Absolutely, Bob. I think we can expect a ruling from the Battle Council on the morrow regarding use of force fields and birth control devices in future matches."

"Well, you know what I say, it is best to make safe war, not love."

Canned laughter rings out.

"Reminds me of the match back in 487, T.T. That is Tore Time for all our off-planet listeners."

"Yes, the Lord Burke - Anthony Savage bout. That was the last time a Terran faced off against a DeTang."

"And the fourth to survive. In the old games, there was no time limit and death could await both victor and defeated. Savage threw everything he had at Burke, but nothing could stop his onslaught."

"It is amazing to think that is the same Burke we are seeing here in the arena. Tarna, the first female G'morran warrior officially sanctioned by the Muridae Battle Commission, is holding her own today against the warrior many consider the best to ever grace the Tore Games."

"Some would argue that honor belongs to ex-tourney winner Red of Roserod. The argument is still a matter of debate and opinion for as we all know the famous grudge match was declared a draw."

"A pity Red is not here today for in the shape Burke's fighting skills are in, I think we could have a final decision on the debate. I fear it is one the DeTang would not appreciate."

"I must concur. Although Tarna has shown both skill and courage in her battle matches thus far she is not considered by insiders to be in the same class as Lord Burke. Yet here she is, holding her own."

"Without the use of unorthodox methods, unlike her squadmate, I might add."

"Rumor is Rick offered her the use of the circlets but she refused, opting instead to carry three traditional weapons of her people."

"Her people in name only. As our listeners may already know, Tarna is a Xile of the Liberty G'morran tribe. Apparently, they did not approve of her liberating ways. Since she began her career just a few scant weeks ago, the Muridae Battle Council has been inundated by requests by other female G'morra who wish to follow in her footsteps. We have tried repeatedly to get an interview with members of her family, but thus far all have declined. Rumor has it her father is very proud of Tarna's accomplishments despite her exile."

"Tarna has also received much support from the male Aprahoe, themselves victims of cultural sexual repression, although not to the same degree as the female G'morra."

"That support may increase after today. Tarna actually shows signs of being able to win today and breaking the undefeated Burke's dynasty."

"Yes, she does. Listen to the crowds and one catches something not heard in the arena in my memory. The sounds of jeers for Burke. The fans seem as confused by the behavior of the highest-ranked practicing warrior as we do."

"We have tried to contact Prince Kerr, ranking warrior and longtime friend and companion of Lord Burke. As warrior fans will remember, Kerr lost a match to Burke back in 488 T.T., so we hoped he might have some insight into today's match, but he apparently has left the arena."

"The reason for that may be that his student, Rick Wagner has also left the arena in the company of the Kroc warrior, Don. Rick may have been hurt more than he let on in that last match. The other warriors may be escorting him to the medics. The closeness of this squad is popular knowledge. Medical care is the only reason this commentator can imagine for two members of this squad abandoning one of their own during a match, especially one as important as this."

"Speaking of notable absences, Muridae overseer Smed'lee, has left the dais for points unknown."

"Perhaps he went to follow the others to see where they went."

"Maybe the match was unable to hold their attention."

"It looks like Dortew has just noticed the absence. That cannot be good news for Smed'lee."

"Sorry to interrupt, but Burke has landed his first successful attack of the match."

"A good attack, but not up to his normal standards. We could go on all about Burke's technique all day."

The commentary was switched off as the desperately driven Hoversine pulled up in front of the Warplex, disgorged its passenger. Troubell hit the ground running.

RICK

"Rick, you were right. I found your human brother's scent."

"He is no brother of mine, Don."

"Don is sorry, Rick. No insult was intended."

"None taken, buddy. Can you follow it?"

"Of course."

"Do it."

"Wait. I also scent Muridae. Smed'lee."

"The scent must be old. He was still up at the match when we left. The rat will get his later. Find Dreg. Use caution; remember, we need surprise. We do not want Dreg using Susie as a living shield."

"He won't."

"Let's go get Susie."

DREG

"No God-damned rat can outsmart the Man. White be right!"

Dreg muttered to himself, pleased at his own ingenuity. After painstaking hours of thought, he realized that the door to the room where Susie lay unconscious had a sensor - a sensor that was inactive while two pieces of metal touched. The moment contact was broken, the silent alarm sounded. Dreg was wedging a bent ten-inch hunk of metal in the door frame. As the door was opened, Dreg straightened the metal. The circuit was kept intact. Dreg carefully slid his body through the open space.

"Yes!" Dreg shouted in triumph, not daring to drop his arms down less he set off the alarm. With the greatest of care, the door was closed and the metal removed as the original connection was reestablished. "Now, sweetmeat, it is the moment we have all been waiting for," Dreg crowed, softly stroking the arm of the sleeping girl.

Coming to the end of her arm and the open end of the sleeve, he tried to snake a single finger under the material. There was not enough room for this to be successful. Dreg was not detoured. Instead, he looked Susie over from head to toe, debating where to begin, what to remove first. With a twisted grin, Dreg took the hemline of the pink nightgown between the thumb and forefinger of each hand. With purposeful slowness, the fabric began to rise as the palms of his sweaty hands brushed against bare calves, soft with the innocence of childhood.

The door which had been so carefully circumvented flew from its mooring, crashing into the opposite wall, driven by the fear, anger, and love of a man and a Kroc.

"Shit!" Dreg spat, suddenly facing down two very angry warriors. "Lousy timing, Rick. You should have knocked. Can't you see we are trying to spend some quality time?" he added with a chuckle. Fear was absent from his eyes. Instead, a belief in immortality shone there. His immortality.

Rick's eyes widened in horror. Dreg hands had gotten as high as Susie's knees and stayed there.

"What the hell are you doing?" Rick screamed angrily.

"Just what it looks like," Dreg replied, coolly

"How could you even think of something so twisted? She's a child!"

"So? What are you, upset you didn't think of it first? It's not my usual style, but I am willing to share."

As Dreg spoke his depravities, he failed to see two very large white forefeet rise as they were placed behind him on the bed. Dreg didn't realize that, although very real, Rick's rage was a decoy. Turning back, expecting to face the child, he instead was eye level to open jaws, filled with rows of razor-sharp teeth. Don let loose a roar that would have shattered glass. In fear, Dreg leapt across the room. For the first time, doubts regarding his mortality filling his eyes to capacity. Don gently crawled over Susie, placing himself between the human beast and the child.

Preoccupied by the approaching Kroc, Dreg forgot about Rick. A tap on his shoulder, a turn of his head, and a two-fisted blow to his jaw reminded him quickly. He reeled away, trying to flee, finding only the snap of a white tail rushing to greet him. The blow lifted him off the ground and tossed him across the chamber, taking a large chunk out of a wall in the process.

Rick rushed forward, lifting Dreg halfway to his feet, keeping him from slumping down to the floor by a constant pummeling. Each blow was designed for maximum pain. Rick had learned much of pain and found himself able to teach every lesson that he ever learned on the subject.

"You will never harm Susie or any other child again. I will make sure of that!" Rick growled, fire burning in his eyes. Raising the deathstroke, he looked down on the half-conscious form he held in his hand without pity. The deathblow had begun when two words rang out.

"Rick, stop."

Shock more than the words themselves stayed the thrust. Susie had spoken. Rushing up to grab Rick's hand, she held on tight.

"Susie! Are you all right?"

"Yes, he didn't have the chance to do anything. Thanks to you two."

"Why did you stop me? Don't you know what he was about to do?"

Dreg, through split lip and broken teeth, spoke. "She stopped you because she wanted the Man."

Rick made to hit Dreg but was beaten to the punch, or rather kick, by Susie. Straight to the groin. With a sharp exhalation and protruding eyes caused by a very tender pain, Dreg quietly shut up.

"Fat chance, dirtbag," Susie said, to punctuate the point made so well by her foot. "I don't care about him, Rick. I care about you. You are too gentle, too caring a person to kill someone. You would hate yourself for the rest of your life."

"I don't know about that."

"I do. Dreg is not worth it."

"You can kill him but part of you would die with him. Susie is right, friend Rick. You know that, down deep where it counts," Don added.

Rick looked down into Susie's deep blue eyes and remembered a time when he pledged to protect her innocence. The role reversal struck him as ironic and funny in a sad sort of way. Turning to face his Kroc friend and looking down at the pitiful mass of flesh he clutched, he knew they were right. That didn't stop him from breaking Dreg's leg before he dropped him.

"How touching," came a too familiar voice from behind. Silhouetted in the door frame stood Smed'lee, Enny in hand. "Pity it amounts to nothing. I will have to kill him now instead of you having the honor. Your weakness has made no difference, save a few extra minutes added to his pitiful life."

"Wait!" Dreg wailed through broken teeth. "You promised! Money and freedom. Sex even. We were partners."

"Dream on. One pointer when dealing with a Muridae and promises: Get it in writing or have it recorded."

Rick was the first to rush Smed'lee, but the push of a button took all the fight out of him. With a battle roar, Don tried to succeed where his friend had failed. The same button ensured he joined Rick in a world of pain. With courage that surpassed that of even the two warriors, Susie ran toward Smed'lee, pounding on his furry chest, screaming.

"Stop hurting them. Stop it now."

Smed'lee merely laughed. With a furry hand, he pulled hard on blonde strands, lifting Susie off the floor by her hair.

"Why are you awake? I gave you enough sedative to knock you out for days," Smed'lee asked, failing to remember that she had woken up early when sedated for the Elucidator to be implanted.

"I only pretended to be asleep."

"You should have kept pretending. Now I will make you wish you had." A twist of frequency and push of a button later Susie's perceptions exploded with a pain unknown to one of her young age.

"Burke thinks he can buy a frequency. He did not even know we had implanted the receiver."

Smed'lee's attention was distracted by the sounds of an injured body dragging itself across a stone floor. Letting Susie drop to the floor, but not letting go of her hair, he added the sound of a second dragging body to the first. A hop, skip, and a jump was all that was required to intercept and block Dreg's escape route. Dreg looked up with the eyes of a mortal and pleaded for his life.

"Please. Don't."

"Beg."

He did... for a good four minutes, Dreg did his best to inspire pity and mercy in the Muridae. Four minutes wasted, but not without a glint of hope to make the despair complete.

"Very well. You are free to leave."

"Really?" said a stunned Dreg, tears of relief dribbling down his battered face.

"No," Smed'lee said with a smile as he hit the pain button of the NG. Still holding onto Susie by the hair, he pulled her back across the room.

"A pity you woke up, girl. Asleep and unknowing, you would have been a point of leverage against the DeTang. Now the only thing I can do with you is make sure your death is as painful as possible."

Susie's mind was in agony and beyond hearing the rat's plans for her; the mind of another was not. Trembling at first, then more steadily, Rick pushed against the floor until he stood upright. Step by agonizing step he moved toward the unsuspecting rat. Heavy footsteps betrayed his presence. Thinking somehow the Nociogenerator had been switched off, Smed'lee moved the knob to Rick's frequency and hit the button. Nothing happened.

Smed'lee frantically pushed the button again and again. Rick did not stop.

"Why aren't you in pain? Why aren't you falling?" Smed'lee yelled, his words tinged with fear. Rick continued his approach in silent defiance, unable to spare even the effort to speak. Stunned, Smed'lee did not even think to run away so when Rick's first blow struck, it hit hard. Smed'lee did not know how to hit someone who hits back. Smed'lee raised his arms to ward off the barrage of blows.

Eyes closed, he did not see Rick grab the NG from his loosened grip. He hit the off button and his pain stopped. Adjusting the frequency knob, Rick tried to end the pain to his friends to no avail. In desperation, he smashed it repeatedly against the floor. With each slam, a cry of pain filled the air from rat lips. Soon the tiny machine was only a mass of wires and digital gears. The mechanically induced pain ended for Don, Susie, and even Dreg. Smed'lee still screamed in agony. The screams were cut off by other louder, angrier yelling.

"You show caring for a pain machine, but none for living people! You don't deserve life. A mistake that will be soon rectified," Rick bellowed.

He then, for the second time that day, raised his hand into a deathblow, poised for the rat's throat.

SAMUEL

Damn Warplex has more twists and turns than the legendary maze at Crete. I keep waiting for a minotaur to pop out. Luckily, I had used the Hoversine's database to print out blueprints of the complex. The only area not currently used is the old dungeons, so I decide to start there. All the entrances on my blueprint were blocked up and I had left my heavy explosives back at the office. Before despair could creep up and grab me, I found what used to be a wall outside of Burke's quarters. Beyond it was a staircase. Looks like someone had gotten the same idea and beat me here. Enough people start thinking intelligently for themselves and we detectives will be without a livelihood. Not that we have much of one presently.

The dungeons drag on for acres. I was ready to begin searching, expecting it to be an arduous process, a search for the smallest trace, the tiniest clue. Instead, all I do is follow the signs and sounds of a struggle. By the time I reached the action, it was all but over. I pull out my Notary Attestant. It is a handy little device, sanctioned by both the Tore court system and the Kentor, which records sight, sound, smell, and radiation levels of events as well as vital signs of individuals. It provides a total record of an event complete with built-in lie detector analysis of the players that will stand up in court. Stores thousands of hours on a one-inch cube. Makes my life a hell of a lot easier. I hit the auto record button and watch the scene unfold before me.

Dreg is laid out on the floor, holding his leg, which is pointed out at a ninety-degree angle. He's not who I am looking for...

Thank God! Susie is alive. The Kroc, Don, is standing over her, mothering her. Amazing in and of itself. Then there is the sight I thought I would never see: a Muridae in actual fear of physical violence. Rick is standing over Smed'lee. The kid looks like he's about to kill the rat. If he does, I'll stop the Attestant and destroy the footage.

"Damn you! I can't do it. No matter how much you deserve to die I can't be your executioner," Rick yells, angry at himself almost as much as the rat.

"Don't be ashamed, Kid. It's a sign of strength, not weakness," I tell him. Also saves me the trouble of having to teach him the finer points of hiding a body. Don't think me cruel or evil. There's only so far a man can be pushed before he snaps. One incident should not have to ruin a life. Actually, let's make that a second life. Often killing may not be right but is justifiable. The Kid has certainly been pushed that far and I'd understand his decision either way. I've been there myself and I'm proud to say I have never killed in cold blood, but Lord knows there have been times I wanted to. I've come closer than I like to admit.

Smed'lee's fear faded slowly as he realized he was not going to die at Rick's hands. A Muridae's view of killing is tainted, as is every other perception, by finances. Killing is only permitted for the very rich to kill the poor. Then they have to make reparations to the deceased's family or corporation for the amount of money he or she would have been expected to make in the rest of their lifetime. It is only considered a crime if the killer is unable to pay. Most Muridae just don't have the capital to afford to kill. Facing down a being who could kill just out of passion must have terrified him. Rick isn't the only passionate being present. We could use that to turn this situation to Rick's advantage.

"Samuel, how long have you been here?" Rick asks, not letting go of the rat's throat.

"Long enough," I said, indicating my Attestant. Smed'lee's eyes widen in horror. I must have missed one hell of a show. If he thinks I have whatever happened recorded, we have a bargaining tool.

"Smed'lee, you want to make it easy on yourself, confess the whole thing."

"Never!"

"So, you admit you have something to confess?"

"No."

"That's too bad. I know you wouldn't have done this alone. I'm sure you were only following orders, but once this gets shown to the Guardsmen, your goose is cooked." I turned off the auto record. "However, should you confess and name names, I might see my way clear to erase the earlier part of the recording," I lied.

"You would do that?" the rat asked hopefully.

"I might. It depends on what you say after," I say.

"What do you mean?"

"You are aware that in addition to gathering evidence an Attestant can be used to form a legal and binding contract." Muridae tend not to use them. The spoken word leaves less room to read between the lines.

"What would you want?"

"It is not what I want. It is what Rick wants."

"Me?" Rick said. "Why not Susie? She is the one who deserves whatever ratboy here can give."

"Susie is a minor. A contract with her would be non-binding."

"But to get out of it, the Muridae would have to admit they knew she was a child and Burke could call down High Justice."

"Wouldn't be that simple. Plenty of ways to weasel out of that. Safer to have you as the primary. Is there anything you want?" I ask.

Rick does not hesitate before he answers. "Freedom. For me and Don."

"Be careful what you wish for. With freedom comes fiscal responsibility. Neither of you has any means of support other than warrioring. Should you leave the arena, the Muridae would not have to take you back."

"True," he answered. Rick thought about the possibilities when an answer must have come to him. "Okay your verminness, here's the deal: you will turn over the contracts of every Warrior and Newbe presently in service to the Muridae on the planet. Then agree to continue the upkeep on each. The division of profits, after approved expenses, will be decided by me."

"Never! You must be mad, Dirtling," Smed'lee screamed.

"Damn right I'm mad! You kidnap me from my home, press me into service against my will, and then try to kill Susie. It is time for a little payback. This will hurt you more than killing you would."

"Rick, I admire your creativity, but Dortew will never agree to that."

"He won't have to. Smedboy here has to. Once we have the confession, Dortew will be much more amenable. If need be, I will negotiate."

"Dortew will eat you alive," I warn.

"Don't bet on it," Rick boasts with a confident grin.

"Forget it, Dirtlings. I will never agree to that," Smed'lee informs, trying to burst our bubble.

"Oh yeah?" Rick said, beginning the violent laying on of hands. I stop him and flash him a wink.

"Pity, then. We have no further use for you," I inform Smed'lee. He fails to be impressed

"What are you going to do about it? Kill me?"

"Well, the kid already has stated his feelings on the matter. Me, I won't be doing the deed. Not my style. But Don here is another matter. You hurt one of his friends. I'm willing to bet he doesn't like that," I said. As if on cue the Kroc turned to the rat and smiled. Very few beings spout more teeth than a Kroc. It riveted Smed'lee's attention and a good deal of mine. Dentists must make a fortune on his homeworld. Probably spend all the profits on life insurance, though. "I'm also willing to bet Don is hungry. Aren't you, Don?"

"Always," Don said, licking his chops to drive home the point. Smed'lee pulled free of Rick's grasp and began crawling backward. Don began creeping after him, slowly, taking his time with each step, accentuating the terror. Smed'lee toyed with the idea that he could flee but that didn't last long as the advancing Kroc neared him hungrily. He looked to a pile of mechanical rubbish that was lying in the middle of the floor as if it held his salvation. Rick saw this and with a chuckle smashed his foot down atop it, crushing it even further. Susie walked to Rick and added her efforts to the task. Smed'lee whimpered softly at the sight, almost forgetting Don. Almost was not good enough and the begging began.

"Stop him! Do not let him eat me... Please!"

"Do you agree to my terms?" Rick asked, doing what looked like a Mexican hat dance with Susie atop the crushed metal.

"No," Smed'lee said defiantly. Rick took Susie's hand and led her away from the junk pile that was their dance floor. As he did, Don's tail came smashing down on the pile, crushing what little remained into dust. An impressive sight when you consider that the rest of Don's body was across the room.

"Bon appetit, Don," Rick said. Don closed the remaining distance quickly and opened his great maw. Smed'lee lost all traces of bravery and began blubbering like a child.

"All right... I agree. Just get him away from me!"

Rick nodded and Don backed off. Everyone else seems to have the nod thing down. They nod, someone else does something. When I nod, folks just wonder what I am agreeing to.

I reactivated the auto record.

"First, the confession," I said. With Don standing nearby, Smed'lee sang like a bird. He told of Dortew's order to kill Susie, then told all about arranging for Dreg to kidnap Susie and his betting scam. If he had pulled it off, he would have usurped Dortew's position by right of wealth and been the head Muridae on the planet.

After he finished, I stopped him and changed the cube for the contract. I would be unable to separate the two if they were left on the same cube. I might need the first to enforce compliance of the second. The cubes are tamper proof, which is why they are accepted as evidence without question. Any tampering is readily apparent or, if it goes too far, destroys the cube. I lied when I offered to erase it earlier. With the new cube in place, we begin the contract. I suggest it be made with Smed'lee as a member of the Muridae Battle Council of Tore, of which he is ranked second, rather than as an individual. That way Dortew and the Council will be bound by it. Soon Smed'lee's individual contracts will be worthless.

Smed'lee gave Rick everything he asked for and then some. Rick made sure the words were chosen carefully. Will be hard to worm out of the contract. Maybe the kid will be able to hold his own in negotiations with Dortew.

"There! You have everything you wanted. Now what are you going to do with me?" the defeated Muridae asked. Dreg still lay silent, but turned his head to listen, for he rightly surmised the same fate awaited him.

"Rick?" I asked. It was his call.

"We leave them here," he said curtly, as he bound them hand and feet so they would be here when he came back. I could see in his eyes he was going to notify the proper authorities and let them handle the matter. Good idea, at least in theory.

"What? Does that mean I have to go hungry?" the Kroc asked sadly.

"Don!" Susie and Rick said in unison, annoyed and disappointed. I do not see why. It was totally in character for a Kroc.

"Just kidding," he said which was totally out of character for a Kroc. I believed him, which is in character for a sap such as myself.

The kid made the right decision, but not for the reasons he thinks. We are not alone. Hearts beat in the shadows. The darkness screams for the vengeance we refuse to take.

We take our leave of the dungeons, rejoicing in Susie's safety. Hugs are exchanged all around. Rick carries her until we exit the door.

I have to know.

"Did the NG stop working back there?" I ask the kid.

"Not until I broke it."

"Then how did you beat it?"

"It was all a matter of pain."

"I don't understand. I thought the NG put you in terrible, unbearable agony."

"It did."

"Then how?"

"I could still hear," Rick said, looking down at the blond bundle under his right arm. "The thought of living in a world without Susie caused me more pain than the NG could ever hope to. So, I did what I had to do to stop *that* pain." The Kid then hugged the little kid, with her still dangling in the air.

At that point, we all mounted Don's back. He was the fastest way back to the Pit. I stressed the need for speed. The match wasn't over yet. We can still save Burke's career.

On the way out, I tip my hat to the shadows as they prepare to devour the sinners we leave behind, who are mercifully unaware of the fate which awaits them.

As we race through the dungeons, we come across Kerr and Nanna whose joy is literally unbounded at the sight of the child. They both embrace the child in their own way.

At the news that Rick just left Smed'lee and Dreg secured but alive, Kerr nods knowingly while Nanna appears furious. They both make to go to the cell where we left the kidnappers, but Kerr stops short as he sniffs the air, picking up the scents even the shadows cannot hide. He looks to me for confirmation. I nod and he returns the favor. At least he knew what I was nodding at. Realizing he will not be needed, he turns back to us.

"Nanna, I will escort Susie back to the Pit," Kerr promises.

"Guard her with your life, Czarrian," she says as if the rest of us didn't exist.

"Of course," the wolf says with a bow and a flourish of four hands. Kerr hopped on Krocback directly behind me and yells "Run, Don, like you've never run before. We go to save a DeTang's honor."

Don hit overdrive and I had to do everything I could to keep from being thrown off. Susie, by way of contrast, was already laughing, her tears half-forgotten. Behind me, the fleabag began to howl, Czarrian style with nary a full moon in sight. It was a victory howl. Rick added his howl to the medley, sounding frighteningly authentic. Don was unable to successfully harmonize, but that didn't stop him from trying. Even Susie joined in with the littlest howl. It was a bizarre situation to be in. I could see the headlines now. "Private investigator, raised by wolves, found." What they were doing was silly, ridiculous, and dumb. They would not stop as the moonsong got louder and louder and the walls flew by faster and faster. Unable to beat them with my rendition of "Freeze Dried Goot" I joined in. Truth be told, I didn't sound half bad.

SAVAGE

Prone and hogtied, Smed'lee struggled against his bonds; it was to no avail. He was caught tight. Opposite him, Dreg was trussed up similarly, but he didn't bother to struggle, just sob quietly. Neither noticed the shadows, but the same couldn't be said of the darkness. A shadow reached out and loosened Smed'lee's bounds. Smed'lee didn't question his luck, assuming it to be a result of his efforts. Dreg stopped weeping when he noticed the Muridae's freedom.

"Smed'lee, what about me?"

"What about you?"

"Free me."

Smed'lee didn't even bother to answer, just shook his head in a condescending manner and kicked Dreg's greenstick fracture directly at the site of the break. Dreg screamed in pain, Smed'lee yelled in pleasure. Savoring the sadism, Smed'lee smiled before turning away. Smed'lee walked over to the shattered pieces of his Enny and gathered them up tenderly.

"They have not killed you, sweet one. I can still fix you. But first, we must go into hiding," Smed'lee whispered, fondling the crunched metal. Rising up to leave, the darkness stood up and confronted him.

"You can run, but you cannot hide. No one will be able to repair you."

"Savage!" Smed'lee gasped in horror, dropping parts of his loved one in shock.

"You have kidnapped a Terran and tried to kill two. That is against my decree. You must pay for your transgression. The payment will be collected in your lifeblood. Make your peace and prepare for the afterlife, vermin."

Smed'lee turned and fled in stark, raving terror. Savage made no move to stop him, content to merely watch him flee. He then turned his full attention to Dreg. Dreg did the same.

"Savage. Thank God you found me. That rat tried to hurt the little girl. I tried to stop him but he did this to me."

"Do not lie to me."

"I wouldn't. Not to you."

"Bullshit."

"C'mon, give me a break. I'm sorry. I will never do it again. I promise."

"You have kidnapped a Terran and tried to kill two. That is against my decree. You must pay for your transgression. The payment will be collected in your lifeblood. By doing this you have lost your standing as a human and all the rights therein. You are now ranked with the vermin for the little time you have left. Make your peace and prepare for the afterlife."

"I am still a man. You can't take that away from me."

"I did not. You did."

"Please!" Dreg begged, screaming for mercy. Savage deafened his ears to the pleas, save one. He did show mercy. The deed was done quickly and painlessly. The screaming stopped and silence returned to this end of the darkness.

But the shadows extend forever and are rarely silent for long, as Smed'lee was about to learn. Smed'lee was running for his life and believed he was winning. Looking behind him, he saw no pursuit and he began to laugh in relief. It was a hollow sound, devoid of any feeling, done solely to build up his conviction that he would live. The conviction was about to be overturned by a second shadow stepping forth from the darkness long enough to speak.

"Vengeance is mine, sayeth the Lord," announced the voice of darkness, fading back to whence it came before the last syllable was spoken.

Smed'lee whirled, his body trembling.

"Who is there?" he demanded. Silence answered him. Turning, he blindly sprinted past rooms of terrors years old, all his focus on a new terror. He ran until he could run no more and had to hold his obese, furry form up by holding onto a wall, gasping for breath.

"The just man shall be glad when he sees vengeance:
he shall bathe his feet in the blood of the wicked.
And men shall say, 'Truly there is a reward for the just:
truly there is God who is judge on Liberty!" the voice said, breathing easily.

"They resolve on their wicked plan;
they conspire to set snares,
saying. 'Who will see us?'
They devise a wicked scheme,
and conceal the scheme they have devised."

"Stop spouting drivel!" Smed'lee screams.

Mad Jake stepped out of the obscuring blackness. "Show some

respect for the Bible. And prepare to meet He who inspired it."

Smed'lee looked at the deceptively frail form before him and underestimated the man before him.

"Out of my way, old dirter," Smed'lee ordered, moving to push Jake out of his way. He might as well grasp for a mist. Jake avoided the clumsy blow as easily as a cheetah dodging a falling feather. Adding his force to Smed'lee's momentum, Jake spun him around and into the air. In an effort to protect his head from harm, Smed'lee frantically threw up his arms, sending a sparkling shower of metal dust and somewhat larger remains up into the air. Smed'lee hit the ground hard, but his primary concern was not on himself.

"Enny!" he shouted, hysterically trying to gather up that which he had dropped.

"So this is the device,
used by you mice,
to cause torment and pain,
on an innocent brain."

Smed'lee looked up confused, as to what the little man was still doing there.

"Attempted pedicide,
is something I cannot abide.
that leaves us with the method of death,
how to prevent your last breath?
The answer comes in a vision,
an act of some precision.
There is only one end for such a beast,
upon those metal remains you must feast."

"No, I refuse."

"Pity."

"I won't do it, I tell you!" Smed'lee screamed. But he did. Jake fed him each piece, one by one directing each one toward his windpipe. Soon each breath was a battle for air, and, by the end of the meal, the battle was lost. Jake took no joy in what he did. He merely was making sure that a monster never harmed another child again.

Savage stepped from the shadows to stand behind Mad Jake and place one hand on Jake's shoulder. It was a gesture Jake would normally never allow, but under the circumstances, it seemed appropriate. Savage asked, "Any trouble, Rabbi?"

Jake shook his head. "You?"

"None. The Nani showed up and devoured the body."
"What a stroke of luck
for you,
for if people found out you ignored your own decree
what would you do?"

Savage didn't answer. He made the rules, so only he could break them. Neither spoke for a moment, almost in mourning. Not for their victims, but for themselves. Each believed they had done the right thing, the only thing justice would allow. Or so they thought. By way of comparison, they both had witnessed Rick's act of mercy and each tried to remember a time when they would have done the same. If there ever was such a time it seemed a lifetime and a world away.

"May I have the rat, so an example may be made of his remains?" Savage asks.

"Yes. But before you start
I must depart."

"Take care, Jake."

"You too, Anthony."

The words were said sincerely, without rhythm, for next time they met the circumstance might be quite different.

They both blended into the darkness. Each carrying the burden of Jake's deed: Jake carried it inside himself and Savage literally carried it on his shoulders.

NED AND BOB

"Ned, I just do not believe what I am seeing. Lord Burke is practically tripping over his own feet. It is almost as if he wants Tarna to win."

"Absolutely, Bob. With less than one minute left, Burke seems ready to lay down and die."

"Excuse me for interrupting, Ned, but listen to that sound."

"A Czarrian moonsong."

"Exactly. And look at who is singing it – Kerr and Rick have returned riding atop the Kroc warrior Don. It appears as if Lord Burke's ward is with them."

"Who is the other Terran with them?"

"I do not recognize him. He certainly is no warrior."

"The lot of them seem to be trying to get Burke's attention."

"They appear to have succeeded. Burke was distracted in the midst of an attack from Tarna. She crashed into his side and rebounded off. She appears stunned by the impact. That is the most damage she has suffered in the match yet. What are they doing?"

"Rick and the unknown Terran are holding Burke's ward above their heads. Why are they doing that?"

"I do not know. But look at the effect. Lord Burke suddenly seems more animated."

"But will it be enough with only thirty-five seconds in the match?"

"Yes, it appears it will be. Tarna is airborne and Burke is upon her before she can reach the ground."

"What could account for this?"

"Perhaps the sight of his ward has inspired him."

"Something certainly has. This is the Burke we have all come to know. Tarna is down and out. With five seconds to spare. He certainly cut that one close."

"Look at this. Burke is deviating from tradition. He salutes only Tarna and the crowd, fully ignoring the Muridae on the dais. He is running to the sidelines directly toward his ward. If he showed that degree of intensity earlier, this match would have been over in five minutes. Now he has lifted the little Terran up. Another shock! Lord Burke is embracing her. I cannot recall him ever doing that before. Let's see if we can get an interview. Stan, are you there?"

"Yes, I am Bob. Tarna's squad is carrying her, albeit gingerly because of the injuries she sustained in the last seconds of the match."

"Excuse me, Stan but I thought they only did that for victories."

"Well Ned, they did it for Rick's draw. I believe they feel doing as well as she did against the ranking warrior is a victory in and of itself. The crowd certainly thinks so judging by their reaction. The G'morran population is here in force and on their feet. The females here are noted to be dressing in the styles Tarna favors, despite the deviation from their norm. The restrooms were full of G'morran women changing out of their traditional garb prior to the Games today. Tarna has made quite an impact in the short time she has been a warrior. We will be broadcasting her interview shortly. But first, let me try to talk to Lord Burke... Lord Burke, Lord Burke, this is Stan'noo for the Muridae Broadcast System. May I interview you about today's match?"

"No. I have other more pressing matters to attend to."

"Wait, here comes Rick Wagner, returning from the Muridae dais. Perhaps we can talk to him. Rick Wagner, over here."

"Hi, Stan."

"Rick, can we interview you on today's match?"

"Perhaps tomorrow. Right now, I have something much more important to do"

"Would you care to comment on what you and Dortew were discussing?"

"Just discussing the beginning of some negotiations."

"Is that what you and Lord Burke have to attend to?"

"No. The negotiations will begin tomorrow."

"Then perhaps you are going to the celebration Mistress Sasha has planned for you at the famous Empirical House."

"Not exactly."

"Then what?"

"I'm going to a tea party."

"And I am bringing the chocolate chip ice cream."

"Lord Burke, why are Rick Wagner and your ward running away screaming 'No'?"

"No comment."

ABOUT THE AUTHOR

PATRICK THOMAS is the author of almost 40 books including the beloved fantasy humor Murphy's Lore series, which includes *Tales From Bulfinche's Pub, Fools' Day, Through The Drinking Glass, Shadow Of The Wolf, Redemption Road, Bartender Of The Gods, Nightcaps* and *Empty Graves* — as well as the future space adventures *Startenders* and *Constellation Prize.*

The Murphy's Lore After Hours spin-offs star the half pixie/ogre Terrorbelle (*Fairy With A Gun, Fairy Rides The Lightning*); the former demon-possessed serial killer Agent Karver of the Department of Mystic Affairs *(Dead To Rites, Rites of Passage);* the cursed magí Hex *(By Darkness Cursed and BY Invocation Only);* Vince Argus, the Soul For Hire *(Greatest Hits);* and Negral, a forgotten Sumerian god who works as Hell's Detective (*Lore & Dysorder* and *Bullets & Brimstone).*

Co-Written with John French and Diane Raetz, his Mystic Investigators paranormal mystery series includes *Bullets & Brimstone, From The Shadows* and *Once More Upon A Time. Assassin's Ball,* his first mystery, is also co-written with John French.

He also wrote the steampunk *As The Gears Turn* and the space epic *Exile & Entrance.* He co-edited *New Blood* and *Hear Them Roar* and was an editor for the magazines *Fantastic Stories of the Imagination* and *Pirate Writings.*

Patrick's darkly humorous advice column Dear Cthulhu has been running since 2005 and includes the collections *Have A Dark Day, Good Advice For Bad People, Cthulhu Knows Best* and *What Would Cthulhu Do?*

His short stories have been featured in over fifty anthologies and more than forty-five print magazines.

A number of his books were part of the props department of the CSI television show and have been spot9ted on the program. Nightcaps was even thrown at a suspect's head. His urban fantasy Fairy With A Gun had been optioned for film and TV by Laurence Fishburne's Cinema Gypsy Productions. Top Men Productions has turned his Soul For Hire Story, *Act of Contrition,* into a short film.

Please drop by www.patthomas.net or follow him at I_PatrickThomas at Twitter or www.facebook.com/PatrickThomasAuthor to learn more.

No One Is Above The Lore...
Even In Hell
Hell's Detective
IT'S NOT EASY BEING HELL'S CHIEF OF POLICE
LORE & DYSORDER
FROM THE PAGES OF MURPHY'S LORE
THE HELL'S DETECTIVE MYSTERIES
"Noir in Hell, with a hefty dash of humor. A fun take on the paranormal detective genre."
—Michael D Pederson, Nth Degree
PATRICK THOMAS
MYSTIC INVESTIGATORS
BULLETS & BRIMSTONE
Patrick Thomas & John L. French
GHOSTMAN AND HELL'S DETECTIVE
TERROR
CASE OF THE MOON MAN
PATRICK THOMAS / BLAIR WERB
FEATURING
GHOSTMAN
HELL'S DETECTIVE
DANTE
MURPHY'S LORE
AFTER HOURS
"Gritty, snappy, very dark and very funny,"
—J. L. Comeau,
Creature Feature
"Dark... and charming."
—ELLEN DATLOW
The Best Horror of the Year Vol. 4

ven the things that go *Bump* in the night will learn that you <u>DON'T</u> mess with...

Terrorbelle.

"Thomas certainly brings the goods to the table when it comes to writing urban fiction...I promise, you will love... Terrorbelle: Fairy With a Gun. Who doesn't love a well-stacked, ass-kicking, gun-toting, woman with bullet-proof, razor-sharp wings that investigates all manner of supernatural spookiness? I know I do, and Thomas's humor shows through in every tale. Jim Butcher and Laurell K Hamilton have nothing on Thomas." The Raven's Barrow

From The Murphy's Lore Universe Of

PATRICK THOMAS

www. padwolf.com & www.terrorbelle.com

The Collected Advice Columns Of DEAR CTHULHU Vol 1
HAVE A Dark DAY
PATRICK THOMAS

The Collected Advice Columns Of DEAR CTHULHU Vol 2
GOOD ADVICE for BAD PEOPLE
PATRICK THOMAS

Didn't your mother ever tell you to listen to your Elders?
CTHULHU KNOWS BEST
The Collected Advice Columns Of DEAR CTHULHU Vol 3
PATRICK THOMAS

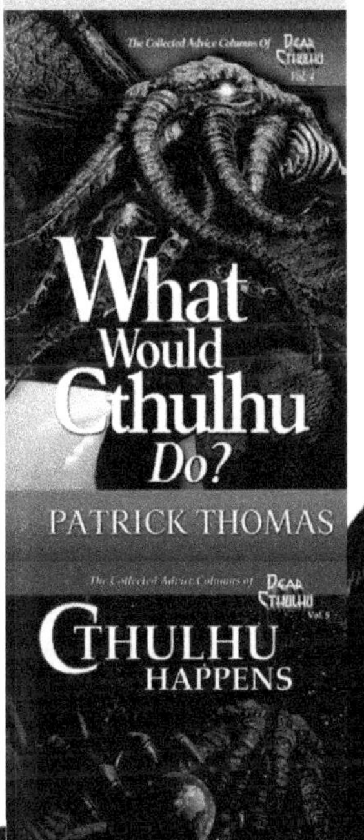

The Collected Advice Columns Of DEAR CTHULHU Vol 4
What Would Cthulhu Do?
PATRICK THOMAS

The Collected Advice Columns of DEAR CTHULHU Vol 5
CTHULHU HAPPENS

PATRICK THOMAS

DEAR CTHULHU
The advice column to END all advice columns

WWW.DEARCTHULHU.COM
WWW.PADWOLF.COM

www.ingramcontent.com/pod-product-compliance
Lightning Source LLC
Chambersburg PA
CBHW071236190726
48292CB00007B/2311